DARKNESS UNCHAINED

(SKY BROOKS BOOK 2)

MCKENZIE HUNTER

This is a work of fiction. Names, characters, businesses, places, events, and incidents are either the products of the author's imagination or used in a fictitious manner. Any resemblance to actual persons, living or dead, or actual events is purely coincidental.

McKenzie Hunter

Darkness Unchained (3rd Edition)

McKenzieHunter@McKenzieHunter.com

ISBN: 978-1-946457-92-9

ACKNOWLEDGMENTS

This is the second time around and I am fortunate to have the same wonderful people supporting me. First, I have to thank my mother. You are always supportive of whatever I choose to do and I am grateful for that. To my beta readers: What would I do without you? I can never express how much I appreciate you for your insightful feedback and constructive criticism. I can't say it enough: Shawn Arroyo, Greg Caughman, April Franks, and London Gibbs—thank you so much for all your help!

Tiffany Dix and Marcia Snyder, I am awestruck by how zealously you supported and promoted my first book, *Moon Tortured.* Was there anyone you didn't try to sell it to? I am appreciative of the time and effort you put in.

Sheryl Cox and Stacy McCright: Every author should have a "Stacy" and a "Sheryl" in their lives. I am always deeply humbled by how much you two help me. No matter how many drafts I send, questions I have, or brainstorming sessions I need, you always find time in your very busy lives to help. I am not sure if I can ever repay your generosity or thank you enough for all that you do.

Thanks to Hampton Lamoureux, cover artist (Stock Artists from DeviantArt: freakingsmg-stock, shelldevil, and Roy3D). John Harten, my editor, you didn't have any qualms about being brutally honest in an effort to help me create the best book I could. I am very appreciative and grateful for your efforts.

Last, but definitely not least, I want to thank you, the reader, for giving me a chance to entertain you with my work.

ABOUT DARKNESS UNCHAINED

~

Darkness Unchained (Sky Brooks Series, Book 2) is written from Sky's point of view (first person) and Chris's point of view (third person). *Midnight Falls* (Sky Brooks Series, Book 3) is written from only Sky's perspective.

CHAPTER 1

The robust smell of French roast coffee met me at the door as I stepped out of my bedroom to find Steven, the Midwest Pack's fifth, in my kitchen, shoving a bagel into his mouth. His full lips curled into that infectious, dimpled smile, enhanced by his wide, olive-green eyes and cherub looks, eliminating any chance of him being described as anything other than adorable. His copper hair was cut short enough to wave instead of curl, an obvious attempt to shed his boyish façade for something that made him actually look his nineteen years. At best, he could now pull off handsome-pretty.

"Do you live here?" I asked, taking a seat at the nook and sipping on coffee he'd made that was stronger than anything I would brew.

"Of course not. You've been to my place," he responded with a grin. It was that same look that made you forget he was the Midwest Pack's very own angel of death. As harmless looking as a lamb, he was the disguised wolf—or rather, coyote. You'd never suspect it, could never be prepared for it, and would have a hard time believing it—but he was the personification of death. When you finally realized that, it would be too late for you to do anything about it.

He was right. I had seen his cramped studio apartment, minimally decorated by his mother, of course, since a nineteen-year-old guy would never consider contrasting decorative pillows on a gray microfiber sofa that complemented a herringbone duvet. It was cluttered with books tossed around the room on the sofa, ottoman, and floor. Clothes hung over the back of the desk chair and occasionally made it on top of the dresser. His was probably less chaotic now, since most of his clothes and books now cluttered my guest bedroom. Every time I opened my kitchen cabinets and refrigerator, they were even more occupied by his favorite foods.

"You can't live here," I said. He was the closest thing I had ever had to a best friend, but I still didn't want him as a housemate. I didn't want a housemate, period.

"I don't."

"Keys," I said, extending my hand. I had given them to him several months ago to let the furniture deliveryman in while I was at work.

Fishing into his jeans, he pulled them out without hesitation and placed them in my hand. I had a gnawing feeling that this wasn't the only set he had, but I didn't call him on it.

He took another sip from his coffee mug before he leaned against the kitchen counter, his brow furrowed as his intense, demanding eyes fixed on me. "Tell me what happened Tuesday."

Shifting impatiently, his eyes narrowed as he waited for an answer. "Well?" He stepped closer. An intense calm engulfed the area, an innate response, as the predator lurked behind the dimples and kind face. He studied my body language, listened for small changes in my vitals and modulations in my voice to detect lies and changes in mood. For a group that toed the line quite closely between unscrupulous and possibly unethical behavior, the pack really had issues with lying. The only reason they cared about changes in mood was so that they could exploit them. It was a behavior so heavily ingrained in them that Steven couldn't turn it off even when dealing with me.

I shrugged. It was now just a hazy memory of breaking glass, screams—mostly coming from me—then the concerned inquiries from the neighbors and, eventually, police sirens. It all seemed like a bad dream seventy-two hours later. The small cuts that had covered my face, arms, and neck from the spraying glass had quickly healed. I rolled my fingers over the small scars left on my palm.

"It was magic ... poorly performed magic. It always seems so easy when Josh does it. But the moment he gives it over to me—Ka-boom. It's like we aren't using the same magic," I admitted.

Josh was a witch and a blood ally of the Midwest Pack. Last year, while they were protecting me from the vampires, he had discovered that I was a werewolf and also part vampire. I wished that were the most peculiar thing about me. Too bad it wasn't. I also hosted a spirit shade, a powerful being that possessed great powers. With Josh's help, I was discovering what that meant for me. Although I didn't possess magic ability, I was able to borrow it from others and use it. I also had the unique gift of being able to convert dark magic to natural magic. As a magic junkie, or rather a magic *enthusiast*—Josh's preferred description—it was a skill that piqued his interest.

He wanted to learn how I was able to do it and hopefully learn to do it himself. He had agreed to loan me his magic and show me how to use it with the condition that I allow him to explore how I was able to convert it from dark to natural. It had seemed like a good idea at the time. It was magic, and when it was performed by Josh, it was beguiling and wondrous. But with me, it was chaotic, clumsy, and destructive.

Steven bit down on his lip as he always did when he held back pack-sensitive information. I had been asked to join the year before, and although I had never formally refused, failure to respond was as good as declining. Now, Steven had to walk that fine line of offering advice without violating any of the pack's rules or secrets, both of which they had a great deal of.

"Maybe that's the way it should be. You're a werewolf—not a witch. Perhaps it's magic's way of telling you that you're messing with things you shouldn't be," he said, frowning. "Next time, it might not be just glass cuts. Windows don't blow out of a house without a reason. And I guarantee it will always draw attention. Josh is talented, but you can only come up with so many creative stories. I can also assure you that questions are being raised by more than those in his condo association."

There was more than concern to his voice. There seemed to be a hint of a warning. Who was raising the questions?

"How's Josh?" I asked, meeting his intense gaze as I made an effort to redirect the conversation.

"Josh is Josh." He shrugged. "He seems to be quite skilled at getting himself out of situations that most people can't. The association decided to allow him to stay and is going to help him with the costs." He grinned and shook his head in disbelief.

Josh was a very charming and talented warlock which was good because he always managed to get himself into situations that required more charm than magic.

"I haven't spoken to him since then. He's been avoiding me," I admitted, unable to hide my battered feelings.

"It's not you. Ethan's been giving him crap about everything."

Ethan was the pack's Beta and Josh's older brother. Although Josh possessed the ability to manipulate people in the same manner he did his magic, with total control, captivation, and skill, his brother was immune to it.

Despite Steven's objections, I doubted I would ever stop working with Josh. Becoming competent in the use of magic was my Everest. At times, I felt like I was totally inept and would never make any progress, but conceding my incompetence wasn't an option with Josh. He pushed and pushed, and sometimes I made progress. I was able to move small objects, but only with a large amount of borrowed magic. Often, it was too much for him to give freely. My protective fields were strong, so at least if I held magic, I could protect myself. This was a huge accomplishment because when we had first started, they were nothing more than lucent glamours that looked stronger and more impressive than they actually were. Even with everything that occurred, having the ability to do any of it was empowering.

Our attention went to the door at the same time. Steven stepped toward it to answer it before the doorbell rang.

It was David, my somewhat-neighbor. He lived five houses down, which was a quarter of a mile away. When I had purchased my quaint two-bedroom house, I had compromised my desire for extensive living space for the ability to throw a rock out the back door without it hitting one of my neighbors' siding. Although he wasn't technically my neighbor, David had somehow finagled his way into my life after approaching me during one of my jogs.

He'd been too persistent to ignore, and eventually, I'd agreed to have dinner with him and his partner. That dinner progressed to brunches several times a month and an occasional appearance or two at the many events he invited me to. David was definitely an acquired taste, but he was so delectably human I found myself drawn to him. Since I'd met the Midwest Pack, I had changed to my wolf form several times without the call of the moon, and the disconnect between me and my animal half didn't seem so large anymore. I was slipping, living on the cusp, toeing the line between my animal and woman. I didn't like it. David somehow made me feel like I was grounded in my humanity.

His smile broadened at the sight of Steven. "Well, hello," he purred.

"Hello," Steven forced out with a smile. No matter how uncomfortable he was, there was always a sense of warmth that surrounded him.

The better to trick you with, I thought.

"Oh, kitten, I see why you want to keep him to yourself," David said, backing into the wall as he ogled Steven.

Kitten, ugh. David changed his nicknames for me constantly. Correcting him, glaring at him with contempt, and subjecting him to fiery rants and tantrums only encouraged him. In the past few months, I had been referred to by a number of cutesy names: pumpkin, angel, precious, cuddle bear (the worst by far, only to be surpassed recently by *kitten*), and cookie. I attempted to do the mature thing and ignore the nicknames with the assumption that he would give up. Maturity wasn't working in my favor, and it seemed like the names were getting more absurd.

He was poised as he stood in the middle of my kitchen dressed in his idea of weekend casual: a V-neck forest-green cashmere sweater and chocolate slacks. More assiduously stylish and groomed than handsome, he still had the remnants of a strong jaw and defined features starting to round off and soften with age. Gray streaks peppered his mahogany coif, but instead of aging him, it lent to his sophisticated style. At the tail end of his forties, he was still tall, lean, and fit.

"I haven't received your RSVP for my party on the eleventh," he said, managing to pull his attention from Steven long enough to give me a disapproving look. "If you are going to decline, then you'll have to do it to my face," he continued playfully.

He immediately went back to ogling Steven as though someone had just put dessert in front of him after being on sugar restriction. Steven didn't like attention, although he drew a great deal of it, from the soccer moms down the street to the teenage girls next door. They all seemed to look a little too long when he was around.

David was known for his parties and small get-togethers. If it could be celebrated, he celebrated it. It didn't matter the occasion: President's Day, Columbus Day, Martin Luther King Day, Arbor Day, Black Friday.

After giving Steven his undivided attention, he managed to

remember I was still in the room and smiled in my direction before focusing on his reason for the visit. "You have to come," he entreated.

"I'm sorry, I won't be able to," I declined, shooting Steven a look. The party was the night of a full moon. While they were enjoying drinks and fine food with friends, I would be in a cage, waiting for my body to betray me as it wrenched, contorted, and stretched, breaking bones in order to reassemble into an animal, which, if left to her own devices, would rip him to shreds. Instead of telling him that, I marshaled a decorous smile and continued to decline.

"Reschedule your other plans. It won't be a party without you," he insisted with a wide grin.

But I only held his attention for a moment as he directed it back toward Steven.

"She said no," Steven said, his tone harsh enough to make David stand a little straighter.

He looked at Steven and forced a pleasant look while Steven's gaze narrowed. The full moon was a source of contention between us. I continued to sedate and cage myself during it. Steven hated that. He accepted it because he knew he couldn't stop me. If accidentally over-sedating myself hadn't deterred me, his anger wouldn't, either. In the past, my mother had always done it for me. I'd never paid attention to how she did it. All I knew was that I was awake and, after a quick shot, I wasn't. After the over-sedation incident, Steven had convinced Dr. Jeremy Baker, the pack physician, to help me during full moons. It was an agreement that both he and Dr. Baker had accepted begrudgingly.

Steven's unresolved anger was turning the small room into an inferno, and the primordial nature that most were-animals had a difficult time suppressing was starting to peek through. I could feel David's discomfort escalating. He quickly excused himself. I promised to call him later, but I doubt he heard me as he breezed out of the house.

~

It was nearly one in the afternoon, and I had left Steven at my house with strict orders that when I returned, his things needed to be at *his* apartment. I waved hello to the owner of the gym. His large, muscular arm shot up in a quick wave as I scanned my membership card. I didn't bother smiling at him; he never returned it. He was of medium height with defined, bulky muscles that covered every inch of his body. An ex-Marine who hadn't truly assimilated to civilian life, he wore his stern face and coarse attitude like a uniform. If it weren't for its prime location, the gym wouldn't have been nearly as successful, given that his personality wasn't bringing in much business.

I walked briskly past him and was moving at a swift trot as I rushed past the typical weekend gym patrons: the Barbie, the "I'm going to lose the weight this year" New Year's resolutioners, the runners too high on endorphins to pay me any attention, the weekend warriors that only saw the gym on Saturdays and were too sore the rest of the week to come back, and the typical muscle-head gym rats. Sprinkled throughout the gym personas were the tried-and-true gym attendants. I cruised past the expensive high-end cardio machines with the small flat screens on them toward the stairway to the basement.

It didn't have a sign to direct you—just a black door. If you were supposed to be there, you knew where it was. I called it the dungeon. I never learned the official name. But it was nothing short of one. Unlike upstairs, it didn't have bright lights, wall-length mirrors, and sleek state-of-the-art equipment. The dungeon was dark and dank. The white walls were dingy and covered by blotches of unpainted drywall mud where the owner had given up patching and painting them after a few too many fists or bodies had punctured them. The only equipment was jump ropes, plyometric gear, and a sled on the left side of the boxing ring. I had only been in that area once when I stumbled into it by accident.

My destination was to the right, a large closed-off room with a small window on the door. Matted walls and floors made the tumbles and body slams a little less painful—but not by much. It was the room where some of the men with UFC dreams came to practice and that others used as an opportunity to pay homage to their favorite cult film, *Fight Club*.

When I yanked open the door, the smell of blood and sweat wafted off the mats, burning my nose. "You're late," said the dark-haired woman in the corner, who kept her back to me. Her movements were lithe, graceful, and fluid, a direct contrast to her crisp voice. She pulled her long midnight hair into a tight bun.

Cursing under my breath, I looked at my watch. I was two minutes late, and she was going to make me pay for every second. Winter turned, smiling, pleased at my tardiness. It was times like this she had the opportunity to be a super bitch without remorse because my tardiness was a slap in her face, a blatant lack of appreciation for her time and talent.

Winter was a were-snake and the Midwest Pack's third. What she lacked in physical strength compared to the canidae and felidae she made up for in exceptional fighting skills. Last year, after several nearly successful attempts by the vampires to abduct me, I had asked her to show me how to fight. A brave proposition on my part because, if she had her way, she would have killed me and relieved the pack of their obligation to protect me.

She didn't like me then because she considered me weak. Over the past months, I wasn't sure if she liked me or not, but she no longer considered me weak. I could protect myself, and that was important to me and even more important to her. She didn't want her pack to get involved with protecting me again. "Your protection should be your responsibility alone," she had stated more times than I cared to admit.

I thought Steven liked being my knight in shining armor. I

didn't. Introduced to a world of vampires, were-animals, fae, elves, and all the horrible things in between, being defenseless in it wasn't an option. Unguarded and unskilled made you prey. I'd been prey before and I didn't like it one bit.

I would have preferred a life of innocent oblivion, clueless that such things existed. But the veil had been lifted and I couldn't go back. I knew what was out there, and I needed to be able to protect myself against it.

Winter didn't give me a chance to put my things down before she charged at me. Her elbow clipped my shoulder before I could block her. She was quicker, but I was stronger. I lunged with a front kick, and she hit the ground with a crash but didn't stay down long. She never did. Winter was fast, as fast as vampires, and she was a bitch. I wasn't sure if that factored into her skills, but it really made her tenacious.

When we had first started, I never walked away without black-and-blue evidence of our sparring matches. It had forced me to become a more creative and innovative fighter because she didn't mind pummeling me.

I punched air as she dodged. When I swiped her leg from the left, she looked surprised and impressed as she hit the ground.

"Thank the gods; I was assuming your left side was paralyzed, since you never used it," she said, jumping to her feet.

"Takes a while, but I learn to adapt."

"Let's see how well." She laid into me with a series of kicks and punches, which I parried with speed and deftness.

"You've gotten much better, but I guess you couldn't have gotten worse," she said.

Training with Winter along with lessons in Krav Maga had improved my ability to defend myself significantly. I wasn't a born fighter, and my skills weren't instinctual. They had developed from fear. I feared being hit, I feared pain, and I feared getting hurt. That was my only motivation to protect myself. What influenced Winter was totally different. The risk of pain or injury only drove her harder. The sadist in her drew from it, and whether or not she cared to admit it, her face always showed it—she derived pleasure from the violence and pain. On my side, I kicked her leg, a tactic I had learned in Krav Maga, a low kick that brought her down to the ground. She moved quickly, coming to her feet before I could react.

A smile curled her lips as she said, "Cool. Dirty fighting." And then she attacked.

All the times I had sparred with her, I assumed she was trying to kill me. Now, I realized she had been holding back. I rolled over the ground, avoiding sharp blows to the ribs. A sweep of her leg and she went to the ground hard, giving me time to come to my feet. Sweat glistened, running down her face. I had made her break a sweat. It was the first time. Punches flew, kicks connected high and low. The air filled with the sound of aggressive, brutal grunts and violence. Tomorrow, bruises would cover the greater part of my body.

I dodged her advances and blocked her punches. A wrist block, then a head-butt to her nose had her staggering. She pressed her finger to her nose, and it came back bloody. I stopped, afraid that I had broken it.

Baring her teeth in a wide grin, she said, "Next time, give it more power. Always go for a break. Never hold back, even with me."

Then she attacked me again. It was as though my giving her a bloody nose had eliminated the very narrow constraints she had put on herself. She attacked with full aggression. I parried and failed. I shifted and dodged her attacks with little success. A combination of kicks, then a final blow to my sternum sent me crashing into the ground. She kicked me in the ribs. I held back a groan through clenched teeth as I rolled to my side to avoid another.

Before I could come to my feet, she slithered around me and put me into a submission hold. My arm was twisted around my back. Pressure from her foot pressing on the joint had the ligaments screaming. I attempted to struggle out of it. She pressed harder.

"Just give before I snap your arm, you stubborn woman!" she barked. Winter had studied many forms of martial arts in her twenty-three years and had combined them to come up with her own style of fighting. Her holds usually placed you in a positional disadvantage. The only way to break them was to break something on yourself as well. She made sure of that.

"Give," I finally conceded with a sharp breath.

"No. Unacceptable."

I gritted my teeth and bit back the pain.

"Say it," she demanded.

Feeling the muscles of my shoulder and ligaments stretched to their limits, I mumbled, "I submit."

Winter didn't just want to dominate you. She needed you to acknowledge that you had been dominated.

She released the hold, slipped from under me, and walked over to her bag. Once I sat up, she tossed me a bottle of water before sinking onto the floor in the corner.

"What do you hate the most: the pack or the idea of it?" she asked before taking a long drink from her bottle.

She didn't often talk to me afterward. In fact, she was usually out the door before I could say good-bye. Her engaging me with something other than suggestions on how to improve my techniques left me baffled. It took a long time for me to answer.

"Did I hit your head too hard, or are you still trying to grasp the complex skill of speech?" she inquired. In spite of her being a snake—generally known for their charm—she didn't really possess much of it. Most men were too enamored by her looks to give a second thought about her less-than-attractive personality. She was Egyptian, with beautiful sun-kissed skin. Delicate features set in a round face made the harsh things that came out of her mouth less offensive. Her pale hazel eyes always seemed cold and even colder when she was agitated; then you were treated to her serpent eyes, complete with intimidating vertical slits.

She cleared her throat, annoyed, as she waited for an answer.

I hadn't officially declined the offer, but there was a part of me that had a hard time accepting. Joining the Midwest Pack meant sharing in their power. They had it in droves, but it also meant a commitment to my wolf half. It was saying to hell with humanity and embracing a part of me I didn't particularly like. For years, I had despised having to share my body with an animal and had just recently upgraded from self-loathing to reluctant acceptance—but it was acceptance nonetheless. However, there wasn't a desire to bond with it. I always felt that if I gave in to her desires, then I was giving up on my humanity. Pack members paid homage to their inner animal. Human form was just the vessel that housed their preferred half. They celebrated it, enjoyed it, and developed such a bond that being around them was the closest someone could get to interacting with violent predacious animals and living to tell the tale.

Yes, they walked around bipedal—most of them highly educated and successful, socializing with the mere humans of the world—but it was just pure Darwinism. The power they had, the assets they enjoyed, the lifestyle they required couldn't be achieved by living on four legs in the woods, so they adapted.

I shrugged. "I don't know. For years, I ignored my wolf half. I don't know how to be part of a power structure that embraces that part so freely." What if I joined and couldn't take it—or like it? Committing to them wasn't like testing out a membership at the neighborhood gym or the local social club. You didn't pay an early termination fee to cancel. Although I didn't have any evidence to support it, I believed the only way out was death. *Isn't that how the mob, drug cartels, and street gangs work?*

She scoffed, "You think ignoring it is going to make it go away? How's that working for you so far?"

A wry half-smile was my only response.

It wasn't working. "Me declining is not a reflection on your pack, but of my own issues. I hope you aren't taking it personally."

Her face held a look of utter dismay. "I'm sorry. Did I give you the impression that I care? I don't. I care more about a cat playing with a ball of yarn than you joining the pack. Join or go play your silly werewolf games alone in a corner. Either way, I simply can't bring myself to care. I am tired of Josh and Steven squawking about you being out there 'alone and unprotected.' Personally, if you don't mind being alone, then why the hell should we?" She used the only tone she knew—harsh.

"I'm sorry. I don't know why it's not an easy choice."

She exhaled. "There is concern over how close you are to Steven and Josh. It's a conflict of interest. You can't deny the pack but expect to be this closely associated with us without it causing some issues. You are aware of where we stand. If you're not one of us and you find yourself in a difficult situation—"

"I know. You all won't help me. And if I become a threat to the pack, I will be treated as most threats are and eliminated," I said, repeating what I'd been told several times. I knew that speech well because it was the last thing Sebastian, the Midwest Pack's Alpha, had said to me when he asked me to join. Steven, on behalf of the pack, had reiterated it on several occasions.

"Do you *really* understand? Despite everything, Sebastian has been kind. You've exhausted it." She sighed.

Sebastian wasn't very fond of me. He didn't mind telling me at every opportunity, but the true indicator was when he'd tried to strangle me. I knew then we weren't going to be friends. He disliked me so much that he'd added that little tidbit about eliminating me when he'd asked me to join his pack. Oddly enough, those weren't the things that deterred me.

Perhaps I showed a certain level of panic and fear at the mention of Sebastian because when she spoke again, there was a soothing gentleness to her voice. "I'm hungry. Let's shower and get lunch."

Distracted by the new information, I followed her toward the locker room, becoming increasingly suspicious with each step. Winter had only invited me to lunch once, and she spent most of it haranguing me over my pitiful skills. "What's really going on?" I asked.

"We'll talk at lunch."

"No, now." I was anxious and didn't have the patience to wait until lunch.

"Dr. Baker won't be able to help you any longer," she admitted in a detached voice.

The anxiety escalated. I felt nauseous. What was I going to do this month? I didn't want to go back to trying to figure out how to sedate myself. Whatever he gave me didn't leave me with the full-moon hangover that I had come to accept as part of hiding from the werewolf. Even my physician mother hadn't been able to sedate me without me waking up feeling like I had been tossing back tequila shots most of the night.

It didn't take a Rhodes Scholar to know what this conversation was about. I considered how much time Steven had spent at my house, the constant and tedious practicing over the past weeks with Josh. It was as though they'd been given a deadline to recruit me, after which I would be persona non grata. It explained why Josh hadn't returned my calls and Steven had willingly given my keys up when I asked for them earlier. Sebastian must have given them an ultimatum, and they were slowly severing their ties with me.

I fell in step with her as we walked to the locker room. "Sebastian controls an awful lot. Can you pick your friends and lovers, or does he pick them for you?" My anger soon found a place right next to my frustration.

Her tone and face shifted into pack-professional mode. "You can't have it both ways: you can't deny the pack yet expect to use our resources. You've been extended courtesies that aren't usual for us. You need to make some decisions." She slipped into the locker room, grabbed her things, and headed for the shower so quickly I didn't have time to say anything else.

Winter didn't waste time showering and getting dressed. I slowpoked around, each moment becoming less enthusiastic about our lunch. I didn't want her to confirm what I had suspected. She didn't wait around for me in the crowded locker room while the weekend gym rats chatted one another up. At first, they had attempted to engage her, asking her questions about her workout, admiring her slim, fit frame. Each inquiry received a monosyllabic answer. Eventually they gave up trying to include the unremorsefully discourteous woman in their gym friendship circle. She didn't seem concerned once they stopped but they remained at a loss. Their Midwestern sensibilities had a hard time understanding and grasping such rudeness.

Every so often, they pulled me into the conversation, asking questions on how I stayed so toned. What was my secret? I felt like telling them, "I'm half animal. You want to trade places?" but instead I gave them one of my many rehearsed responses. I caught a glimpse of Winter leaving the locker room and rushed to catch up with her.

The dark-haired serpent looked bored, leaning against her white Navigator. "Meet me at Panera, the one near that café you like on 10th Street," she said as she opened the door. Stopping abruptly, she looked around, scanning the area. She stepped to the back of the SUV and opened it. As she reached into it, a tall, scaly slate-gray creature, something I hadn't encountered before, stepped into our line of sight. Its massive arm struck her, sending her crashing back into the brick wall of the building. The sword she had managed to grab out of the trunk skidded across the ground. The creature struck at her again before she was able to block it. Its clawed hand swiped across her chest, slicing it open and spilling a deluge of blood. Despite the injuries to her chest and abdomen, she fought it off aggressively. When it loomed over her, she kicked the large reptile away with all the force her injured body could muster. It plodded back several feet. Coughing up blood, she raked at the wall, pulling herself up to stand.

I ran for the sword, picked it up mid-stride, and swung. It cut through the thin top layer but became impacted in thick tissue. I tugged hard. By the third jarring pull, I dislodged the sword and plunged it into the creature again, where I left it.

Grabbing the key that Winter had dropped at the back of the SUV, I jumped into the driver's seat and careened into the monster. I pushed the car into four-wheel drive, reversed, and slammed into it again and then again, pinning it under the vehicle. The SUV rocked as the thing attempted to move from under it. The Navigator started moving. I jumped out of it as it rolled back and the creature began to crawl from under it. I ran to Winter, lifted her as gently and quickly as possible, and brought her to my Honda Civic. I had to shove her into the backseat in order to quickly get in the driver's seat and back away from the creature. It limped, but it was still plodding toward us faster than anything that had sustained such injuries should have.

I backed away far enough to turn around without hitting the thing and damaging my car. It stayed in my line of sight for a few minutes before vanishing. I half expected it would just pop up in front of me. I had learned the hard way that many things in this dreadful world traveled in more ways than on foot. That was the worst feeling, when you thought you'd gotten away—and poof, they were standing right in front of you.

After I had driven several miles and was sure the creature wasn't going to reappear, I gave Winter my undivided attention. She looked like hell. Blood oozed from her wounds, her skin was blanched, and her breathing was just sharp gurgles. I pulled over and did my best to stop the bleeding and compress the wounds that bled with anything I could find in my gym bag.

Please don't die. Please don't die.

I grabbed my phone as I started to drive and scrolled through the call log until I came to Dr. Baker's number. It was near the top because I had spoken with him less than two days before to schedule a time for him to sedate me during the next full moon.

He responded after the first ring. "Skylar—"

"Winter is hurt ... bad ... I think she's ... she's bleeding a lot." I couldn't bring myself to say that I thought she was dying.

"Where are you?"

"On Westin Street ... just past the Midway intersection ... I can be at the retreat in thirty."

"Okay, I'll meet you there."

I hung up and looked back at Winter in the rearview mirror. Her breaths were so shallow that I considered taking her to the hospital just five miles away instead of the pack's home. The only thing that deterred me was what the doctors would find when they examined her. I could only imagine what type of weirdness she had going on as a were-snake.

That was the reason most were-animals joined packs. It was not just for the innate need to be around their familiars, but for the convenience. Each pack had their own physicians, which made life a lot easier when members needed medical attention.

When Winter's breathing paused too long, I pulled over to give her rescue breaths. I had to stop three times. Between stopping to help her, slowing down any time her breathing pattern changed, and trying to avoid the massive potholes in the road to keep from causing her further pain, I had only driven seven miles.

A dark blue sports car darted in and out of my line of sight in my rearview mirror. I maintained my speed, driving through the traffic, but the car kept its pace, barreling down the crowded street, closing in on me. The cars in front of it scattered. I expected to see a trail of flashing police lights behind it, but undoubtedly they couldn't keep up. Once it was closer, I got a glimpse of the driver: Gavin, the pack's fourth. Of course Sebastian had sent someone to retrieve Winter. He wouldn't leave the job of bringing her safely to them to someone like me—a lone were-animal. I was sure the very thought of it left a bitter taste in his mouth.

When Gavin leaned on his horn, I pulled over to the side. He glared at me from the driver's seat, and Josh jumped out.

Josh took one look at Winter and let out a string of expletives as he pulled her closer to him. He closed his eyes, his teeth grinding, and remained still for a few moments. Inhaling a long breath, he slowly opened his eyes to find that she had slipped out of consciousness again. She lay limp and broken in his arms. The extent of her injuries forced a worrisome scowl on his face that he didn't seem to be able to relax.

"I'll see you at the house," he mumbled. Then he disappeared with her.

Being a witch had its benefits.

CHAPTER 2

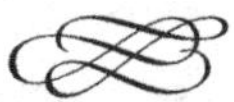

By the time I arrived at the house, I was grateful that Josh and Gavin had shown up. The pack's retreat was tucked away and camouflaged by mature trees that created florets in the landscape cloaking the surrounding area. A GPS wouldn't locate this place. They made sure of that. No one stumbled on this house by accident. If you were here, it was because you wanted to be. It had been a year since I had been to the retreat, and it was harder to get to than I remembered. I had gotten lost twice trying to find the obscure single-lane road that led there. It was a palatial three-story brick home, hidden from the road and the surrounding neighbors by hundreds of acres of foliage and coppice that acted as a bastion and habitat for both wildlife and were-animals. They could change into their animal form and run through the wild undetected by the distant neighbors or anyone else that happened to stumble upon the deserted road.

I pulled into the only available parking space in the crowded driveway. Trails of splattered blood met me at the breezeway. I negotiated around them as well as the puddles of sanguineous fluid that covered the living room floor. Sebastian moved past me toward the clinic, carrying another injured were-animal. Three others followed behind, holding more battered bodies.

The first time I saw the pack's in-house clinic, I thought it was grossly impractical. Set up better than any hospital I had seen, there were nine medical beds aligned against the white walls, each surrounded by floor-to-ceiling privacy curtains. The high-gloss rubber flooring made the room seem sterile and cold. Several vitals-monitoring machines were in the far left corner, a portable x-ray machine stood in the other. A microscope sat next to the large oak desk that was positioned in the center of the room to allow easy observation of each bed. Now it seemed like it would be impractical not to have such a well-equipped clinic.

For the next few hours, there was a steady flow of injured people brought into the house. Dr. Baker moved with composed confidence as he triaged, gave orders, and quickly determined who needed to be taken to the clinic and who could be treated in the living room. They were quickly running out of space in the former.

Dr. Baker controlled the situation with deftness and precision, unaffected by the constant influx of injured. Only after he lost the first were-animal did his steely composure crack. He took in the moment with a long pause, observing the state of his pack, and sighed. The smell of blood inundated the air; splattered trails of it soiled the floor. The constant sounds of monitors beeping and clicking were as much a distraction as the painful groans that pierced through the chaos of the clinic. The soft sound of someone taking their final breath resonated the loudest. Dr. Baker masked its effect on him, seemingly immune, but Kelly, the nurse practitioner and the only human I was aware of who had such an intimate knowledge of were-animals, didn't possess such skills.

She was faltering under the stress. Distressed lines formed along her delicate features to the point they seemed harsh—troubled. Large brown eyes glistened under examining lights as she fought back her tears. When she placed another white sheet over someone, she leaned in, whispering what I assumed was a prayer. Tears splattered on the sheets, and this time she was slower at wiping them away.

"Three gone, eleven injured so far," Kelly said once she finally forced herself to move from the body.

"Let's get back to work," he said with clinical detachment. It was what she needed, a reminder that they didn't have the luxury of dwelling on the travesty. She went back to the beds, checking orders, writing things on a clipboard, and moving throughout the clinic on autopilot.

It had been nearly three hours and the situation had come to an abrupt calm. Those who lived were stable, but there were still so many injured that I was recruited to assist. Crouched on the other side of the living room, I applied a compression bandage to the lacerated abdomen of a were-hyena. The skin was so inflamed that it warmed my fingers through the gauze. Perspiration pooled as he drifted in and out consciousness. It didn't take an MD after my name to realize he had been poisoned. Dr. Baker came over and immediately had someone take him back into the clinic. He rambled off instructions to Kelly, who was scribbling things down.

But the calm was short-lived. Minutes later, the front doors swung open again, and Ethan, the pack's Beta, carried in someone whose torso and face were so battered and bloody I barely recognized him as their sixth. Josh came in not too far behind, stopping abruptly at the entrance. His gaze swept over the room, a gasp catching in his throat as he took in the scene; blood and injured, mangled bodies made him pause and take a breath. It seemed like an eternity before he could exhale, and it was a slow ragged one. Killing a were-animal was hard, so difficult that it was easy to consider them invincible. That was why it was even more devastating when you saw one die or linger on the cusp of death.

Things were a mess, and though Dr. Baker seemed like he had it all under control, it was hard to hide the concern and curiosity over who could have done this. I couldn't imagine things getting any worse.

Dammit. Never say it can't get worse—because it always does.

A short Hispanic man rushed through the door; a limp body lay in his arms, wrapped in a bloodstained white sheet. As he came closer, I could see the battered body. Pale skin with light freckles speckled along her nose and cheeks, slight frame, and russet-colored hair. It was Joan—Steven's mother.

Both Sebastian and Steven took a step forward and stared at the body. For a brief moment, neither of them moved. Steven opened his mouth but words wouldn't come out. Sebastian was the first to respond. "How many?" he asked, leading the man toward the clinic.

Wincing at the question, the Hispanic man's voice was like sandpaper. "Everyone's gone except Taylor. Joan was like this when I got there," he said.

The short blonde behind him—I assumed it was Taylor—stayed close. She barely gave him enough room to navigate around the furniture. She was coiled so tight I didn't want to be in a twenty-mile radius when she finally snapped.

"Taylor, stay here," Sebastian instructed. She stopped midstep. After a long moment, she sank into a corner and gnawed at her fingernails.

I split my attention between her and Steven, whose eyes grew distant, slipping into whatever place would offer him comfort. It was hard to look at him. He already had had to deal with the deaths of his birth parents from an automobile accident and his sister from a vampire's bloodlust. Death—he deserved some form of reprieve. Joan had to live.

He followed Sebastian to the clinic. "You have to stay out here,"

Sebastian insisted, backing into the room and handing her off to Dr. Baker. Steven's gaze swept over her, closely watching as she struggled to take breaths that were reduced to fluid-filled gurgles. Large claw marks covered her chest, abdomen, and legs. His attention stayed pinned on the gash across her neck, which gaped open. He started through the door again, trying to push his way past Sebastian.

"Steven, stay out of here, okay?" Sebastian urged.

He hadn't heard a word Sebastian said and kept trying to force his way past him. When Sebastian ushered him back, he made an attempt to push his way through again. All he wanted was to be close to his mother, but if he was like this now, he wouldn't be any better once in the clinic and Sebastian knew it. "Steven," he said again softly, but his voice was laden with command. It was only a matter of time before he lost his patience.

Stepping forward, I took hold of Steven's arm. He pulled it away and started for the door again. Sebastian held him back, pressing him against the wall, trying to get Steven to focus on him, but he was too far gone, his attention lost on the other side of the double doors.

"Steven, look at me," Sebastian said in a low, firm voice, but all Steven could do was shake his head, unfocused and uncontrolled. Sebastian didn't have the patience at this time to deal with him in such a state, and it was starting to show.

"I have him," I said, sidling up next to him. Surprisingly, he nodded and moved aside before disappearing into the clinic.

Just a few feet away, we could hear Dr. Baker giving instructions, instruments ringing on their tray, hisses of pain, Kelly's soft reassuring voice, and the sharp grunts of bones being set. All the noise and commotion could have been distracting, but there was a distinct silence and calm between Steven and me.

"Steven," I said softly, but it still didn't get his attention. My hands slipped over his, and I held them until he forced his gaze to meet mine. Slowly, I led him away from the door. "There isn't anything you can do right now. Let Dr. Baker handle this. It will be fine." I had a hard time saying *she* would be fine. The way she looked, I felt like that was a lie—and I couldn't lie to Steven.

After minutes of staring at the clinic doors, golden brown waves rolled across his olive eyes as he directed his attention to me. The horror vanished and sorrow shed, he slipped into a place of quiet resolve—traumatized to the point where he seemed defeated. I could feel all eyes on him—on us, and I wanted to get him out of there.

"Come with me," I continued in a gentle voice. If he heard my emotions—the sorrow, desperation, and immense fear—it would make things worse.

"Steven, when she's stable, I will come get you," Ethan assured as Steven reluctantly followed me out of the living room. The crowd of people parted, clearing a path for us to leave. At first, I felt like a child trying to get a distracted mastiff to follow me, but as I continued to talk softly to him, he eventually complied.

With lumbering movements, he trailed me upstairs into one of the bedrooms and plopped facedown on the bed. I leaned against the doorframe. I didn't expect him to say anything, and for a long time, he didn't, until he mumbled, "She's going to die. I've been through this enough times, but I still don't know how to prepare for it."

I didn't know what to say, and each time I blinked, my tears fought harder to escape. I reminded him of the year before when he was injured and close to death, how Sebastian and Dr. Baker saved him. I hoped more than ever they could do it again for his mother.

For nearly an hour, Steven stayed in the room in virtual silence, and then he closed his eyes. Message received—he wanted me to give him some space. I couldn't bring myself to leave him; so instead, I sat on the floor outside, near the door.

The house was now calm. Most of the rooms were soundproof. I couldn't hear anything if people were in them, but I gathered most of my information from the chatter downstairs and from talk in the hallways.

The atmosphere was intense—and became even more so as I felt Ethan's hard presence coming toward me. His anger and frustration hit me like a blast of wind. You never had to guess his mood; you could feel it. It was an ineffable thing that sent me into flight mode whenever he was around. Deep cobalt eyes always held a hint of steel gray, a true sign that his wolf was always present, skulking and ready to be released. He padded rather than walked. "Can we talk?" he asked.

I peeked into the room where Steven still lay facedown.

"He'll be fine. Come with me."

I didn't move initially, but when he turned back around and beckoned, I glanced back into the room at Steven before I followed him down the hall to one of the empty bedrooms. It was the same one I had stayed in the year before, when the were-animals had kept me a virtual prisoner to prevent vampires from abducting me. Soft yellow walls were faux painted to make them look aged and delicate. Deep mahogany furniture was placed neatly throughout, and thick floral drapes were slightly open to allow the sun to illuminate the room. I took a seat in the chair across the room as he quietly paced. Each movement was lithe and predacious.

Although he wasn't angry with me—just noticeably agitated and stressed—I could barely suppress that urge to leave the room. Self-preservation made me want to distance myself as much as possible from violent beings.

He eventually stopped pacing. He scrubbed his face with his hands; strong jaws clenched so tight it made his prominent cheeks stand out. Rigid lips turned down into a frown, but despite his distressed appearance, Ethan still managed to look handsome. This was something that was a battle to admit each time I saw him because his personality was far from appealing. So intense and powerful, he seemed to always be at odds with anyone and everyone about anything. I believed even the subtle passage of oxygen and carbon dioxide bothered him.

Last year he had kissed me, and I had never experienced anything like it before. It was like being swept into a wave; just when you thought you had control over it, you were pulled under —drowning. If you survived, you felt exhilaration about conquering something you otherwise shouldn't have. Lips pressing against someone else's shouldn't have felt that way.

He stepped closer to me. "Tell me about the thing that attacked Winter." His attentive gaze making it hard to focus.

"I've never seen anything like it before," I admitted, taking several steps back until my back rested against the wall. That wasn't saying much. I was new to the otherworld, and many of the things that peopled it were still new to me. I didn't know of their existence until last year when I read stories in a book in the retreat's library about gods, were-animals, demons, vampires, elves, and fae.

"What did it look like?"

I tried to focus my thoughts and remember everything about the creature. "It stood upright and had a massive body. Its arms were similar to a human's, but instead of fingers, it had claws, long sharp ones. That's what got Winter. And its face was short and scaly—"

"Like a snake?"

I nodded slowly, frowning. There was something about the creature that was vaguely familiar—a scent that I had encountered before.

"Was it a were-animal?"

I considered the question for a long moment, remembering what they looked like midform. Were-animals were gruesome looking in midform and didn't possess the ability to stand upright. Stuck in the liminal position between man and beast, they took on the worst features of both. Oddly mutated during that phase of transition, the vertebrae protruded from the spine into a distorted arc, forcing the changeling into the quadruped position. The forehead bulged too far from the body while the lower jaw moved awkwardly over the misshapen face. Seeing a were-animal in mid-change is a life-altering experience. You saw it once, and you weren't in a hurry to do it again. I believed that was why most of the were-animals I knew could change in under a minute.

"It wasn't a were-animal. If it were, something went terribly wrong with their change."

"Did it say anything?"

"I doubt it could. When I crashed into it, it groaned, but it was just a guttural sound."

He exhaled, taking that well-needed breath as his body relaxed slightly. Frustration still radiated off him in waves as he washed his hands over his face several times. "Twelve different attacks with seven different descriptions of the creatures. I have no idea what these things are," he admitted, and it seemed to pain him to do so. Ethan prided himself on his knowledge of most things. I knew if he didn't know now, it was only a matter of time before he did.

He lowered his head and started to pace slowly. "The Southern Pack is virtually destroyed, and three of ours are dead. Three more may not make it," he said, but he wasn't speaking to me, just assessing the damage and trying to make sense of it, moving slowly as he paced in a circle before me. In silence, his gaze cruised in my direction over my bloodstained jeans and t-shirt and then the bruises on my hands and forearm. "Are you hurt?"

I shook my head. "No, just the typical mementos from sparring with Winter."

Stepping closer, he gently took my arm and studied the bruising. Once satisfied with the results, he released it. "If you weren't there, I doubt she would have survived the attack." It was a realization that didn't seem to bring him much comfort. Winter had been defeated. There weren't many that could do that.

Something changed. His nostrils flared and his cobalt eyes changed to graphite and cold as his body tensed into a defensive stance and his lips pulled into a disapproving sneer. When his attention went to the door, so did mine. Gavin stood there, glaring at me. If I could say I had a nemesis, it would be him. Saying he hated me was a gross understatement. He despised me not for *who* I was but *what* I was—an anomaly that he felt shouldn't exist. He wanted to remedy that. He was angry that his pack had chosen to protect me—even from him. It only fueled his hatred.

Gavin's face was distorted with menacing scorn and acutely fixed on me. "Why is it that whenever she's around, someone gets hurt or dies?" he asked. "She's a thorn in our side—a poison without an antidote. Get rid of her."

"Gavin, leave," Ethan said, focusing on the hostile were-panther standing at the door.

"No. She is no longer under the pack's protection—no longer our problem. Why is she still here?" His voice was hard as he inched closer to me demanding a response that Ethan wouldn't dignify with an answer.

"It wasn't a request," Ethan said.

Gavin didn't move.

I started to inch toward the door, hoping to slide past him and leave.

"You stay right there. He's going to leave," Ethan said, stopping me in my tracks as he kept his attention on the petulant were-panther, who had taken a few more steps into the room.

Gavin broke his gaze from Ethan just long enough to look at me briefly before returning his hardened stare to him. From what Steven had told me, Gavin was a skilled single-target hunter in both animal and human form. When he set his sights on obliteration, there wasn't much that could be done to discourage him. It was great when he was acting on the pack's behalf, but when he wasn't, it was an unnecessary hassle. "I won't ask you again," Ethan warned.

"If Winter dies, so do you," Gavin promised as he backed out of the door. Too bad he didn't take the air of rage that lingered behind with him. As he stormed away, he nearly crashed into Kelly. I'd only met her once during the surprise birthday party he'd thrown for her, which I attended as Steven's guest. She seemed nice, and judging from the way Dr. Baker and his wife doted over her, they admired her.

"Hello, Gavin," she said in a soft, firm tone as he pushed past her. When he didn't respond, she repeated herself in a genteel but persistent voice, urging a response. After he grumbled something, which I assumed was a greeting, she let out an exasperated sigh. "He is quite *intense*." She shook her head, her gaze trailing after him, her full lips pressed into a moue.

No, not intense—bat-shit crazy.

Kelly didn't strike me as one who became easily flustered, and I doubt anyone would if they spent as much time as she did with the pack. But now, she seemed uncomfortable, fidgeting with the dark brown corkscrew ringlets that formed a thick halo around her round face. Soft deep-set walnut-colored eyes focused on Ethan. "Josh is—" she started slowly.

"In the way?" Ethan interjected.

Her lips curled into a small sympathetic smile. "I know he's trying to help, but—"

"I'll take care of it." He followed her out the door, but stopped short. The traces from the altercation with Gavin still emanated off him in waves. "Stay away from Gavin," he warned me.

Did he expect me to go skipping behind the ill-tempered maniac that wanted me dead? Perhaps he thought I was dying to ask him out for coffee and biscotti.

Just as Ethan was about to go downstairs, Kelly gently touched his arm, and she looked in my direction with an apologetic smile. I knew she wanted a few minutes of privacy with him. Perhaps she was aware that he and his brother sometimes didn't play well together, but I doubted she possessed the skills to help them with that.

Steven was still where I had left him, lying on the bed pretending to be asleep when I returned to the room. I didn't take offense. He wanted to be alone, and I knew from experience that the last thing you wanted when you were grieving was someone standing around gawking at you. I walked downstairs and looked through the house, trying to familiarize myself with it again. The dual staircases spiraled. One led you to the back of the house, placing you near the kitchen. The other led toward the living room. I went to the kitchen, where several were-animals that I didn't know had gathered. The air was stifling as stress, anger, concern, and even fear fused together.

The moment I walked in, all eyes turned to me with blank stares. As long as I remained a lone wolf, I wasn't going to receive an open-armed welcome from the were-animals. I was an interloper, a trespasser, a person who dared to deny their pack and still had the audacity to hang around. Their narcissism and arrogance wouldn't allow them to take the rejection lightly. But I had helped them, so instead of looks of contempt, I received cool glances of disinterest.

I quickly navigated through the kitchen to the other side of the house, hoping to gather more information about Winter's condition. The last thing I had overheard was that she had a fever they couldn't manage. She wasn't responding to any of the treatments, and they were considering putting her into a medically induced coma.

The house was just as I remembered it. Despite the care taken by whomever had decorated it, you couldn't overlook that it was a residence for purpose, not style. Large, sturdy, dark-colored furniture filled most of the rooms. The walls were painted in varying colors with one thing in common—faux finish to hide any imperfections from where they had been patched or replaced.

They had changed the great room. They didn't have a choice but to do so. Last year, Sebastian had destroyed the couch during one of his fits of rage, and what *he* didn't demolish, Josh and Ethan did during one of their fights. The new furniture was slightly smaller and more rugged than the previous furniture. They had removed the ottoman and spread the furniture out, giving the large room more open space. I guessed that the next time Ethan and Josh or anyone else wanted to destroy the furniture they would really have to work at it.

Josh barely acknowledged me as he rested against the wall just adjacent to the clinic. He was still dressed in the bloodstained t-shirt from earlier, his hands shoved deep into his pockets, his face pensive and withdrawn. I assumed he had been locked out of the clinic. I was about to warn him that Ethan was on the way and to be prepared, but I was too late. Out of my peripheral vision, I could see him slowly approaching Josh. I stepped out of sight around the corner, hugging it. There wasn't anything I or anyone else could do. When it involved Ethan and Josh, everyone knew to step back and hope there wasn't too big of a mess to clean up when they were done.

Josh looked up and frowned at Ethan's approach. "I'm not leaving," he said adamantly.

Ethan shrugged. "Okay," he said softly as he took a place next to his brother. It was when they stood next to each other that both their differences and similarities were apparent. They both had brown hair; Josh's was caramel while Ethan's was a deep chestnut. Even after the perils of today, Ethan's was still neat while his brother's was always mussed. I had always assumed

Josh's style was the result of extensive and tedious grooming, an effort to pull off the bedhead style. But after I had gotten to know him, I found out that his morning routine included a shower, and the closest thing his hair came to being styled was when he towel-dried it. Shaving was optional and done infrequently, so his appealing looks were often shadowed by a light beard. Ethan was clean-cut.

Ethan's eyes were cobalt but usually looked gunmetal, a constant reminder that his were-half dwelled too close to the surface. Josh's deep arctic blue eyes managed to be just as penetrating as they were welcoming.

Covered in blood as well, Ethan didn't look as shambolic as his brother. His tailored blue khakis and white shirt were stained in crimson but remained unwrinkled, the sleeves rolled mid-forearm, each cuff an even, crisp fold. His brother's attire always consisted of jeans and graphic t-shirts that displayed the multitude of tattoos that decorated his forearms and the greater part of his shoulders and back. "Staying here isn't going to make things any better. You know that, right?" Slightly taller than Josh, he rested his forehead against his brother's.

Josh moved away, pacing the floor. "What should I do, go home and wait for a phone call telling me she didn't make it?" His voice was harsh, laced with concern and anger that was misdirected toward Ethan. He shook his head slowly. "You didn't see her. She didn't even look like herself—like a person."

Ethan leaned back against the wall, his head turned toward his brother. "She'll be fine," he said softly.

Josh's gaze shifted to Ethan as he studied him for a long moment. He would never be as perceptive as a were-animal, but when it came to Ethan, he exceeded their ability to detect lies. "You don't believe that," he finally said.

Silence. And it remained that way for such a long time that Josh gave up on a response, but finally, Ethan exhaled a long, ragged breath, shaking his head in quiet resolve.

"I'm not leaving," Josh said firmly, taking a place next to the clinic door.

Josh was in a bad place, and asking him to leave would have led to a disastrous display of obstinacy and will, of which both of them possessed far too much. It would have erupted in violence, which was the last thing they needed.

Ethan nodded his head slowly, watching his brother carefully. "Fine, we'll stay until we know something. Okay?" He seemed to have found an odd acceptance of death, violence, and the uncertainty of life. Josh hadn't.

~

It had been nine hours since I had arrived at the house. I should have left hours before, but like Josh, I just couldn't do it. I needed to hear something, or at the very least, to know that everyone was stable and going to make it. I spent most of my time upstairs with Steven, and when I grew restless, I idly roamed the house.

Taylor, the blonde who had accompanied the Southern Pack's physician, was still in the same spot as earlier, nestled into the corner, wallowing in her own torturous bubble of self-doubt and guilt as she worked on chewing the nails on her left hand to nubs after spending the previous hour working on the right. Based on the tidbits of information I gathered, Joan had been injured protecting her.

Each time she lifted her eyes from the floor, shimmers of light gold rolled across the pupils. The severe look on her face made her cold and unapproachable, extinguishing any thoughts I had of talking to her. Instead, I watched her from the other side of the room as she became restless, pushing herself from the wall to pace a small area only to return to it within minutes.

A light knock on the front door half an hour later pulled my attention away from the barely stable Taylor. Light footsteps entered the door before anyone could answer it or invite her in. A familiar scent wafted through the large house—floral and intensely human. It was Chris, Ethan's former lover and a Hunter. *Hunter* was a misnomer—she was a mercenary and human only according to the loosest definition of the word. She traded with Demetrius, the Master of the Northern Seethe, offering him her blood, and, in return, she fed from him, gaining temporary use of his strength, agility, and speed. But there was something about her lithe, calculated movements, intense gaze, and élan for violence that led me to believe that even before she started trading with Demetrius she was just as dangerous and vicious as the company she kept.

"So the rumors are true. Your pack is under attack," Chris said, taking one look at Sebastian as he cleared the corner.

He was starting to show the stress of today's events and with the most recent reports that four other pack members had been killed earlier, I doubted he was in the mood to deal with her.

The moment Chris sauntered into the middle of the great room, Taylor's head snapped up. Her gaze locked on Chris. Light brown eyes became rapacious and violent, as a distinct feline glare homed in. She lunged, pushing Chris hard enough that she skidded several feet back across the room. Recovering from the attack quickly, she countered with a strike to Taylor's jaw, flooring her. Taylor swept Chris's leg and she crashed to the floor.

All the pent-up rage that had plagued Taylor went into her strikes as she hit Chris. She parried several of the blows and quickly gained control of the situation, pushing Taylor off her. Then there was the distinct sound of a gun being cocked. Chris pressed the barrel firmly against Taylor's temple and said between gasps, "I know you're fast, cheetah, but I doubt you can dodge a bullet at this range."

Her attention remained on Taylor as she addressed Sebastian. "I've come here as a neutral representative for Demetrius's family, which has been compromised, as well. My intentions aren't to hurt anyone, but I will if forced to."

Neutral? Who was she kidding?

Taylor's gaze kept shifting to the barrel of the gun with such defiance it seemed like she was calculating her speed and that of a bullet.

"Let her go," Sebastian ordered, stepping closer to them.

She moved slowly, but before she could move to a full standing position, Taylor knocked the gun out of her hand and grabbed her by the throat. Chris grabbed Taylor's arms and fell to her back. Taylor tried to break the fall, but Chris held her forearms in an iron grip. She grunted when she hit the floor with Taylor's weight on her, and then threw a leg up and locked it across her other ankle. It was a perfect triangle choke, the legs scissoring Taylor's neck. Taylor struggled as Chris slowly strangled her, holding her tightly by the arms.

Sebastian walked over with an immense calm that made me nervous. It was during his calmest moments that you were hit with the most severe storm. His face was stern and portentous as he pushed them apart. When Taylor lunged for Chris again, his arm hooked around her waist and pulled her back. She made several more unsuccessful attempts before she turned to Sebastian and snarled. I expected him to respond with the type of virulence that could clear a room. Instead, he took her face between his hands, forcing her gaze on his. Her face held a grimace as an internal battle between beast and woman tore through her. It tensed as she attempted to keep her eyes on Sebastian. But she kept breaking her focus to look at Chris, which only incited her rage.

Chris wasn't the real problem, just an outlet for the frustration building in the young woman. Her Alpha was dead, her Beta fighting for her life, and she was having a hard time dealing with the combination of emotions. Control was far from her grasp, and she was unable to manage her anger.

Her face trembled in Sebastian's hands as she blinked back tears. His forehead rested on hers. His words were soft, gentle entreaties for her to calm down as he kept her face firmly between his hands. But she was too far gone. After a few moments, he nodded his head. "I know," he admitted in a whisper. He continued to speak to her in a low, soothing voice. Her face flushed as the trembling persisted. He sighed at her friable condition. "Okay, Taylor," he conceded, stepping away. She dropped to her knees, and her clothing shredded as she shifted into animal form. Steven, along with several others, had come into the living room in response to the noise. As Taylor ran toward the door, Steven reached it just in time to open it for her.

"Watch her," Sebastian instructed. Steven and a few other were-animals went out behind her in a fast run.

"Let's talk," Chris insisted once she had Sebastian's attention.

CHAPTER 3

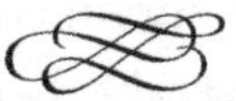

As Steven and I stood next to Sebastian and Taylor in front of the restaurant, watching as the valet took Ethan's keys from him, I considered the string of events that had led me to this potentially catastrophic moment. I blamed Chris because she had acted as the intermediary. She had foolishly thought it could be handled over the phone. Instead, it resulted in the trading of malicious insults, threats, and verbal attacks. She had finally intervened and suggested that they meet, but Sebastian refused to allow the vampires to come to the pack's house, and Demetrius felt the same way about the were-animals coming to theirs. Finally, they had reluctantly agreed to play nice—or their distorted version of it—and meet in a neutral location.

Even with Chris's assurance that she could easily mediate the situation, neither one felt comfortable meeting alone and wanted a buffer. But anyone they chose to accompany them would be closer to a double-edged sword than a buffer. If things went bad, they would want their best present—and the best weren't often known for having an amicable side and a good temperament.

Before I could make my escape from the pack's home, Sebastian made a peremptory request, informing me that Steven would pick me up at nine. Like Joan, Steven could be diplomatic when necessary, but it was something difficult when it came to the vampires. Sebastian was under the impression that I had a calming effect on both Ethan and Steven, which was the first time I'd witnessed a true lapse in his judgment. Steven responded to me, we got each other, but Ethan spent most of his time either being annoyed or enraged by me. I didn't calm him in any manner.

For Steven's sake, I agreed to go. But there weren't many things that I would prefer less than being in a room with two powerful men who, at some point in my life, had wanted me dead or had tried to kill me.

Steven walked back and forth, agitated and restless. I was glad I was there, at least for his sake. He didn't want to be there any more than I did. His skin was ruddy, his eyes tense, and his breath uneven hisses as he paced the small space in front of the restaurant. Each time he looked at his watch, he tensed. When he passed me, I grabbed his hand and gave it a quick squeeze. Giving me his trademark dimpled sideways grin, he stopped pacing, linking his fingers with mine. He exhaled slowly, his body relaxing into calm.

"How long do you think it will take before Sebastian tries to stake Demetrius with a spoon?" I whispered.

He chuckled. "I give it fifteen minutes," he said just as softly.

I looked at Sebastian. He was calm, collected, and somber. "Five minutes tops." Then I directed my attention to Taylor, standing next to him. "I give *her* two."

"Thirty seconds," he said. He was probably right. She fidgeted too much, strung too tight to allow even the slightest insult to go without retaliation.

I didn't know a lot about their seventh, Hannah, who stood next to Ethan, other than she was the vice president of the "Let's Kill Skylar" club informally initiated by Winter last year. Completely composed, she seemed like she was the only person who was going to enjoy herself. A hint of a smile showed on her face as she waited patiently for Demetrius and the others to arrive.

The restaurant had been on my list of places to try. It had opened to rave reviews citing its chic ambiance and exquisite gourmet meals as some of the best the city had to offer. The exorbitant prices and waitlist made it easy to pass on. Now I was finally here but probably wouldn't have the opportunity to enjoy my meal because two of the most powerful men in the otherworld would be trying *not* to rip each other apart over dinner.

"Sebastian?" inquired the hostess as he started to become restless waiting for Demetrius, who was now officially late by three minutes. Dressed in a simple black dress, she wore her hair pulled back in a neat twist that drew attention to the welcoming smile that remained plastered on her face as she waited for him to respond.

"Yes." He turned to face her. His deep baritone voice was melodious, his smile charismatic. He possessed a confidence that only a man who commanded several hundred were-animals could. His dark blue tailored suit, pale sky blue shirt, and silk-printed tie complemented his flawless espresso-colored skin. Despite his less-than-agreeable personality, you couldn't ignore that with his distinct oval-shaped eyes, broad enticing features, wide, defined cheeks, and full lips, Sebastian was a beautiful man.

As he approached her, the look on her face reflected the same way I felt so often when dealing with him. You were intrigued by the dichotomy of his nature: a masculine beauty that compelled you, making him hard to resist, while his primal virulence triggered your internal alarms, urging you to retreat. Did you flirt or run?

"Demetrius said I would recognize you," she said, still smiling, but with a tinge of apprehension. "He and his party will be late. Please allow me to escort you to your dining area."

We followed the hostess through the beautifully decorated restaurant that held a flagrant air of exclusiveness. The waitstaff was uniformed in designer suits as they catered to the patrons' needs. Contemporary oil paintings decorated the walls, marble tiles covered the floors, and rich natural-colored silk drapes cascaded over the windows. Asymmetrical-wave pendant lights illuminated the spacious room. Freshly cut lilies decorated each table.

The faint aromatic scent of the food inundated the air, laced with the decadence of chocolate, vanilla, caramel, and fruit from the desserts. I tried not to be drawn in by the enticing scents, positive that I wouldn't have a chance to taste the wine, let alone eat the food and desserts. The olfactory overload was becoming too much of a distraction as we followed the hostess past the other patrons, who stared as we were led to the private room tucked away at the far end of the restaurant.

The restaurant was especially suited for Demetrius and his family: pretentious, opulent, and indulgent. We were welcomed by a large bouquet made of lilies, carnations, and exotic flowers placed on the table next to several bottles of aged red wine, a gift from Demetrius. Sebastian looked at the setup and frowned. "Please clear the table," he requested in a low, thin voice that barely veiled his irritation.

Yeah, this night is going to go well.

We waited patiently for nearly fifteen minutes and were about to leave when we saw Chris heading in our direction. The couture strapless peach satin dress complemented her dusky pecan tone as she eased her way toward us. Her neckline was accented by a dainty diamond necklace, bringing attention where she wanted it, while the dress clung to her curves. Dark, loose curls framed her face, drawing attention to her full lips, high cheekbones, deep-set eyes, and delicate, refined features. She was the embodiment of sexy, and the assured way she glided through the room showed that she was well aware of it.

Demetrius entered just behind her. His hand was placed lightly on the small of her back as they moved through the restaurant.

His tall, slight body kept in step with hers. His movements were so fluid and smooth it was as though he floated. He watched the crowd, welcoming their stares but daring them to last more than an acceptable amount of time. He was striking: well-defined cheekbones and a strong jawline flattered modest lips that drew back into a slight smile, just shy of exposing his fangs. Anthracite, wavy hair spilled slightly above his onyx eyes where flickers of red rings danced around the pupils. Unreasonably long lashes that were too delicate for his striking features drew you to him. His surreal appearance could have easily made one forget that he was a ruthless, horrid creature of the night that saw you as nothing more than a sex object, food, or an occasional toy, and sometimes all three.

He wore a finely tailored black suit with a coral shirt that accented Chris's dress. They were quite an attractive pair, but I wasn't sure if they were an actual couple. Demetrius remained extremely close, attentive hands lingering at the small of her back, but she seemed distracted. When she entered the room, her gaze immediately went to Ethan, and then she smiled. They stared at each other for a long moment before he came to his senses and looked away. Ex-lovers that had threatened each other's lives on more than one occasion, they now seemed to regret their decision to break up.

Behind them walked a shorter, thinner woman with long, voluminous mahogany hair pulled back with a decorative hair tie, showing off her features. Hollow cheekbones were deeply set in an oval-shaped face with crescent-shaped lips that disappeared into a thin line when she smiled. She hid her fangs to play into the demure façade she presented to the rest of the world. Opal eyes held that distinctive shimmer of crimson that seemed to be a trait in the older vampires. Michaela was the Mistress of the Northern Seethe, but instead of Demetrius's arm, she held on to the arm of the average-height, athletically built vampire I had come to know as Quell—Quella Perduta—the *Lost One*.

Not far behind them walked the horrible duo—Chase and Gabriella. They had made it into the VAMPIRE book, the sole purpose of which was to document the most heinous vampires. They were *lynked,* a couple for over fifty years, and unlike Demetrius and Michaela, they didn't find pleasure in the arms of others. From what I had been told, their love for each other was strong and strange. It was common knowledge that if you tried to kill one, you needed to kill the other because if you didn't, you would spend the rest of your short life in fear of the torturous end you would receive from the remaining lover.

When I had first encountered Gabriella, she had short unnaturally orange-colored hair, cut into messy spikes, completing her androgynous look. Now she sported long blond extensions with highlights of pink that framed her heart-shaped face. Sharp angular features made her appearance look exotic. I stood by the notion that exotic didn't necessarily mean pretty, but for her it did, although she seemed to go to great lengths to look less attractive. She could easily offer someone a torturous death as they looked upon her face: a great beauty with large dark eyes that had lost all remnants of humanity.

Chase, like his partner, had abandoned his androgynous look. He had changed his black spiked hair and settled for a trendy buzz cut, which drew focus to the tattoos that decorated his neck. He had replaced the earrings in his lips for one through his eyebrow. Chase's classic broad features put me in the mind-set of old Hollywood, a Cary Grant kind of masculinity.

The odd duo was dressed in his-and-hers matching dark blue suits. A butterfly clasp held her suit jacket together, which barely covered her breasts. One wardrobe malfunction and we all would be intimately acquainted with Gabriella's two friends.

Still angry over our last encounter, when I had staked him, Chase fastened his dark eyes on me with the same level of disdain for my existence that I had seen in Gavin's far too often. He wasn't in the room long before he slid next to me and planted a wet kiss on my cheek, making a loud, exaggerated smacking noise.

"Hey, wolfie," he whispered. I slipped the stake from my purse and gripped it tightly in my hand. Before I could give him the welcome he deserved, Steven shoved him into the wall and held a knife at his throat. It was then our waiter walked in, took one look at the scene, and left the room, shutting the door behind him. He didn't even seem shocked, as though this were a typical occurrence during a meeting in the private room.

"Steven," Sebastian's stern voice urged. Steven hesitated, his hard gaze drilling into the mischievous vampire. After several seconds of contemplation, he let Chase go and returned to his seat.

"If you can't control him, then I will," Sebastian warned Demetrius.

"Chase," Demetrius said, but he seemed more amused than agitated by his minion's antics.

"Sorry, I was just trying to greet my old friend. How does one greet the half-pups?" he asked in a cloying, polite voice.

I glared at him. In anticipation of this potentially disastrous evening, instead of the typical things in my purse (makeup, brush, perfume, and incidentals) I had concealed a knife and two stakes. Right now, I had an overwhelming urge to introduce Chase to both of them.

He grinned. "Gabriella, isn't she cute? She's like a little poodle. All bark and no bite," he said.

Sebastian shot Demetrius another warning look, but he simply responded with a genial smile as he looked in Chase's direction.

Chase grinned and took a seat next to Gabriella, directly across from me.

"Sorry about our tardiness. I hope the accommodations meets your standards," Demetrius said as his hand rested on Chris's leg, which didn't go unnoticed by Ethan.

"I would expect nothing less. It's shocking you didn't have

your own score playing during your entrance," Sebastian responded.

I smiled. Sebastian was funny when his sharp tongue was directed toward someone else.

"Oh, the dog has a sense of humor. This evening should be quite entertaining."

I sighed softly. This was going to be a very long night.

"Call me a dog again and I'll show you just how humorous I can be," Sebastian said in a mild voice, but the wave of amber that rolled across his pupils made his point.

"Gentlemen, I thought we were going to play nice. Please do so," Chris interjected in a dulcet tone, her lips curled into a welcoming smile that she directed toward Sebastian. "Thank you so much for agreeing to meet with Demetrius."

Sebastian graciously returned her smile, subtly letting her know her charms didn't affect him.

"Tell me, Sebastian, what you have done that has caused this unholy attack on our families?" Demetrius asked, releasing his hold on Chris as he leaned back in his chair.

Sebastian's lips pulled back, baring his teeth. "I would be remiss if I didn't inquire the same thing of you. What careless, self-indulgent thing did you or"—his gaze slid in Chase's direction—"your Seethe do that has angered someone to this extent that they have misdirected their wrath?"

They engaged in a caustic back-and-forth of blaming each other for indirectly causing the attacks. It was odd that when people despised each other, they couldn't navigate their way through the murky waters of logic. I knew why Demetrius hated the Midwest Pack. They had stopped him from performing a ritual that would have lifted all the restrictions that bound vampires. I wasn't sure why Sebastian hated Demetrius. Was it a natural instinct to despise and even try to dominate anyone that he perceived as a rival?

As they went back and forth with their accusations, my attention was focused on Quell. His weird eyes left me peculiarly fascinated.

"He's beautiful, isn't he?" Michaela purred, her finger sweeping along his cheek as she watched him with adulation.

"No," I blurted.

She raised her eyebrows, astonished at my response. Like the others, many would consider him beautiful: short dark brown hair, strong, delicate jawline, prominent cheekbones, and refined features complete with the classic Mediterranean nose and supple, bowed lips. As he sat next to Michaela with an off-putting, vacuous stare, he reminded me of those dogs that were so ugly they were cute. It was the opposite with him—he was so beautiful that he lost some of his attraction. He was missing the very qualities that I find attractive in others—flaws. Those quirky little intricacies that we all had that gave our looks character.

His strange eyes commanded my attention. Among the varying degrees of onyx and anthracite vampire eyes, his fluorescent green ones stood out. And then there was the low, indistinct beat of his heart. He was a vampire. I was almost certain of that. Well, he wasn't human, that was definite.

"Oh, darling, the half-breeds won't mind if you admire his beauty. It's nothing more than appreciating art and rendering compliments to the artist. He is indeed one of my best creations," she boasted, studying him for a long moment as though she was seeing him for the first time and finding a new appreciation for her work. Her eyes roved over him, tracing every inch of his limestone face.

Wow, someone had a big bowl of herself this morning.

"Since the only thing you did was chomp on him until he was nearly dead and then give him a dab of blood afterward, shouldn't I render compliments to his parents?" I wasn't sure what all went into creating a vampire, but I was willing to bet I was pretty close.

Instead of being offended, she laughed, throwing her head back and making a light harmonious sound.

"His eyes ... They are ... disconcerting. Why are they so green? In fact, why are they green at all?" I asked.

Demetrius laughed first. It was a deep, throaty, amused sound, and then the others joined in. I regretted my question once I realized they were laughing at him. What was so amusing to the undead?

"Go ahead, *Quella Perduta*, tell her why your eyes are green," Michaela urged with a smile, finding a cruel delight in his ignominy. She was my third least favorite person sitting at the table, closely falling behind Chase and Gabriella. After all, when we had first met, she'd tried to kill me, but not before telling me that she found me entertaining and would like to keep me as her pet.

He turned to look at her and nodded politely. His gaze held mine as he spoke, gauging my response. "Vampires do not necessarily need blood to survive, just the essence of life, which, in humans and animals, is blood. When we feed, our eyes reflect the source of life we choose, which is why it's deep red when we have recently fed but darkens after years of feeding, the result of aged blood in the body. We can survive on any life source: animals, humans, and, surprisingly enough, even plants."

Did I just hear him correctly? No, I had to be mistaken. I stared at him for a long time, waiting patiently for him to laugh, grin, smile, chortle, or give any indication that he was joking—but there was only silence. Finally, I asked, "You feed from plants?" My voice was tight as I bit back my own amusement, swallowing the giggle lodged in my throat.

He nodded once. "I use one particular plant, *Hidacus*. It seems to be the only one that can sustain my existence."

"He has a greenhouse and has these silly little plants flown in yearly and pays a gardener a ridiculous amount of money to tend to them. All this he endures when food is all around us," Michaela interjected, showing a mixture of amusement and disgust.

"You're a vampire that doesn't drink blood?" I asked, fascinated, and like the vampires, oddly amused.

"A creature of the night that doesn't feed on humans. Is it possible that you have a civilized one among you?" Sebastian coolly remarked. "Perhaps there is hope for you all."

Demetrius smiled, but he was far from entertained. "You've never seen him in battle. Civility has no place in his heart. His adoration for torment and violence is absolutely exhilarating. If I weren't so proud of his abilities, I would be envious. Please don't underestimate him based on his unfortunate choice of sustenance. He is indeed one of us, and there is nothing civil about him." Demetrius had responded conversationally, but there was a menace behind his eyes. He didn't take kindly to Sebastian questioning the ruthlessness of one of his Seethe members.

I couldn't drop the subject, as I should have. "You are able to survive like this?"

"Yes. You should see it sometime—its stem looks like a human neck. Does that comfort you?" He smiled, pulling his lips back to expose fangs, as if by some chance I had forgotten he was indeed a vampire. I didn't care if it smelled like human blood and the chlorophyll was red, this so-called *vampire* ate plants to survive.

"Is she finished interviewing Quell, or shall we continue to cater to her insipid curiosity?" Demetrius grumbled impatiently.

"No, let us continue our conversation. I am curious to find out what mess of yours I am left to clean up," Sebastian shot back.

I thought they should have just tried to resolve this over the phone instead of agreeing to meet. Sure, a couple of phones might have been smashed against the wall and occasionally they would have been yelling at dial tones, but at least I wouldn't have had to be present for it. Now they were lashing out at each other. Neither one knew how to communicate without feeling the need to exert their power. It didn't take long before they had come to their feet and were leaning into the table inches from each other.

Chris displayed a level a diplomacy that brought the raging storm to a low calm.

The turbulent emotions that filled the air were harsh and hard to take. I excused myself to the restroom. Walking slowly through the restaurant, I took in the beauty of it again. There were two restrooms, but I chose the one farthest from our room. Even this was elaborate and excessive. The stalls were the size of small dressing rooms. Two earth-toned tuxedo sofas were placed toward the back with an ornate curio between them. Opposite the sofas were a lit vanity and a chaise lounge. Chaise lounge? Who came to the restroom to take a nap?

"Bad date?" the elderly attendant asked as I dropped my head back against the sofa. The lines on her weathered skin deepened as she smiled. The various scents of perfume and makeup that wafted from the sofa made me queasy. I turned my nose up at both the smells and the question.

"If only it were just bad," I said.

She laughed. It was a deep, throaty, and jubilant sound that resonated throughout the large space. "I'm sorry, honey," she responded with rehearsed sincerity.

"Do you mind if I hang out here for a minute? If I go back too soon, I'm likely to slit my wrist with a butter knife or intentionally choke myself on the appetizers."

She nodded and handed me a magazine. We were the only ones in there, so at least I didn't have to endure the questioning looks from other patrons as they wondered how horrific my date had to be that I would rather hang out in a restroom than indulge in the fine dining experience.

I flipped through the magazine idly as we talked. She did most of the talking, but I enjoyed hearing about her grandchildren, her trip to Florida with them last year, and the trials they were having trying to house-train their new dog.

I had been in the bathroom for fifteen minutes when I politely excused myself. I left her a generous tip to show my appreciation for her making the night enjoyable, even if only for a few minutes. Heading out the door, I wondered if Demetrius and Sebastian had attempted to kill each other yet. Could I sneak out of the restaurant unnoticed? Between their snide remarks and hostile posturing, I doubted I would be missed.

As I fantasized about my great escape, I turned the corner and found myself face-to-face with the weird, plant-sucking, green-eyed vampire with the odd heartbeat.

"I have three dimples and a scar behind my ear," he offered quietly.

"I have ten fingers and ten toes, five on each limb," I quipped back, sliding past him and keeping my brisk stride toward the room. Quell fell in step with me.

With a look of confusion, he stopped walking. "What?"

I shrugged and continued toward the dining room. "Oh, I thought we were telling pointless anatomical facts about ourselves."

He laughed. It was a deep rolling sound that didn't fit him. It made me stop midstride and look at him. "No, Michaela prides herself on my perfections, but I assure you I am not. I have three dimples: One on each cheek, and a smaller one on the left, near my jaw. Asymmetrical, which is often undesired in beauty," he stated smoothly. "And I have this." He turned, showing me a scar that ran from his ear to his chin. A barely noticeable ridge of raised skin that was so small I had missed it the two times I had seen him in the past and would have missed it then if he hadn't pointed it out.

"So you're not perfect. Join the club—population size: everybody."

"I notice you keep staring."

"Your eyes—they're weird. It's like looking at a green fluorescent light. It doesn't matter the reason. They're odd and really creepy." It wasn't polite. In fact, it was downright rude, but I just didn't have it in me to be cordial. Surprises were annoying, and being surprised by the odd vampire with the absurd diet was even worse.

"Most find it disconcerting," he admitted. "I still haven't gotten used to the looks people give me."

"Maybe they're staring at your three dimples or that massive disfiguring scar."

He chuckled.

"If you don't like the stares, then go eat like a real vampire" was my snarky rebuttal.

"Are you offering?" he asked in a deep drawl, slipping effortlessly next to me. I shuffled back away from him so quickly I lost my footing and barely caught my balance. *Damn heels!*

His hands quickly went under my elbow, trying to steady me. I pulled it away and started back toward the private room, mumbling a quick apology for my rudeness. It didn't take long for him to catch up and fall in step with me again. As we neared the door, we both hesitated before entering. Like me, he was reluctant to enter the hostility riddled room. I hoped by now they would have gotten out all their insults and subtle threats and were ready to play nice.

Quell opened the door for me. "Ten fingers and ten toes," he whispered with a chuckle, "you're funny."

When we entered the room, all eyes turned to us. Had we just committed a were/vamp social faux pas? I quickly left his side and sat in my chair, looking down at the table. The snide comments and subtle threats hadn't subsided one bit since my reprieve. It was getting late, and I had spent far too much time with salacious vampires, irritated coyotes, angry wolves, and ill-tempered felines and I wanted to go home.

Chris leaned back in her chair and gave a long, lingering look in Sebastian's direction, and then focused her slanted gaze on Demetrius. After a moment of contemplation, she blew out an exasperated breath. "You two can put them back in your pants and quit the pissing contest. I can assure you they are both quite impressive," she finally asserted, obviously tired of playing mediator to a pair of power-hungry men who had very little desire to be in the same room with each other, let alone work together.

"You two don't like each other. Some might be as bold as to say you hate each other. Your people are being slaughtered. We can stay here another two hours and be entertained by your witty insults and unsubstantiated blame and let more of them die, or you can put aside your differences and agree to work together. It's not a difficult decision."

And there she was, the woman who dared to stand between two charging bulls and whack them on the nose with a newspaper while telling them to stop misbehaving. Refusing to soothe their egos and hostility, she simply told them to pipe down and get it together. I didn't want to be impressed, but there was a part of me that just couldn't help it.

Demetrius sat back in his chair. His hand rested on Chris's leg as an amused smirk flourished across his lips. "I do believe we are being chastised for our unbecoming behavior," he said as he glanced over in her direction again before directing his attention to Sebastian.

Sebastian smiled. It held that incontrovertible charm that put you foolishly at ease, warm enough to melt the walls of hostility that had been erected. "She's right," he said, then directed his attention to Chris. "'Pissing contest'? I expected something with a little more subtlety from you."

She shrugged and smiled, pulling off a sweet innocence that could easily disarm the most hostile person. "I couldn't think of anything clever that involved behaving like children, a time-out, and a sandbox fast enough, so I went with obvious. It was crude. My apologies."

What a load of crap. Chris didn't strike me as the type of person who was ever at a loss for words. She had called it for what it was: a hostile display of power that was getting in the way of progress.

Sebastian still seemed tense, fighting his way through his aversion to Demetrius and the very idea that he needed to be amicable with him.

"Joan, how is she?" Demetrius asked. There was such earnestness in his voice. It made me focus on him, waiting for the callous or crude remark that never came. Surprisingly, it was a sincere inquiry.

"She will recover," Sebastian responded.

"Good. She has always been an asset to the Southern Pack and worthy of her position. It would be quite unfortunate for something to happen to her." It was obvious that he held a level of regard for her. Unlike most were-animals, she was gentle, kind, poised, and friendly. It was hard to believe she was a were-animal and capable of holding the position of Beta in her pack. Her placid brown eyes could put anyone into a state of ease. And her personality could soothe the most enraged beast. But it was a persona that she could shed with ease as she ripped out someone's throat with such skill and malice it left you awed. It was only then that you stopped questioning how she had achieved her position. The year before I had witnessed her do just that when she punished one of the members for pack betrayal by tearing him to pieces. Joan was the only were-animal I knew who could speak in animal form, which spoke volumes about the level of control she held over her animal half. While most were-animals were ruled by that part of them and only capable of subjugating it on minor levels, she had complete control of hers.

The room stayed quiet for a long moment. The very things that made them power players in this world where they were feared and revered were the same things that made conceding to the idea they needed each other difficult.

Sebastian asked, "Have there been any attacks on the Southern Seethe?"

"No, they were left unharmed," Demetrius admitted.

"Good. Perhaps they can be used as a resource if necessary."

Michaela laughed. Demetrius simply smiled politely. "I assure you that if we are in need of the Southern Seethe, then we are far worse off than I imagined," she said.

The Southern Seethe weren't known for their skills as fighters, nor were they as organized as the Northern. Although Demetrius and his family prided themselves on indulging whatever whim they fancied, they were still a force to be reckoned with. The Southern Seethe was a fraternity and sorority house gone wild: unstructured, careless, and undisciplined. Demetrius hid his embarrassment well. Although the Southern Seethe's behavior shouldn't reflect on him, it did. He had created their Master and given him the South with the expectations that their Seethe would mirror his, but his protégé had failed substantially.

Sebastian exhaled a slow breath. "Then it seems like we really need to work together to ensure we find out who's responsible. I am not willing to lose anyone else just because"—he shifted his gaze over to Chris and grinned—"we're too busy seeing who's going to win the pissing contest."

"I couldn't agree more," replied Demetrius.

Gold stars for both of you. Give them some cookies!

But there wouldn't be any cookies involved, nor was there dinner, just pseudo-pleasantries as they attempted to remain cordial and tolerant of each other for a socially acceptable amount of time.

Finally, after nearly twenty minutes of discussion on how things would be handled, Sebastian smiled. It was forced, but he managed to make it look sincere. He extended his hand to accept the agreement, and it took a moment before Demetrius reached for it. Sebastian offered a quick but polite good-bye and headed for the door with the rest of us not too far behind. The were-animals departed the meeting looking as if they were doing the walk of shame, feeling sordid for having to deal with the vampires on this level but handling it with exceptional poise. Demetrius quickly returned his attention back to Chris, leaning into her to whisper something. He became so distracted by her I doubt he would have noticed if we stayed or I was set aflame while standing in front of him.

Ethan almost made it, but before he could exit the room, he took another glance over his shoulder, focusing on Demetrius and his ex. It took him too long to take his eyes off them and even longer to leave the room. I slipped my hand behind him and urged him out the door. Hannah, who accompanied him, fell in step with Steven as they left the restaurant.

"I'm taking you home," Ethan informed me while we waited for the valet to bring the cars up. My preference would have been to leave with the person I came with, but I knew Steven wanted to get back to be with Joan.

On the drive home, there was an obdurate silence between Ethan and me. There was always an awkward uneasiness between the two of us that was rooted in the fact that he was unpredictable. Last year when Sebastian had extended an offer for me to join the pack, Ethan suggested that I decline because he didn't want me as a member. He never gave me a definite reason. All he said was that I wouldn't be good for the pack. It had caught me by surprise. I thought he liked me, especially after we had shared a kiss that was so intense it left me breathless. But I guessed wanting to suffocate someone with a kiss and having them in your pack were two different things.

As he zoomed the Porsche Cabriolet down the street, darting around cars and riding others' bumpers until they moved over, he finally turned his attention to me. "They don't work," he said, referring to the imaginary passenger brakes I kept hitting each time he drove too close to a car. My comment about speed limits being the law and not a mere suggestion was soon substantiated by the flashing lights behind us. Ethan pulled over. Shifting, I moved my leg to allow him access to his glove compartment to get his registration and insurance information, but he didn't move. Nor did he take out his license. Instead, he lowered his window, sat back, and looked surprisingly at ease for someone driving twenty-four miles per hour over the speed limit.

"Hello, Ethan," said the officer, his lips curving into a welcoming smile.

"Tim," he said cordially.

The officer flashed his light toward me. He shined it on my face, and then it slowly drifted down over my body, making an uncomfortable situation worse.

"I need to get her home. It's past her bedtime," Ethan stated with a wry smile at the officer's questioning look.

Please give him a ticket—a big one.

The officer chuckled then flashed his light on me again. "One of ours?" He scrutinized me, inching closer to the window to get a better look.

Ethan's lips curled into a bemused smirk. "No. Just a friend of the pack."

Was I? I didn't consider myself their friend, but rather the annoying friend of a friend that you tolerated and made sure didn't die under your watch.

The policeman's gaze lingered in my direction, and the overt look of censure was hard to ignore. "She's different. Not your usual," he said in what I assumed he thought was a whisper.

Hello, werewolf here, too.

Ethan looked at me briefly, giving me a quick once-over. "How's your wife?" he asked the critical policeman.

"Still pregnant and getting more irritable by the day." But the giant beam on his face made it obvious that he didn't care.

"I have a new partner. That's the reason I stopped you. You were going pretty fast, and he noticed."

Ethan nodded, reached into his coat jacket, pulled out his wallet, and gave him the license. Then he reached over my left knee to get his registration and insurance information. After Ethan handed the officer the registration, he kept his hand pressed firmly on my leg, which had been tapping nervously since the moment we were pulled over. I'd been pulled over once since I started driving, and I'd been so nervous that the officer let me off with a warning. I had a feeling this wasn't Ethan's first time being stopped, and he was probably going to get off with just a reprimand.

His hand was still resting on my leg long after it had stopped bouncing. I slid my leg closer to the door, forcing his hand to fall from it. The officer looked at the license and registration, went back to his car, and returned with a warning ticket. "Be careful the next couple of exits. We are out quite a bit, and they are not ours or pack friendly," he cautioned.

"You've heard what happened?" Ethan asked.

The officer nodded. "How is Winter?"

"She's not dead," Ethan responded in a callous tone.

The officer nodded his head but looked at a loss for words in response to Ethan's insensitive remark. He handed him back his information, wished him a good night, and went back to the patrol car, but not before tossing one more disparaging glance in my direction.

As soon as the officer was beyond earshot, I yelled at Ethan, "What's wrong with you? Just stop it!"

"Stop what?" he asked in that same cold, detached voice he had used with the officer, which further enraged me as he pulled back into traffic, his eyes intently focused on the road.

"Being that way ... being like you ... cold, heartless. I know you probably don't care whether she lives or dies, but can you at least act like it?"

He swallowed hard. Eyes fixed ahead, his teeth clenched together as he gripped the steering wheel so hard the muscles on his hand rose. The silence between us was stiff and cold and both of us seemed reluctant to break it.

"I care. I care very much whether she lives or dies," he admitted softly. He didn't turn to face me, but his lips pressed down into a pronounced frown, then he bit down on them. It looked as though he had done what I had a few moments earlier and let an image of Winter's crushed, broken body drift into his head.

My angry outburst left an odd protracted silence that worsened with each moment. I couldn't get away from him fast enough.

He pulled up to my driveway and quickly got out of the car. I looked at him suspiciously when he walked over to the passenger side to open the door. I kept the same apprehensive look when he extended his hand to help me. I stared at it as though it were poisonous to the touch before taking it and letting him help me out of his car.

He walked me to the door but didn't leave. Instead, he waited for me to open it. When I hesitated, he asked, "Did you forget how to disarm the ward?" with a voice heavy with condescension.

"Would it matter if I did? Aren't you able to break them?" I turned to face him.

His face was impassive, his expression so null it wouldn't betray any of his secrets. If he were about to lie, I couldn't tell. Last year, he had broken a protective field of Josh's, apparently something were-animals couldn't do. Ethan had admitted nothing, shrugging off the incident, and referring to the protective field as nothing more than an overrated ward, which were-animals broke all the time. Josh hadn't been convinced and neither had I. Ethan was hiding something. But I had no idea what.

He responded with a forced smile. "I suspect you could, too, if necessary. All wards can be broken or disarmed by someone, even the ones created by my brother. His magic is strong, but not indestructible."

I studied him closely as he spoke, watching for that *tell,* that one thing I needed to confirm he was lying. He remained emotionless. His vitals were all normal, his face passive. If this were anyone else, I would have safely assumed they were telling the truth, but with Ethan, it only meant he was just a really good liar.

When I opened the door, I expected him to leave, but instead he came in behind me and started to walk around. At first, I thought he was making sure it was safe to enter, but then I realized it was just him. He was just taking a tour of my new home that he hadn't been invited into. Being that he was a narcissist, I was sure it didn't occur to him that it was rude to invite himself into someone's home.

As I scrutinized him, he assessed me with interest. His coarse, penetrating gaze roved over me, focusing on my violet single shoulder dress that touched just above the knee. Under his intense leer, it now seemed too short. I could have sworn he could see the edge of my pink hipsters. Makeup that I had spent more than my typical five minutes applying in order to transition from a daytime to an evening look now seemed lascivious.

Then his gaze trailed off to my three-inch heels, which, at the beginning of the night, I had thought were a perfect complement to my dress. They enhanced the curves of my long legs and were a nice mix of style and function. I could walk in them with ease, run if necessary, and if imperative, use the long, sharp heels as a weapon. Now they seemed salacious and too high. I felt like I should be gyrating seductively around a pole with inebriated men throwing dollars at me.

I fidgeted, wringing my hands, waiting for him to direct his attention elsewhere. After a long awkward moment, he spoke in a low, terse voice. "You're a very pretty woman."

Pretty? I was never one to be self-deprecating, but I would never be among the pretty people. My thick, coiled waves of mahogany hair were relaxed and attacked daily with an arsenal of straightening aides in order to manage them. My deep-set, moss green eyes complemented my olive skin tone. Described as exotic or unique, I often wondered if it was the socially polite way of saying I had all the right features—full lips, deep-set cheekbones, oval face, slight edged nose—but somewhere things had gone terribly awry and now I was stuck in that place where I would forever be considered exotic or unique looking.

My lips parted to thank him for the compliment, but the words didn't come. Instead, I gawked at him. I hated that Ethan had that effect on me.

"Oh." *Great response! Skylar you are indeed a wordsmith, a true artist of linguistics, an auteur of the spoken word. Your next career —poet.*

He turned toward the wall, focusing on the art that covered it. As he walked through the open area, he seemed so comfortable that he ignored my "please leave" looks. He turned once to glance at me and returned his attention to the pictures. They probably looked familiar because I had purchased them all from his godmother's gallery. I had gone there with the intention of purchasing a portrait that had captured my attention the year before when I'd first met her. But she wouldn't sell it and had directed me to similar pieces.

"What do you have to drink?" he asked as he shrugged off his jacket and laid it across the sofa.

Had I invited him to stay? Did something in my uncomfortable stance, awkwardness, and confused, befuddled actions somehow lead to a nonverbal invitation? When he asked again, I walked into the kitchen and ducked my head into the fridge. "Water, apple juice, orange juice … Wait … Steven finished that off.… Cranberry juice."

"Do you have anything stronger?" He gave me an amused smile.

At that moment, he reminded me of his brother. It was a bright wayward smile that held hints of mischief and coquetry, but I didn't know what to read into it. *Well, you can have the wine while I have a big glass of "why the hell aren't you leaving?"*

Instead, I said, "Cabernet and this." I showed him a bottle of

Scotch that his brother had given me. "It was a gift for my birthday."

He chuckled. "Let me guess—Josh? My brother gave you a bottle of *his* favorite brand of Scotch on *your* birthday." He laughed and shook his head. "That's my brother. I've received that same gift every year since he turned twenty-one." He nodded toward the Scotch.

I took out two tumblers, filling mine with enough ice to water it down, and tossed a few cubes in his. I filled his glass then poured enough in mine to barely cover the ice. He took the bottle from me and filled my glass more.

As I stood next to Ethan at the nook, sipping Scotch, I still didn't feel comfortable around him. Our pseudo-cordial interaction didn't inspire the same cozy feeling you got when you drank with a friend, nor did it possess that uneasy self-assurance you had when you knew you were drinking with an enemy—with them you knew where you stood. This was stranger and more uncomfortable. The unknown was always a strange place to be, and it was hard to be at ease when you found yourself there. "Can Demetrius be trusted?" I finally asked, breaking the silence.

"No. He's an egotistical bastard and will cooperate with anyone that can help find the person responsible for the attacks. Right now, his arrogance is the only thing I trust and the only thing we can count on."

Don't hold back. Tell me how you really feel about him.

Demetrius had been the face of my would-be death last year. The vampire with the cold soulless eyes, provocative appealing features, and lascivious ways was now an ally. It was hard to imagine and even harder to accept. Would his betrayal be quick and unexpected, subjecting the pack to a new brand of cruelty that they hadn't anticipated?

Ethan's attention had drifted and I wondered if he was thinking the same when he returned his focus to me. "Your help during this situation has been greatly appreciated and it will not be forgotten." He started off in a cool, despondent voice as he looked into his nearly empty glass. When he lifted his eyes to meet mine, I felt exposed, as I always did. He made me feel like he had broken all barriers and saw things that I wasn't even aware of. I hated that because it made me feel vulnerable and cautious. But I didn't think being cautious around him was a bad thing. "You can walk away now. No one will think any less of you if you do."

The acrid liquid slipped down my throat, choking me when my mouth dropped open. It took a minute for me to respond. That was Ethan in a nutshell: he could flatter you with one breath and use the next to tell you to go to hell, beat it, get lost.

"I would ..." I blurted, finding my words after being blindsided. "I would think a lot less of myself if I walked away without doing what I could to help find out who did this to Winter." I gripped the glass harder, glaring at him. I fought the urge to toss it in his face.

His eyes were stern, his voice low, concentrated, and rough. "Skylar, consider this fair warning. If you keep getting involved with pack business, you'll find yourself so heavily entwined that becoming untangled will be impossible. The life you want, the normality you desire, will no longer be an option."

I placed the glass on the counter and slid it away from me before I gave in to the urge to throw it in his face. Perhaps I had been drinking with an enemy. "Do you ever just give people friendly advice? Does everything you say have to be a 'fire-and-brimstone' type warning with growls, snarls, and impending doom?"

He turned up his glass and emptied it, then stepped closer to me, his hand slipping around my waist, crushing me into him. His lips pressed firmly against my ear as he whispered, "Here's your friendly advice: you were given a choice whether or not to join us, and you made it—and it was a wise one. If you stay involved when you have the chance to bow out gracefully, then you may no longer have that option—that is *not* wise. Go back to your so-called normal life."

I stepped away, distancing myself as the animal dwelling just below his surface peeked out—it was intense and malicious, forcing an urge to retreat. I couldn't quite put my finger on it, this hint of primordial cruelty that nicked at my self-protective instincts.

I accepted that I had been pulled into a world that I could not ignore or escape. Whether I chose to accept it or delve into denial, I was part of it and it still existed. "I think you got your 'friendly advice' voice mixed up with your 'fire-and-brimstone' voice. You should work on that."

His lips curved slightly as his intense gaze bored into me. "That *was* my friendly advice, Skylar."

"I thank you for that. You won't be offended if I ignore it?"

"I wouldn't ignore it if I were you."

"Are we watching the same channel? I can't go back to normal. The moment you all came into my life, it was changed. Normal—faked or otherwise—is no longer an option for me!"

The tension between us couldn't have been leveled, even with a bulldozer. We stood staring at each other—no, glaring. I sighed and made an attempt to reason with him. Something, at times, I wasn't sure he was capable of. "Turning my back on this world is turning my back on Steven, Joan, and even Winter. I can't do that."

He stepped toward me, backing me into the counter as he towered over me. There was a strange intensity about him that made me want to step away, to find a spot across the room where I could force faux bravado. "You seem to have a hard time turning your back on my brother and his magic, as well. You're not just staying in this world. You're stomping around and making as much noise as possible while you're in it, and it is being noticed and drawing attention that you don't need."

"Attention from whom?"

As it always did with Ethan, my question went unanswered.

I blew out an exasperated breath. "You asked me not to join your pack and I didn't. What more do you want from me?"

His gaze was harsh and penetrating. This was the time in the East African savannah when the gazelles' gaze set on the predator and they scattered. I didn't have that luxury because he still had me pinned against the counter.

Placid features with an attentive leer made keeping my attention on him difficult. I jumped when he touched my face, his long fingers trailing down my cheek then tracing along my jawline. His voice was low and surprisingly soft. "You asked for friendly advice. I gave it. Walk away from it all. There is nothing here for you." And as quickly as he was in front of me, he was at the door with his jacket in his hand.

Maybe he wasn't an enemy, but he definitely wasn't a friend.

CHAPTER 4

Later that night, after Ethan had returned home, Chris pulled into his driveway. She stayed in her car for a few minutes, trying to decide if she should go to the front door. She hadn't dealt with him since she had threatened to kill him and his brother. Threats to kill Ethan weren't unusual. She'd done it before so many times during their tumultuous relationship it had almost become a form of foreplay. But their relationship had never suffered the complexities that it had now. When she had threatened to kill his brother, she knew she had crossed a line. Things had escalated to a point of no return. That was when Ethan threatened to kill her if he found her. And she knew that if he had, she wouldn't be here now.

There hadn't been a way to salvage the relationship after that, and she doubted she wanted to. Ethan was standing in the way of the completion of a job, and she swore that she would never let their relationship, even when they were dating, affect her job. Yet somehow, it happened. If it had been anyone else, she wouldn't have hesitated about threatening or even eliminating him if he got in her way. Josh and Ethan were in her way.

I need to get it together, she thought, frustrated, taking slow, controlled breaths to calm herself. The rapid heartbeat, ragged breath, and cold sweat that beaded on her forehead were all signs of her nervousness, discomfort, fear. She hated that, and she knew that Ethan would find intense pleasure in it. She wouldn't give him that joy. She took several more long breaths in an attempt to pull herself together before she got out of the car.

She knocked on the door, looking at her watch, which indicated 11:13 p.m. *I've been hanging out with vampires too much.* Before she had started dealing with the vampires on this level, she would have considered it an insult to show up at someone's home at this time of the night, unless it was an emergency. She had already decided that if it took too long for him to answer, she would leave. It meant he wasn't alone, but probably entertaining himself with Skylar, who seemed to have struck his interest.

She waited, and when he didn't answer on the second knock, she turned to leave.

"What do you want?" he asked when the door swung open. Like her, he had changed and was dressed in a pair of jeans and a t-shirt. Hers, form-fitting and a lilac color and his, a black V-neck cut close, accentuating the defined muscles of his chest and arms. His face didn't show any signs of having been asleep or even relaxing. Knowing Ethan the way she did, she thought he had probably stood at the peephole watching her as she knocked.

"We need to talk," she stated, attempting to slip past him as he blocked the door.

"We've said enough." He shifted his hip to nudge her away.

When she took a step forward, he placed his hand gently on her stomach, preventing her entrance.

She looked down at his hand and waited patiently until he moved it. "We really should talk," she said firmly.

After long consideration, he stepped aside. She took one sweeping look around the large open space of his house. He had redecorated since the last time she was there—the day of their breakup. Switching from his previous urban chic décor, his home was now decorated in a modern style. Lush cognac-colored Italian leather sofas and deep mahogany tables were placed throughout the room. The walls were a muted latte color. Unique bronze lamps decorated the side tables. A cream cocktail ottoman was placed on top of an opulent Persian rug that covered the hardwood floor. Ethan—or rather his interior decorator—had changed everything she remembered about his house. Everything was new: the stainless-steel appliances, dark cherrywood cabinets, and granite counters in the kitchen. Had he done this to erase all the memories of her from his life? The house seemed foreign to her, and she hated it. This wasn't the place where she had spent most of her weekends and numerous nights.

He crossed his arms and studied her in silence, his eyes roving over every inch of her face. "What exactly do we need to discuss?" he asked in a low voice, directing his attention to the wall just past her. She was glad that he did. Aware that their relationship existed far too deep in carnality, she wanted to keep it professional, or whatever counted as professional between them.

She took another look at the rooms, hating the tinges of pain she felt, knowing that he had purposely redecorated her existence out of them. Finally, she turned to face him with inexpressive eyes—a mask that served her well. "Are we going to have problems working together?"

His supple lips curled into just a hint of a smile, holding a combination of condescension and amusement. "Hmm. Will I have a problem working with my ex-lover who threatened to kill me and my brother? A woman who attempted to kidnap a person who was under my pack's protection, in order to help the vampires perform a ritual that would have left them invincible—a true threat to me and my pack. What do you think?"

He inched closer, narrowing the small space that she consciously kept between them. Despite the increasing intensity of his gaze, she held it. She smiled. "I don't know. That's why I'm asking. We might as well lay all the cards on the table. Can I trust that you aren't still holding a grudge?"

"What's the matter? Is Chris having trouble determining who she can trust? Who will betray her, the vampire she's feeding and doing—well, let's just leave that up to the imagination—or the man she used to sleep with? What a dilemma she's gotten herself into."

She sidestepped him. "It's not a dilemma. Are you going to be petty, or are you going to get over it?"

"Me not 'getting over' you trying to kill my brother and me is far from petty—"

"If I'm not mistaken, you threatened to hunt me down like an animal and kill me. Rumor has it that you were quite devoted to your search. I can't help but think that if you had found me, you would have carried out your threat. You are taking it personally. Don't. It was a job," she said coolly.

There was a long, protracted silence of unresolved anger that still left an air of animosity between them.

"Then hunting you like an *animal* was just an occupational hazard. You shouldn't take that personally."

"I need to know whether or not I can count on you when we are out in the field. I don't want to have to watch my back for fear you will have a personal vendetta to settle."

It took a while for him to answer. "We're fine," he finally said.

"Good. I already assured Demetrius of that, but I needed to hear it from you."

He made a dark, cynical sound. "It's good to know that you two are able to talk about business between your extracurricular activities."

Ethan stepped back, leaned against the wall, and watched. Each movement, twitch, and nervous reaction seemed to be scrutinized by him. He bit down on the side of his lip, as he always did when he was irritated with her. She didn't know why. It never helped him hold his tongue. "Why did you leave?"

She wasn't prepared for this conversation. She knew he wasn't just asking why she left him. He was asking, "How could you leave me?" No one ever left Ethan. And she doubted anyone slipped out in the middle of the night and ended all communication with him. She swore under her breath several times, wishing she had more time to come up with an answer—two years just wasn't long enough and the answer she had was utter BS. Their relationship was the most indefinable thing she ever experienced. The complexity of what they had was both elating and devastating. Together they were pyromaniacs setting ablaze something fierce and that destroyed everything in its path. Drawn to the devastation created by their coupling, they were unable to extinguish it as they should, allowing it to continue until the point they were both left charred, injured, and choking from its poison along with anyone else that happened to witness it.

Ethan should have come with a warning or, at the very least, a disclaimer: "Proceed at your own risk." Rumors had him painted as a self-indulgent, womanizing narcissist. She had soon realized that they weren't rumors—they were truths. Yet in contrast, as she got to know him, he was gentle, intense. The harmonious bond he had with his beast transferred well into the bedroom. Attuned to her body and desires in a manner that she didn't believe was possible, he made her feel like she was a stranger to herself, as though he were the only one that could truly know her. She adored and hated him and realized the true dysfunction in it. With him, she lacked control, and every moment, the intensity was like sand between her fingers. She couldn't grasp it.

He stepped closer, the warmth of his body pulsing against hers as he waited with determination for an answer. His touch was delicate as he held the gem on her necklace, then it moved to her cheek, gently stroking it. She closed her eyes for a mere second, turning her head into his touch. She wanted to move but her body didn't want to cooperate.

"Answer," he urged in low voice.

"Because it was time" was all she could offer.

His lips spread, not quite a smile or sneer. It was a wry grimace of disappointment with her answer—with her. "Have a good night," he said. His hands slipped around her waist as he kissed her lightly on the lips. It was a wisp of a touch that left her yearning for more.

She should have left then—but she didn't. Instead, she remained pressed close against him. He kissed her again, his lips pressed firmly against her, deep and ravenous as he pulled her closer. Long, warm fingers kneaded into her skin, entreating her body to respond to him in ways that it always had.

Her hand ran under his shirt, feeling the warmth of his skin against her fingertips. Slipping her shirt over her head, he laved his tongue over her exposed cleavage as he tossed the shirt to the ground. Impatient fingers played with the clasp of her bra before tearing it from her body. He stopped kissing her long enough to look at her, naked from the waist up. A deep throaty growl reverberated as he tugged at her pants. As if they had been too far away too long, he returned to her lips, kissing her hungrily. With quick tugs, they helped each other out of their pants.

They slid to the ground, skin pressing against skin, unable to be close enough to satisfy their urges. It was like a new discovery as his lips trailed over every inch of her mouth then her body, brushing over the delicate parts of her breasts, traveling down to her stomach, where he stopped. She knew what he saw—a scar. Ethan knew her body. Every mark, no matter how subtle, he was aware of. He wouldn't have missed such a scar, no matter how small. Light webbed markings stretched from across her abdomen toward her back. With the help of a lot of vampire blood and a very skilled plastic surgeon, it was now a light mesh that most would have missed, but not Ethan. It might as well have been deep welts rising like Stonehenge from her. She glanced down at him, meeting his inquisitive gaze.

She pulled him up and pressed her lips against his, working to make him forget whatever questions were dwelling in his mind. He didn't need to know how close to death she had been and how she wouldn't have survived had it not been for Demetrius. She would never reveal to him that sometimes she got dressed in the dark because, no matter how slight, the scar was a constant reminder of her mortality, and at times, she couldn't bear to look at it.

He was very easily distracted. When her lips pushed against his again, her tongue licking at his lips, he responded frenetically. Soon, they were sprawled on the floor, naked and heatedly caressing, clawing, and kissing each other as primal sexual urges consumed them.

As he slid slowly into her, he exhaled a ragged breath and held her gaze. Her fingers sank into his skin. A deep moan escaped as he moved rhythmically against her in deep commanding movements. She had forgotten how he made her feel, the intensity of his touch, the sensuality of their bodies linked together, moving as one and making everything around them inconsequential. Each groan captured by his demanding lips as they covered hers, his tongue caressing her in exigent lust. Any resistance that logic forced was subdued as her body shuddered against his repeatedly, leaving her sated with each moment.

After Ethan dropped me off and left his "friendly advice," I took a hot shower, but I couldn't sleep. I rolled over in the bed, looked at the clock, and cursed under my breath. It was a little after one in the morning. I should have been asleep, but instead, I was thinking about the creature that had attacked Winter. Something about it was familiar to me—its scent. I couldn't remember where I had smelled it before, and it was bothering me.

By one thirty in the morning, I was dressed and driving toward the scene where everything had occurred with a knife

Steven had given me for my birthday sheathed to my leg. A sword that Winter had loaned me was on the backseat. The Sig 9mm, which I had purchased eight months ago—just in case—was in my jacket pocket. I wasn't sure why I had brought it. It didn't work against vampires, and without silver bullets, it was useless against were-animals. I doubted it would injure the beast we saw earlier. But I had all my just-in-case weapons, including a nine iron.

Using a nine iron didn't cement my position as a tactical or skilled fighter, but it made my point—back off. Some might have considered it a cowardly weapon and distastefully crude, but I didn't care. It did the job. At the end of the day, when the would-be assailant was writhing and lurching in pain, he wasn't pondering how tacky and unskillful it was for me to use a golf club.

I drove around the empty parking lot several times, making sure that I was the only one out. With all the buildings closed, the lights from the street and cars offered only minimal illumination. But once parked, I didn't need the lights to find the area where everything took place. The strong smell of Winter's spilled blood still flooded the air. A large volume of it had seeped into the concrete, leaving it stained. My chest tightened. How could someone lose that much blood and still live? The bleakness crept up fast and it took a great deal to push it aside. I quashed the images of Winter's battered body and concentrated on the other scents that drifted through the air. The smell of asphalt, pine, dirt, gas, and emission fumes made isolating that one familiar scent difficult. I closed my eyes in an attempt to let that distinctive smell jar whatever memory had made me forget it and force it back to the surface. Nothing.

With the sword in my hand, I slowly walked through the area, lifting my head slightly to inhale deeply, acutely aware of the silence broken only by loose gravel that scraped under my feet from time to time. I wasn't the most skilled with it, but a sword allowed me to stay at arm's length while protecting myself.

Honestly, how much skill did you need to swing a double-edged blade? You just kept swinging until you hit something that made them hurt. When I heard light footsteps behind me, I turned, swinging the sword hard toward the intruder. Long, pale fingers grasped the center of the blade just millimeters from the sharp edge. If I had been just a little faster, the blade would have sliced through his hand.

Smiling, Quella Perduta—the Lost One—looked at the blade in his hand. "Sebastian would send his littlest wolf to hunt for the creatures that have injured his best. Very confident of him," he stated in that distinctive, cool northeastern monotone dialect. He had changed and looked out of place in dark brown chambray pants and a mustard button-down that contrasted rather unflattering against his pallid skin. The odd green fluorescent eyes were bright and inquiring, with a hint of amusement.

"I've proven to be quite proficient. Sebastian has no worries." There was no need to tell him that if Sebastian knew I was out here, I would be engaged in a verbal fencing match that I would never win. That wasn't any of Quell's business.

"The scent, I've smelled it before but I can't remember where," I stated, walking past him as I continued to assess the area.

"I don't smell anything." He walked up close behind me. It was disconcerting that they moved so silently and quickly. I kept a steady eye on him as he stepped nearer.

He was right. Perhaps it was the compilation of the various scents that overwhelmed it or maybe it had just dissipated, but nevertheless—it was gone. It had been a day and a half since the attack and the scent was untraceable.

"I haven't disposed of the body of the creature I killed earlier, maybe that will help you. I can take you to it if you would like," he stated, doing a thorough visual sweep of the area.

"You were attacked?"

There was a small smile on his face. "I don't sleep at night. I get bored, and I prefer to be the hunter, not the hunted." A menacing dark cast swept over his face.

You may not feed like a vampire, but you damn sure are one.

Quell drove my car after a fairly long, spirited debate in which I conceded when he pointed out that he knew the location. You dealt with were-animals long enough and you learned to pick your battles. When it was a battle worth fighting, I was usually quite obstinate. Driving to an unknown destination just wasn't a battle worth fighting.

He was careful as he drove, but the way he handled the curves and dark single-lane roads gave me the impression that he usually wasn't.

"Little Wolf, you don't seem like the type of person whom Sebastian would allow to go on an endeavor like this alone." He kept his eyes on the road, his voice sounding curiously amused with a hint of condescension.

"My name is Skylar, not Little Wolf. If you can't address me that way, you probably aren't going to get a lot of answers from me."

"Skylar." He said my name slowly, tasting each letter, every syllable in a peculiar manner. He regarded me for a long time, saying my name over and over. For every second he kept his gaze on me, I wished he dedicated that time to keeping his eyes on the road. "You don't look like a Skylar."

"What does a Skylar look like?"

He kept his eyes on me then tilted his head slightly in introspection. "Not like you."

"You don't look like a Quella Perduta," I shot back.

His sharp cool eyes cruised over in my direction, but he didn't say anything.

He still held a look of amusement that irked me. Why did he just assume I wasn't the type of person Sebastian would send out? "I have proven myself quite often. Sebastian has no concerns when it comes to me." I was taking creative license with the truth, but he didn't have to know that.

Finally, we came to our destination and parked. As we walked through the verdant area, crowded by thick florets of pine trees and oak, I slowed my pace after losing my footing in the broken patches of soil that got worse the farther we walked. Quell's movements were quicker, and he gracefully negotiated the uneven acclivous area. I approached cautiously but didn't smell anything, nor did I see a body. Even Quell looked surprised by the empty space. As he did a sweep of the general area, a tall figure plodded toward us. It looked entirely different from the creature that had attacked Winter. Its body was thick and bulky but that was where the similarities ended. It looked human—not serpentine, but primitive: broad face, wide brow, disproportionately small nose, and a skewed jaw, the most hideous depiction of human features imaginable mixed together, forming an atrocity.

Quell smiled, displaying genuine pleasure instead of fear. I was too familiar with that smile because I had seen it often on were-animals. It was in response to the adoration for violence and the knowledge they were about to engage in a bloody fight. They reveled in it, seeing it as a challenge to sharpen their skills, never considering the possibility that this fight could ultimately end in their death. I suspected that losing a battle was something they never considered. It was probably a sign of weakness they weren't willing to accept.

Quell moved quickly, pulling a dagger from a sheath. Dropping to the ground, he slashed the thing's Achilles' tendon. He moved so fast it was hard to keep track of him. Its clawed hand caught him on the shoulder as it collapsed to the ground. He slit the creature's throat. Then he went on to systematically dismember the thing. This wasn't his first time doing something like this. I stared, disgusted, watching the vampire with the strange eating habits. He was working on autopilot. Whatever grossly insignificant form of humanity he'd displayed before had washed away.

When he finished with the creature, he looked up and started toward me. I heard the sound just a fraction of a second before he had. I should have moved—should have run—but instead, I turned to look. Another creature stood just inches from me. I expected it to attack immediately, but instead, it stood frozen, its face tilted to the side, studying me.

I distanced myself enough to plunge the sword into its chest. The sword was sharp, but the thick fascia gathered around the blade, restricting real damage. Pulling it out, I went for another thrust, harder and faster, hoping to hit an organ as I used the force of my body. Its massive arms swung out, raking across my abdomen, leaving four deep gashes that trailed around to my back. Pain seared through me so deep and forceful that I had to suck in a deep breath to keep from crying out. It swung again and I jumped back, barely missing its strike. It started to swing again and something jerked it back, stopping it in midswing. It remained still for a long time—unable to move. Then it vanished.

Holding my side, I gawked at the empty space. *That can't be good.*

Quell surveyed the area as he walked toward me. "How did you do that?"

"I had nothing to do with that."

He walked around, assessing the vacant area, brows furrowed as he crossed his arms over his chest, giving the surroundings another sweeping, inquiring look. When his attention shifted to me, it immediately went to my claw-ripped shirt. "You're injured."

"Just a small cut," I managed, pressing my bunched t-shirt, damp with blood, firmly against the injury, an effort to slow the bleeding.

"Skylar, that is not a small cut. Small cuts don't gape open. You will need to see Dr. Baker for this." He came closer, bending his head down to get a better look.

I became very aware that a vampire was dangerously close to an open, profusely bleeding wound. I took several steps away from him. "No, it's fine. I can take care of it," I stated hastily, wincing when I made a sudden move. "I heal pretty fast."

"I heal fast," he declared confidently, showing me a rapidly healing wound on his shoulder. "But with a wound like that, I would have our Seethe healer look at it."

They needed medical care, too. Good information to know.

"I'll be fine," I reiterated as I picked up my sword and headed for the car. Quell was leaning against it waiting for me when I got there. I was going to have to get used to how effortlessly and quickly they moved.

"If you choose to be so stubborn, then at least allow me to help you."

The blood loss was starting to make me feel ill. I shelved my pride and reluctantly accepted his help.

As he drove to my house, I kept a close watch on him. Trapped in a small area with the scent of blood inundating the air, he seemed undistracted by it. I had been unimpressed when I learned he refrained from drinking human blood, but now I sat in complete awe of his restraint. When he arrived at my house, it didn't escape my attention that I had never given him my address nor provided directions to get there. It also dawned on me that he knew the pack physician's name and was able to spew out other little details about the pack that were rather unnecessary for him to know.

"How do you know where I live?" My words came out harsh and cold as I watched his movements carefully. With an inconsistent heart rate and breathing pattern, it was hard to tell whether or not he was lying. I had to rely on his body language.

His strange green eyes flickered with humor. "Our kind make it our business to know where the members of the pack reside. It is quite disturbing to find out—too late—that you are neighbors with a were-animal. You all seem to meddle more than most, making living near you a rather unnecessary hassle."

I didn't correct him by telling him I wasn't part of the pack. It was probably safer that way.

He stopped at the threshold of my home, waiting to be allowed entrance. Hesitating, I wondered if I should allow him in. A vampire had tried to change me in-vitro, forever linking me to them and preventing me from having a natural barrier that others enjoyed. Josh's ward kept vampires and pretty much anything that wasn't wholly human out of my home. "No funny business. If there is, I will stake you," I stated before dropping the ward.

He smiled as he stepped over the threshold. He handed me my sword. "Behead me instead. Cut out a step."

I thought it was supposed to be a joke, but as with most of his speech, it lacked inflection, just a dry deadpan. I pressed my hand to my stomach trying to assuage the pain. It was so warm I could barely keep my hand against it and the pain was becoming intolerable.

"Do you have an icepack?" he asked, walking over to the refrigerator.

"Yes."

He opened the freezer, pulled out the cold pack, and went to press it against me, but I moved out of reach. I still had a problem with a vampire being close to my injury. He smiled. "I haven't had human blood in all the years I have been in this life. I assure you I can resist yours," he said smoothly as he handed me the cold pack. "Here. Put this on your *small* cut."

I hissed at the pressure of the ice against my skin, it was too tender. I needed to clean and bandage it.

"I'm going to take a shower and clean the cuts," I informed him in my politest attempt at asking him to leave.

"Very well. I will help you bandage it when you are done." He took a seat.

Apparently, subtle social cues didn't work on Quell. I

conceded because I was going to need the help. The cuts felt like someone had rolled hot coals over them and ached with the slightest movement.

Sharp pains wrenched through my abdomen as I stepped into the shower. No, this wasn't a small cut. When the water hit me, I doubled over, and my body temperature rose to an intolerable level, turning into an inferno as the room whirled out of control. I held on to the shower curtain, which gave under my weight, and I crashed onto the shower floor. The only thing I felt was cold wet ceramic against my face as I drifted into darkness.

I awoke wrapped in a blanket, reclined back on the passenger side of my car as Quell raced down the dark street. "Not a small cut after all," his tight voice muttered when my head dropped to the side to look at him through blurred vision.

Just what I needed, an "I told you so." Closing my eyes, I drifted off. When I opened them again, his arms were looped under me, carrying me. Instead of knocking, he kicked at the door. I parted my eyes just enough to see Dr. Baker standing there.

"She's broken," Quell stated in his typical impassive voice.

"What happened?" Dr. Baker's rushed out as he pulled me into his arms.

Quell let out a quick harsh sigh. "Fix her. Question me later."

He must have vanished because Dr. Baker made an irritated growl before taking me into the house and closing the door.

Dr. Baker's face, which was rough from too many missed shaves, pressed against my forehead. "You're burning up," he said in a fatigued drawl.

I tried to tell him what happened, but everything was starting to feel numb and too heavy to move. I mumbled a couple of words, but he didn't seem to understand me.

"You will be the death of me," he grumbled as he carried me to the clinic. I tried to keep my heavy lids open but quickly gave up.

~

"Is she okay?" asked Sebastian's rough baritone voice.

"She was poisoned, too, but she should be fine. Her injuries were minor compared to …" Dr. Baker's voice trailed off. My injuries weren't as bad as Winter's and Joan's. He didn't say it, and no one really wanted to be reminded of it.

Sebastian's face hovered over mine, eclipsing the bright light that filtered through my closed lids. I could feel the turbulent unease of his anger and wasn't ready to face it.

Play possum and he will go away.

But he didn't. His presence still lingered just above me.

Okay, snore. Don't snore, you idiot. What are you, twelve?

The only thing he could do was yell. How was that any different than any other time? I opened my eyes. "Hi," I said in a spritely voice.

Look at that, his frown brought friends—two deep veins on each side of his forehead. His frown dipped so deep it looked painful. I remembered that face. It was the same one he had last year when he had attempted to snap my neck. He inched away just enough to give me space to sit up. I shimmied my hips along the bed until I was sitting near the head, increasing the distance between us. I clung to the blanket that Quell had wrapped me in earlier.

He sighed heavily. "Tell me why Quell was at this house at three in the morning, dropping off an injured Skylar when she should have been tucked away in her bed. You are really a busybody, aren't you?" he asked in a gruff voice.

It was seven. Time flies when you're poisoned and unconscious.

"Are you in trouble again?" Josh asked, leaning against the frame of the door, his lips twisted into a sideways grin.

"I wasn't being reckless," I countered, defending myself. "I went back to the gym, just to check it out. There was something familiar about the creature—its scent. I've been around it before. I wanted to see if smelling it again could jog my memory." Maybe it was the way that Sebastian was staring at me, the somnolent awe etched on Josh's face, or the utter dismay at my stupidity, but it jarred my memory. "Lemon and brimstone," I blurted.

Dr. Baker stepped in front of me, took a penlight and flashed it in my eyes, then started taking vitals and performing a quick evaluation.

"I'm fine," I told him as I inched away from him and directed my attention to Sebastian, trying to explain myself. "Last year, when I visited Gloria, she smelled like brimstone and lemon. Each one of those creatures had the same scent. I think Tre'ases are involved. They can alter their appearance at will. It makes sense."

Gloria was a Tre'ase whose nature I was still trying to figure out. Some speculated demon, others fae. Last year, when I had visited her, acting as a foreteller she had shown me images of my "evolution," or the things she predicted I would become based on the choices I made. I wasn't sure what was more disturbing: the image of the demonic creature she presented me with or the version of myself as a vampire. That day, I experienced every possible debilitating emotion and walked away without any better understanding of what I was.

Were-animals can't be changed to vampires, and I had no idea what choices I had to make or what series of events needed to take place for me to be changed into one. I wasn't a true were-animal—I wasn't a *true* anything—technically, I was dead, so some of the rules didn't really apply to me. I wasn't immune to vampire entrance into my home. Silver didn't bother me. I had a *terait,* which was only seen in vampires during bloodlust. And it seemed to be the general consensus that I didn't smell like a were-animal. I was an anomaly, all because my mother had tried to save my life when a vampire saw fit to take it.

Josh shook his head. "Not possible. There are only three Tre'ases in our area. Joan and her Alpha killed two creatures, and Gavin was attacked this morning the same time you were."

And then, if I added the two that Quell killed, that would be at least five.

"But Gloria could be involved," Sebastian added. "I wouldn't put it past her."

Josh looked worried. Certain entities he really didn't like to deal with. I was never sure if it was a magic thing or a healthy dose of fear.

"We should look into this," Sebastian affirmed as he started toward the door. "Josh, check it out, and take Ethan with you."

"Heaven forbid that I actually do something without my big brother," he mumbled at Sebastian's back.

"He can hear you," I informed him in an extremely low voice. But of course, he knew. Growing up with Ethan and being around were-animals all his life, he was aware of how acute their hearing was. I doubted he cared. He was becoming less careful with concealing his irritation with living in his big brother's shadow.

"Do you mind if I go?" I really didn't want to see Gloria again, but I needed confirmation that my suspicions were correct.

"I think you should stay here."

"No, I'm fine."

He hesitated for a long time, something he wasn't known for doing. Finally, he agreed. I guess he suspected that I had every intention of tagging along whether he agreed or not.

I eased off the bed, and pain made me wince. Josh frowned and looked like he was about to rethink his decision. I assured him I was okay, but he didn't look convinced. Once I started walking, it felt better. At least my skin didn't feel like I was being seared on a grill. Now it was just a dull ache. By tomorrow, it should be healed —I hoped.

CHAPTER 5

I showered and dressed in the last outfit from my overnight bag in the trunk of my car. Quell had left it parked in front of the pack's home with the keys on the seat. I was thankful that Steven had harassed me into being prepared for virtually anything. Okay, maybe not anything, but anything that would have me otherwise naked if it weren't for my little stash of clothing.

Josh had called Ethan several times to tell him we were on our way, but kept getting voice mail. By the third call, he was noticeably panicked when he hung up the phone. He pushed his Wrangler to speeds it wasn't used to as he headed for Ethan's house, periodically calling him. By the sixth call, he was driving over ninety miles an hour, the beating of his heart as erratic as his driving.

He drove up the long driveway camouflaged by the large oak and pine trees that grew alongside it. It formed a *J* that allowed access to the front door and curved around, taking you to the back of the house, to the garage. The large open lawn was surrounded by tall trees that swallowed the sunshine, shading the area. In the center of the sward was an enclosed gazebo with large picture windows that overlooked the small duck pond that surrounded it. It was probably just for decoration. I was sure Ethan had given the ducks their walking papers long ago.

Josh ran up to the door. He didn't bother knocking. Instead, he took out his keys and opened the door, but stopped abruptly as soon as he entered. I slammed into his back. Rigid muscles tensed and felt like bricks against me.

He moved a little farther into the house, and I got a glimpse of what had him upset and quickly spiraling into a well-deserved rage. Ethan and Chris lay naked on the floor, entwined, scarcely covered by a chenille throw and surrounded by discarded and ripped clothes.

Ethan awoke with a start, sitting up quickly. A twinge of color shaded Josh's cheeks and jawline as his glare switched from intense anger to abhorrence and right back to anger. Awakened by Ethan's sudden movement, Chris sidled in closer, hiding her bare breasts, her lips gently brushing against his shoulder.

Josh stared at them for a long time, trying to control the anger that was brewing. "Threatening and trying to kill each other is what ... foreplay?" he asked, his voice surprisingly calm and a stark contrast to the strife that marked his face.

Chris smiled impishly and kissed Ethan on the shoulder before gathering her clothes and backing up to the stairs. Josh's gaze fastened on her until she disappeared up them, and then he focused his attention back on his brother.

When he started up the stairs behind her, Josh pointed his finger at him and shouted, "No, you stay right there!"

Shock had Ethan freezing midstep before he turned to face him, moving stiffly as he pulled on his underwear. "I need to shower and dress," he finally said, his voice still rough from being abruptly awakened.

"It can wait."

Ethan's eyes narrowed as he crossed his arms over his chest. I wondered how long he was going to allow Josh these liberties. It was a strange change in dynamics. Ethan usually attempted to dominate and even control Josh at every chance. Josh was skillful enough in dealing with his brother that he bucked at his control mostly, submitted if necessary, but ignored him usually. Josh's anger had reversed the roles between them. If I hadn't been so disturbed at seeing a naked Ethan and Chris entwined, I would have been amused by this situation.

"What? Life isn't dangerous enough for you? You've decided to spice it up by sleeping with Demetrius's lover?" Josh asked, stepping closer to his brother, his gaze intensely focused on him. The last time he was this angry with Ethan, it ended in an epic fistfight, an immense demonstration of power and emotions. It seemed like they were heading in that direction again.

Use your words, boys.

"She's not Demetrius's," Ethan stated in a strained voice.

"Really! I'm not sure he got the memo. Whether she accepts it or not, she is *his*. What do you think happens when they trade—they have tea and talk about the weather? You can't seem to have dinner with her without getting in her pants. You think he's any better? You just screwed Demetrius's lover! How do you think this is going to play out?"

Ethan's gaze slipped in my direction before returning to Josh. "We are not going to have this discussion now."

"When should we have it, when Demetrius is trying to see what your insides look like as he rips you apart?"

"It'll be fine," Ethan said confidently.

Josh sighed. "He will try to kill you over this out of principle because you dared to touch something of his—"

"She is *not* his!" Ethan snapped.

Josh looked incredulous, lost for words as he shook his head.

"Drop it."

Josh seemed like he was having a heck of a time doing so. But whether he wanted it to be or not, as far as Ethan was concerned, the conversation was over. The quiet resolve on Ethan's face said it, even if you denied his posturing that demanded an end. "Why are you two here?" he asked, changing the subject.

Josh took the cue—reluctantly. "Skylar thinks that Gloria's involved with the attacks. We're going to check it out."

They were playing nice, but Josh kept shooting Ethan cold glances that he ignored.

Switching his attention from Josh, there was something peculiar about the way he looked at me—it wasn't guilt or shame. It was amusement. He smiled at me and a sparkle of mischief shone through gunmetal pupils. "Give me ten minutes to shower and dress."

"Are you going to be able to *just* shower and dress, or will you need a chaperone?" sniped Josh.

"Screw you," he responded with a smirk as he trudged up the stairs.

"It's not me I'm worried about you screwing," Josh shot back after him. When he disappeared upstairs, Josh rubbed his hands over his face several times before he looked at the clothes scattered over the floor. He kicked them over into the corner along with the blanket.

Minutes after Ethan had made his way up the stairs, Chris came down in one of his shirts, her skin still damp and glistening from the shower. "You don't mind if I join you on your visit to Gloria?" she asked as she started toward the back of the house.

Josh lifted his gaze to meet hers—cold and reproachful. "I mind very much, but I won't stop you."

She smiled, letting his coarse words roll off her as she continued to the back, going out the backdoor and opening the trunk of her tan BMW. She rummaged through it and pulled out some clothes. Dressing quickly and skillfully, she slid on her underwear and bra under Ethan's shirt without exposing skin.

Ethan came down the stairs before she was completely dressed. He started to say something to Josh but became distracted by the view of Chris from the window behind him. Josh huffed a long-defeated sigh, rolling his eyes in frustration as Ethan's attention remained fixed on Chris, watching her wiggle into a pair of jeans, take off his shirt, and replace it with a button-down. Hair tousled, no makeup, and dressed in a lightly wrinkled shirt and worn jeans, she still managed to keep Ethan's unyielding focus.

Chris shoved two knives into her boot sheaths, added one on her right thigh, and put a pocketknife into her back pocket. Two guns were placed in shoulder holsters and one at the hip. It looked like after we visited the Tre'ase, we were going to take over a small country. When she looked up to see both Josh and Ethan looking, her full lips turned up into a slight smile. She might not have been a were-animal, but her movements were stealthy, predatory, and captivatingly feline as she sauntered back to the house.

They watched her as she approached. Ethan had a look of sheer longing while Josh's was of aversion and a reluctant understanding of whatever it was that seemed to have his brother enthralled. He took several long glances at him. "This has disaster graffitied all over it," he said with an exasperated sigh.

"It's hard to stay away from her," Ethan admitted quietly.

"Maybe when Demetrius breaks your legs, it'll help."

Josh and I followed Ethan and Chris down the same deserted road I remembered from last year. Chris took her small sports car down the road and around its curves at speeds that would ensure that she and Ethan would arrive at the Tre'ase's home before Josh and I would. We arrived at the red and white house, which still reminded me of a peppermint. The curtains were drawn, and fallen leaves gathered at the first step. Chris gave three brisk knocks on the door. No one answered.

Ethan placed his shoulder against the door, preparing to break it when Chris slipped next to him with locksmith tools in her hand. After less than a minute, she had unlocked the door and let us in. She went through all the rooms, giving a brief rundown of what she found in each. "She's gone," she finally said after she had inspected the whole house.

"You think she was taken?" Josh inquired, looking around. The place was very neat. Everything meticulously placed the way a woman did when she knew she was leaving for an extended period.

She shook her head. "No, her things are too neatly placed. Just her necessities are gone. She's in hiding." She walked out the door. "We should visit her son. He may know something."

"Son?" Josh asked, stunned. There weren't many things that he didn't know, but he seemed shocked by this information.

Chris grinned. "It's a 'not-so-secret' secret."

We followed Chris, staying close behind as we drove onto an unpaved country road bordered by open fields, which, by late fall, would be obscured by stalks of corn. Pastures and a few small farmhouses were tucked behind broad maple trees with large, low-hanging branches that obstructed our view. We drove deeper into the trenches of no-man's-land, where people probably went only when necessary. The road curved into a dead end that was blocked by a cluster of large trees. If that didn't deter you, several road barriers blocked any visible trails. It couldn't be any clearer. *Stay out!*

The Tre'ase's home was tucked away—hidden from the world. The were-animals lived in seclusion, encouraging the privacy they desired, but this person resided in the shadows, squirreled away from civilization entirely.

We parked near the roadblock and had to travel the rest of the way on foot, following Chris along the murky path. Branches broke under my feet, and leaves crunched, announcing our arrival as we made our way through the forest. I tried to be stealthier, especially when Chris shot me sharp looks.

Nature's beauty always put me in a state of awe: the rich greens during summer and fall, and now, in the middle of October, opulent orange, greens, and russet often colored the surroundings. Somehow, it had abandoned this area. Everything was stygian and desolate, buried away from civilization, shunned by nature, forcing even the sun to retreat. Yet we continued traipsing through the wooded area until we reached a sienna brick house.

Chris didn't knock. She opened the door and walked in with Ethan close behind. A figure kept to the shadows, hiding, for which I couldn't blame him after we barged our way in.

"Thaddeus, I need to talk to you," Chris said.

He remained still for a long time, and then he stepped into our line of sight.

There was a reason why he was kept a secret. He was grotesque. A tall, broad build, his lower half made like a goat, and his upper half curved to the point he was unable to lift his head all the way. Small horns that reminded me of a lamb's protruded from his head. His face was humanlike. Josh told me that Gloria was a subspecies of demon, but she had the gift of morphism. When I had met her, she was a stout, salt-and-pepper-haired, very human-looking woman. But I wondered if she had used her gift to present that to me, and if something like her son was what she really looked like. I tried not to stare.

"What do you want?" he asked, his voice soft and melodious, a surprising contrast to his appearance.

"Where is she?" Chris demanded.

"Who?"

"This isn't the time for games. Where is your mother?"

"I wasn't aware she was missing." He sounded sincere, but she didn't seem convinced.

"If she's in trouble, we will help," Ethan offered, taking a step closer.

Instead of answering him, Thaddeus focused on him with such intensity and abhorrence it seemed violent.

Ignoring whatever was going on between Thaddeus and Ethan, Chris spoke in a terse, low voice. "Do you hate your mother so much for bringing you into this world that you wouldn't help her if she's in need of it?"

Once again, his attention went to Ethan. He frowned and backed against the wall. He addressed Chris. "Make him leave."

Last year, when I had visited Gloria, she had had a similar reaction to Ethan. In fact, she could barely hide her disdain. When Chris looked in Ethan's direction, he nodded once and stepped outside. Intense curiosity obscured Josh's face as his gaze trailed him out of the house.

What the hell is going on?

Chris smiled grimly as she stepped closer to Thaddeus. Dipping her head down to catch his gaze, she spoke, her voice satin soft and gentle. "I know it's hard to live like this, unable to walk between the two worlds. It's unfortunate not to be gifted with the ability to change your form, destined to live in this way because of a mother who is too selfish to relinquish or even share her gifts." Her hand rested on his shoulder. "I am sorry this is your life. But I will be even sorrier once I tell Demetrius and Sebastian that you were reluctant to offer assistance with finding the culprit responsible for attacking and slaughtering their people. I cannot imagine the downward spiral your life will take with them as your enemies."

"Are you threatening me?" he asked through clenched teeth. His grotesque appearance made him seem more harsh and confrontational.

Her voice was tepid, her demeanor impassive as she simply stated, "No."

She waited for a response and when there wasn't one, she headed for the door.

Thaddeus exhaled deeply. "I don't know where she is, but she advised me to leave because people would soon start looking for me."

"Was she taken by force or did she leave willingly?" Chris asked, turning to meet his rueful gaze.

"My mother is stronger than most people realize, but greedier than I care to ever admit or understand. I believe self-preservation is what drives her absence, and possibly a very good payoff."

"If she is in any way responsible for the attacks on the vampires and were-animals, then you will get the gifts you've desired."

Upon the death of a demon, fae or witch, their gifts are handed down to their eldest child. It seemed to take a great deal of effort for Thaddeus not to smile at the thought. "Contrary to what you may believe, I would rather have my mother safe at home than her gifts."

"If she isn't willingly involved, then you will get that wish, but if she is, then you will get your true desires," Chris stated perceptively before heading out the door.

Fifty feet from the car, Ethan hesitated as Chris went for the gun holstered at her side. The crowded branches separated, pushed aside by the two creatures that stalked toward us. Bristly gray fur barely covered their massive bodies. Ill-formed canines protruded from their mouths. One snarled with its disfigured maw; sharp-angled claws that should have formed its front legs swung wrathfully as it made its way toward Ethan. The creature that charged toward Chris continued to morph into a grossly disfigured humanoid. The features were all in place, but there was something terribly wrong with the way it looked. The nose was twisted like a poor imitation of a Picasso: thin, furled lips were disproportionate to the face. Pulling a knife out of its sheath, Chris tossed it to Ethan. They moved quickly and synchronized with a fluid rhythm deeply rooted in violence.

Chris's first shot went into the humanoid's chest, the next into its stomach. She watched, assessing how it responded, each shot calculated to determine the monster's vulnerabilities. It kept advancing, its pace swift but mechanical. Ignoring Ethan's commands to get out of the way, she locked gazes with the creature, smiled, and shot it in the eyes. Blood gushed as the creature stumbled back and fell. It was still alive, taking deep, ragged breaths. Taking the knife from the sheath at her thigh, she started toward it to finish the job, I assumed to behead it. I wasn't sure if every being needed to be beheaded to ensure death took, but it was a good practice. I doubted anything could survive very long without a head. Before she could strike, however, the creature disappeared.

Her lips parted and she stared at the empty space. When the creature that Ethan fought fell, it, too, disappeared before he could finish the job.

"What was that?" she asked, looking in Josh's direction. He looked just as lost, staring bewildered at the empty space.

"That wasn't a demon. They don't have powers like that," Josh replied. "Most of them look scarier than they actually are, possessing minimal magical skill, defensive tricks that aren't strong enough to stop an inferior were-animal. And those gifted with the ability to change their appearance have mated so much with humans that their magic has been diluted to the point it is negligible. Whatever those were, they possess abilities greater than anything I have seen. When injured, most of us cannot travel." His focus lingered over the surrounding area, looking for either more creatures or clues.

"I need to go back to the house to do some research, Chris. Should I contact you or Demetrius if we find anything?" Josh asked as we all started back toward the cars.

His brother frowned at the very mention of Demetrius.

"Call me," she said.

"What part of me telling you to stay back didn't you understand?" Ethan asked her as they approached her car.

"Just the *telling* part. The rest I ignored," she stated coolly.

"Demetrius's blood doesn't make you invincible. What you did was reckless and amateurish. If you want to work with us, you won't do anything like that again. Do you understand me?"

He continued his rant, describing her response to the situation as incompetent and amateurish to the point it could have gotten her killed. She regarded him for a surprisingly long time, listening calmly as a frustrated and angry Ethan continued to berate her tactics. Then she just stopped. Dismissing him with a roll of her eyes, she slid into her car and drove off without waiting for him to move out of the way.

When he started walking toward Josh's Wrangler, I wished we could ignore him as well and speed off. Chris had lit the fire of his rage and left us to deal with it. *Thanks.*

"Some things never change," Josh mumbled under his breath as Ethan continued toward us, his jaw clenched hard and set with frustration, his eyes cold and steely. And I thought *I* rubbed Ethan the wrong way.

"Did you two lovers have a quarrel? I can't believe it. You two usually get along so well," Josh said as Ethan got into the backseat.

Ethan's eyes narrowed to sharp lines. "Just drive the damn car."

"Maybe this time you two will learn it can't work and stay out of each other's beds," Josh mumbled.

Chris took a long draw from the glass of carménère. She spit it out and emptied the glass and bottle into the sink. Its strong spiced taste made her think of Demetrius's blood. She didn't want another reminder of what her life had become and what he had become to her.

Grabbing a bottle of Riesling, she opened it and filled the large wineglass just shy of the top. She gulped down a fourth of it in one large swallow before going back to the den. No matter how she tried, she couldn't get Ethan out of her mind. Hindsight being exceedingly profound, she realized she shouldn't have gone to see him. They had never been able to be around each other without it becoming physical—mostly sexual—and also violent at times.

She placed the glass on the coffee table, one of the few things in the sitting room that wasn't white. The monochromatic space was her place of solace, untainted by the life she lived outside the four walls. White walls and delicate flowing curtains softened the hard edges of her ultra-contemporary furniture. Lavish gifts of appreciation from Demetrius were placed throughout the room, adding a subtle palette of color. They had started to appear regularly after she had commented on a tribal mask she once saw in his home. Appreciating it for its unique elegance, she never thought anything of it. From that day on, her payments for services were accompanied by one of his distinctive gifts. The pearl and ocher blown-glass vase was the first gift he had given her and had become the thing she valued the most. It wasn't the vase itself, but the *Ipomoea alba* or moonflowers that filled it. Ethan had introduced her to them when they first dated, and it wasn't often that she didn't have a bouquet of them in her home.

The rest of the house was tainted, tarnished by the long nights she lay sprawled across the sofa with her Mac in her lap doing research, sullied by the numerous times she sat at one of the tables or sofas cleaning blood from her weapons, loading her guns, or sharpening her knives. The rest of the house was a constant reminder of what her life had become.

With a sigh, she turned up the glass, emptying it before leaving the room, grabbed her laptop off the kitchen counter, and headed for the living room. She plopped onto the large overstuffed chair and opened her Mac to do research on the creatures they had encountered. There weren't many things that surprised her. Through the years, she had collected extensive dossiers of the many creatures that occupied the otherworld. And just when she thought she knew all there was about the various species that populated it, she was thrown another subspecies or anomaly that was a result of interrelationships, mutation, or a complicated version of Darwinism.

She managed to keep up with the changes and had an impressive knowledge of the many dirty secrets out there. When people hired her, there was an implied confidentiality that she adhered to, but there wasn't a conflict of interest in keeping records and using them to her advantage. The were-animals were the hardest group to gather information on because they rarely went outside the pack for assistance. Since they had become allies with Josh, things had become harder. Through the years, they had acquired enough allies and established enough pack-friendly associates that they could keep their secrets tightly sealed. And if a were-animal went rogue, they went after them, never seeking outside help. Chris always suspected it was out of embarrassment. Most of the time, it was handled before too many people knew about the situation. However, when one did turn for whatever reason and gave in to their violent nature, the mayhem and savagery usually sent a swarm of people to her, wanting her to capture it. Fae and elves weren't typically malevolent, but when crossed, they could be as vicious and malicious as any were-animal or vampire. They didn't enjoy the hunt, just the punishment.

At one time, Chris never would have considered witches part of the otherworld because, technically, they were wholly human. But over the years, as she gained better knowledge of them, she found that they weren't much different than vampires, exhibiting the same superiority complex that led them to do some radical things to eliminate those whose existence they viewed as being unacceptable. They had a special contempt for were-animals.

Although they hid well under the deceptive veil of humanity, they had proven themselves to be as cruel, cunning, and deplorable as the others that dwelled in this world. Whenever something atrocious and horrific occurred, witches often were on her list of usual suspects.

Even with her meticulous records, her store of knowledge still didn't compare to what she had found in the pack's library. They had had a wide selection of books and information on mysticism and thaumatology even before Josh became an intricate part of them. The library had volumes on the history of elves, fae, and vampires, meticulous chronicles of the major players, leaders, consorts, and alliances. If it ever made a significant ripple in the fabric of this world, the were-animals had it documented. She was sure that when this was over, she could go to their library and find it listed somewhere. It wasn't always their strength that made them a force to be reckoned with. It was their knowledge.

Chris was working on a list of all the possible alliances Gloria could have formed when Demetrius's familiar knock at the door pulled her from her work. She glanced at the clock. Four hours she had been drilling away at the information. The knocking persisted and her attention went to the door. "Nightfall and he appears," she mumbled under her breath.

"Come in," she yelled from the sofa. Hospitality had long left their relationship. He entered slowly, gliding across the floor with masculine grace. Demetrius was 160 years old, yet he managed to blend into the modern world with little effort. Stylishly dressed in a pair of dark slacks and an English-cut button-down shirt, he looked like a model for an upscale designer. She was so used to his overwhelming beauty it no longer fascinated her. He smiled, exposing fangs. That, too, was something that no longer fascinated her. They didn't seem so deadly anymore.

After Demetrius had saved her life, she wasn't sure what to

expect from him. Would he treat her like she was an indentured servant or his possession? When neither one had occurred, she wasn't sure how to deal with him. It was during that time that she saw a less arrogant, more genteel, kinder side. In another life, she could have imagined them becoming friends. But it was hard to befriend someone when you knew the body count of the lives they had taken.

"I haven't heard from you today," he acknowledged, slowly pacing as he kept an inquisitive look in her direction.

"Do I need to call? I typically see you every night."

"A less narcissistic person would think you had a problem with that," he said before he walked over to her. Kneeling down in front of her, he took her hand and kissed the palm of it.

"No," she said, turning her head away when he leaned forward and attempted to kiss her on the lips.

As he made his way to the sofa across from her, there was that same look of bemused intrigue he gave her far too often. Holding his dark gaze, she couldn't help but revisit the night that had linked them into this odd arrangement.

For nearly a month after the "incident," he had been a daily visitor. When she was finally well, things returned to normal. Weeks passed and she hadn't heard from him. She didn't miss him, but she did miss his blood. For those weeks, she tried to deny it because she hated that she had become dependent on vampire blood. It wasn't the dependency on the blood that repulsed her. Everyone had something they were dependent on. Some dependencies were as benign as chocolate, sweets, or caffeine, while others were severe and damaging like drugs or alcohol. It was a dependency on someone she couldn't control that bothered her. Her pride took a hit when she asked to trade with him. Now it had been a little more than a year when Demetrius sat relaxed on the sofa across from her with his fingers clasped behind his head as he listened attentively to her proposal.

Her hands wouldn't stop sweating, leaving streaks on her jeans each time she wiped them across the worn fabric. Smug condemnation shad-

owed his face. "Why would I agree to such a thing?" he asked after long consideration.

"You'll get me," she blurted. When his brow rose in miscreant interest and he licked his lips, she quickly rephrased. "I will drink from you and you will do the same."

He looked thoroughly disinterested and she knew that wasn't a great bargaining tool. And if by chance she didn't know, he quickly informed her of it. "I have a house full of wonderful people at my disposal willing to meet my needs, and if I'm ever bored with them, I have a whole city. Do you think what you offer will surpass that? I never considered you to be so arrogant."

There was that part of her that was afraid to go back to her life without that supernatural strength, speed, agility, and healing ability. After seven years, she had grown accustomed to the daily dose of fear that came with her job, but now, the fragility of her humanity made her nervous. Yes, that was it. She had never been nervous about doing her job, but now she was.

"I need you." It came out in a barely audible whisper before she could clench the words back.

His eyes lifted to look at her. A hint of a smile curled his lips. He had gloated over things more insignificant than this, and she expected that along with his trademark smugness. But he did nothing of the sort. Instead, in a gentle voice, nearly as soft as hers, he agreed with a simple "Okay."

He was standing next to her before she could look up again. When he leaned forward to kiss her, she turned her head away. "I'm not agreeing to anything more than just us trading." Chris was aware that his garden, a group of people who lived in the vampires' common home, met more than his nutritional needs, but she didn't want that. For her, this was nothing more than a barter deal.

"Fine," he said with an amused smile. "Is there anything else you aren't willing to do?"

Emboldened by his tacit agreement, she continued, fully aware that this was merely a gentleman's agreement that he didn't necessarily have to comply with. But she knew him well enough to know that if he gave his word, he would never go back on it. That was one of the things that she admired about him. He gave his word seldom, but when he did, he kept it. She needed to establish clear-cut boundaries because something this delicate could head south quickly.

Knowing his propensity to try to seduce during his lascivious feeding practices, she limited it to her wrist at the radial vein.

"Add the jugular and the saphenous and you have a deal," he stated with a grin.

She wasn't sure where the saphenous vein was, but because of the ribald grin on his face, she figured it wasn't something pleasant. She didn't agree. She later discovered the saphenous vein was located in the inner thigh.

"Under no circumstance will you ever call me," she added. The very idea that she was opening herself up to having that done was appalling. When vampires called, your volition was yanked from you, your will expunged, leaving them masters of your actions. It was vile and demoralizing, and though it wasn't brute force and violence, it was still a blatant violation. Chris couldn't stop him from reading her thoughts as he fed from her, which was annoying enough, but at least she had some control. It wouldn't be long before she learned to block him from doing that. But she wasn't aware of how to prevent him from calling or resisting it if he did.

When she was finished with her stipulations, he smiled, exposing the edges of his fangs as he circled her in slow, deliberate steps. "Let me understand: I can't have you. I can only feed from your tiny wrist, and I can't call you or use you for any of my own pleasures. This is quite perfunctory. I doubt either of us will enjoy this."

"It's not for enjoyment," she said in a low voice, half expecting him to laugh at her proposal and walk out the door.

Instead, he stepped closer to her, just inches from her face, his finger stroking along her jugular vein as he mulled over the information. Seconds turned to minutes, minutes turned into even longer minutes, and finally, they had been in that same spot, in silence, for nearly ten minutes. "Agreed," he finally stated. Chris exhaled.

"May I?" he asked, pressing his cool lips against the skin of her wrist. At her assent, his teeth pierced her skin, and she shrieked. It had been years since she had fed a vampire. She had forgotten how painful it was. She watched him closely. For someone that said he would gain no pleasure from it, he seemed to be in a euphoric state. Sinking in deeper, he seemed pleased as she groaned and hissed at the pain.

The day before marked a year since the first time she had fed him and neither of them seemed disappointed with the agreement. Now Demetrius sat across from her inquiring about her day, and the trading between them was so routine it seemed mundane.

"We went to see Gloria today," she informed him.

Last year, he had used Gloria as a source to track down Skylar, whom he had planned to use in a ritual that would have given him and his Seethe the ability to walk in the daylight unharmed and be immune to *reversion,* a process that occurred once a vampire was staked, causing them to putrefy and revert physically to a dead state. They could survive it if they were fed in time before the process was completed. In this state, they were the most vulnerable and unable to defend themselves. It was during this time that most were decapitated and killed.

Gloria had also informed them that Skylar was linked to magic —strong magic. If the ritual had been completed, all the vampires would have acquired the same magical abilities. They were inherently able to borrow small amounts of magic through feeding, and a select few were gifted with more, allowing them to *travel.* Usually those vampires were linked to a common creator, either Demetrius or Michaela. Demetrius wasn't known to share his gift with his *created.* Michaela was the only one whom he had chosen to gift with such abilities, and he hadn't been happy when she extended the gift to Quell. Chris suspected that this had led to the fall of their relationship. It had somehow violated the sordid, obtuse agreement between them.

Vampires preferred to stay single. A few were like Gabriella and Chase, monogamous and satisfied with the situation, becoming lynked, a vampire version of marriage. Most vampires preferred and functioned best in polyamorous relationships. But they were not without complications, and were often plagued with jealousy, bruised egos, and violence. Still, polyamory remained a popular choice among the vampires. Michaela and Demetrius's relationship was a sordid mélange of lynked and polyamorous. They proclaimed an undying love for each other but indulged with others and very often lived apart. Chris didn't understand how they managed, but somehow it worked for them. While most of the Seethes were controlled by either a Master or a Mistress that preferred to stay single, allowing them to indulge their desires without consequence or complications, the North was controlled by both, although most considered Demetrius the true leader.

Chris wanted to believe they loved each other and what they shared with others was just physical. Michaela loved beauty in both men and women. It was the very reason their Seethe was an homage to her appreciation of it. She collected beautiful people like trophies, and if during their human lives they hadn't lost their humanity, when they crossed over, she did whatever was necessary to chip away at it until there was nothing left. It was the reason she loved and valued Gabriella and Chase. They were beautiful, cruel, and exceedingly deviant. Quell held her attention with his looks, but not her interest. There was still a light of humanity that dwelled deep in him, and Michaela hadn't figured out how to extinguish it. Chris suspected he wouldn't be around much longer.

Demetrius leaned back on the sofa, his midnight eyes deepening at the mention of the Tre'ase. "You think she is involved?"

"She's gone, so, yes. Her son has no idea where she is, but she did urge him to leave."

"Is he involved?"

Chris shook her head. "He's scared of you and Sebastian. Even if he actually possessed any significant gifts, I doubt he would ever use them against you two."

There was an inscrutable look on his face, a cross between pride and arrogance. He derived a certain pleasure from knowing people feared him.

"I plan to see Josh tomorrow to see if he found anything else."

"You are able to be around Ethan without any problem?" he asked, concerned, his features quickly shifting to a grimace, distorting his appearance.

"We both have tried to kill each other. It can only get better from there," she said with forced nonchalance. *It helps that we are sleeping together again,* she thought acridly.

He pushed himself up from the chair and knelt in front of her. "Be careful. If Gloria is involved, don't underestimate her. She can be very dangerous. I do not want you hurt on my behalf, and I don't trust that wolf to keep you safe."

"I don't hold Ethan any more responsible for my safety than I hold you. I'm a big girl. No need to worry."

"So much bravado. I do believe it is more stubbornness than skill that has kept you alive for so long." He grinned as he leaned forward to kiss her on the lips. She turned her face, offering her cheek. He hesitated for a long moment before his cool lips pressed against it.

"Maybe I am a fool, but I worry about you as though you were one of mine."

"Yes, you are a fool. And if you hold me in such high regard, then I have more than Gloria to worry about. I've seen how you've treated those whom you consider yours. I would rather you consider me something else."

He chortled. "I punish as lavishly as I reward. Is there anything wrong with that?"

No, there wasn't anything wrong with that. He needed to be loved and feared to maintain the control of his Seethe. Chris was aware of that. His punishments were so cruel and brutal they turned her stomach and sent shivers through her. She never wanted to be on the receiving end of his anger.

Fear of his wrath was what kept many of the vampires in line. But she knew he derived pleasure from most of his punishments, and there was something very wrong with that. He took her long silence as a tacit agreement as he leaned forward to kiss her again. When she attempted to turn away, his hands held her face firmly in place. His lips pressed against hers, but she didn't respond, keeping them tensed into a disapproving moue. His tongue brushed across her lips, beseeching a response that never came.

His obsidian gaze remained fixed on her the whole time. With any other vampire, especially one as old as Demetrius, she would have never held their gaze so long and with such intensity. It was through that extended gaze that vampires could capture the minds of most humans and make them slaves to their desires. He had promised that he would never do that to her and hadn't broken it, even when he was angered that she wouldn't bend to his will.

She continued to watch him as he walked across the room, a stern frown marring his face. The constant attempts to seduce her were one of the most tiresome and annoying things about dealing with Demetrius. His delicate ego was bruised because very few people denied him. Maybe once, maybe even twice, but it wasn't long before he had his way. He had been trying to get Chris into bed since Ryan, her trainer and mentor, died. Each refusal had been met with more persistence and even more immature responses. Far too many times she expected him to jump up and down in a tantrum while yelling, "Why won't you let me have you? Everyone else lets me."

That was the problem. Everyone else did. He was denied so seldom, this was just a game of conquest for him, and Chris was well aware of it.

"When was the last time you fed?" Demetrius asked.

"Four days." She didn't need to keep up with it on a calendar because she could feel the absence of his blood in her. Everything seemed to be off, as though she were now living life in 2-D, a sluggish, less spirited version of herself.

"Are you hungry?"

She nodded slowly, her eyes lifting to meet his inviting smile.

It wasn't a hunger, but a craving. When his blood filled her veins, she could feel it pushing through her, making her reflexes sharper, her senses keener, healing her faster, and enhancing her strength. It was like a veil had been lifted off her eyes and everything seemed clearer, objects around her moved slower, and she became more focused. The feeling was so exhilarating she could never refuse it.

He pulled out a small knife and took a seat on the sofa next to her before handing it to her. "What about you?" she asked.

"I've fed already."

As she swiped the knife across his wrist, he moaned. Only a sadomasochist like Demetrius could find pleasure in such pain. She lay across the sofa on her stomach, her mouth covering his wrist as she took long draws from it. Resting his head back against the sofa, he stroked her hair lightly, urging her to continue.

CHAPTER 6

The odd green-eyed vampire with the strange eating habits stood on the other side of the door while I debated whether I should open it. It had only been twenty hours since the last time I had invited him across my threshold, and I could have gone a couple more. He was peculiar, but I hadn't decided if it was in an interesting way. His distant personality, vacuous appearance, odd eating habits, and vicious, murderous ways made it difficult to determine if he was a pleasure or pain to be around.

He wasn't going away. After he knocked again, he stood like a mannequin, staring directly at the peephole.

When I finally opened the door, he waited until I invited him in and made an attempt at a smile. Lips barely moved to offer any warmth or incitement. Quell might not have been quite a vampire, but he didn't seem to have lost all his humanity, either. His behavior was distant and mechanical, as though typical human behavior was foreign to him and vampirism was just a welcomed escape from it as he teetered in between the two.

"Sebastian didn't know you were out playing hunter, did he?"

His tone lacked inflection, and I couldn't determine if he was upset or impressed by my deception.

"He wasn't aware of the particulars," I stated evasively.

He looked away for a brief moment. Irritation quickly flickered then disappeared from his face. "Did he know? Yes or no?"

I couldn't understand why people who lived as they did possessed such an affinity for the truth.

I shook my head. He smiled. It was a real smile, which nearly floored me.

"Covert activity amuses you?" I asked.

"You lied." For some odd reason, that disappointed him. I didn't know if I should have been flattered that he didn't think I was capable of doing such a thing or worried that he held me to such standards.

I stared at him, trying to make sense of his inquiry. The silence continued for such a long time it was starting to feel uncomfortable.

"Have you ever killed anyone?" he asked, taking a step closer. His eyes were intense, displaying an odd curiosity

"What's wrong with you?"

"Answer the question," he insisted.

For a few moments, fear had its way with my imagination. Had I been wrong to invite someone that possessed a peculiar interest and pleasure in violence, lies, and murder into my home?

He waited patiently for an answer.

"Yes," I admitted, looking at the door several times, wishing he would take the hint and leave. I wanted the green-eyed vampire with the death obsession as far from me as possible. Whatever comfort I found in him that led me to inviting him in was gone.

"Did you enjoy it?"

Moving several steps back from him, I frowned at the question. If I said yes, then what? Was he going to invite me on some type of killing spree? "No. Not at all." The memory was hard to deal with. I had killed a member of the Seethe's garden after they had attacked Ethan and me. Driven by a rage that I hadn't realized dwelled in me, I had mercilessly assaulted and killed another human being. The thought of it still made me sick.

He nodded slowly as he watched me from across the room in silence.

"The smell of blood doesn't bother you?" I asked. I should have chosen a different topic—anything that wasn't in the death, blood, and violence family. But I couldn't ignore my curiosity.

"No, not human blood."

"Why? You're a vampire. Isn't that what you do?"

"How old are you?"

"Why?"

He shrugged a response.

"Old enough to know there was a time when it was considered rude for a gentleman to ask a lady such a thing."

"Gentleman?" He chuckled modestly. "Has this world ever created such a person?"

"Twenty-four."

"Not very long," he said softly, turning his back to me as he slowly paced the space in front of me. "If you live long enough you will learn that humans are despicable, vile creatures. They start wars, murder, violate people's rights because of things they didn't have any control over such as race, gender, or the location in which they were born. These so-called *humans* perform betrayal of country, others, values, and beliefs for money and power. I've cringed, watching violence inflicted on humans by other humans far more abhorrent than that of vampires, yet we are considered monsters. I can resist human blood because they disgust me."

Awe-struck, I gaped as I took in his response. His denial of blood wasn't out of love for humanity but out of disdain. There was a naïve part of me that wanted to believe he denied his bloodlust because he was a vampire with a soul, a kind-hearted creature that valued human life and regarded people as more than food and entertainment. Instead, Quell was a vampire who denied his kind's usual urges out of his complete disdain for humanity.

"I've seen people come together to help others who are victims of natural disasters, fight wars to give people rights that were brutally taken away, create inventions and perform research in efforts to improve or save lives. There are people who dedicate their lives to find the people responsible for such perverse acts of which you speak. Humanity has its flaws, but it has its good points as well," I retorted.

I wasn't advocating for him to feed from humans. In fact, if his non-sanguine feeding habits could rub off on the rest of the Seethe, especially Michaela, who had a penchant for feeding from children, it would be great, but pure disdain for humanity bothered me. He hated the very thing I wanted desperately and wholly to be.

His words were stiff. "Humanity hates itself. With each decade that passes, they drift further away from any remnants of humane behavior. As the years pass, I loathe them even more."

Really, I didn't gather that from your speech.

"That's rather hypocritical coming from an undead that is part of a Seethe that has done far worse," I responded coolly.

"We do not cling to any moral codes that dictate whether or not we are vampires. But humans are quick to categorize someone a monster or inhumane for acts that they themselves indulge in regularly." He finally moved, walking slowly across from me, bearing a perceptive look on his face that quickly turned into a frown. "What can be said of a population that prides itself on its civility, which is rooted in human nature, but behaves not much different from us?" he countered, stepping so close to me it was invasive.

I stared into the cold green eyes of the misanthropic vampire, seeing them for what they really represented—his disdain for humanity. "You've placed all humans in a box, prejudging them by the worst of their kind and ignoring those whose acts are altruistic, selfless, and kind."

He forced a smile and it seemed as though he was struggling to remain pleasant as I gave my little spiel. "I am well aware a few perform acts of civility and commend those who actually behave as a human should. Maybe at some point their humane deeds will surpass their vile acts, but I doubt that. They have yet to impress me."

Thanks to my numerous dealings with Ethan, I had learned when it was time to drop a topic. "This Hidacus, how are you able to survive on just it? You are strong. I can't imagine it giving you the necessary sustenance to survive."

"It serves its purpose well. Would you like to see it?"

Hell yeah! I nodded slowly, attempting to seem indifferent, but my intense curiosity poked at me.

Quell lived nearly forty miles away from me. I had to drive because he hadn't fed, and he couldn't travel with the both of us. The radio played as we drove in silence, but he soon grew annoyed with the pop princesses crooning at the top of their studio-enhanced voices about their promiscuity and dysfunctional views of love and romance. When I changed it to a classic rock station, he made an aggravated sound before turning the radio off.

The vampire that despised humanity ensured that, despite living among them, his interactions were very limited. His old farmhouse was in a rural area, surrounded by acres of open space and cornfields. The nearest neighbor was driving distance away and the two closest houses were vacant.

In the heart of the Midwest's humdrum of cornfields, farms, and uncultivated land he'd found a little piece of countryside that made me forget that we were in any part of Middle America. He didn't just live in solitude. He lived in isolation, hiding from the world and staying as far from humans and their reprehensible ways as possible.

A moment of clarity hit me as we got out of the car. I was about to follow the Lost One into his home, in the middle of nowhere, to look at plant that was strong enough to sustain the life of a vampire that I had watched kill and dismember a creature that had slaughtered and injured the pack's best. This was the beginning of every slasher flick imaginable. Common sense had me frozen in place just a few steps from my car.

Quell continued toward the house. It took a while before he realized I wasn't following him. "If I were going to hurt you, I have had more than enough opportunities."

He had a point. I followed him inside and stopped in the foyer to admire his home. Every time I found myself wandering through the home of a vampire—which over the past year had been far too often—I was amazed. Because they were creatures of darkness, predators of the night, I expected their homes to be stygian, and Neolithic. On the contrary, they were usually impressively decorated, exquisite combinations of aged refinement and modern flair.

Quell's home wasn't any different. It was Tuscan influenced with a décor of rich browns and terra-cotta. Rustic furniture claimed a large amount of the space. The textured plaster created intricate designs on the crown molding, and earthy clay-colored floor tiles added authenticity to the room. Surprisingly, his home felt warm and comfortable.

He was silent as I followed him through the house. The stealthy and lithe way he moved was a constant reminder that he was a creature of the night—a predator, a murderer. And foolish curiosity had me walking behind him to get a look at this elusive plant. He stopped at the back door and waited patiently for me to catch up while I browsed through the house as though I was on a museum tour. He must not have many guests because he seemed to enjoy my appreciation.

The greenhouse that held the very plants that allowed him to survive was just a few feet away from his home. It seemed too small and simple. I had expected something grand and captivating. "You can only feed in the evening?" I asked, looking at the glass that surrounded the vestibule. He shook his head as he pressed a control on the wall and shutters enclosed the small area, forcing us into complete darkness. My night vision was pretty good, but Quell still took the lead, his hands cuffed around my wrist, and led me down the dark pathway.

Beautiful budded flowers were entrenched throughout the greenhouse: rich fragrant lavender plants, pungent orange marigolds, and sundry chrysanthemums. The various smells were a delightful distraction, inundating my senses. I walked throughout the greenhouse so absorbed by the enticing aroma and the various displays of beauty that I had forgotten the purpose of this field trip.

With his hand in the middle of my back, Quell redirected me, guiding me toward the plant. Its rough jasper presence looked misplaced surrounded by such delicate beauty. It was large, towering over the other plants, an odd cross between a willow tree and flowering plant. The veined stems were long, stout, and swayed steadily. Wide nodes along the petioles thumped rhythmically, like a pulse. Instead of blooming flowers at the tip of the expansive leaves, there were tiny buds filled with a sappy fluid. I stared, engrossed, disgusted and slightly intrigued as it pulsated at a steady beat. Quell stood to the side observing my reaction.

He took a stem into his hand and pierced it with his teeth. It flickered, moving ever so slightly as though it felt pain when the fangs invaded it. He fed from it for a long time. When he finished, it blanched and fell from the branch withering and dissolving into dust before it could hit the ground.

"How did you find such a thing?" I asked.

"Many of us have known of its existence, few use it. Blood, for many of us, is the preferred choice," he admitted as he licked his lips, removing the green trail left behind.

"Try it," he suggested. He broke off a stem. A low moan resonated throughout the space—I believe it came from the plant. I looked around for a better explanation: there wasn't one. *The freaking plant moaned.* I shook my head vigorously, declining. I didn't have any desire to eat from a plant that moved as though it were alive, had a pulse, and was potent enough to sustain the life of a vampire.

He insisted, pressing the plant to my lips. "Open," he urged.

I turned my head away. The silky deep rasp of his voice was a tempting invitation, and if he were offering anything other than a pulsating, moaning plant, I might have agreed.

He broke the stalk in half, squeezing a viscous green gel onto my finger, easing it to my lips and pressing it into my mouth. I took a quick taste, anticipating something bitter and vile. Instead, I sampled it again. It had a sweet, light metallic flavor with a hint of spice, a cloying version of blood. Watching my expression change, he handed me the remainder and I finished it. Its taste lingered on my palate. "Do you find my diet so strange now?" he asked with an amused smile.

At that moment, I wasn't sure. I had tasted blood before—mostly just my own. But last year, when the Tre'ase had showed me what I would be like as a vampire, I had experienced bloodlust, and for the first time, I had tasted blood from an unknown donor. I was drawn to the flavor, seduced by it. After tasting the Hidacus, I wondered if this could truly satisfy a bloodlust, or if Quell was just fooling himself.

I studied the vampire with the same intensity he had set on me. "How long have you been a vampire?"

His contempt for humankind seemed rooted so far back it predated the progress that had been made in the past few decades.

If he were a century or older, then I could understand his disgust because he had seen the worst of mankind.

Stepping closer, he showed just a hint of an amused smile. "Longer than you've been alive."

I waited for him to elaborate, but he never did. There was still a light smile on his lips as he started to circle me in long, deliberate steps.

He was a strange one, and his enigmatic ways pulled at my curiosity.

"You are an inquisitive one, aren't you?" he asked in a low voice once he was in front of me.

Most people called it *nosy,* but *inquisitive* sounded better. "I find you interesting," I admitted.

Leaning in just inches from me, he angled his head and studied me. "Are you flirting with me?"

Flirting? That was flirting? Does he even know what flirting is? "No … no … um, no. You make me curious," I fumbled out, taking several small steps away. The greenhouse seemed crowded. No matter how much distance there was between us, it still seemed too close for me. "You don't feed from humans because their immorality disgusts you, but you allow them to live—unharmed, never forcing them to do penance for their crimes against humanity. By all logic, you should be society's greatest murderer, making them atone for their evil ways. Based on your beliefs, wouldn't it be just?"

I waited patiently for a response but was met with silence. Instead, he stared at me with an undecipherable expression. I continued, "You won't feed from humans because you find them deplorable and choose to have nothing to do with them. But you are a vampire, the people in your Seethe have done things just as, if not more, heinous."

He took a moment before he spoke, considering my words. "You think I should revere them because I am a vampire and interact with those whose behavior is considered inhumane?"

"Well, the whole pot and kettle thing does come to mind." The odd green eyes, a reminder of his feeling for humankind, were penetrating as they stared back at me.

"Vampires do not have codes of morality that they live by. Humans apply so many to themselves as an effort to feel superior, yet most of them fail to meet the very basic requirements placed on them," he said in a tenuous whisper.

I said, "A human found a dying woman and tried to save her. When she realized she couldn't help the woman, she saved the child and raised her as her own. And when she found out the child she had raised turned into a wolf once a month, she didn't abandon her. I've seen the best of humanity and that is what I choose to color my view. Despite all the bad that exists, there is still a lot that is really good."

He clung to my words but was obviously unmoved. The crimes humans had created against his perception of humanity were so egregious there wasn't any redemption. I could praise the many good deeds that I had witnessed for the rest of the night, and I doubted I would change his mind. But the gentle smile remained.

He was quiet for such a long time I needed to end the silence. "How long have you been like this? Your parents didn't give you the name Quella Perduta. What was it before?" I just couldn't ignore my curiosity.

"Does it matter? Is who I was as important as who I am?" he asked quietly.

I nodded.

He'd moved back to the Hidacus, and once again the odd whimper came from it as he removed a stem. Breaking it in half, he pressed another piece to my mouth, and the sap moistened my lips. He kept it next to them until I sucked in my bottom lip to remove it. Then he handed me the stem.

His voice was a gentle timbre as he spoke. "Sixty-nine years ago, I became Quella Perduta, leaving behind Andrew Fletcher, who I am glad no longer exists."

Then there was the odd silence again. The impassive look didn't offer any more information. I was just as curious about the things that Andrew Fletcher had endured, things that had resulted in the Lost One, Quella Perduta.

"Thank you for coming, I have enjoyed your company" was his final response before he vanished.

As I let myself out of Quell's home, I knew that Michaela was wrong. He wasn't the Lost One—he was the complicated one, and I wanted to figure him out. What had happened to him that was so bad that he had turned away from humans and into the clutches of the vampires?

CHAPTER 7

Josh and Chris were sitting at the library table with a collection of books scattered over it. She blew out an exasperated sigh as she slouched down in the chair across from him, propping her legs on the table. She seemed so relaxed in the pack's home with Josh as her partner in research. When I finally walked farther into the library, she acknowledged me with a smile, while he seemed too engrossed in their conversation to give me anything more than a quick wave of his hand.

"We have to rule out the fae, period," he said. "Few are skillful fighters, and their magical abilities are limited to cognitive manipulations, premonitions, and minor spells. The most nefarious thing I found they could do is compel someone to harm someone else, but they require physical contact with them to do it."

"Rule out the elves as well. They're rarely violent like this. Just mischievous jackasses that derive too much pleasure from mayhem and chaos," she stated with confidence.

"I wouldn't rule them out yet. In the last year Mason seems to have a new thirst for power that I haven't seen before. He's attempting to form an alliance with the witches."

Chris leaned into the table. "With the witches?"

Her look reminded me of the way Josh looked when he was trying to make sense of an abnormality. I had been on the receiving end of that look many times.

After several long moments of thought, she stood. "I need to speak with Gideon."

"Why? He will never give you any useful information," Josh said.

"Never underestimate him just because he turned down his candidacy for leadership. He cares what goes on with his people and he likes to play clueless, but don't fall for it. He's a lot more astute than people realize."

"If he knows anything, I doubt he will be very forthcoming with any information."

"He will with me. Over the years, we have come to understand each other quite well," she admitted with an impish grin.

"I'll go with you," Josh offered.

"No. Then he'll just show off and posture. We've developed a good working relationship past that stage of name-calling and idle threats. We understand each other."

"Hmm, and yet you can't seem to get past that stage with my brother," he said with a smirk.

She smiled. Her eyes danced with amusement. "Your brother's a narcissistic, arrogant, stubborn person who is impossible to reason with," she pointed out as she started for the door. "If we can't get past that stage, it's because of him, not me."

"Yet you can't stop sleeping with him," he rebutted.

With her hand on the door she turned to look at him, her laugh a light musical sound that lingered. "Even the smart ones can make really stupid choices." Then she slipped out the door.

Josh was still chuckling after she was gone, his attention still on the door. Like his brother, he had somehow been disarmed by her charm. Maybe it was jealousy that fueled my curiosity, but I wondered if there was something a little supernatural about

Chris. Could she be a fae, possessing the ability to control another's mind and emotions? There had to be something more to her than just a charismatic personality.

Being around predators to the extent that I had, it was easy to consider her one. She seemed quite harmless in comparison, but she was a quiet storm, a predator in her own right. While most stalked their prey, tracking them, exulting in the hunt before the kill, Chris did nothing of the sort. Her approach was far more elusive. She captivated, disarmed, and lured her prey with the impression that she was innocuous. They trusted her. Then, before they were aware of their fate, she struck, leaving behind a surprised but dead carcass. Soft eyes, a gentle smile, and an intoxicating personality lured them willingly into the predator's trap.

Josh had gone back to his book, oblivious to my presence. "Is Chris just human?" I finally asked, attempting to sound indifferent and casual.

Flipping through pages, he scanned over them. "As far as I know. Except for trading with Demetrius—there's nothing special about her. She's just well-trained and knowledgeable." He kept his head buried in the book, engrossed in things that were far more important than my odd curiosity. Perhaps he heard the disappointment in my sigh, or maybe I distracted him enough that the perceptiveness that he was known for had been piqued.

He looked up, his lips kinked slightly into a small smile. "She is charming. But she has to be or someone would have killed her long ago. She was trained by the best. Ryan's reputation took her further than her personality ever could. I will admit, there is something about her that seems—"

"Enchanting," I finished.

He nodded. He returned to his book, then lifted his eyes to meet mine. "My brother"—he rolled his eyes in dismay—"has always been drawn to her in a manner that I can't understand. When she shot him, I think he fell in love."

"What?" Nothing about that sentence seemed to lead to a then-they-fell-in-love story.

"A couple of years ago, we had a were-animal that went rogue. That's the official word they used. I say he went rabid-ass crazy. It happens rarely, but when it does, it's a tragedy. No one knows how or why it happens. The thing killed several fae in a very torturous and cruel manner. Fae are typically harmless, but when they are angered, they can be merciless. They hired Chris to capture and bring him to them so that he could be punished. Ethan and Winter were already looking for him. Both Ethan and Chris found him at the same time. When Ethan wouldn't back off, she shot him in the leg with a silver bullet. I think he asked her out a couple of days later." He shrugged off the absurdity of the situation.

"So that's the way to Ethan's heart: a silver bullet and poor anger management skills."

"Are you trying to get to his heart?" he inquired with a faint smile, his gaze probing and inquisitive.

No, I wasn't trying to get anywhere near that thing, which I was sure had atrophied from lack of activity, but strangely, Ethan was an enigma who intrigued me. Of all the women he could have and the ones he'd had, what was it about Chris that held his attention so thoroughly?

Josh's gaze was so curious, I dropped my eyes and directed my attention back to the book in front of me. "Do you believe some people are so wrong for each other that they can actually be good for each other?"

When he spoke, his words were weighted. "No. I believe some people are so wrong for each other that it's only a matter of time before everything explodes into a fiery mess. Please don't misunderstand me. I like her—more than I wished. But they are horrible together. A disaster waiting to happen." He sighed. "Any objections I make only seem to make her hotter to him. So I have to wait in silence until it ends again—and, hopefully, the wreckage won't be as bad as the first time—then clean up the mess," he stated with a smirk.

~

Chris knocked on the door as a low rumble came from the sky, which shadowed to a deep gray as clouds crowded the once sunny day. Thunder crackled, water sprouted from the clouds as a hard, torrential rain started, drenching her. Wiping away the hair that matted to her face, she smiled and pounded on the door harder.

When the door swung open, a lanky man blocked her entrance and handed her a thick towel.

"Gideon, stop playing," she said, drying herself off as best she could. The brisk wind blew against her back, sending shivers through her. He handed her another towel, wider and more absorbent than the first.

A miscreant grin sharpened his thin, angular features. Short butterscotch-blond hair was an odd contrast against his desert-sand color. The king of mischief and mayhem was often hailed for his good looks, but Chris had always thought he was too effeminate. A slim aquiline nose that usually made him look aristocratic and regal was diminished by lips that were too full and supple, cheekbones too high and rosy, and wide, expressive violet-colored eyes. There wasn't much of a difference between his appearance and that of his twin sister.

"Didn't your mother tell you it was rude to come to someone's home uninvited?" he teased, holding the door open as she continued to dry herself off.

"Yep, just like I am sure your mother told you it's extremely rude to drench someone."

She slid in past him as she entered the house, making sure to rub her sodden shirt against him. His movements were always quick and lithe, but not fast enough to place the other towel he held in his hand on the chair before she plopped down into it. She grinned when the miscreant smirk quickly vanished as her wet jeans squeaked against the leather.

"I am sure you know why I am here," she said.

"I figured I would be receiving a visit sooner or later. Someone's trying to kill off the vampires and were-animals." He shrugged. "A huge waste of time, in my opinion. If you give it a couple of years, they are likely to do it themselves," he said as he played with the white streaks of electricity that he created. Sparks flared and he rolled them over his fingers. Chris considered elemental elves freaks among monsters. Shape-shifting immortals that survived on blood and people who could perform magic by merely speaking words all paled in comparison to those with the ability to control the weather. The world, even for just a mere moment and in a limited space, was under their command, bending to their will.

That realization, even when there wasn't any threat, caused her to always cling to the iridium cuffs that she always kept near when she was dealing with magical beings. Named for Iris, a goddess that linked gods to humanity, iridium reduced magical beings, who often considered themselves gods, to mere mortals by inhibiting their use of magic. Chris considered it one of the most useful weapons she possessed.

"Do you know who it is?"

He shook his head. "Nope, but I suspect they aren't someone you want to mess with."

She watched him for a long time as he continued to play with the flashes of electricity he created. "You're sure the elves aren't involved?"

"We aren't fond of the were-animals and vamps, but our issues aren't enough to start a war that would surely leave us in worse shape than them. If I am not mistaken, the creatures are shapeshifting, right? None of us possess the power to shift."

"What about the *others*." The *others* wasn't their official name. They were referred to by less flattering terms by many. They were the self-proclaimed elite of the elves that had created a new society to separate themselves from the mainstream. It wouldn't have been considered a big deal except that they were the strongest of the elves, those untainted by intermixing with humans.

"I would love to tell you yes so that you could destroy them, but even with their powers combined they do not have the power it takes to create beings that can shapeshift. Whoever is involved has a level of power and skill I haven't seen in my lifetime."

"That's the part that is most frustrating. They can shift to anything and increase in size."

Gideon didn't have more information to give. She was confident he would have spilled it if he had. It had to be in the back of his mind that if this person or persons were coming after the were-animals and vampires, his kind could be next.

"Thanks for your help," she said. They weren't friends, but their tumultuous past had put them in a good place. Gideon was expected, like his father, to lead until his death. The elves would love him if for no other reason than in remembrance of his father and his excellent leadership. But Gideon was too busy partying and living a life free of the responsibilities that most twenty-nine-year-olds had. She knew it was just sheer defiance and insecurity that had led to him declining his nomination ten years before. Although she hadn't experienced his father's leadership firsthand, his reputation remained fifteen years after his death. Elections were next year, and once again, he would be nominated by their council. She hoped he wouldn't decline. She was confident that eventually he would accept the position, and she hoped it would be sooner than later. She had spent so much time trying to establish a civil working relationship with him, which would be far more beneficial with him as the leader of the elves.

"I wish I could have been of more assistance. I don't want this to get worse and my people to be swept into it."

His people? This was the first time she had heard him speak in such a way. She smiled. It was only a matter of time before he was the new leader of the elves.

The dour look on his face was followed by a change in his mood. Lightning crackled outside and the room chilled. "Your boyfriend's here," he said.

She stood up quickly and went to meet Ethan at the door. She wasn't sure what problems Gideon had with him, but she assumed they were the same as most people had.

"I don't know if this will help, but the *genums* are missing," Gideon said.

"I thought they were extinct," she said, stopping short of opening the door.

Genums were small creatures with the ability to shapeshift. Unlike were-animals, they weren't limited to one animal, species, or object. The problem was they were restricted by size. Chris couldn't imagine the massive species that had been attacking the vampires and were-animals could be genums.

"No, not extinct, not yet," Gideon said. "I used to see them all the time. We can usually spot them when others can't, but I don't see them anymore. They aren't as harmless as people believe, but I can't imagine them being responsible for this level of violence."

"Okay, thanks," she said, slipping out of the house and meeting Ethan several feet before he got to Gideon's door.

"What are you doing here?" she asked him.

"Josh was concerned about you."

"Oh, how sweet. Now I have two of you worrying about me unnecessarily." She continued walking to her car.

"Did you get any new information?"

"Yes, but let's discuss it back at your place," she said, ignoring him, and then stopped, listening.

Ethan had heard the sound before she had and turned as the furred creature soared in their direction. Its massive arm struck fast and hard against her as she reached for her gun. An audible pop was followed by searing pain as her arm dislocated. She winced and grabbed for the gun, which had fallen under the car. She expected a quick attack, but the creature wasn't after her. Once she was out of the way, it went for Ethan.

It swung its large claws, and he jumped back. It missed him by centimeters. He charged the animal, pushing it back, drilling punches into its stomach and chest with enough force that the thing lost its footing. He grabbed the knife from his ankle sheath and plunged it into the creature, and when he pulled it out and attempted another jab, it disappeared.

Chris was on her feet, gun in hand, when Ethan approached.

"How's the arm?" he asked.

She held it close to her side, forcing back tears brought by the excruciating pain. "It's fine." She could hear the strain in her voice, so she knew he could as well.

"Are you going to let Dr. Baker look at that shoulder, or are you going to pretend it's not hurt?" he asked in an even voice.

"Do you think he will?" She fought the urge to cradle the arm at her side as it started to throb. When Ethan and Chris had ended, Dr. Baker had taken the breakup the hardest. He had called her several times, but she knew if she had to break from Ethan, it had to be clean. She had severed all ties with the pack, including with Dr. Baker. It was the hardest part of the breakup because she had developed a fondness for him.

Ethan gave her a sideways smile. "For you, of course he will."

Chris sat on the exam table holding her arm as Dr. Baker went through the medicine cabinet. She hated being in here surrounded by the sterile white walls, metal trays, and glossed floors, inhaling the scent of blood, sulfur, and disinfectant. It reminded her of the ER and the many visits she had made to them as a child. Even now, sitting on the table watching Dr. Baker examine her arm, she had the overwhelming urge to come up with a convincing lie for the injury, just as she had done when she was younger. When the images and the memories forced their way to the surface, she shrugged them off and focused on the narrow face, distinct structured jawline, and bristled gray hairs from several days of missed shaves. His silver hair was tousled from worried hands running through it. A deep frown creased his regally handsome face.

There was something paternal and kind about him that made forcing bravado as she declined pain medications or anesthetics very difficult. She ignored his stern look. Pain was an unexplainable comfort to her. Where there was pain, eventually there was a respite.

"How often does it happen?" he asked.

"Not often."

He frowned at her lie and gave a warning look. "How often?"

"About six times a year," she admitted.

He made an irritated noise as he shook his head. "I can fix it for good if you can lay off it for a week."

"I can give you three days."

"Fair enough. I only needed two." He shrugged.

She fought the urge to tell him how much she had missed him as he smoothed a thick yellow substance into her shoulder. The burn along her skin was tolerable, but she hissed when he first applied it. "I see you are still very creative with your medical treatments." *Creative* was an understatement. Dr. Baker was a genius. There weren't too many treatments he hadn't heard of in both the traditional and alternative approaches. He had made several trips out of the country for training.

He shrugged. "I have the least number of permanent injuries of all the packs, and it's not because they are injured the least. They challenge my skills at every chance," he stated exasperatedly. In his attempt to sound irritated, he couldn't hide the pride he felt at being there for them.

She kept her arm hugged against her body, refusing to wear

the recommended sling. She just couldn't do it. It made her feel broken. Pressing the arm to her chest, she promised to keep it protected.

"If you dislocate it again, you will wear a sling, and there's nothing you can say that will change my mind," he said with paternal authority.

She nodded.

Chris had almost made it out the door, when Ethan called her. With a heavy sigh she thought, *I really don't need this right now.* Ignoring him just wasn't an option. The long day had already chiseled away at her patience, and she didn't want to argue. "Yes."

"I want you to stay here, or at the very least, at my place."

"Why?"

"Because you're injured," he said.

"This? I've had worse."

"I know. It's quite unfortunate, but I need to make sure you're protected while you are injured."

"I won't heal any faster here or at your place than I would at my home."

"You're right. But at least I will make sure you won't get any more injuries," he said.

She had dealt with him so much that she realized arguing with him was pointless. To him, his decisions and desires trumped all others and a person's autonomy was rarely considered.

"Ethan," she said in a soft tone, as soothing as she could, stepping closer to him.

She kissed him, a gentle brush against his lips. At first it was soft, but quickly it progressed to something she needed to rein in before it went too far. A kiss was never just that with them. It couldn't be. It was too simple, too tame for what they shared. Resting her hands on his cheeks, she said, "I am not staying here nor am I staying with you. I'm going home *alone*."

His lips parted to speak but she shook her head. “We aren't going to fight about this.”

His eyes dropped to her injured arm, which she guarded against her body. “As if you are in any condition to fight with anyone,” he said.

There was never a calm silence with them. Such banality between them just couldn't exist. The battle of wills was ongoing, neither one possessing the desire to gracefully concede. Chris had learned early on in their relationship that no one ever won a battle with Ethan. Sometimes he just chose not to pursue the fight, which he had done at that moment.

Pressing her arm closer against her body, she opened the door. “I'll see you later,” she said as she left.

Chris's arm was angled and propped on the small pillow at her side as she lay on the couch. It was the most comfortable position she had found, and she wasn't in a hurry to move out of it in order to answer the knock at the door. When it didn't stop, she knew who it was and reluctantly answered the door.

Demetrius didn't wait for an invitation. He breezed past her, taking a seat on the sofa. *How comfortable he is in my home,* she thought bitterly as he relaxed into the chair, legs crossed and arms spread out across the cushions. Far too often these days she wished she could *un*-invite him. But once you invited a vampire into your home, they had access until you moved, or better yet, they died.

He watched her as she walked into the living room, her arm cradled close to her body.

“What happened?” he inquired so low she had to strain to hear him.

She exhaled a harsh, ragged breath, irritated. Injuries, usually minor, were part of the job, and it was something she accepted.

Ever since the *incident*, he had handled every injury with an overreaction. He was the guardian angel that she didn't want. She took too long to answer and he quickly came to his feet and was next to her before she could move another step.

"Answer me," he whispered, his voice laden with command.

Her arm was throbbing and she was already on edge from dealing with an overprotective Ethan. She definitely wasn't in the mood to deal with a domineering Demetrius.

He patiently waited for her to answer, and when she didn't give him one, he edged her closer to the wall. His eyes narrowed, flicks of irritation pranced across his face. It was then she felt the full force of his anger. Cool breath bristled against her ear as he spoke. "Christina, I am losing my patience. Don't push me."

She wanted to push him—push him right out the damn door. Instead, she dropped her gaze, taking a minute to get a hold of her own anger, anger that was about to get her into a situation she wouldn't quickly get out of. Peering up, her gaze, soft and tenuous, met his. Demetrius didn't need to breathe, but now he was taking long controlled breaths to calm himself. It was rare that this level of anger was directed at her.

"I injured myself—"

"I can see that," he snapped. "How did you injure yourself?"

"I was attacked by one of those creatures while at Gideon's."

"Why were you there in the first place?"

"Because I needed to talk to him."

"I was never informed of this. Why didn't I know of this?"

"Why would you have to? I am *not* part of your Seethe. My whereabouts or who I talk to are not your concern. Completion of this job should be the only thing that you worry about. Don't tie my hands by overreacting to everything. Then perhaps this can be resolved quickly."

She met his angry gaze with aggravation. It was times like this she felt as if she were walking a tightrope. One misstep and she could easily plummet to her death. Finding that balance between being strong enough that Demetrius didn't feel the need to subjugate her and acquiescent enough that dominating her seemed almost undignified was a delicate task. It was a skill that had improved over the years, but she still had her share of mishaps.

"I won't be responsible for further injuries to you."

"What options do we have? Send Chase and Gabriella, who are restricted by natural light? You hired me because I am competent and can get the job done. I have access to places you and your Seethe don't. How comfortable do you think a member of your Seethe would be hanging out at the pack's retreat helping with research? Let me do my job."

He smiled. "Is it wrong for me to worry about you?"

Chris's attention stayed on him. "Yes."

Throughout the years, she had learned to deal with him amicably and with great skill, but recently, it had become difficult. Far too often, she felt like she was just winging it.

"Was the wolf there?" he asked, disdain dripping off his words, as he stepped back to give her room to move.

"Yes. But I hold him no more responsible for my safety than I do you. I am the only one responsible for keeping me safe."

His lips pressed firmly together, clenched by his fervent anger. "Why did I hire you, Chris?" he asked brusquely.

"Because Sebastian hates your guts more than you hate his. I was hired as a buffer. He hates me a little less. I doubt you two could spend any amount of time together without trying to kill each other."

"Right. You weren't hired for your skills as a Hunter, so I don't expect you to act in that capacity. I will allow you to continue to investigate, but before you proceed with anything, you will consult with me first. Then I will determine how involved you will become."

She snorted. At the moment, resolving this amicably didn't matter. Unable to tame her tongue, her words came out harsh.

"You think I am going to ask you before I proceed with anything? That's not going to happen."

"I will not warn you again. We do not want a repeat—"

"Don't you dare bring that up!" she snapped. She winced when she wrenched her shoulder to aggressively point in his direction. It ached horribly as shrill pains shot through it. She hoped she hadn't undone Dr. Baker's work and would have to have him repair it again. He would definitely make her wear the sling. *Me walking around in a sling? Yeah, that won't make things worse,* she thought.

"Why? Because you want to forget it happened? You were as close to death as one could be and be capable of coming back. Don't forget that night, because you don't need a repeat of it."

That incident wasn't something that he needed to bring up because she would never forget it. It was a pivotal moment of her life when she realized she was really fragile, that she had a shelf life—she could die.

"If you are going to restrict and micromanage me, then go ahead and fire me because I can't work that way. I am not part of your Seethe, and it's about time you grasped that."

They were at an impasse, drilling each other with hard stares, just inches from each other. When he stepped closer, a gasp caught in her throat. She wasn't sure what to expect.

His glare faded. His words were gentle—too gentle. "You have to be more careful with yourself."

Cold swept along her injured arm. She hated to admit it. It felt good against her inflamed skin. Her gaze drifted to the floor. He stepped closer. The coolness of his body enveloped her. He leaned in to kiss her but she turned her head. Gentle fingers lifted her chin so that his eyes once again met hers, then his lips pressed gingerly against hers. She stilled, unresponsive to his commanding lips. After another failed attempt, he stepped away, giving her space, but not enough to move freely.

Demetrius enjoyed the act of seduction and prided himself on the fact that few refused him. But she had denied him far too many times for his ego to take. It wasn't that she was immune to his charms—she wasn't. She just refused to be among the many that had fallen for him only to be whimsically discarded when he was done.

Ryan had warned her about getting involved with anyone in the otherworld. Professionally, it was unwise, but socially, it was inevitable. She had managed to date casually, never allowing the relationship to linger or become emotionally involved—until Ethan. She broke every rule she had set for herself by dating him and violated everything Ryan had warned her against. It may not have been a career-ending relationship, but it was career-altering. When it became known, she was forever linked to the were-animals and was constantly having to prove that the Midwest Pack didn't hold her loyalties.

Demetrius studied her. "Look at you: so mature, self-assured, and inured to the dangers of this world. Do you remember the first time we met? How old were you, fifteen?"

"Seventeen."

"Ah, you seemed much younger, standing over that vampire, feeding him just to bring him back so that I could punish him properly. Before Ryan took you under his wing, did you think such things existed?" he asked, smiling fondly at her.

She wasn't sure why he was walking her down memory lane. Perhaps when a person was immortal and stuck at the age at which they were turned, they missed the inevitable changes that humans endured and, at times, even envied or resented what they had missed.

Her body tensed at the mention of Ryan's name. It seemed sacrilegious and distasteful for his name to pass through Demetrius's lips. He didn't have the right to force the images of him into the forefront of her mind. "I'm tired," she whispered as she stepped away from him. "I need to rest." She backed away from him, her attention on the door she wished he would use to leave.

He followed her over to the sofa then knelt over her, invading the small space she left between them. "You shouldn't be left alone in such a vulnerable state," he said, stroking her shoulder gently. Cool lips pressed against her skin, chilling it.

"Is Michaela okay with this level of concern for me?" she asked, cautiously scooting farther back onto the sofa away from him.

"She is. Michaela hasn't bothered to be concerned with me or the people who hold my interest for some time."

Chris knew that couldn't be any further from the truth. Michaela maintained a certain level of control with Demetrius's interactions with others, effortlessly directing his lovers in and out of his life. His affections were fleeting but still meticulously controlled by Michaela. If he bothered to care enough, he would have missed them as she eliminated them from his life.

He never seemed concerned with those that kept Michaela's interest. However, if Chris had to guess, Quell would be the first who had ever piqued his concern. He didn't like Quell, and she knew that it had less to do with his abhorrent eating habits and more to do with how smitten Michaela was with the Lost One.

"Maybe your concern is misdirected. Since the were-animals and vamps are the ones being hunted, your worries should be for Michaela's safety, not mine."

His lips curled into a tense smile. "I assure you, she is quite safe. If not Quell, then Chase, Gabriella, and Sable will ensure that she is protected at all times. They would gladly give up their existence to protect hers."

She saw he was having a hard time disguising his irritation. They had stripped him of the role of her protector that, at one time, had been solely his. "The pain pills that Dr. Baker gave me are starting to really kick in," she lied. "I need to rest." She stretched and then closed her eyes. Instead of leaving, he remained in front of her, brushing his hand over her hair gently as he kissed her lightly.

She kept her eyes closed, feigning sleep.

"So stubborn," he whispered with a heavy sigh before he vanished.

She opened her eyes to look at the empty space where Demetrius had stood and finally admitted something that she had refused to accept for some time: her life was coming apart at the seams.

Rip.

CHAPTER 8

Ordinarily, when I don't hear from someone for three days, it doesn't bother me, but since none of the calls I made to Steven or Josh were returned, I went to the pack's home. Josh answered the door and I was grateful. If it had been anyone else, I would have been met with the same inquiring look they always gave me. The deep, penetrating uncomfortable look that always wanted to know why I was there.

He beckoned me in and said, "Why are you here?"

As I followed him into the house, I was met with the sound of loud voices coming from Sebastian's office just to the side of the great room. It was a big room with two large, sturdy, deep ruby sofas—perfect to hide bloodstains—sturdy handcrafted hardwood tables, and modern-styled accent chairs. Nature-themed pictures, mostly of wildlife, covered the walls. The room was so nicely decorated in a contemporary-modern style you often forgot that this home's only purpose was to provide a hideaway from the world. They had several throughout the states, but this was the only one I'd seen.

I walked slowly across the hardwood floors, unable to ignore Steven's frustrated voice. As the conversation continued, I was surprised to hear that one of the voices was that of Joan, his mother. I figured it wouldn't be long before she was fully healed. Joan was a felidae, a jaguar and superior species, which meant she healed extremely fast.

"No! She can't leave. She isn't ready," Steven said.

I moved closer and quickly wished I hadn't. The level of intensity in the room sent goose bumps up my arm.

"Steven," said Joan in a low, soothing voice. She managed to always remain composed no matter how heated a situation became.

"Sebastian, you can't let her do this! She's not ready," he continued. Being a man—or rather a teenager—of action, Steven rarely raised his voice. Now it was a tight booming sound that reverberated through the door.

"Calm down," Sebastian said gently, but he wasn't able to match Joan's gentle, mesmeric tone.

When Joan had adopted him, Steven had begun spending his summers with Sebastian. He was Steven's mentor and the closest thing he had to a father or role model. Because of that, he was one of the best pack members, always seeking Sebastian's approval.

"She's barely healed and you are going to just let her leave? There is no fucking way I am going to let that happen!" Steven continued.

"Steven!" they both snapped almost simultaneously.

"What? I'm the only one who seems to be thinking here. You are so preoccupied babysitting Demetrius and his Seethe. We don't need to babysit them, nor do we have anything to prove. Screw them!" Then he directed his anger to Joan. "And having your ass handed to you again or worse isn't going to prove anything except that you have poor judgment and allowed your pride to compromise it. Who the hell wants an Alpha like that?"

Wow, he's on a rant, and if he doesn't tame his tongue, he's about to have his *ass handed to him.*

"You're not leaving. No damn way!"

"Leave," Sebastian finally ordered. Steven must have taken too long, moved too slowly, or even refused, because he was soon hauled out of the room by the neck. When Sebastian tossed him to the ground, he crouched over him. "I've been more than tolerant of your little tirade because she's your mother and you're upset—I understand that. But you will not speak to either of us that way, do you understand? Don't push my patience. I guarantee you will not be happy with the results of that," he cautioned before he returned to the office.

Steven panted angrily. Eventually he pulled himself to his feet and stormed past me toward the basement. I assumed he was going to take his frustration out on a punching bag or someone. I couldn't reason with him while he was like this, and I doubt he would want me to try. It was wise to let him have his tantrum in his angry place.

Sebastian's voice was calm as he continued his conversation with Joan. "You aren't leaving," he said firmly.

"Sebastian," she said, her voice losing its usual mellifluent tone.

"You have a mess to clean up when you go back. Putting yourself in harm's way will not make it any easier. You are the Alpha now; you'll need to demonstrate it. You will be challenged more times than I can even prepare you for."

"The longer I stay away, the more credibility I lose. It'll look like I ran. They need a presence there—my presence. The longer I stay, the weaker I look."

There was a long silence. "I will make it known that you had no choice. If anyone has a problem with that, they can take it up with me."

"Oh great, the Elite came to my rescue. I assure you that will work well in my favor," Joan challenged with derision.

"The South is destroyed. If you want them to trust you, follow you, and reduce the number of challenges you have, then return with the person responsible for killing your pack found and the situation handled. Then no one will doubt your ability to lead. You will return with more than a 'presence.'"

I couldn't see Joan's face, but I could hear each deep, controlled breath she took. She hadn't left.

Sebastian spoke, and his voice matched hers in calmness, but it was firm, ending any further prospects of a debate. "This conversation is over. You can let yourself out."

Joan left the office, but it took a long moment before she shut the door. When she finally did, small golden embers of feline rage sparked along her pupils. She started up the stairs but stopped as though she was considering going back. It was a long contemplation, but, finally, she gave in to reason. I was sure she had dealt with Sebastian enough to know that once his decision was made—that was it. You could scream, yell, threaten, and in the end, you had just wasted breath and energy that would have been better spent on other things. The status of Elite, the Alpha that headed the other Alphas in the country, was given to the one that was the most dominant and strongest, but I was pretty sure stubbornness had something to do with it as well.

I decided to give Joan and Steven time to calm down and went to see Winter. She'd been moved down the hall from Dr. Baker's office. I hardly recognized her when I stepped into the room. Her deep olive skin was now pallid. Her long, sleek black hair was a tangled mess, and she had IVs attached to every available space on her arm. The constant hum of the machines made the room seem noisy. I hated looking at her like this.

I combed through her tangled hair, giving her a detailed summary of everything that was going on. I spoke to her uninterrupted, but I longed to hear one of her biting quips about how she "couldn't care less if a cat was playing with yarn." It was a stupid response that she used a lot. I had never thought I would miss her scoffing at me about being considered a "greater species," but I did.

After spending a little over an hour with Winter, I went to look for Steven. Before I left, I was going to tell him that Sebastian had decided that Joan was staying and make sure he didn't put himself in a predicament with Sebastian that he couldn't easily escape. I searched for him in the kitchen, the media room, and the library. When I didn't find him, I knew he had to be in the gym. I heard the sounds of heavy pounding and deep breathing as I descended the stairs toward the gym. I knew he was taking his aggression out hard on one of the heavy bags or a sparring partner, who now probably regretted their decision to participate.

When I nudged the slightly ajar door open, instead of seeing a battered were-animal or punching bag, I found Steven leaning into the corner of the wall, his pants dropped to his ankles. Taylor's arms and legs were wrapped around him. Red-welted scratch marks covered his sweat-drenched back. His right hand dug into her thigh while the other grabbed a fistful of her hair, pulling her to him as his hips moved rhythmically against her. He kissed her roughly on the lips and neck, as his movements became increasingly frenetic. He moved fiercely, thrusting her back harder into the wall. As guttural, primal moans filled the room, the only thing I could do was stare with my mouth gaping open in awe and shock.

It was so carnal and intense that it seemed depraved. Too preoccupied with pawing at each other, they didn't hear me shriek, and I was sure they definitely missed the door slamming so hard the frame shook.

The sight of Steven and Taylor didn't seem to be as easily buried with the other things in my head I never wanted to think about or see again.

. . .

"Nothing has happened," I heard Josh say as I passed the library to leave. He'd spent so much time in there that he'd added a large leather club chair in the corner in which he was slouched with his legs crossed. The library was his domain, and as far as I was concerned, his office. It was where you could always find him. "Three days and there hasn't been any movement from these things, not a single attack."

I thought he was talking to me, but his comment was directed to the figure leaning against the corner of the bookshelf—Ethan. When I stepped in the room, Josh, as usual, greeted me with a smile. Ethan just watched in silence.

"Did you need something, Sky?" Ethan asked, his tone just as uninviting as the sharp look he gave me.

Shaking my head, I ignored him as I waited for Josh to continue.

"I just spoke with Chris, and there hasn't been any activity with the vampires, either."

Something that should have been cause for elation troubled him. His arms crossed over his chest, and crinkle lines formed across his brow. Then he engaged in his most obvious nervous habit that signaled he was concerned, nibbling at his nail bed.

Ethan paced the immediate area, his hands rolling languidly over each other. "You think we should—"

Josh nodded his response before he could finish the sentence. Now if only I could get in on that conversation. I hated when they did that. They were so in tune with each other they rarely needed to hold a detailed exchange.

"Are you going to Gloria's?" I asked. I knew the answer before Josh confirmed it. It was where the investigation had started. Somehow, she was involved and we needed answers.

When Josh stood, Ethan was close behind as they headed out the door. "Are you sure?" Josh asked as I fell in step with them, his brow furrowed.

I nodded. Being on the sidelines was a horrible place to be. Most information was relayed to me by Steven or Josh, if at all.

Ethan came to a halt before taking hold of his brother's arm. "I don't think that's a good idea."

Josh shrugged off his hold. "It'll be fine. An extra person can't hurt."

"I assure you that around her finger is not a place you want to be," Ethan shot back over his shoulder as he picked up his pace and walked past me.

Maybe it was frustration with the situation or I had finally just reached my limit with him, but before he could make it out the door, I shot back, "Perhaps you'll remember that advice when you find yourself twisted around Chris's."

A sharp gunmetal glare was his only response.

Our approach toward Gloria's house came to a painful halt as I was slammed back by a powerful force. Josh kept walking through it—the benefits of being considered wholly human. Most wards wouldn't stop a human. I pressed into it, and it countered, exerting a force twice as hard, shoving me back. Each step I made toward it made it hiss and shrill as black and gold embers danced off the translucent wall. Josh stepped away from the house and stood next to me, pressing his hands against the invisible borders, reciting incantations. Lambent lights flicked then fizzled, undulations rolled over its surface. Sharp, angry sounds rang through the air in retaliation. It was a strong ward. After several long, turbulent moments, it hissed at the assaults, sparks crackled along its surface, and finally Josh gave me the okay to proceed. The force that pushed me back wasn't nearly as bad as the first time. He had managed to weaken it, but it was still holding.

I leaned against it with force and a keening sound whipped through the open space, scaring away any life-form that might have been within a three-mile radius. Josh blew out a frustrated breath, placed his hands against it, and concentrated, his lips moving quickly as he recited spells. Ethan barely looked in our direction as he went around to the back of the house. Before the last word spilled from Josh's lips, the ward shrilled. As its last act of defiance, it sparked small embers of lavender and then collapsed.

When Ethan came around the corner, Josh's gaze darkened with curiosity and suspicion as Ethan passed him and headed up the stairs. Josh remained planted in his spot, his gaze wandering over the collapsed ward, then moving toward his brother. I walked past him as he continued to drill his brother with an inquiring glare.

The door was unlocked, definitely not a good sign. The air roiled with the sordid smell of death, honey, and a combination of unfamiliar spices.

"She's dead," Ethan announced as he walked into a room just to the right of the kitchen. I didn't bother to go back and check. I had seen my share of dead bodies, and I was trying to keep that count as low as possible.

Two teacups sat on the table: one empty, the other a quarter full. The aromatic scent of flavored tea and lemon wafted from the cup. Was someone so heartless as to have tea with her before they killed her?

"Was she murdered?" I asked Ethan.

"If so, it wasn't violent," he replied nonchalantly.

"It wouldn't have to be," Josh commented as he slowly walked through the house. His body tensed as he walked farther in with his hands splayed out. "There is some really strong magic in here, powerful," he acknowledged.

As we drove home, silence voiced our collective thoughts: the creatures were dormant, Gloria was dead, powerful magic was involved. What was going on?

~

The only thing Chris could see were the lucid amethyst eyes with the backdrop of fawn-toned skin. When he stepped back, her gaze ran listlessly over the strong broad features, pronounced jawline, arched nose. She didn't know this person and gripped the Glock closer to her body. "May I help you?" she asked.

He chuckled. "Yes, Chris, you can."

She recognized the voice, but the face was too different. "Thaddeus?"

When she opened the door, he hesitated, focusing on the weapon that she pointed in his direction. "You really know how to make a person feel welcome," he stated, smiling with perfectly aligned teeth.

He really went all out on this form, she thought as she tucked the gun in the back of her pants. "You look … different."

"Do you like it?" he asked, wide-eyed and patiently waiting for her approval.

She smiled. "You look very handsome." He followed her to the kitchen and took a seat in the chair she pulled out for him. Staring at him for a few more long moments, she relaxed back into her chair.

"I guess you know about your mother." She had just been given the information about Gloria's death less than an hour ago, but she wasn't sure how long Josh had had that information before he decided to share.

Thaddeus nodded his head once. His eyes drifted to the ground, sorrowed and shamed. Shame? Perhaps shame for indulging in his new gifts and sorrow that his mother had to die for him to receive them.

Chris studied him for a long time, a plaintive face reflected back at her. His lucent gaze followed her as she went to the minibar in the corner and returned with two glasses and a bottle of Scotch. "When did you see her last?" she asked, pouring him a drink and sliding the glass toward him.

He took a long drink. The gulp was too big and the drink too strong. He choked back words and suppressed a cough before he was able to speak. "Yesterday, I could tell something was wrong. She seemed troubled. There weren't many things that troubled her," he admitted, taking a sip.

She took a long draw from her glass and then leaned in, watching him carefully. "Was she alive when you left?"

"Despite what you care to believe, I loved my mother, even though she forced me to live as I did. I would rather have her alive than any of this." His hand swept dismissively from head to toe. The body he had chosen for himself was as impressive as the face he had created. Tall, slender, but sturdily built, he flexed lean muscles with even the most minor movement.

She admired his ability to love Gloria despite that fact she hadn't deserve it. If her own mother died, she would only go to the funeral to make sure it was true. She realized that was what she and her mother had in common: she didn't think giving Chris life obligated her to protect her or love her, and Chris didn't believe that giving birth to her warranted Chris's unconditional love.

"Did she tell you anything?"

"Nothing useful. She advised me to leave again. But where would I go looking like that? I had found a space I liked away from everyone. What did she expect me to do, just traipse off to the next city undetected?"

"Well, you can go anywhere now, and I think it would be a good idea if you made yourself less visible."

"Why?"

"Because whoever persuaded your mother to assist them will come after you, as well."

"I'm not as easily persuaded," he admitted stoutly.

"Everyone has a price."

"Even you?" Curiosity flourished along with his smile.

"Especially me," she admitted, meeting his intrigued gaze.

"And what is that price?"

"Depends," she admitted with a shrug. There was an inscrutable smile on his face that she didn't like. "Why are you here, Thaddeus?"

"I don't want enemies in the pack or the Seethe. I wanted you to know my mother was no longer involved."

"A call would have sufficed," she stated, but she knew he was aching to show off his new form. She was glad he did stop by. Now she didn't have to waste time looking for him.

He seemed too interested in her place, studying it for too long. "May I request a favor?" she asked.

"Depends on what it is."

"You're a decent person, Thaddeus. I don't think you would do anything to hurt the Seethe or the pack—"

"But you would need my blood to do something to make sure," he interjected.

She nodded. His blood was needed because then she could always find him, trace any use of his magic back to him. She couldn't do it, but Josh or any other powerful witch could. Walking into the kitchen, she pulled out a vial, bandages, gauze, and a small knife. His hand was lying palm up on the table when she returned. His full attention was on the knife. Air hissed through his teeth, and he sucked in a breath at the pain as she slid the knife across his hand. Squeezing his hand into a fist, he trickled blood into the opening of the vial. Once it was an eighth full, she placed it aside, cleaned the cut, and began to bandage it.

He watched her dress the cut with clinical detachment. "You've always intrigued me," he admitted.

"What's so intriguing about me?" She smiled, challenging him.

"The vampires and the were-animals respect you, the fae adore you, and the elves fear you. That's quite an extraordinary feat for a human."

"Not extraordinary. Demetrius and his Seethe are varying degrees of arrogant, impertinent asses that most people don't care to deal with. I don't mind a challenge. Sebastian and his pack are ill-tempered jerks that make working with them nearly impossible, but it amuses me more than it annoys me. The fae are the sympathetic type. It's not adoration they have for me. It's compassion because I have to deal with all the creeps of the otherworld. And as for the elves, yeah, they fear me because I can't stand them, and they know it. They like me only because I've saved their mischievous asses more than they've deserved. If it were up to me, I would inject them with iridium and neuter the little troublemakers. I am not that extraordinary. I just have a high tolerance for bullshit."

His smile was so broad he exposed his perfectly aligned pearly whites. "Protest as you will, but you are quite a fascinating woman."

"We aren't that different. The result of unexpected pregnancies, with fathers that cared less about our birth than our mothers and skipped out on them, and hiding from the world because they see us as monsters. If I'm extraordinary, then so are you."

She wasn't sure why she was sharing with him, and as his mouth parted in surprise, she wished she hadn't. Her stomach lurched at the frivolous way she had exposed her personal life to Thaddeus—a stranger. Her life was really coming apart at the seams and parts of her were slipping out.

There was gravid silence. The bright amethyst eyes retreated, becoming saddened and withdrawn. "My mother told me he died right before I was born."

Chris winced, cursing under her breath. *Why do people do that?* she thought angrily as she watched the pain of his mother's lie engulf him. "I'm sorry. I wasn't aware that you didn't know."

"No … no, it's fine." He shook his head as he clumsily came to his feet. "I hope you find out who is responsible for this," he mumbled as he started for the door.

She took hold of his arm. "Don't look for him," she urged firmly. "Please take my advice and just don't. He's not a good person. You're better off not knowing him."

"You know who he is?"

It took a moment before she answered, as she considered how much information she should disclose. She nodded. "You're named after him. He's an elf, and the bounty on him is so high that if I were to make the effort to find him and capture him, I could easily retire. He's been quiet over the past two years, so I haven't pursued him. Perhaps he's changed, but I am sure he's just too afraid to bring attention to himself. If you find him, I'm afraid he'll hurt you. I think you deserve an opportunity to enjoy your life and the gifts you were denied and not be burdened with someone like him in it."

The sag in his shoulders and frown that was etched deeply on his face made her feel guilty. "I'm so sorry." The breath she took was difficult. Her chest was bound too tightly.

"No ... it's okay … it's closure … I needed to know," he managed before making his way to the door and quickly ducking out of it.

He's not my problem, she thought. But she felt that he was. Thaddeus, without his knowledge or active participation, had become everyone's problem. She couldn't let him out the door to either be found by whomever was really responsible for this or by his father, who would exploit his powers before disposing of him. It was her job to fix this and she needed to contain the problem.

"Thaddeus, come back!" she yelled after him. He stopped abruptly, hesitating for so long she thought she would have to go after him.

When he returned and took a seat at the table, she filled his glass, then hers. "Gloria screwed you. Mourn her, pretend to love her, or forget her, but a mother's love isn't something you can replace, even with your father's love," she said softly.

He nodded, but she knew he didn't understand. There was a level of naïveté that came with secluding yourself, and she knew he would be vulnerable in this world. She exhaled. "You're very strong now."

"But I don't know how to do a lot of things," he admitted. He waved his hand over his body. "It took me all day to do this and sixteen failed attempts."

Chris smiled. Most would have given up after five or so, but he had lived so long in his prison of seclusion, tenacity was now his motivator. He was powerful but unskilled. The alcohol was starting to have its effect. His lids fluttered erratically before they started to droop, and he struggled to continue to listen to her.

She filled his glass again and waited until he took another long draw before she continued. "This world will exploit you if you let it, and in order to become the person you need to be, in order to ward it off …" She sighed. "You become jaded, evil, an indomitable asshole, a user, and a manipulator."

He smiled. "You don't seem to be any of those things."

"I'm all of those things, and when I need to be, I am worse. You aren't any of them. But if you try to find your father, you'll become your mother; and you see how things ended for her."

She needed him to break through his intoxication and take her advice. Whoever was responsible for the attacks was going to approach him. She knew he would be exploited because he wasn't tarnished and cruel enough to ward it off and see through the manipulation and lies.

"Go lie down on my couch. Sleep off the four glasses you stupidly drank," she suggested.

He stood and managed to stumble over to the sofa, where he collapsed just seconds after she made the offer. Half-lidded eyes quickly closed, surrendering to his drunken stupor.

For several long moments, she stood over him waiting patiently for him to shed his magically modified appearance and was stunned when it held. Without the call of the moon or Mercury, the were-animals had difficulty keeping their alternate forms. It only became easier with practice. She considered how strong and talented he could be if properly trained. Like his mother, he would possess a level of power that could easily make him dangerous. Innocent and inexperienced, he was ripe to be picked and exploited by anyone in the otherworld.

She knelt down next to him, examining his features, feeling the sparks of magic that surged off him, rolling over the hairs on her skin. She leaned in and whispered his name. When she called him louder, he mumbled something, batted her away, and snuggled closer to the sofa, the snoring becoming increasingly loud. His slim body, diametrically different from his true form, looked innocuous.

Inhaling a deep breath that lingered in the back of her throat, she had a difficult time exhaling it. She walked over to the console and pulled out the Berretta with the silencer attached. She closed her eyes, convincing herself that doing this was the right thing—no, the best thing. If he were dead, no one would approach him. He couldn't be seduced by the money, the anticipation of acceptance and love, or the hope of an alliance in which he would never experience equality.

"This is best," she tried to convince herself softly.

This was the first time she would kill in cold blood without cause. She aimed the gun with her right hand while the left cradled it in an effort to stop it from shaking so much. She knew her breath needed to be slow and steady because if she jerked, it would make a bigger mess. The trigger felt stiff. The light press didn't discharge the bullet. She was panting short, hard, desperate breaths, unable to slow them enough to make a clean shot.

Her chest tightened too much to expand, making breathing impossible. She dropped her hand at her side, gasping for fragments of breath.

She retrieved a .22 revolver, which, in the past, she had used solely to interrogate. Putting one bullet in the chamber proved to be a great motivator to talk because most people didn't like the odds of Russian roulette. Now she would use it for a different purpose: to determine Thaddeus's fate. She didn't want to make the decision herself. She convinced herself to believe that whatever happened to him now was fate. But the guilt gnawed at her. In the back of her head, she knew it was an assassination of someone that was harmless and whose only crime was possessing power that others could exploit.

She removed all the bullets except one. Pressing the cold steel against his head, she was surprised he didn't feel it and try to move to save himself.

For nearly three minutes, she stood, the barrel pressed against the back of Thaddeus's head, unable to do something she had done more times than she would care to admit out loud.

Her hand wouldn't stop shaking as she attempted to steady it against the back of his head. Beads of sweat formed at her temple.

"Pull the fucking trigger," she scolded herself. Her body froze, staring at the person whom she needed to kill to help the situation. It had to be done. Her finger clung to the trigger as she closed her eyes and took a deep breath....

"Dammit," she growled under her breath. She dropped the gun along with the bullets on the side table next to him.

Chris was exhausted from raking herself over the coals for the past three hours as Thaddeus slept. Disappointed in herself, she sat at the kitchen table, waiting for him to wake up. He stirred slightly before wiping the drool from the side of his face. When she called his name, he responded, his voice groggy but more alert than before. When he sat up, she handed him a bottle of water and an aspirin. Turning the bottle up, he didn't bring it down until it was empty, then he took the aspirin. He sipped the next bottle that she handed him.

"You're going to leave tonight. Don't piddle around. Just go somewhere far away, okay? A large city will be best. You'll blend in among the crowds, making it harder to find you. Pretend you're not what you are. Be normal. Get a boring job, live a boring life, and find an equally pretty boring girl and enjoy the rest of your life," she instructed him. She tossed an envelope at him. It hit the floor, but he quickly retrieved it. He looked confused as he flipped through the bills in it.

"I would like that" was his only response.

It was as though she had granted him permission to live a normal life. Was that possible? Would he suppress all that dwelled in him and live among the insipid, cloaking himself, becoming just another sheep that the wolves perceived as too docile to use?

"Good." She smiled. "Don't drink. You don't handle your liquor well." As long as he was gone and hidden, then she had succeeded, she convinced herself. If he were gone, then the person responsible for killing the vampires and were-animals would be neutered.

She looked at the front door but he didn't move. In silence, his manufactured, amethyst eyes looked back.

"I would have liked to know you better," he admitted with such sincerity that she couldn't look at him any longer.

"Look to your right."

His gaze drifted over to the gun and bullets lying on the table. He stood, keeping his attention on the table, biting down on his lip hard. "You have a good night," he said, coming to his feet as the sun broke through the darkness, illuminating through the blinds. He looked over at the clock. "I mean morning."

She didn't have much more to add as he moved toward the door. He hesitated for a brief moment, taking another look at the table, then at her. He grinned. "You may have thought about it, but you didn't do it," he said quietly.

"I considered it. Doesn't that bother you?"

"No."

His naïve optimism will guarantee his death, she thought bitterly. She didn't do it, which was something that she should have been proud of because it meant there was something left inside of her that was actually humane, but her failure made her feel deflated. It was a betrayal of who she was. "Bye," she said, closing the door.

CHAPTER 9

The pack's house smelled like freshly spilled blood, reminiscent of the first day of the attack. I had gotten used to seeing the red stains on the floor and no one seemed to bother cleaning it out of the rugs anymore. Like the others, I'd found myself in a sustained state of rage since the first attacks. Two more were-animals had been killed and five severely injured.

Josh wandered throughout the house, tension and concern heavy on his face, marring his features. His frown deepened and the color quickly drained from his face when Ethan, his hand clutched around his torso, stumbled and limped into the house. When he saw Josh, he stood taller, walking slower and making the limp less pronounced. His flushed skin was damp with sweat. Josh was by his side before he could take another step. He took Ethan's arm and draped it around his neck, helping him to the clinic. Josh insisted on looking at the injury.

Ethan's crooked grin mirrored the one that often covered Josh's face most of the time. "Of course I'll show you. As soon as you show me a medical degree," he joked.

Josh shot him an aggravated look before they disappeared behind the double doors leading to the clinic. He stayed there for nearly twenty minutes before Kelly emerged, her smile broad and unassuming as she escorted him out. She had taken to wearing bright pink scrubs, perhaps in an effort to add cheer to a desperate situation. Josh didn't look affronted as she closed the door with him on the other side. It was hard to be indignant toward someone dressed like a life-sized Jolly Rancher.

After moments of silence, he declared, "We need to find out who's behind this."

Before I could respond, Chris eased through the door. She didn't bother knocking any more, as though she belonged there, and the fact that the were-animals didn't agree with her assertion didn't bother her.

"Yes, we do. Six more vampires are dead, and from the looks of it, you all aren't faring well." She handed him a vial of blood, saying, "This will help find them."

Josh hesitated. His eyes narrowed suspiciously as he scrutinized her. His lips parted slightly to speak but he decided against it, as though he had given up any expectations that she would offer the truth willingly. Devoid of any emotions, her behavior was that of one who had long traded her conscience for whatever she could get for it. Josh was past denying the obvious. Chris had intimate knowledge that most didn't have.

Instead, he gathered supplies from a small closet tucked away on the other side of the living room, one easily missed, as it blended with the wall. The only giveaway was the small silver handle. This was the first time I had seen him perform magic that required the use of supplies. The unwavering confidence he had when performing magic was missing. He was tense, his insecurity poorly veiled. He placed everything neatly on the table over a map that he had spread out: coarse salt, a blue crystal, tannin, three candles, and a small cauldron. He bit down on his lower lip, and tense furrows formed along his brow as he poured a small amount of the blood over the crystal and placed it in the cauldron. Then he sprinkled the tannin and salt over it. The candles formed a tight triangle around the cauldron. He whispered an incantation as he lit them. The thick vapor that formed in the cauldron drifted slowly over the map next to it, spreading over it. It flickered bright bold colors, flashed, then died out like a blown bulb. Josh groaned under his breath and tried it again. Again, sparks of light flickered then squelched, but nothing came of it.

After several unsuccessful attempts, Josh and I headed out of the house with an uninvited Chris close behind.

An hour later, we stood at the door of a small town house in the middle of the art district. People walking their dogs politely acknowledged us. A pale guy with matted ash-blond dreadlocks toting a guitar smiled as he bustled past. A group of women, eclectically dressed, headed into a small coffeehouse across the street from where we stood. I loved this side of town but rarely had a chance to visit. Too trendy to be a place I would consider living in, it was a little enclave in the city where the artsy, bohemian, hipster types dwelled. It was a fun place to visit, but since the only thing I could offer was my mediocre flute skills, I would never fit in.

Josh's hard knocks went unanswered the first three times. On the fourth attempt, a petite Hispanic woman in her early twenties answered the door, brushing back her asymmetrical, short blush-cinnamon-colored hair. Her gaze shifted to Chris and me and then abruptly back to Josh.

"The answer is 'no' to whatever you're about to ask," she said brusquely as she started to close the door. He pushed himself through and kept it open for us to follow.

"London, please," he entreated in a low, urgent voice.

London's penetrating russet brown eyes was set on his as he attempted to temper it with an errant smile. Ill-defined cheeks softened the frown on her face, and the small nub of a nose that flared with annoyance made taking her anger seriously a little difficult. She stepped aside, giving us space to enter, moving with such precise and graceful sweeps it was easy to imagine that at some point in her life she had twirled across a stage adorned with a tiara, tutu, and pointe shoes. She was an adorable pixie of a woman, and I had a feeling Josh imposed on her a lot, as she, too, fell victim to his warm, entreating eyes, captivating smile, and alluring personality.

"You are running out of favors," she said sternly, her lips quivering as she fought the smile starting to form. "You know you wouldn't need me so much if you hadn't dropped out of the training. Your mother was far too lenient with you. She should have made you finish."

Josh was a magic school dropout—why wasn't that surprising?

He handed her the vial of blood. "I need this *sourced.* Try to take it as far back as you can. I have tried several times, but I can't get anything."

She slid back the sleeves of her yellow quarter-length shirt, exposing a detailed tribal tattoo on her forearm and a small one on the side of her hand as she eyed the vial. When she turned from us, she bared another one on the nape of her neck. I assumed, like Josh, she considered the body a canvas for art.

"Whose is it?"

He shrugged an answer, and suspicion fell over her heavily lined eyes as she glanced once more at the vial. She pulled out a cloth, several herbs, and a tiny cauldron from the small closet in her sitting room. She brought them closer to her computer and the projector next to it. Short, nimble fingers swept over the keys and a lit map of the city covered the wall. She shot a long, suspicious look in Josh's direction before returning to the task.

Particles whirled around her, the lights dimmed, and she took command of magic in a manner that made Josh look like he was in the minor leagues. The way they commanded magic was quite different in appearance. Flickers of light bounced around as her short, slender fingers swiped over the map. Josh presented magic—she made it perform in an imaginative and engaging manner. While Josh had magic at his fingertips, easily controlled, she wrangled it into submission and trained it to carry out her demands. If their magical styles were dance, hers was ballet—smooth rhythmic, lithe, fluid, precise movements of beauty—while his was modern dance—improvised, rushed, solid, sharp movements. Both styles effective but vastly different.

Josh stood back, watching her in impressed silence, his lips crinkled into a grin.

The house shook briefly and something flashed on the map then disappeared. London looked perplexed. She tried the spell again then looked at him, bewildered. "The blood is *unsourced.* Whose blood *is* this?" she asked again, her voice losing the gentle timbre it held earlier.

He took too long to answer and irritation flourished on her face. "I think you should leave. Why don't you stay away for a while," she suggested, walking to the front door and opening it. When no one moved, the room rumbled as a force migrated from her, creeping through the open space as it nudged us out the door. His eyes widened when he felt it, too. It was apparent he hadn't been on the receiving end of her power and seemed startled by the sheer intensity of it.

Chris didn't need the supernatural nudge. The moment London announced the blood was unsourced, she couldn't get to the door fast enough.

Unsourced. Chris's thoughts ran over every possible scenario that could lead to blood being unsourced, and there was only one. Nearly blinded by anger, she drove around the first bulwark that separated Thaddeus from a world that would hate and fear him because of how he had looked; despite the fact he was innocuous and powerless. Her car couldn't navigate around the verdant bastion, his second defense. She jumped out and ran at full speed to his house, aware that no matter how quickly she got there, she would be too late to do anything.

It didn't surprise her to find his body lying in a puddle of blood. She thought she was immune to the gory ways of the world, but sometimes, it was still hard. Looking at Thaddeus's mutilated, battered body, she realized immunity to it all just wasn't possible. You grew a tolerance, not immunity. Right now, her tolerance was too low not to cringe at the scene.

His murder was different, unnecessary. A brutal assault that sickened her to the core. The various scents of the home inundated the air, but nothing strong enough to smother the smell of blood. One scent stood out—Demetrius. He had been there. Even with the trading, her sense of smell wasn't as good as a vampire's or were-animal's, but she was very familiar with his.

Forty minutes later, Chris pounded on the front door of Demetrius's private home. The neo-Mediterranean stone building was a distinct piece of architecture among the large nondescript houses in the neighborhood. A few of them were owned by other vampires, and the rest by their unsuspecting neighbors who had no idea such creatures populated their small suburban community. A combination of large pillars and stucco enclosed the entrance, creating a bleak archway, darkening the path as it led you into the home. Some would enter, never to see the light of day again. Others came willingly, hoping for another invitation.

This was Demetrius's place of refuge. He only frequented the Seethe's home when new vampires were created. The recent attacks had caused him to put them on restriction because he was unable to give the necessary attention to the newly changed. Attention that he prided himself on delivering to each new vampire because he believed he didn't just make creatures of the night, but gave life to masterpieces. He considered himself an auteur, and his progeny weren't just a Seethe, but a collection of his perceived greatness. Vampires created by anyone other than his family were regarded as spurious, the bastard children of the prosaic.

When he opened the door, the inviting smile quickly disappeared when he saw the scowl on her face.

"Did you do it?" she demanded through clenched teeth.

He stepped aside. "Come in," he offered, his voice so soft and level, it fueled her anger.

"No. I don't want to come in. I want you to answer my fucking question. Thaddeus is dead. He was slaughtered mercilessly. Did you do it?"

He stared at her with steely silence.

"Answer me," she demanded. "Now!" She was having a hard time saddling her anger, although she knew she needed to.

"In," he commanded quietly.

She hesitated before entering. He waited impatiently, his arms folded across his chest in hushed hostility. His dark, cold eyes bored into her until she made the decision to enter. She knew she had overstepped his very lax boundaries. When they had first started dealing with each other, being more obstinate than wise, she'd done it often. She had learned quickly that an enraged Demetrius was too hard to deal with.

The moment she stepped over the threshold, his hands closed around her throat as he slammed her so hard against the wall her head rebounded off it. Before she could reach for the knife secured in the sheath around her thigh, he grabbed her hand and pinned it above her head. The left hand received the same treatment when she went for the dagger concealed in the back of her pants as he momentarily released the hand on her throat. His left hand pinned both of her hands overhead. Virulent dark eyes glared at her. "I've been too tolerant with you," he whispered in a low, stringent voice, his lips pressed firmly against her ear. "And you've taken far too many liberties because of it. You forget yourself."

She indeed had forgotten herself. In the past, she never would have come near Demetrius without being armed sufficiently with a stake or two, a gun holstered, and several blades within reach from either side. She had grown careless in dealing with him.

Her nails dug into his skin, entreating a release. No matter how she tried, it was hard not to show fear when it was pulsing through every bone in her body. His hand pressed harder around her throat, his thumb massaging at the pulse, the pressure so tight she could barely swallow. She gasped for any air that managed to make it through. Most of the brutal things she had seen him do started with his hand wrapped around someone's neck. It had been a long time since she'd ever thought she would be on the receiving end of his wrath.

His eyes narrowed, his gaze sharpened and loomed as he studied her through his long dark lashes. Inching close to her, his face rested in the curve of her neck, his cool breath brushing against her skin as he spoke. "Why have you chosen to stay like this—weak, fragile, and dreadfully human? I could kill you now with little effort. Vampire blood makes you better, but *being* a vampire makes you superlative. What you become surpasses the frivolous things you think you'll miss: the taste of food, the sun rising, breathing, a heartbeat. Such foolish things you revere now will become irrelevant once you cross over."

It was a change she didn't want. Last year, when the vampires could have continued to live virtually human lives if the ritual had been successful, it wouldn't have been such a sacrifice. But being a true vampire with all their restrictions was a life she wasn't ready to accept. He knew that and she made no secret of the fact that she didn't want to be changed.

Demetrius respected her wishes because she was clear about her stance. He hated those that were undecided. It was then he made the decision for them. And it was never vampirism. He chose death for them. Hate them or love them, he would never fault humans for their stance, but he hated in-betweeners. Most vampires were like that. They rarely changed those who didn't want it. Of course, they weren't above seducing you into that decision. And then there were the times when they were driven by pure unadulterated bloodlust and accidentally killed their donor. As an act of penance they changed them—giving that person the gift of eternal life—their idea of the most divine gift they could bestow on someone.

His fangs grazed across her neck, near her carotid. He was angry with her, revoking her right to choose. This was the most enraged he had ever been with her. Cool lips opened over her neck. Hard, sharp enamel pressed harder into her, breaking the skin, spilling blood down her neck.

"Don't," she whimpered. Her eyes stung from tears that would not shed as she clenched them shut. His grip stayed firmly around her neck. "Demetrius, please."

She was scared. It wasn't as though she were a stranger to fear. She thrived on it. But this fear was debilitating, and she hated it. Just when it heightened to the point it triggered desperate angry tears, his grip loosened enough for her to gasp some well-needed breaths. Fear—he wanted to make her feel it. To reacquaint her with the fact that he was the face of danger. He was death, torment, and pain wrapped in a lovely package, and he wanted her to recognize that, to remember not only the cruel things she witnessed but also the crueler things that made him infamous.

He released her, dropping her to the floor as he stepped away. She gulped hungrily for air as she came to her feet.

By the time she was composed, he was seated comfortably on the couch. "He was dead when I got there," he admitted, leaning back.

Chris massaged her throat. It was sore, and even swallowing was painful. Holding his gaze, she fought the urge to glare at him, curse him, and tell him that of all the monsters she had dealt with in her career, he still remained king. But she bit her tongue and swallowed her words.

Truth—Demetrius always gave it, but not out of any intrinsic sense of ethics or anything of that sort. It was because he was arrogant and powerful, challenging anyone to try to punish him or hold him accountable for his actions. He didn't have a problem telling whoever would care to listen that he would do whatever he wished without consequences.

"Why were you there in the first place?" Chris inquired. She wasn't sure why this bothered her, but it did. Rarely did she feel sorry for people, but for some reason, she did with Thaddeus. She identified with him, understood what it felt like to be brought into a world where the people responsible for your birth constantly reminded you that you weren't wanted and penalized you for it as though it were your doing. And when things had finally taken a better course for him, someone killed him. Life wasn't fair. She knew that, but she was tired of it being shoved in her face constantly.

"I wanted to speak with him," he responded, his voice flat and bitterly cold. "There have been far too many losses of mine. This can't be tolerated. I wanted to make sure he had revealed everything he knew."

Chris nodded. His rage was all consuming, and she truly wished she had handled things differently, especially now as he came to his feet and paced back and forth. His ire was still palpable.

"They've killed my strongest but I haven't been attacked," he said gravely.

"Nor has Sebastian. Whoever is involved wants you all weak, compromised," she added, staying close to the door. It was a perfect plan for someone that was going to execute a massive attack. But who would do that? The list of enemies that both the vampires and were-animals had made for various reasons was extensive. But this was beyond the capabilities of anyone they had provoked.

"Could the witches be involved?"

She shook her head. "I doubt it, but it wouldn't hurt to confirm it."

"Perhaps I should speak with Marcia." His tone held a hint of amusement. Chris knew that would be catastrophic. Demetrius was a steamroller when he dealt with people, plowing over anyone who didn't bend to his will. It was the very reason he and Sebastian didn't get along. They had the same manner of dealing with people. If the witches weren't involved, Demetrius would not handle it amicably enough not to enrage and insult them. The last thing they needed was the witches' wrath.

"It would be a good idea if Josh handled the matter. He is trustworthy and would deal with the situation in a manner that you would approve of," she stated in a tepid tone.

He was silent for a long moment, intently watching her, taking long pseudo-breaths, the trials of the situation causing his dense mask of impassivity to falter. "Speak with him on my behalf. I would rather not deal with him."

He was being diplomatic. He would love to deal with Josh. In fact, if Josh weren't an ally of the were-animals, he would have dealt with him after he had stopped Demetrius from performing the transference ritual last year. Demetrius had never been fond of the were-animals, and their involvement only sealed that disdain. But they never would have been successful in preventing it if it hadn't been for Josh.

She nodded. "Okay, I will speak with him tomorrow."

He seemed calmer, but there was still a trace of tension along the lines of his face as he rose and approached her. His face remained rigid, eyes severe, cold, and distant. Thin lips dipped ever so lightly into a frown. His approach toward her was languid and graceful. She stood frozen in position, uncertain what to expect. Just inches from her, his cool thumb ran rhythmically along the angle of her jaw then along her neck. "You do that," he said in a low voice.

For a long time, his eyes lingered over her, briefly coursing over her face before remaining fixed on her neck, which had started to tint with bruising. He admired his handiwork. His fingers brushed against it lightly. "I did not enjoy that," he whispered.

Liar, Chris thought angrily, her attention placed on the delighted smile that brandished his lips. He'd enjoyed every moment of it, and she had no delusions that he wasn't exulting in her fear and reveling in her capitulation. Demetrius liked confidence and strength, but enjoyed stripping people of it even more. Blood nourished his body, but it was pain, anger, and fear that truly fed his sadistic mind.

As his body pressed against her, she relaxed into the wall, feeling the weight of him against her. His lips were a light touch against hers, as though he expected her to resist. Instead, she pulled him closer, kissing him. His response was fervent, and soft breaths escaped as the weight of his body draped over her.

He looked content as he pulled away, self-assured. Arrogance swathed his exotic appearance. Nipping her bottom lip with his teeth, he licked away the blood that welled. He kissed her hard. She could barely catch her breath. Her legs curled around him as he lifted her. She molded against him as he backed into the sofa. His mouth coasted over hers, refusing to release contact. Languid, cool fingers slipped under her shirt, kneading at her skin as she sat astride him.

He pulled away, his thumb traced over her full lips as he basked in the moment. Leaning back, his gaze was lustful as it cruised over her body. A hint of a smile formed as his attention rested on her breasts, and then traveled to the long sleek curve of her neck and over the light bruising that formed along it. He smiled. The tinted coloring encouraged him. As he tugged at her shirt, her hands closed over his.

"Let me," she said softly.

He nodded and smiled. Her fingers trailed along the well-formed muscles of his chest. The palm of her hand stopped over his heart, where she waited, knowing she would never feel the rhythmic thump of it beating. The tips of her fingers continued to explore him, running down the grooves of his abs when his hands cuffed around hers. He brought them to his lips and kissed them gently.

"Your clothes," he reminded her, leaning back and delighting in the bravura of her submission and the carnality of his desires.

His pleasure, confidence, and conceit were all wiped away in an instant when she plunged the knife she kept in her ankle sheath into his shoulder. Pushing it in to the hilt, she angled her weight forward and held it there. Any blade jabbed into a vampire's flesh was painful. If it was laced with holy water, it was torturous. Her knife had the next best thing—*thalim*, its gelled equivalent. A compound that she had overlaid on most of her knives. No matter how the vampires worked to dispel it as a myth, holy water did work. It was like acid on their skin. Chris spent too much time around vampires not to have something that would get their attention and make them behave. Right now, she wanted him well behaved and in extreme pain.

He gasped, taking hard, short, ragged breaths in an attempt to assuage the pain. His lips pulled back, exposing fangs as crimson spilled and stained his dark blue shirt.

Her hand firmly gripped the knife as her gaze lifted to meet his. "I was rude earlier, and I apologize for that." She wrenched a handful of his hair, pulling his face closer to hers. Sharp cool breaths battered against her lips as his gasping continued. "But you will never do anything like that to me again. Do you understand me?"

He responded with rapid, deep pants of pain. She twisted the knife. "Do you understand me?" she barked angrily. Ripping out the knife, she held it to his throat, and pressed it into his skin. "Answer me, or so help me, I will end this right now!"

He nodded once, shoving her hard from his lap and sending her sliding across the floor to the other side of the room. Her back slammed into the wall. She scrambled to her feet and assumed a defensive crouch, knife in hand. Taking slow, controlled breaths to abate the fear, she waited for him to retaliate. It had been several days since she had traded with him. Human frailties put her at a disadvantage, but she refused to slide down that slippery slope she was heading toward by allowing Demetrius to undermine, threaten, and hurt her without consequences.

As they held each other's gaze, she wondered if he would kill her. He'd saved her life. She assumed it was because he thought, at some point, it held value to him, but now, she wasn't so sure if he still felt that way. He cast menacing looks in her direction. Chris realized, at that moment, it didn't matter whether or not her life had value to him. He could change his mind in a matter of seconds, depending on how he felt. She had witnessed his angry and violent retaliation against those he had *created* for acts far less egregious than this.

With the knife clamped firmly in her hand, she maintained her defensive posture, waiting for a response. Her reflexes amped into her fight mode, ready to do whatever damage she could. Her heart pounded, cheeks inflamed, the pit of her stomach grinding as she waited for him to react. It seemed like an eternity before he even moved.

His teeth slipped over his lips, his attention acutely fixed on her. He sagged deeper into the sofa, his anger so negligible it was nonexistent. The muscles of his neck were still rigid as he warded off the pain, but a smile of bemused interest coursed its way onto his lips. "Perhaps I overreacted," he admitted.

She stood, trying to slow her paced breathing. Nodding slowly, she kept a look of indifference, refusing to show her relief that things hadn't escalated to something that she might not have survived. Chris backed out the door and left before he could truly grasp what she had done and become enraged again.

~

Chris took one look at Ethan's car parked in her driveway and walked past it toward the front door without giving it a second look. When he stepped out of the car, she turned with a sigh. "You already know that Thaddeus is dead. Demetrius didn't have anything to do with it, and that is all I know. Why are you here?" she snapped when he started following her toward the door.

"You changed the locks." He tossed her a set of old keys.

"Did you think I wouldn't?"

"Bad day at the office?" His brow furrowed at her bloodstained shirt. His jaw clenched at the bruising around her throat and the swelling of her lip where Demetrius had bitten her.

"Demetrius and I had a *misunderstanding*," she admitted, entering the house with Ethan close on her heels. Not ready for another fight, she let him in.

"Did you stake and behead him?" he asked, closing the door behind him.

"No." She continued through the house as Ethan stopped abruptly, his gaze following her as she went into her bedroom. When she backtracked, she found him still standing by the door in an odd state of dismay.

Then his anger quickly ignited, uncontrolled and unrestrained. Chris didn't have it in her to pacify it or to console him into a calm. "He better stay that way. Don't touch him," she said. Then she closed the door to her bedroom and headed for the shower. She hoped by the time she finished, he would have found a way to manage his anger, although she doubted it. Emotional control had never been one of his attributes, and she doubted anything had changed, but she hoped he could control his temper enough to adhere to the alliance with the vampires. If Demetrius showed up beheaded tomorrow and the vampires even suspected she had something to do with it, there wouldn't be a place she could hide to escape their retribution. Chase would gain the position of Master that he'd been vying for over the past ten years, and they would hunt her down. Even if they discovered it was Ethan, she would be held accountable by association. They might still go after Ethan, but he had his pack behind him. She didn't have that luxury. She knew Ethan still had an unresolved grudge over her involvement last year with the Gem of Levage, and the pack wouldn't be quick to come to her aid, despite her relationship with him.

She stood under the showerhead, forcing her mind to be clear of the events of the night. She had finally washed all evidence of blood off her. Stepping out of her shower, she glanced at her reflection. "Bad day" was an understatement. Blotchy bruises covered the front of her neck. Her bottom lip was slightly swollen and the bite mark on her neck was still open and bruised from spilled blood. She pulled her eyes away from her image, wrapped a towel around herself, and went into the bedroom.

As she suspected he would be, Ethan was sprawled across her bed, his legs crossed, arms folded behind his head, waiting for her. "There was a time when if you had a *misunderstanding* with a vampire, he wouldn't be around long enough for there to be another," he stated, rising to look at her.

"Those vampires weren't Demetrius. His status as the Master of the most ruthless Seethe in the country affords him more consideration."

"Are you sleeping with him?"

"Does it matter?"

"If we are going to be together, then yes."

She laughed, "Is there a *we?* And when has monogamy been important to you? You have always had a rather distant acquaintance with it."

"With you, I have always been faithful—"

"Until you weren't. Should we talk about the two bimbos?" she asked in a crisp voice as she started to dress. Pulling the t-shirt over her bare skin and slipping into a pair of jeans, she ignored his intense gaze. She turned to face him.

He stood in silence, his arms crossed over his chest. The

unequivocal look on his face told her what she already knew—he would never show remorse over such a thing. She doubted he ever had a problem confessing to his infidelity because he had always been forgiven for it. He shrugged. "It had been three weeks since you took that job. I asked you not to because it was too dangerous. For all I knew, you were dead."

"You have a strange way of grieving."

"And you overreacted, as usual."

"You pay that much for a car, you wouldn't think a little splash of brake fluid would ruin a custom paint job or a few licks with a tire iron would damage the body so much. And I thought the negative effects of sugar in the gas tank was simply a myth." She watched the same anger erupt that had happened when he'd found that she had destroyed his '03 Aston Martin DB7 Vantage Zagato. That night, she'd listened to his rant for hours that only ninety-nine of them had been built and he had waited years for one to become available. It was his most prized possession, but when she was done with it, it wasn't fit to be sold off for parts.

Chris waited with a smirk as Ethan made peace with his anger again. Leaning into her, his face nestled into the crook of her neck as he inhaled the soft floral scent of her bodywash. When his lips brushed against hers, she pushed him away. "Have the witches contacted Josh?"

"Why would they?" he asked, stepping back, his arms folding over his chest again, poised to give her as little information as possible.

"I have no idea what deal you have with them to keep Josh as an ally. But I assure you, as strong as Josh is, they are always aware of what is going on with him and your pack. If they aren't concerned, perhaps they are involved in the attacks."

He was silent for a long time, then he shrugged a response. She studied him, trying to read between the deceptions. The stolid looks and vague answers were just a smokescreen. She recognized how ridiculous their relationship was at times. They created walls of deceit to protect their personal interests. If there were truths between them, they were so heavily veiled by the keeping of confidences and lies of omission that they were nearly nonexistent. Yet, through the complexity of their relationship, the lies and deceit, the violence and threats, they managed to care for each other. Chris often saw the absurdity in it but could not deny that the feelings existed.

"Demetrius thinks of you as his. You're his possession." Ethan's voice was rigid with anger and revulsion.

"Hmm, then you two aren't as different as I thought."

He smiled. "The differences between the two of us are not by any means subtle. Don't ever compare me to that thing." He focused on the mementos of her night with Demetrius. His features hardened and cobalt eyes gleamed with glints of graphite. "Quit. Come work for us."

"Switch teams in the middle of the game. Quite admirable of you to make such a request," she responded with biting sarcasm. Once again, an insensate face reflected back at her as though what he had just asked wasn't one of the most reprehensible things he could have requested. "I have ethics. Whether you approve of them or even understand them doesn't mean I don't have them. Go home."

Instead of leaving, he stepped closer, eyeing the marks on her neck. His gaze narrowed and drifted down to the thin layer of cotton that covered the scar on her abdomen. When he finally spoke, his voice was gentle and languorous. "Most Hunters retire after five years because by the sixth year they have more enemies than allies, and by year seven, if they haven't retired, someone retires them for good. You've done this for nine years."

She thought of pointing out that Ryan had exceeded that timeline by a decade. As though he anticipated her argument or sensed her thoughts, he added, "Ryan, by all accounts, was exceptional. Seventeen years as a Hunter, before he came along, was unheard of. It's your time, Chris. Trading with Demetrius isn't helping you. You have more enemies than you have allies."

"What exactly do you propose I do? The real world is just a little too vanilla for me. It won't let me capture the naughty, shoot or stab the deserving, and be an overall badass without a badge."

Many times, she'd considered reemerging into the world from whence she had been pushed just shy of her seventeenth birthday. Ryan had recruited her into this world, and most of it had been a rude awakening, even traumatic at times, but it had saved her. She needed to know there were things that existed that were far worse than what she had encountered in the "normal" world.

This world had become her prison, but it was all she knew. Leaving it and assimilating back to the world of humans, with their convoluted morals, distorted ethics, self-indulgence, and heartlessness all disguised as human nature was not an option. For most humans, it was the otherworld that took away their innocence. For Chris, it was the opposite.

She accepted the violence, deprivation, and cruelty because they all existed to ensure survival. The denizens here were so far removed from the human world they had lost all fragments of humanity. She could accept that from those who weren't quite human. But from those who dwelled in a postlapsarian world defined by altruism, charity, love, and all the other platitudes that existed in the so-called normal human world, she expected better. It left her disappointed when she realized they were even more removed from humanity than those who no longer lived in it.

"Isn't there a distressed damsel somewhere waiting for your help? I don't need it," she said coolly.

He headed out the bedroom door and then stopped. His back was to her, but she could feel the harshness of his scowl in his voice. "I think you should retire and get a hobby. And for the record, being obstinate and bitchy isn't considered one." He slammed the door behind him.

She waited for him to come back. Calling her a pigheaded

bitch was him flirting with her. Too often, they castigated each other with such angry, virulent remarks that others would have considered abusive. For them, it was foreplay that ended with them naked, clawing at each other like animals in heat as they made their insincere apologies and empty promises to never let it escalate that far again. The lies had become their ritual.

When she heard the front door close behind him, she waited. After a long moment, she eventually locked it.

CHAPTER 10

Taking another sip of the two-hour-old coffee, I waited for Josh to answer what seemed like an easy question: besides the vampires, who else would benefit from wiping out the were-animals? His fingers tapped against the wood table in a slow rhythm.

"It's not a question of who would benefit as much as what person has that type of control and power. If Gideon is correct, someone has power to use multiple sources of magic and to control the magic to shapeshift creatures so massive and powerful that they can easily kill a were-animal or vampire."

The click of Chris's high-heeled boots gave away her arrival before she actually came into the room. Did she own a pair of gym shoes or flats? *We get it, you're a bad ass, but can you be one in comfortable footwear and yoga pants, too?*

"Perhaps it's not what *person* but what *group*," she said.

"Why would you think that?" he asked.

"Besides the vampires, who else finds the were-animals' existence abhorrent?" the queen of badass fashion mused.

The corners of Josh's mouth tightened and his eyes narrowed

to slits. "They aren't involved," he answered, far too quickly for it to be given any serious consideration.

"*Who* isn't involved?" I asked.

Chris's eyes drifted from Josh to me for just for a moment. "The witches. Josh, I get it, you don't want to believe they would be capable of trying to kill your brother and friends, but it is careless not to consider them. It wouldn't be the first time they were responsible for mass killing of were-animals."

"You're bringing up something that happened a century ago. Things have changed."

"Not all of them. Witches have always considered themselves gods and are self-proclaimed regulators of who should and should not exist. Maybe some of them are letting their egos control their actions."

Josh leaned into the table. "Holding people accountable for past misdeeds, especially something that happened so long ago, is a dangerous precedent. You, of all people, should want to be forgiven for past misdeeds and mistakes. We all have things in our pasts we aren't proud of. Things we would like forgotten and never brought up again. If I'm not mistaken, around this time last year, I was staring down the barrel of your gun."

"I never asked for your forgiveness, and I definitely don't want you to forget what I am capable of doing," she replied. "If you start forgiving and forgetting, you're likely to start underestimating me as you are doing with the witches."

I wasn't sure why he was digging in his heels on this, but they were dug in deep and he didn't seem like he was ready to budge. I wasn't sure what was causing such insolence, the accused or the accuser.

I decided to jump in. "Josh, their history can't be ignored. And if they are stronger than you, can we really rule them out?"

"We can't create creatures," he refuted.

"*You* can't. There are those that are stronger than you, more skilled. It wouldn't be the first time they were involved in massacring the were-animals and vampires—"

"We detect one another's magic. Like a fingerprint, it leaves a distinct mark. It is so strong that I can sometimes determine the witch that performed it."

"You were around the creatures for such a short time, not nearly close enough to sense anything. How can you be so sure?"

"It doesn't matter, because Ethan was exposed—" Josh's mouth clamped shut. His face flushed.

Something had just gone terribly wrong but I didn't know what it was.

"I just know," he blurted out.

Chris and I looked at the door around the same time to find Ethan there with the same odd look on his face as he caught the tail end of the discussion. I couldn't quite place it. Was it caution? Had Josh disclosed something that otherwise should have been kept a secret? Or was it suspicion? Could Chris be trusted? Or anger? Had she crossed the line and gotten involved in something that was pack business only?

Her eyes narrowed. She turned her attention to Josh, eyeing him perceptively. "Why does Ethan being around it have anything to do with it? Were-animals can't perform or detect magic," she said slowly before directing her attention to Ethan.

Josh swallowed his answer, ignoring her question. His gaze shifted to his brother.

"He knows the witches are not involved. That is all the information you need," Ethan stated. She started to respond, but he interrupted. "That's all the information you will get. No more questions."

Cold eyes pushed into him as he matched them with the same harshness. "No. That's not enough. I need more," she demanded.

"That's quite unfortunate for you."

She stepped closer to him. "You will not shut me out. Tell me what you know."

His lips crooked into a disparaging smile. "I'd like to see you make me," he challenged.

Disagreements between them had now reached an all-time low, reduced to playground antics and threats of "make me." What did he expect her to do, give him a skin twist or kick him in the shins?

After a tense moment, she realized neither brother would offer any more information. Her stony gaze held Ethan's as she walked out the door.

"Stop sleeping with her," Josh commanded once the door was closed. He stepped around the table closing the distance that separated them.

Ethan's tensed lips turned down into a deep scowl, cold eyes focused on his brother. "This again? Are we advising each other on who we should or should *not* pursue now?" His gaze cruised in my direction.

Ethan had become so accustomed to his dysfunction with Chris, I supposed he had forgotten that a man and woman could have a relationship that could be platonic and consist of more than a warped combination of loathing and lust.

"She's your Achilles' heel," Josh asserted with a frown, "your weakness, and you don't seem to realize it."

Ethan chuckled, cynically amused at the very idea of Chris or anyone being a weakness. "We aren't so inept that we would allow our other activities to compromise our ability to do our jobs. I do what is necessary and best for my pack—even if it called for eliminating her, and you know that." Last year he had proven that when he had vowed to kill her.

Josh didn't seem convinced. "Those were just words. If anyone else would have threatened to kill us, betrayed the pack, and adamantly worked against us, like she did last year, what would you have done? You definitely wouldn't have warned them and given them a heads-up before dealing with them. But with her, you extended such courtesies." His deep azure eyes scrutinized his brother as he waited for a response.

A response came in the form of a jaw clenched so tightly the muscles of Ethan's neck became taut. He crossed his arms over his chest. A grimace encroached over his face.

"The very reasons you find yourself drawn to her are the very things that will become our problem. She is smart, resourceful, and inquisitive." It was then that Josh seemed to realize that I was still in the room. He lowered his voice, but not enough. The were-animals had perfected the barely audible whisper—he hadn't. "The flimsy excuses you have given me about your peculiar abilities won't be as easily explained away to her. Your secrets won't be your own anymore. When she knows, so will Demetrius. Once again, leave her alone." Although he accepted the explanation Ethan had given him when he had broken his protective field, he wasn't happy with the secrets and the lies.

Ethan smiled. "I guess if I am too preoccupied with her to do what is necessary, then finally, you will have to. That will be quite interesting to see." Then he left without another word.

Winter slept peacefully, even though she didn't look that way. Her skin was blanched, her lips cracked and barely tinted with color, and the solemn look on her face seemed fixed in that position. The room smelled distinctly of peppermint. For five days, I had placed peppermint oils around the room. Peppermint was used to arouse the senses, but I wasn't foolish enough to think it would do anything but prevent the room from smelling like a hospital. Despite being one of the bedrooms across from the in-house clinic, it still had a clinical feel. A floral duvet covered the large hospital bed. A small cherry nightstand was next to it. The TV covered the greater part of the opposite wall and was offset by an oddly placed floor lamp next to it. Nature-themed pictures and a decorative rug were all failed attempts to make this room appear to be a well-decorated bedroom. They had even abandoned the boring high-gloss white hospital walls and painted this room a warm, earthy taupe.

"The vampires are on the way. This should be fun," I said, walking farther into the room as I started in on my usual updates. My last update was about the fight between Ethan and Josh two days ago, once again about Chris. Now I had to tell Winter about the strong words between Josh and Sebastian. Surely if any gossip would get her up, that would. Sebastian had been adamant about never allowing a vampire to pass through the pack's door, let alone several. Josh, with the gift of charm and diplomacy, had pointed out the advantage of the meeting being on their playing field, allowing them better control of the situation and the vampires. If things went badly, he could cage them like the monsters he considered them to be. Sebastian wasn't as easily manipulated by Josh or softened by his charms and had continued to refuse. He only agreed after Josh had pointed out the urgency of the matter and that Demetrius wasn't capable of being the better person, so it was up to Sebastian to do the right thing. Sebastian wanted to find the person responsible for the attacks as well as sever his alliance with the vampires more than adhering to a rule that only existed because of his disdain for the vampires.

Josh had called a meeting with the were-animals and the vampires, requesting the presence of their most skilled hunters. *Yeah, place the strongest, most skilled murderers in a room together. Nothing can possibly go wrong with that situation, right?*

I was surprised to find Kelly standing in the shadows by the bed, watching a syndicated nighttime dramedy. She placed her fingers against her lips and smiled. "It's her guilty pleasure. Let's just keep it between us girls."

We focused on the television for a long time. I couldn't believe Winter would ever watch this campy soap opera with actresses whose faces were pulled so tight they looked like they were windsurfing. If she pulled through this, I was never going to let her live this down.

Kelly looked in my direction. "Trashy, isn't it?"

I kept watching in bemused silence, occasionally looking in Winter's direction, unable to believe this was her guilty pleasure.

"Did you do this?" she asked, taking one of Winter's braids between her fingers.

I nodded.

"You did a good job. I secured the ends so they wouldn't unravel." She began to work with the machines that Winter was hooked to, making adjustments, changing the IVs, and flushing the lines. When she finished, she just looked down at Winter, concerned. Kelly's gentle oval face and brown eyes didn't look nearly as refreshed and pleasant as they did the first time I had met her. There were bags around her eyes, barely concealed by her deep cinnamon coloring. The pack liked her a lot, and I could see why. Surrounded by predators, anomalies, freaks of nature, she seemed at ease, even comfortable.

"Is she going to be okay?" I finally asked.

I had asked Dr. Baker that question many times and only received a series of answers thickly obscured by medical terminology as he detailed Winter's current condition. It was his way of avoiding the question.

"Yeah, she's tough. Besides, heaven isn't ready for her, and the devil just wouldn't know what to do with her." She gave a mild, reassuring smile.

I think she was just a few years older than me, but she seemed so confident I was willing to believe anything she said. Or perhaps it was wishful thinking on my part.

"After this goes off and you tell her about the vampires, turn it to ESPN."

ESPN sounded more like the Winter I knew.

She started toward the door then stopped. It took a while before she spoke. "What are they like?" she inquired, her eyes burning with inexplicable curiosity.

Her face held such inquisitiveness that I really wanted to give her an accurate answer. If she hadn't been around vampires, then she probably hadn't been around fae, elves, demons, or dark magic, either. She was lucky. She had successfully found a haven where those things didn't exist in her world, despite working for were-animals. I wanted to urge her to hold on to that little piece of innocence because she would miss it once it was gone.

"How do you feel around the were-animals? Uncomfortable?"

She shook her head slowly.

"Like prey?"

Again, she shook her head.

"So overwhelmed that you feel like you're suffocating under their power and control?"

"Not at all. Being around the were-animals is no different than being around anyone else."

There it was. The reason the were-animals respected her in such a manner. Her level of acceptance of what they were was refreshing to them. She represented that part of them, no matter how small, that hoped if they had to go public, there would be people like her who openly accepted them.

"Well, when you're around the vampires, you will feel all those things. It's subtle but definitely there. Your senses are awakened because self-preservation forces you into a state of high alert, urging you to protect yourself, as well you should." They weren't all that bad—Quell was an exception.

"If you ever find yourself around them, be cautious, be careful, and be alert. But the best advice I can give you is don't be around them at all."

She nodded perceptively, backing out of the room, but there was still that shadow of curiosity that covered the soft lines of her face and enveloped her deep-set eyes. An interest that words just couldn't satisfy.

~

I waited in the background, leaning against the wall as the vampires spilled into the pack's home. There weren't as many as I expected, only eight, including Demetrius and Michaela, yet their presence consumed the space, making the large room feel cramped. I thought I had done a good job shrinking into the background unnoticed until I felt Michaela's gaze on me. She focused on me for a long time with her hard, cold, debilitating stare and then smiled, exposing her fangs. I despised her and I wasn't sure which reason was the best. Perhaps it was the fact that, after meeting me last year, she had stroked my hair like I was a dog and wished she could keep me as a pet. Or the fact that she was responsible for populating the VAMPIRE logs with the most notorious vampires ever known because of her sadistic draw to unconventional behavior and beauty. The person's ruthlessness or viciousness didn't matter as long as they had a beautiful face to accompany it.

As everyone settled, Josh looked around at the many faces in the room. I wasn't sure if he was doing a head count or assessing threats. No, he was looking for someone, because his gaze quickly darted around the room. When he looked at Sebastian, whose face held the same look of irritation as his own, Sebastian shrugged and nodded for him to proceed.

Josh took several slow, measured steps toward the middle of the room, waiting patiently for everyone's attention. As he stood in the center of a room full of predators, he seemed unfazed that on one side was a group that would protect his life as their own, and on the other a group that still held a grudge against him for his involvement in stopping them from completing their ritual and would rejoice in his death.

All eyes turned to the witch dressed in relaxed jeans and a bright blue t-shirt with the Sesame Street characters posed on the front, displaying in bold black block writing: I WAS RAISED ON

THE STREET. His hair was mussed and chaotic. He didn't exactly inspire confidence, but he held the stares with a stony calm. As one of the strongest witches on this side of the country, he demanded their respect.

"Nice shirt," Chase said with a grin as he leaned against the wall.

Demetrius didn't share the same amusement. He watched Josh with sheer abhorrence, disbelief, and even disdain that this was a person they were entrusting to find out who was responsible for the attacks.

Just as Josh was about to speak, Gavin sauntered into the house. The look of anger and censure from Sebastian only increased his enjoyment. Whether he was dealing with Ethan or Sebastian, there was always a level of contention, a subtle challenge. Gavin was the pack's problem child—reckless, unruly, obstinate, and ill-tempered—and an overall douche extraordinaire. He was a transfer from the East Pack, and the reason for it seemed to remain the pack's well-kept secret. The only thing I knew was his transfer, a process that usually took several weeks, had been expedited over the course of two days.

Sebastian controlled him barely and with great effort. I believed that Sebastian had taken him in because he was the ultimate challenge and would truly demonstrate why he was the Elite Alpha. He was going to break the incendiary panther or die trying, but Gavin wasn't going down without a battle.

As he sauntered over to a spot near the were-animals, a dark-haired, parchment-toned vampire with large round eyes followed his every step, seemingly mesmerized by his sinuous movements. When his severe, dark gaze met hers, it didn't deter her. She made a beeline for him, approaching him quickly with a look of avid interest etched across her face. Gavin gave her his version of a smile, a cross between a smirk and a sneer—never inviting or pleasant, but definitely wicked. He waited for her to make a move.

Does she know what she's getting herself into?

As he waited, he appeared innocent and unassuming. She was thoroughly unaware that this might be the last time she approached anyone.

Quell reached out, intercepting the charging vampire, and pulled her close to him. She didn't look at him. Instead, she kept her attention fixed on Gavin.

"Sable," Quell soothed in an effort to tame the ravenous vampire. Recognizing the voice, she looked up and smiled.

So *that* was Sable. She had made it into the VAMPIRE logs. Created by Chase, she'd become his and Gabriella's little protégée. She was not only infamous for her acts as a vampire. Her most nefarious deeds were those done when she was human. I was young when she made the front page of the Chicago papers and headlined the news for weeks. Fifteen years later, people still talked about it because it was one of the most horrific crimes ever committed.

Nineteen when she was turned, she was barely old enough to stand trial as an adult for the crimes that ultimately led to her conviction for nine counts of murder and one for manslaughter. Prior to becoming a predacious vampire, the doe-eyed girl had made headlines as the grieving survivor of a home invasion that left her parents dead and a sister so badly brutalized she died two days later. For two years, Illinois's finest couldn't find the invaders, but eventually she did.

She found not only the two guys who had committed the crime, but also their best friends, girlfriends, parents, and children. She tortured their friends and families, making them watch every horrifying moment. To further the torment, she kept them alive long enough to grieve for their lost loved ones and wallow in the fact that those deaths were a result of their actions. Then, in front of the neighbors, who would testify against her at her trial, she stood on the front lawn, put a gun to their heads, and executed them. Afterward, she sat next to the lifeless bodies and waited for the police to arrive.

Her violent acts were still referenced when describing heinous crimes. People often speculated whether or not she was broken before or after she was a victim. The only consensus was that she was unremorseful and was indeed a damaged person.

During her trial, she was frequently shown sitting next to her lawyer, playing with whatever piece of lint, pen, hangnail, or banality that caught her attention. She was either oblivious of or callous to the severity of her crimes.

Gabriella and Chase were enamored of her. How could they not be? She was a psychopath—the very criteria needed for their affections. They didn't have to bring her over to the dark side. She was already there, had set up camp, and was roasting marshmallows over an open fire. Of course, a person with such bloodthirsty qualities was a perfect candidate to imbue with supernatural strength and eternal life. Chase and Gabriella wanted the juvenile psychopath as their own and went through great lengths to get her, including staging the death in her cell that led to a media frenzy only one month after she had started serving her life sentences.

Demetrius wasn't happy about her joining the family. He always practiced a level of discretion with those he turned, considering his choices nothing but assets to strengthen his family. Unfortunately, a great deal of his family didn't feel the same. His Mistress was drawn to bad and undesirable behavior, populating their family with members that eventually had to be put down like rabid animals by him or the Seethe. On rare occasions the pack intervened when the Seethe failed to control the situation in a timely manner.

I was still having a hard time believing she was responsible for those heinous acts. But why wouldn't it be that way? Steven was the pack's angel-faced assassin; Winter often ensured death at the hands of a supermodel. Demetrius was death in its most beautiful form. So why couldn't I believe that the cute round-faced girl with wavy brunette hair and chocolate eyes that made you think of Bambi could be capable of anything less?

"Quell," she said, hugging him. She lifted onto her toes to give him a kiss. He leaned down and the young girl's lips covered his hungrily in their version of a platonic kiss. Had these undead creatures never heard of the forehead kiss? Watching them lip lock in that manner turned my stomach. I realized that she had been undead for fifteen years, but she still looked nineteen.

"It's a were-panther. I've never had one of them before. Look at him. He's so beautiful. I want him," she admitted in a small longing voice and laid her head against Quell's chest to get a better look at Gavin. She, along with Gabriella, had a penchant for feeding from were-animals. One that I was sure Gavin was itching to remedy.

I couldn't describe him as beautiful because he was a certified jackass. Beauty to me was more than just physical, but I was willing to concede to his being handsome and very sexy. Standing at five ten, he had a lean stealth build, broad jawline, sensual wide lips, and flawless fawn-colored skin. Midnight chin-length hair messily dangled, drawing attention to his brilliantly seductive almond-shaped eyes, his greatest asset. They drew you in, captivating you in a manner that, for a brief moment, caused you to forget that he was depraved and malicious.

He enjoyed how his presence provoked the young vampire. She would never make it far enough to feed before he slaughtered her. Killing a vampire would mean nothing to him. He'd done it far too often, but he would gain a special pleasure in the chaos and contention it would cause between the were-animals and the vampires.

"Yes, he is quite intriguing. Do remember the mean wolf that you despise?" Quell asked her softly. I wasn't sure which wolf he was speaking about, but I was willing to bet it was either Sebastian or Ethan, since they both fit the description. Neither was known for being pleasant and most vampires held a special form of hatred for them. Her genteel face puckered and she nodded. "The panther will be a hard one to feed from. Compared to him, the mean one is as gentle as a pup," he cautioned.

She continued to look at Gavin with yearning as Quell guided her to the other side of the room. He sat on the floor near Michaela. Sable lay down on the floor and propped her legs on him, keeping her eyes on Gavin the entire time. Quell gently kneaded her legs as she snuggled closer into him. Vampire interactions always seemed too intimate even if their intentions were supposedly innocent. Chase started toward her, clearly agitated by her behavior.

"I have her," Quell informed him confidently. Chase relaxed slightly and nodded before returning to his place next to Gabriella.

Whether or not it was intentional, the were-animals and vampires systematically distanced themselves as they stood on opposite ends of the room.

As the room settled again after Gavin's tardy arrival and Sable's antics, I noticed that Kelly had slipped in quietly. Avid curiosity covered her face like a mask. It was at that moment I questioned why she found so much comfort being around the were-animals, who were innate predators. Could she be some weird adrenaline junkie, looking for the odd high you get from being in a perpetual state of immense fear and just seconds from death? I scrutinized her for a long time—no, not a junkie, just curious.

She sank into a corner of the room. A small smile covered her face, pleased that she had crept into the lion's den unnoticed. But she had indeed been noticed. Sebastian's sneer turned to a frown, which he worked at erasing as he watched her in his peripheral vision. She had wanted to see the vampires. Well, they definitely saw her, but it was Demetrius's attention she held. He closed his eyes for a mere breath, inhaling as he listened to something—perhaps her heartbeat or the calming sounds of her breathing. He opened his eyes again, his gaze piercing and intensely focused on her. Did she think she could really go unnoticed? He inhaled again. Her scent was noticeably appealing to him, but the only thing I could detect was the smell of human with a hint of peach body spray.

He smiled in her direction, hiding his fangs. It was deceptively innocent and pleasant. The same type of smile abductors used to lure you into captivity. Kelly hadn't blinked for some time. Her gaze was fixed hypnotically in Demetrius's direction. His lips parted slightly and I could see the edges of his fangs as his attention remained transfixed on her. Suddenly he ripped his gaze from hers violently, his features rigid and strained as he kept his head down, eyes focused on the floor.

For that odd disturbing moment, I identified with the vampires. We were called by the lunar cycle periodically and then we were given some form of reprieve, but what called to them was intrinsic and constant. They didn't have days where they could forget what they were—or deny their lusts. It was difficult to control—most of the time they didn't care to do so. But when they had to, it was a struggle. The act of calling to his prey, charming them, seducing their minds was so heavily instinctive that it was a struggle to deny that need.

But Kelly's gaze remained in Demetrius's direction as she chewed on the left side of her lips. Short bursts of breath escaped as she struggled with some unseen force. When she started walking away from her little corner toward him, there was an obscure look of panic on her face.

"Stop it. Now!" Josh commanded the unfamiliar vampire standing next to Demetrius. He looked amused and didn't appear to have any intentions of stopping whatever he was doing to Kelly. Sebastian charged toward the vampire in a full onslaught of rage, but Demetrius grabbed the undead by the throat and slammed him into the wall before Sebastian could make any significant distance. Before anyone could react, speak, or even comprehend what was going on, Demetrius had staked the vampire, and then quickly pulled out a knife to finish the job. It happened so fast that my mind could only seem to grasp seeing the vampire against the wall and then lying on the floor in a pile of ashes.

Josh had Kelly's face pressed firmly between his hands, forcing eye contact with him. He leaned in closer and whispered something that seemed to either calm her or remove whatever held her captive. She was trembling, her eyes glossed over with tears as she gasped softly, barely able to walk as Steven ushered her out of the room. She stopped briefly and turned back to look at the vampires standing against the wall. Revulsion quickly shaded her face. Her curiosity was stifled, now replaced by fear.

Demetrius looked at the ashes as he addressed his Seethe. "We are not here for games or to indulge our desires. Our Seethe is being hunted like animals and I won't tolerate anything but compliance until the person responsible is found and punished. If you don't behave, there will be consequences."

There was a very uncomfortable silence in the room and a level of uncertainty and hostility tainted the vast space. Periodically, the vampires looked at the pile of ashes, a constant reminder of the struggle between their alliance and their needs. The destroyed vampire was a vivid reminder to the were-animals of what the vampires truly were—slaves to their bloodlust.

Sebastian hadn't taken his eyes off Demetrius. It was apparent that all that was keeping him from retaliating were his principles, which forced him to adhere to the alliance.

Demetrius expelled an agitated sigh as he turned to face Josh. "You have our attention. Get on with it." Kelly remained in the house and because of it, Demetrius no longer wanted to be there, fighting a lust that he barely controlled. Sebastian noticed it and looked briefly at the room Kelly had been ushered into. You could still smell her scent, feel her panic stifling the room, the inundation of her fear—the very things that caused a predator's afterglow.

I mourned for the independence that she had once enjoyed and would no longer have. The life she once knew, the freedoms she once enjoyed, were now squelched by her curiosity. She had Demetrius's attention and would soon have Sebastian's overbearing protection. Demetrius looked tortured as he fought his urges, which wasn't missed by Sebastian. No, he was going to go full-bore crazy. The poor woman wasn't going to be able to go to the bathroom without an escort.

Once the room had finally settled to a substantial calm, Josh spoke. "I have a task for you all. I need one of the creatures."

This piqued the interest of everyone in the room. He had just asked a bunch of predators, hunters, and killers to go on a hunt. Merry Christmas to them.

"But I need it alive and unharmed," he quickly added.

Deflated, all eyes turned to him, some in awe but most in disgust. A hunt without a kill wouldn't interest them.

"Those of you who have killed or injured one realize that they fade when injured. That is why I need it alive."

"For what?" Demetrius inquired.

"To source the creature. To track it back to its creator," he replied quickly, meeting Demetrius's intrigued gaze.

"And you can do this?" Demetrius asked, his brow rising with interest.

Josh nodded once, apprehensive.

"He's more gifted than I imagined," Demetrius admitted to Sebastian in a cool voice, but his attention remained on Josh with implicit admiration and curiosity.

"Yes, he is an asset, one that we are happy to have," Sebastian stated diplomatically, but everything about his mannerisms screamed: *He's ours. You go near him, and I will rain hell until there is nothing left of you and your Seethe.*

"Whoever's successful, bring the creature back here," Josh continued.

Everyone, apparently attaining their fill of being in the presence of people they simply loathed, began to inch away from one another. Just before Demetrius and the others could reach the door, Josh added, "You should pair up, vampire with were-animal." When he slipped in the less-than-desirable request, all movement ceased.

"Why?" Gabriella asked, frowning.

"With the were-animals, they shift to match their appearance. I assume it does the same with you all. Shifting, no matter how strong the magic is, can be difficult. If it has to shift quickly and too often, it will be easier to apprehend."

Gabriella started to say something, but he continued, "We agreed to help each other, which is an impressive sacrifice by both parties. Not much of a sacrifice if you never really deal with one another, now is it?" His voice was cool and professional.

Her lips pursed together as she bit back her words. "Of course."

"I think that's a grand idea," Michaela added with a smile, but it was tainted with an air of mischief. "Confuse the creature. One could only imagine how it would respond if we complicated the equation even more." She shot Chris a quick glance. "Perhaps adding a human would improve our chances" Her sly gaze shot to Demetrius, whose face remained vacant.

For a brief moment, he stared at his Mistress. If adding Chris to the mix bothered him, it remained a mystery to anyone looking. Finally, he nodded in assent. "That is a strategy worth considering."

Chris looked indifferent, professionally stoic, as though Michaela making her the sacrificial lamb meant little to her. With a placid face, her eyes traveled over the room, over each person who returned her gaze, intrigued as they waited for her reaction.

"Or perhaps adding her would further endanger whoever she's with. This isn't her fight," Ethan added gruffly.

"Ethan, you're insulting her as well as underestimating her skills. If nothing else, she is efficient in wiggling herself in and out of all types of complicated situations, aren't you?" Michaela stated in a low shrewd tone, her eyes fixed on Chris.

When Chris looked in her direction, she forced a genteel smile, as she nodded politely at Michaela in response to her pseudo-compliment.

Ethan's glare narrowed into thin slits, lips curved slightly into a disapproving scowl as he resigned himself to the idea that if Michaela had anything to do with this, Chris wouldn't sit this one out.

"Fine, then she partners with me," he declared.

"If I am not mistaken, the last time she *partnered* with you, her shoulder was dislocated. Perhaps she would fare better if she was partnered with someone more capable of making sure she isn't harmed," Demetrius responded.

"Well, if your comfort with the situation is of utmost importance, perhaps I should demonstrate how capable I am of keeping her safe." Ethan pushed himself from the wall.

"Perhaps you should," Demetrius challenged, walking in his direction.

Chris's attention jumped between the two. Her stolid mask fell, and her skin grew flushed with anger and embarrassment, I assumed over them coddling her. "Gavin, do you mind if I tag along with you?" she asked.

"There aren't too many things that would make me happier," he admitted. A smug grin shadowed his face as his gaze lingered in Ethan's direction. Still angry with Ethan for preventing him from exacting his revenge on me, he was more than happy to do anything that would gall him.

"Look at that. It's settled then," Michaela interjected, fueling the fire. "Josh, would you care to do the honors of pairing us off?"

she asked, eyeing him in a sultry manner. He held her interest and I was sure it wasn't for his magical ability.

Josh shrugged. "I don't think it really matters. I asked that you invite your strongest and most skilled. Pair as you like," he said dismissively.

"Then I choose Gabriella," Gavin added confidently, smiling in Chase's direction. They held each other's regard as Chase bared his fangs, unable to feign nonchalance. Gavin was in mischief heaven, igniting flames and standing back with pure delight as he created chaos.

The pairing off continued until every were-animal had been matched with a vampire. The vampires needed to feed before the hunt and agreed to meet back at the house before they went out.

As the vampires departed, Gabriella stayed close to Sable, guiding her toward the door. They had almost made it out when she quickly turned and headed straight for Gavin. She lunged at him, but before she could strike, he darted to the side, turned, and grabbed her from behind. He was advantageously placed, with a strong handhold around her neck while his other hand was placed around the crown of her head. With one move, he could easily snap her neck. It would be a quick kill.

The room stilled. Everyone's attention focused on Gavin and Sable.

"She attacked me. It is well within my rights to kill her," Gavin stated, his voice sharp ice, chilling the room. He looked at Sebastian, whose face was pulled so tight that the tense lines that ran along his neck became increasingly taut, a clear sign that Gavin was right.

Demetrius nodded his head in Gavin's direction. "Do as you see fit," he urged and turned toward the door. He didn't want Sable in his Seethe, and he was going to allow Gavin to fix the situation, leaving him blameless.

Sebastian could have commanded him not to, but then it would have made him look weak in front of the vampires, especially if Gavin disobeyed. But if Gavin obeyed, it would only have incited his inflammatory tendencies, forcing him to keep provoking Sable until she attacked him again, and then he would kill her without a second thought, whether he had the right or not. That was the type of person he was, and that was the type of sick, malicious crap he was known for.

"Please don't," Gabriella pled softly. Concern settled on her face the way it would if someone's child were in danger. I wasn't aware she was capable of that type of consideration. She and Chase stood in the middle of the room, staring at their protégée, helpless as her fate lay in the hands of the were-panther, who wasn't known for being compassionate.

He held her close, staring intensely at Gabriella and Chase, the sharp look of contempt unyielding. Chase seemed calm, but Gabriella was on the edge of an emotional break. The seconds lingered as the expression on Gavin's face transitioned from anger, mischief, to ignobility, making the moment all the more intense. No one had any idea what the troublesome panther was thinking, but I imagined it wasn't nice. Would he kill just to spur drama and discord?

Removing his hand from her neck, he placed it in front of her turning it palm side up, exposing his forearm. "Go ahead," he encouraged in a rough voice.

She hesitated.

"Do it," he urged, bringing his wrist to her lips. She wrapped her pale finger around his arm, pulled it closer, and parted her lips slightly before sinking her teeth into him. When Chase had bitten me last year, it singed like fire, but Gavin didn't seem bothered by the sharp enamel invading his skin. His expression didn't change. If anything, he looked bored. Perhaps pain had little meaning to him.

"Sable, that's enough," Gabriella said firmly after she had fed for what seemed like an eternity. The room remained quiet while the vampires stared longingly at them and the were-animals looked on, vastly uncomfortable.

Gavin continued to stare at a spot on the wall, finding little interest in what was being done as a captivated young vampire continued to feed from him, ignoring Gabriella's request.

"She's okay. I'll stop her if I need to," he stated in a low, smooth drawl. Sable continued making sounds of pleasure that should have been left in the bedroom.

She finally pulled away. Smiling, she stared at Gavin as she licked the viscous fluid that ran down her lips.

"Don't leave me marked," he commanded, making eye contact with her for a brief moment. She leaned down and ran her tongue over the area, taking far longer than necessary. Her tongue bathed his forearm until the marks were removed completely.

A thoroughly enthralled young vampire walked backward toward the door, barely able to keep her eyes off Gavin. Unyielding coal eyes held hers.

"You've had a were-panther now. Don't attack me again, because if you do, it won't end so favorably next time. I will kill you. It will be the most painful thing you will ever experience. And if you *call* me at any point, you will suffer the same fate," he stated calmly.

Gabriella nodded graciously while Sable's bright ruby lips curled into a demure smile as though he had whispered earnest words of love and devotion to her.

Too engrossed by him, she didn't seem to hear his threats. Her eyes fixed on him, a wistful yearning eclipsing her face.

"Sable, do you understand?" asked Demetrius's hard voice, yanking her out of her state.

She looked at him once and nodded, having a hard time pulling her attention from Gavin. She once again directed her gaze back to him. Gabriella grabbed her roughly by the arm and pulled her out the door.

CHAPTER 11 (CHRIS)

Hunting with Gavin wasn't something Chris necessarily wanted. But he was one of the few in the pack that didn't mind ignoring Ethan. Gavin played by his own rules, which he made up as he went along. Watching him irritate the members of his pack in the manner that he did was entertaining, but it made her realize he barely operated in the realm of sanity. As she hunted with him, she realized that her ego had gotten her into a bad situation.

They had been out searching for a creature for nearly four hours. The search areas were divided, concentrating on areas where the creatures had attacked or been spotted. Chris followed close behind as Gavin darted through the woods, assessing the area as though he had truly given in to the panther and its primal ways.

Now they traipsed through the bosky area near Thaddeus's home, where she and Ethan had been attacked. The deeper they trailed into the woods, the less visible they were but the harder it was to negotiate the uneven, crowded area. The fallen autumn leaves crunched under their feet along with numerous broken branches.

Somehow, Gabriella and Gavin had slipped away from her. It was the animalistic sounds of the brawl that identified their location. Gabriella fought the creature, moving fast around it as she engaged it, but had difficulty subduing it without spilling blood. *This is one hell of a task,* Chris thought angrily.

Gavin had shifted to his panther and stalked toward the creature. It changed to mimic his appearance but stood upright in a peculiar duplication. As Gabriella continued to try to wrangle it to the ground, Chris slipped in closer, Tasering its leg then chest. Instead of disabling the creature, it just enraged it. Hoisting Gabriella by the throat, it tossed her several yards across the meadow. Her arm angled in an odd position behind her, possibly broken. When Gavin charged toward the distorted thing, it pushed him out of its way and aimed for Chris.

Drawing her weapon, she hoped that the tranquilizer gun would work the way she intended. But as the creature shifted, changing its appearance again, her finger froze on the trigger. It looked human—a very familiar human. Of all its morphing, which had barely resembled the type of creature hunting it, this one had the most intricate and precise face yet. Staring back at her were refined, classic Mediterranean features that belonged in a museum on a sculpture. Penetrating hazel eyes stared back at her. She knew that face, those eyes, and those features all too well—Ryan. Chris gasped at the image in front of her, barely managing to point the gun in the creature's face, but she couldn't pull the trigger.

The moment of distraction was all it needed. Snatching the gun from her, it tossed it out of reach. She moved back just in time to dodge the fist swinging in her direction. Using the arm as leverage, a hip toss landed the creature on its back. As she ran for the discarded tranq gun, it shifted again, to a massive feline form whose clawed fingers sank into her leg, pulling her to it as she gripped the ground and used her free leg to strike back. It was nearly on her. She accepted the reality that they weren't bringing this one back uninjured. She pulled both guns out of her holsters. After the first shot, the feline creature fell back, and moments later the body, along with the splatters of blood, disappeared, a light mist left behind in its wake.

Gavin extended his hand to help her up. "You hesitated," he said, keeping hold of her hand as he scrutinized her for a long time. He released her. "Why?"

She shrugged it off. Gavin hadn't been part of the Midwest Pack long. Perhaps he didn't know about Ryan and didn't know the effect he had had on her. She had just realized it herself. It had been too long. The memory was now dredged up and it was the only thing that occupied her thoughts on the way back to the pack's retreat.

You didn't kill him, the voice of logic scolded. But she hadn't believed it, nor had his fiancée, who had refused to speak to her since his death five years earlier.

That night, Chris had wished a thousand times over that she could have that moment in time back. The thought of it made her heart ache, her stomach churn, and mournful tears form, distorting her vision. The memories were too forceful to ignore. That night, he had told her that after that job he was going to retire and marry his fiancée. She couldn't do anything but stare at him—shocked and unable to speak. Wasn't that the type of thing you told someone over coffee sitting on a couch or at dinner?

Five years they had worked together. He had trained her and molded her into what she was. She loved him so much that it was distracting. There was something between them and she wasn't sure why he chose to ignore it. Why didn't he want her? It didn't help that his fiancée, Melani, was just a slighter older version of herself. He was going to leave her and live the rest of his life with a woman who could easily be mistaken for her sister. That night, he should have killed her. At least then she would have been in a better state.

~

The next evening, she stood to Gavin's left, feeling his cool gaze piercing the side of her face. He didn't trust her plans and didn't hide his doubt in her capabilities. She needed this to work, not just to capture the creature and for the sake of the job, but for her confidence also. Never before had she questioned her skills as a Hunter or her abilities. But now, she did—often.

Gabriella stood in the midst of the wooded area, her eyes closed as she focused on the sound of the approaching creature. "It's here," she sang as her lips curled into a deviant smile. It was the thrill of the chase, the challenge, the appeal of a capture but not a kill. Chris always wondered what Gabriella's life would have been like if she weren't a denizen of the night. What career, what life would appeal to a woman who adored violence and turmoil in a manner that was both strangely alluring and disturbing?

Gavin stayed back in the shadows as the thing approached, and then he soared forward, crashing into it. He was smaller than the creature, and his speed and force weren't enough to send it to the ground, but it unbalanced it enough to allow Chris to take several well-placed shots with the tranquilizer. Shed no blood and cause no injuries. That was the only objective. The impact of the shots was enough to send it to the ground with a thud.

They worked fast and strategically, tying up the creature and getting its massive form into the SUV. Josh had the door of the pack's home open for them by the time they had pulled up into the driveway. At the sight of the creature, Josh looked as though he were ready to jump up and down with joy.

Ethan, Steven, and Sebastian were there to assist with the thing that had started to wake up in the car. Chris shot it two more times with the tranquilizer gun, careful not to do anything that would injure it. They were too close to have it disappear.

"Good job," Ethan said as he helped put the creature in a cage.

In spite of all the moving, jostling, and rough handling, it stayed unconscious.

Gabriella didn't stay long. Surrounded by a room full of were-animals, her discomfort was apparent. It was nearly one in the morning, but Chris was too charged with adrenaline to go home. Instead, she stood next to Josh and watched as he set up in order to source the creature's magic.

Before he could finish setting up, Skylar came down the stairs. Chris thought it was peculiar that Ethan was always extremely agitated and tense when she was around. Everyone seemed hushed when she brought her name up. Nor would anyone confirm whether she was part of the pack or not, but she assumed she had to be because of the amount of time she spent there. Josh smiled as she came down the stairs. There was something about her that didn't sit well with Chris. It all stemmed from the fact that the year before, the vampires had planned to use Skylar for a ritual that couldn't be performed on were-animals. And a couple of days ago, Chris thought she had seen a terait on her. Were-animals didn't have teraits.

Chris held Skylar's gaze for a long time, searching for whatever it was about her that made the pack create a bastion of secrecy on her behalf. Skylar had a hard time holding it; her vibrant green eyes seemed too wide, naïve, and benign. *She will never survive,* Chris thought, as Skylar turned away and focused her attention on Josh. She was out of her depth, struggling, and eventually, this world would destroy her, leaving a broken person and battered spirit in its wake.

But Ethan reminded Chris that she was struggling, too. "What happened last night?" he asked. "Gavin told me you froze when the creature morphed into Ryan."

She glanced in his direction but ignored his question, returning her attention to studying Skylar. She had finally admitted to herself that Ryan's death still affected her, but she doubted that she would ever be ready to admit it to Ethan. As the creature stirred, she gripped the tranquilizer gun holstered at her hip and positioned it.

Before Josh could start the spell, the massive thing came to and began to hit against the cage, rattling it. Large trunk-like arms pushed at the bars, trying to get to Josh.

Then suddenly it stopped and morphed, but not into a wolf or anything animal-like or human. Instead, it turned into a scaled creature, rough skin the color of charcoal. It held Skylar's gaze, then it hissed a name, "Maya." It said it again, holding Skylar's wide-eyed, bewildered gaze as it screeched the name. Chris said the name over and over, hoping it would jar her memory. Maya. Who was she and what was her relationship to Skylar, the peculiar woman in the Midwest Pack's life?

The creature said the name again, then in one quick act, it turned its claws on itself and plunged them into its stomach, spilling blood.

"No!" Josh yelled, opening the cage and grabbing it before it vanished.

"What are you doing? Get the hell out of there," Ethan yelled, moving toward the cage. He was too late. The creature slashed into Josh's arm, but it didn't deter him from trying to stop it. He gripped its massive arm. The lights blinked erratically, and then shut off for a few seconds as Josh's eyes changed to an odd opaque color, something she hadn't seen before. She watched with interest as the cage trembled and the lights flickered. Ethan yanked Josh out of the cage. She lunged at it with a knife, hoping to get a sample of the blood before it disappeared, but she was too late. It vanished, and whatever blood spilled from the self-inflicted wounds disappeared with it.

Josh let out a string of expletives before he realized that he was in need of medical attention. Ethan grasped his arm, assessing the wound. He frowned, exhaling a ragged breath as Josh's blood stained his hand.

"Whoever is involved in this is stronger than I am," Josh admitted.

But not by much, Chris thought to herself. He was stronger than she realized, and it was only then she understood why Ethan was so vehement about protecting him.

Ethan looked around the room. Only a couple of the lights were still on, and the others flickered several times, trying to recover from the surge of magic that had disabled them. Then his focus went back to Josh's arm, which was split open and bleeding like a geyser.

"You did what you could, more than you should have," Ethan said in a low voice. He was still examining the wound when he looked up at his brother. "Don't do anything like that again, okay?" he said in a low voice.

"You're doing it again," Josh said firmly.

"You asked me to give you room, I'm doing that. I am just asking that you be more careful." Ethan's voice was hard, strained, fighting his nature to avoid going into one of his enraged rants.

He returned his attention back to the claw marks. "You're going to need stitches—several."

Josh looked down at his arm. His eyes widened as he took in the full extent of the injury. It gaped open. Blood ran down leaving a claret trail along his arm. He grinned and cradled it against his chest. "I guess I should get it over with. You want to bet I get to hear another one of his speeches?" He shrugged. "This should be fun."

Ethan chuckled but it was a forced, tight sound—insincere. He couldn't take his eyes off Josh's arm, seemingly more upset by the injury than his brother was.

CHAPTER 11 (SKYLAR)

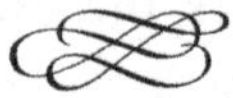

Gavin and Chris carried the massive creature down the stairs. Gabrielle was supposed to be helping, but she was too distracted watching Ethan and Josh with contempt, her face scrunched into a grimace that she couldn't seem to relax. Once the thing was locked in the cage, both Gavin and Gabrielle made a dash for the door. She was more cordial as she politely excused herself. Gavin simply said, "I'm out" and was up the stairs and out the door before anyone could object to his leaving.

With the creature locked in the cage and Josh preparing to source it, Ethan scrutinized Chris before approaching her. Usually she was relaxed but watchful, focusing on everything and studying it with great intensity, but now she looked sad and distracted. Something or someone had her preoccupied. She ignored Ethan, who was now standing next to her, but I didn't receive such treatment. She stared at me, as she always did when I was near. There was never disdain in her gaze, just immense curiosity that made me nervous. *What is it about me that fascinates her?* Last year, she knew that I was the only were-animal able to be used during a ritual that would have lifted all the vampires' restraints.

As with the were-animals, she was always glancing at the corners of my eyes for the terait, that odd orange line around my pupil that was usually only present in a vampire that needed to feed. I didn't need a lot of blood. Just a few bites of rare steak usually worked to make my terait disappear. The stress of recent events made eating less of a priority. My terait had showed up a couple of days before but I wasn't sure if it was present now. I turned to look at Josh, shifting my body at an angle, making it harder for her to look me in the eye. The less she saw it, the more plausible deniability I had.

Ethan quickly noticed that I garnered an extensive share of Chris's attention and started to talk to her. Although they seemed to work well together, there was an odd detachment and distrust that lingered. At times, there was even annoyance as though they forgot they were supposed to like each other.

She half listened to him as she switched her attention between me and the creature that was starting to stir. Soon it was rattling the cage, chewing at the bars, and doing everything possible to escape. Its movements were mechanical and obviously controlled by someone else. It stuck its oddly misshapen face against the bars and stared at me. Its change happened quickly, to the coal-colored reptilian creature I had encountered last year when I visited the Tre'ase.

All movement stopped as it hissed my name. I thought it was too low for the others to hear, but I could feel their intense gazes on me. Again, it whispered my name. No, it wasn't my name. It was Maya's, the spirit shade that lived inside of me. The next time it made a guttural sound, it was my name that was uttered.

Don't look back, don't look back, I commanded myself, but I couldn't help it. There was Chris, eyes narrowed as she watched me. I dropped my gaze, although I knew I shouldn't have. I was a werewolf, a greater species. A human shouldn't have me cowering, but she did. The intensity of her gaze was devoid of the warmth that most humans possessed. Instead, it was replaced by unquenchable curiosity.

When the creature called out "Maya" again, the polarizing pull of its command was harder to ignore. It beckoned me and I felt a desperate need to respond. Outstretched fingers stayed at my side, but the desire to touch it, comfort it, and even help it kept increasing with each passing moment. I took a small step forward before forcing myself to stay planted. It finally moved, poking its face through the bars a final time as it murmured Maya's name again. When I failed to respond, it turned its claws on itself. Josh rushed into the cage and grabbed it, attempting to restrain it with magic, but whoever was controlling it was more powerful, and it disappeared.

I wasn't sure who else had heard the creature call my name and Maya's, but I knew who I wished hadn't—Chris.

CHAPTER 12

The keys of my laptop were clicking away as I rushed to catch up on two reports due in less than a week. I couldn't afford to lose my job because I knew I would never find anything that was better suited for me than my current job as a contract healthcare auditor for a private company. I had worked hard to prove myself to the owner in order to negotiate my current position and worked from home. Office life just didn't work well for me. I knew that if I spent enough time in one, people would eventually want to know more details about my life. All the lies I would have to tell to explain it were an unnecessary hassle.

Now as my fingers swept across the keys and I flipped through my notes trying to catch up on my work while worrying about the fate of my job, I realized that once again, the pack, which I was *not* a part of, had somehow taken priority in my life. For the past two days, instead of working, I had spent most of my time waiting for them to bring in another creature, but no one had. But there hadn't been any more attacks, either.

When the door rattled, I suspected it was Quell. For the past three nights, I had been greeted by him standing on my porch. We talked. Well, I talked. He listened. And the conversations were as dull as watching boiling water. Yesterday, I finally asked why he kept coming over, and he simply shrugged. If I could have found a polite way to ask him to stop coming over, I would have. But there was still a part of me that needed to see him because his existence tugged at my curiosity. What had happened during his human life that turned him against humanity? Sixty-nine years was a heck of a long time to hold a grudge.

Three impatient knocks tapped at my door. Before I could answer, it shook, along with the house. The hinges of the door creaked in an effort to stay intact. After several blasts, the door swung open. It definitely wasn't Quell.

"Let's talk," requested the stranger. His pale skin and platinum hair looked odd as a backdrop to the distant amethyst eyes that locked with mine. I didn't know him and there wasn't anything about his cold, penetrating gaze that made me feel hospitable.

As he stepped toward the threshold, the ward shuddered. Lilac sparks flickered as an unforgiving hum resounded, piercing the air as it withstood the force with which he pushed against it.

Grinning, he spoke with immense confidence. "It's a good ward, but I can break it."

That was exactly what he would have to do, because I wasn't letting him in. I slammed the door and then locked the double bolt. It blasted open again; the sparks shone brighter, flaring off the doorframe as the ward fought to stay intact. I covered my ears at the howling screech that resounded, a cry of defeat as it started to waver. It rolled, bulging in. Crinkles formed in the diaphanous wall.

"Don't make this harder than it has to be," he warned, his hand resting against the ward as it worked to prevent its demise.

"What do you want?"

"To talk."

"Then start talking."

"Drop the ward," he demanded.

"No."

He sighed impatiently, but his irritation wasn't directed at me. Quell appeared at the door. When Quell attempted to grab the stranger, he vanished and then reappeared behind him, yanking him back as he plunged a stake through his heart. Quell's lips parted in a gasp, his eyes rolled back, as he collapsed to the floor, grasping frantically at the stake.

"Quell!" I started to disarm the ward, which had managed to hold despite the relentless assault, to help Quell, but stopped at the threshold. What exactly could I do while the violent stranger was standing over him, ready to finish the job? Sensing my dilemma, he turned toward me, giving me his haughty grin and a challenge I would not accept.

"I spared his life. Remember this." Then he was gone. His strong magic left remnants of its existence to cloud the air.

I disarmed the ward, ran out the door, and pulled Quell into my house. Deep, pained gasps lodged in his throat as his legs turned a dark color: the early stage of reversion.

This is sparing his life? How about not staking him? That would help.

I called Quell's name several times but he didn't respond. His eyes began to lose whatever form of life once existed in them. A vacant cloud crept over them, his face relaxing as he accepted his fate, eyes fluttering as he tried to keep them from rolling back. I wondered how long it would take before the process was complete and he was a dead undead. Last year I had staked Chase, and he actually drained his donor, killing her to revive himself. Is that what it took or did they just need a little blood? I figured some blood was better than nothing. I could give him enough to slow down the process until I could get help.

I started for my phone, but the reversion process happened fast, creeping up from his legs and covering the upper part of his thighs as they became rigid. I was afraid that if I touched them they would crumble.

He needed to feed. Crouching over him, I placed my wrist at his lips. With a painstaking grunt, he turned his head away and shook his head. Was he freaking kidding me? I was trying to save his life!

Fine, just die!

Indignation made me want to just walk away and let his reversion continue. Having a conscience sucked. I pressed my wrist in closer, pushing past his lips forcing them apart.

"Do it," I commanded.

He didn't.

"Quell, I won't let you die. Now do it," I insisted, shoving my wrist under his fangs and piercing the skin. Blood swelled and dropped into his mouth.

He responded slowly. After several long moments, he swallowed, pressing harder into my wrist and taking deep draws from the vein. It was painful, but tolerable. I gritted my teeth. Eventually the pain eased. Minutes after he started feeding he became whole, reverting quickly to his natural form. But he didn't stop. His fangs sank in deeper, the pulls became harder and more intense. I panicked, tugging my arm away, but he kept a firm hold on it.

His eyes changed to a deep red color. Far too accustomed to his green eyes, I stared, disgusted by what it signified—what he had truly become. Closing his eyes, he licked his lips and inhaled deeply, tightening his grip on me.

"More." He moved quickly and, grabbing a fistful of my hair, he tugged me into him and sank his teeth into my neck, taking sharp, painful pulls.

My fist pounded at his shoulder, nails clawing into his skin as I struggled to pull away. Afraid of severing a vessel if I moved too abruptly, I was cautious as I tried to get away.

"Quell, stop!"

He pulled away with a start. But it was far too late. My vision blurred. I forced my eyes to stay open, my hand pressed against my neck, but that soon was sodden with blood.

"I am so sorry." It was the last thing I heard as Quell hovered over me.

~

I opened my eyes to find Dr. Baker's face right over me. Golden brown sparks flooded his eyes. Dr. Baker was a were-tiger, but it was always hard to imagine that such a warm, kind-spirited personality could house a vicious apex predator. But now, as he gazed at me with those excoriatingly hard and intense eyes, I couldn't see him as anything else.

"How do you feel?" he asked, his voice stiff and raspy. There was so much anger it overshadowed the apparent concern. My neck and wrist were throbbing and felt scorched.

"You lost a lot of blood. I had to give you a transfusion. Sit up, slowly."

I hadn't lost the blood. I knew exactly where it was—in Quell.

He helped me up and I focused on the intensity of his face. Something was wrong, but it wasn't until I sat on the side of the bed and saw Sebastian, Steven, Gavin, Taylor, and Ethan on one side of the room and Demetrius, Chase, Gabriella, Michaela, Quell, and an unfamiliar vampire on the other that I realized just how very wrong things were.

Quell stood next to Demetrius, bearing a look of guilt and shame that made me feel worse for him than I did for myself. Surrounded by a room full of angry were-animals, Quell should have been afraid, but instead, he looked plaintive. His odd eyes and indiscernible heartbeat were gone. He wasn't teetering in between anymore. He had crossed over, and I was responsible for it.

My gaze drifted to the floor. I couldn't look at him—it was disturbing—he was disturbing, even more so now. Once he had stood out like a sore thumb among the vampires. Now, he blended, truly one of them.

"Skylar, what happened between you and Quell?" Demetrius finally asked, his accent, usually light and barely noticeable, was thick, difficult to understand. There wasn't any question about how he felt. He was angry, but I wasn't quite sure why. Quell feeding from me? Such a thing would be of little concern to him. In fact, he should have been proud. Quell was no longer the "Lost One." He was one of them now. Or was Demetrius angry that Sebastian looked like he was ready to rip Quell to pieces and anyone who attempted to stop him?

The room was thick with hostility, and I found it a little hard to breathe. Anger reeked—it always does. How I answered this question was very important. It could end our alliance with the vampires and possibly Quell's existence if I said the wrong thing. I wasn't sure at whose hand, but, from the way Chase looked at Quell, I determined it would be by his. It was interesting that the vampires held little regard for much, especially the loss of life, but honored their agreements and alliances. It made me respect them at that moment. I still didn't like them—well, with the exception of Quell. The verdict was still out on the unknown vamp, but based on their track record, it was safe to assume if I got to know him, I wouldn't like him, either.

I started out slowly, editing the story into the most favorable light. "Someone tried to break in, they were forcing down the ward when Quell showed up. Quell tried to grab him when he was staked."

My attention stayed on Sebastian and occasionally moved in Demetrius's direction. "I didn't think Quell deserved to die because he wanted to make sure I was safe, so I made sure he didn't." I waited a minute before continuing. "He refused at first, but I made him feed." My gaze darted to Quell, who was now staring at me with despondence.

"You made him?" Steven asked in disbelief, condensed rage reflected on his face.

I nodded. Okay, it didn't take a hell of a lot of persuasion, but I urged him nevertheless, and at that moment, it didn't seem like such a bad idea to let them think that. I had taken creative license with the story, but it wasn't a lie, and everything would remain intact: the alliance and Quell. I looked at Sebastian, attempting to hold his iron gaze. The features of his face had hardened, his lips were clenched, and rolls of amber seemed to continue in erratic bursts. He was trying to control the anger, which was a good sign.

"I couldn't let him die," I admitted, as I attempted to appeal to their understanding.

Sebastian finally nodded in acceptance but not understanding.

"Hmm. Why is that, Skylar?" Michaela asked. Disdain dripped from every syllable as she pronounced my name, sending sharp pricks along my skin. She liked me about as much as I liked her and she had no qualms about showing it.

"If the roles had been reversed, I believe Quell would have done the same," I stated softly.

"I would have," he admitted, his repentant eyes fixed in my direction.

Both Demetrius and Michaela shot him baleful glares.

"Sebastian, your reaction was unnecessary. There wasn't a need for me and mine to be called here. I can assure you that Quell hasn't become so besotted by your precious little pup that he would abandon his way of life," Demetrius stated smugly.

Chase relaxed, which cued the others to do the same, with the exception of Michaela, whose daggered gaze was pressing into me painfully. She seemed aggrieved by what I had done and didn't look like she was ready to offer clemency anytime soon.

Quell started toward me, but Steven blocked his approach. Quell put up his hands in surrender. "I am going to remove her marks. I believe it would be best if there weren't any reminders of what has occurred," he stated in a soft, distressed voice.

Steven reluctantly stepped aside, keeping a watchful eye on him. While Quell approached, I stared at the audience. He was quite brave or stupid. Sometimes people mistake the two. As he stood inches from me, I kept my face blank. Grasping my wrist, he put it close to his mouth, and I heard some of the were-animals' breathing patterns change, becoming rapid thrusts.

Whatever you're about to do, make it quick and get away from me, I urged with a look.

His lips pressed against me before his tongue laved across the mark, leaving a cool, moist breezy tingle against my skin. When he pulled away, I looked down and the bite marks had vanished. Even the bruising, etiolated, was barely visible. I turned my wrist toward Sebastian and Steven so they could see, but they didn't seem nearly as impressed as I was.

"Why didn't you do that in the first place?" Steven said.

"Hiding the evidence of what was done would not have helped in exonerating me," Quell stated, his focus on me. He leaned in and did the same thing to my neck. A rumble erupted in the room. Well, several rumbles erupted that sounded like rolling thunder right before a torrential storm. I decided that Quell wasn't brave, which left the alternative—stupid.

When he pulled away, he lingered near my ear. "Thank you," he whispered low enough for only my ears.

"You should move, quickly," I warned in a whisper just as soft as he did as I watched an enraged Steven slowly inch toward us. He gave me a small nod, smiled, and stepped away. I didn't look at the were-animals. I knew they weren't going to be happy. Demetrius had a very smug look on his face, and Michaela divided her glare between Quell and me.

"That will be enough, Quell," she stated in a harsh, crisp tone. "I believe you have entertained yourself with her enough for the day."

"Very well, the matter is handled," Sebastian stated. Translation: Get out. The faster the better.

Sebastian watched the vampires as they dispersed. Ethan followed behind them, ushering them out the door. Once the room was empty, Sebastian turned toward me. "Follow me," he commanded without looking at me. I didn't plan on following him anywhere.

He made it to the door when he realized I hadn't moved. "Now."

I hopped off the table and followed him down the hallway, around the corner, then through his office to a room in the back. He punched in several numbers on the keypad then opened the door. It opened into a bedroom—his bedroom, and it looked utterly depressing. Pewter-colored walls with sky-gray trim. The hardwood floors of the large open space were covered with a Persian rug. With the exception of the rug and the damask designer accent chair in the corner, the room was bland. Like the other rooms in the house, the walls were complemented with unique and extremely detailed pictures of wildlife and nature. In his room, right above the bed, was an oversized canvas painting of a pack of wolves—of course. I expected a picture in a bedroom would depict an animal sleeping, in a state of rest, or something similarly soothing. Instead the wolves' teeth were bared, eyes intense and ravenous as they adopted the attack position. This was the image Sebastian wanted to look upon before he slept.

"Sit," he stated, his hand directing me toward the chair next to the bed. "Please," he added when I hesitated.

Once I was seated, he stood in front of me. He stared at me for a long time. "You look like hell," he finally stated. "When's the last time you actually slept?'

"Last night." With everything going on, sleep never came easily when I tried. Instead, I lay in the bed tossing and turning.

There were several minutes of silence; he frowned at the lie but didn't call me on it. "What happened between you and Quell?"

"I found Quell in the process of reversion…."

His eyes narrowed, amber eclipsing them for a brief moment.

His lips pressed firmly together, tightly coiled muscles raised along his neck, chest, and forearms. "Not the politically correct contrived bullshit you spat out earlier. I want the truth."

There wasn't a need to cause unnecessary discord so I settled on using the same version of the story I had told earlier. It was a relatively harmless account of the truth.

Sebastian, anticipating my response, sighed. "Either you think you are cleverer than I am or you believe that I am quite stupid."

He knelt in front of me and took my right wrist into his hand. "The marks here were clean, no hesitation marks, which meant he initiated and stopped on his own volition." He released my wrist and then ran his finger over my neck across the bruising. "The marks here were slightly jagged where you either struggled or he did. You also have bruising on the back of your neck, indicating you were held firmly at some point today. If you forced him to drink, then why is there bruising on you, and why did he have scratch marks on the back of his neck? Stop lying to me."

I inhaled a jagged breath. "I told you how it happened and I was there," I stated firmly.

For a long time he didn't speak, and holding his intense gaze was getting more difficult. I just waited for the volcano to erupt, but it didn't.

"Skylar, what were you thinking?" he asked softly. Through the tone of his inquiry, I could detect a hint of concern.

"I didn't want him to die," I admitted. "I like to think you would have done the same."

"He's still dead and no, I would not have done the same."

We were at an impasse; nothing I said would have changed his mind and he wouldn't change mine. It was expressed prolifically on his face. Whatever concern he showed over a vampire's death was a result of the alliance and it had its limitations. Quell meant nothing to him.

"Quell is new, rabid and now will have the ability to call. You aren't strong enough to ignore it. Most aren't," he said. "Tonight you will stay here. His ability to call you will decrease significantly over the next few days and then you can return home."

Sebastian was calmer than I had ever witnessed, which led me to believe his mind was made up and wasn't likely to change, but I wasn't going to let a thing like that stop me. I trusted that Quell had enough control that I didn't have anything to worry about.

"I trust Quell and I'm sure I will be fine at home."

Sebastian pulled a chair up in front of me and then sat. "You shouldn't. I assure you he is not the same. Newly changed vampires are impulsive, bloodthirsty, and very difficult to control. Demetrius has been more responsible over the years in controlling the damage they do, but it is not his priority. The next time Quell feeds from you, things could go quite differently. If he kills you, it forces my hand to retaliate. I don't trust Demetrius to control Quell, so I will have to."

Then I realized this all boiled down to politics and not my life. "So it's not really about my life, is it?" And it wasn't. If I was wrong and Demetrius or Michaela failed to intervene and Quell fed from me again and killed me in the process, Sebastian would be forced to handle the matter. Maintaining an alliance would be rather difficult after that.

Sebastian was finished with this conversation even if I wasn't. The piercing amber gaze, the stern look, terminated the conversation immediately. "There is a shower over there." He looked over to the left. "Use it. You smell like him," he said with a frown.

I stayed on the bed, even after he glanced at the shower again. He stopped at the threshold, his back to me, his arms clutching the sides of the doorframe, his thick, defined muscles straining against his shirt. When he spoke, his tone was gentle. "Winter would not be alive if it weren't for you. So it's not just politics. I protect your life because you saved hers." And with that, he closed the door.

. . .

I stared at the closed door, then the keypad next to it. A room this size should have had several windows, but it didn't. Once again, I found myself locked in the pack's home, for my safety.

After taking a long shower, instead of Quell, I smelled like vanilla bean shower gel and fragrant floral shampoo. The entire time during the shower, I kept thinking about what Sebastian had said about Quell. Was he going to be different? Would he be like the others now, with a bloodlust that he could no longer control? For once, since I had met him, I found comfort in his disdain for humans. He would never become like the others because of it.

After I got out of the shower, I found a waiter's table covered with food, and looking over at the bed, I saw a robe draped across it. I slipped on the robe and ate all the macaroni and cheese and steakburger on the table. I fell asleep soon after.

Firm knocks pulled me out of my sleep with a start. I lurched up. "Come in," I said in a rough voice. *Because I can't let you in.*

The placid look on Sebastian's face dulled his appearance. I wondered if he had stayed up all night worrying if I would try to leave to get to Quell.

"How long have I been asleep?" I asked, rubbing the sleep out of my eyes as I sat up.

"Twelve hours."

Yeah, that seemed about right. A couple of hours before I had woken, taken another shower, and dressed in my jeans from the day before and a t-shirt that I found in the closet that sort of fit me. It hung unflatteringly, nearly swallowing me, making me look like a child playing dress up. Then I had curled up on the bed and fallen asleep. Apparently, feeding an odd vampire and worrying about a pack was taking its toll on me.

He looked at me in the oversized t-shirt and wrinkled jeans and the odd twisted bun on my head and chuckled. "Let's get you more clothes."

. . .

At the door of my home Sebastian spoke for the first time since we had left the pack's house, and it was a low grumble about the small splatters of blood at the entrance. He stopped me at the door and walked in, searching through each room, taking more time in the bedrooms than the other ones that were easily seen from the door.

"Put the ward up," he said once he was satisfied with his findings.

I whispered the words to erect it.

"You should pack enough for three days," he said, as he rested against the wall near the door. His appearance was wry. The strain of the past couple of days blemished his striking face. The sharp lines of his flawless cocoa skin were rugged, and a hint of a beard shadowed his jaw.

Now his state was the result of the current situation, but he was a tense person on an average day. I was sure that even if he were on an island, surrounded by palm trees, umbrella drinks, and the soothing sounds of the ocean, he would still be at full-threat mode. I couldn't imagine why anyone would battle their way to such a position.

I had no intention of staying at the retreat for three days, but I would deal with that later. "Are you able to break wards?" I asked.

He nodded. "Most were-animals can break wards. It takes practice and a lot of effort, but they can be broken."

Nice and rehearsed, the very thing Ethan had said to Josh last year.

"What about protective fields?"

"Only a witch can erect and break a protective field."

"Ethan broke Josh's protective field last year," I pointed out. "So Ethan's a witch."

Not one thing betrayed him. Not even the cadence of his voice, the beat of his heart, his respiration, or his demeanor. By all means, I should have been given the truth.

"I am sure you are incorrect. I've known Ethan a long time. He cannot break protective fields, just wards. I will admit that he is more skilled than most."

Okay, I'll play your game. "But it really would be quite advantageous for you to have two witches: one as a blood ally and the other as a pack member."

He smiled. "If Ethan were a witch, it would be more of a disadvantage. In animal form, we are immune to their magic, which is quite advantageous for us. It has always been a point of contention for the witches. One with the ability to perform magic and immunity to it would be considered quite dangerous to them. For that reason, they have always frowned upon relationships between were-animals and witches. The offspring have always been perceived as problems. It has been quite fortunate that children that didn't demonstrate any magical ability seemed to live. The others ..."

"Died," I whispered.

He nodded once.

The moment the question was asked, I wished I hadn't asked it. Sometimes being oblivious to certain horrors was the way to go. "Did they die at birth?"

"No, usually accidents or peculiar illnesses. The witches have always blamed it on coincidence. Odd thing about coincidences: they smell a lot like BS."

I didn't have any more questions. Well, I had plenty, but at that point, each time a layer of this world was peeled away, it never presented something beautiful and alluring. It was always disturbing and morbid. More and more, I wished I could jump out of the rabbit hole and back to a world where all these horrid things just didn't exist.

I closed the door to my room and sat on my bed. I needed a minute. I realized Josh had shut down when discussing the witches' potential involvement. It was a strange place for Josh to be, torn between his inherent loyalty to his brother and expected loyalty to the witches. Did he suspect that his brother was a witch? Was he obligated to divulge such information? If it were ever found to be true, would Ethan all of a sudden become the victim of numerous "coincidences" until one of them actually killed him?

"Are you packed?" Sebastian's baritone voice was a welcome distraction from my bleak thoughts about the world that I was starting to hate. Ethan was right: I was becoming so entangled that exiting it quietly would no longer be an option.

"In a minute." I grabbed the overnight bag out of my closet and started stuffing a few clothes into it.

Sebastian stepped into the room. "We're leaving in ten minutes."

For several uncomfortable minutes he stayed, making small talk, which wasn't a skill he'd mastered. He threw out a couple of random questions and then settled on asking inane ones that I knew he had the answers to. Like most people in the pack, he believed knowledge was power. And he always had a firm hold on it.

His presence was a distraction, and after several minutes, he realized it, too, and eventually stepped out.

There was a change in the air: magic, strong and potent, stifled the room. The platinum stranger's presence was overpowering the large space. He stood just inches from me as he brought his finger to his lips. "Shhh. I thought he would never leave."

The startled gasp slipped out before I could stop it. He'd broken the ward effortlessly, without alerting me or Sebastian. Josh was right. You could feel magic. If I were ever in the presence of this form of it again, I would be able to identify it. There wasn't any denying the unique fingerprint it left, the surge of power that crawled over my skin, pricking at the hairs on my arms.

He bared all his teeth when he smiled. "My amphora," he whispered.

Taking several slow steps backward, the overnight bag clutched close to me, I angled myself just right in order to make an obstructed escape out the door, if necessary.

He rolled his eyes and let out an exasperated sigh. "He ruins everything. We'll talk later."

Then the visitor disappeared just as Sebastian lunged at him, but he only grabbed air. After he erupted in a string of curses, he shouldered my bag and guided me out the door.

"Is that the same person from earlier?" he asked once we were in the car.

I nodded.

The imposed lockdown was a lot more stringent than the night before. Sebastian now was just as concerned about the platinum-haired stranger as he was about Quell. As I moved throughout the house, there was always a were-animal just a few feet from me. I couldn't help but have fun with it. I went to the gym, changed my mind and went to their media room and watched a few episodes of the *Real Housewives of Whatever,* then I went to the kitchen, fixed a sandwich, and took far too long to eat. When I went to the bathroom, I could hear the impatient pacing of a were-dingo as I sat on the edge of the tub and caught up on my reading.

It was a good distraction, but I couldn't help but wonder what a rabid vampire was like. The VAMPIRE book was filled with atrocious acts by vampires, most by newly made ones, but I just couldn't imagine that could ever be Quell.

I had been asleep for a couple of hours when the door of Sebastian's room swung open. His features were more relaxed than they had been in a long time.

"Winter's awake," he informed me, holding the door open for me to leave.

The clock on the nightstand displayed 12:44 p.m. I seemed to be making up for the many sleepless nights.

The door to her room was slightly ajar and Dr. Baker's voice spilled from it with authority and agitation as he scolded her for trying to take out her IVs. "What am I going to do with you?" he finally asked, exasperated.

"I don't know. Bitch at me some more? It's going well so far," she said in a raspy, sluggish voice.

His slender, stern face was flushed, holding that strained look in the immense dichotomy of happiness that she was well but discontent that she was still Winter—strong-willed, antagonistic, and rambunctious.

Her harsh personality didn't deter him from chastising her for a few more minutes while she laid her head against the wall, rolling her eyes.

"If I slip back into a coma, will you stop?"

His lip kinked into a snarl. "Welcome back, Winter," he huffed out, but his face was bright and calm as he breezed past me. "She's her typical pleasant self," he warned.

I slowly walked into the room, and her dark gaze moved in my direction before looking at the mirror on the opposite side of the room.

There was a weird silence. Both our gazes swept across the room as I tried to figure out how to react. I wanted to hug her, but I had a feeling it would have been met with sharp words and probably a sharp hit as well.

"Skylar, can you tell me why I woke up feeling like I was being coddled by a peppermint patty with my hair in these two ridiculous braids?" She tugged at them. "I look like Pippi Longstocking."

"More like Pocahontas."

"Semantics. Why do I have fucking pigtails in my hair?" she snapped. "When someone is unconscious, it doesn't give you permission to play dress up with them."

"You like your hair," I said softly. It was the only thing I'd seen her take time with. "You would have had to cut it if it had matted and become too tangled. I didn't want you to have to do that. Peppermint is strong and alerts the senses. Your room was starting to smell like a hospital. The peppermint covered it."

With her hard, penetrating gaze piercing me and her harsh personality shoving me out the door, it was hard to believe I cared so much.

Her gaze dropped from mine to her hands, where it stayed. "Thank you," she hissed in a barely audible whisper.

I shrugged. "You would have done the same."

Her head jerked up. "No. I wouldn't have."

Wow, what a piece of work. What a tool.

"I'm glad you're okay," I mumbled as I started out the door, ready to get away from the inhospitable snake.

"I'm sorry. I wouldn't have done any of the things you did, but I would have been a jerk because of that," she admitted.

I had just received an apology from Winter. I leaned against the doorframe, bracing myself for the apocalypse that was surely on its way.

She took a deep breath. "So we are allied with the vampires, Ethan's back together with Chris, and you're friends with the Lost One. What else have I missed?" she asked with a small smile, scooting over to make room for me to sit next to her. She patted the bed, urging me to sit.

I filled her in on the fight between Ethan and Josh over Chris, me feeding Quell to stop his reversion, and the strange person who wanted to talk to me. When I finished, her mouth had curled into a small *O*, and for the first time since I had met her, she seemed at a loss for words and shocked.

"What do you mean, you stopped his reversion?" she asked slowly, regarding me with profound intensity, her mouth turned down into an odd frown—she looked worried.

"I fed him and he reverted back." It was an easy concept. I

couldn't understand why Winter, of all people, was having a hard time getting it.

"Skylar, we can't stop a vampire's reversion. Only true humans and—"

Before she could finish, Josh rushed through the door, a broad smile on his face. Hesitating for a brief moment, he pulled her to him, crushing her against him where he held her until she finally pushed him away.

"Okay, I get it. You missed me."

He grabbed one of her braids and held it in his hand. "What's going on with your hair?"

"What's going on with this pack? She's befriending vampires." She jerked her head in my direction. "We're snuggle buddies with Demetrius and his Seethe, and Ethan's back with Chris. I didn't realize I was the glue that held this place together."

"It's not like I—" He stopped abruptly. "I can't have a serious conversation with you looking like this." He started to unravel the braids. Once her hair was loose, he ran his fingers through it a couple of times until the deep waves of raven black cascaded over her shoulders. "Better," he stated.

It was better. Although her face was still pale, her eyes a dark hazel, almost walnut, her lips a little rough and chapped—she still looked more like herself.

Then Josh washed his hands over his face. "I don't know how it happened. We need Demetrius and his Seethe on this. I have no idea what Skylar's doing. And one minute, Chris and Ethan are threatening to kill each other, as usual, and the next, they're back together," he admitted, exasperated.

As they continued to talk, I felt like I was eavesdropping on a conversation between friends. Josh was the type of person who could charm the most hostile, and with Winter, it was very evident. Taking small steps backward, I just couldn't leave without satisfying my curiosity.

"Why can't were-animals stop reversion?" I blurted from the door.

Winter's gaze shifted in Josh's direction as a placid look covered his face. He spoke gently. "It's always been that way. Your blood doesn't seem to be a viable sustenance for them. No one knows why."

He was being very cautious with his information, skating around some truths, hiding something. I wasn't sure why. He went through great lengths to protect me, but omission of information was more harmful than truths.

"But Gavin fed Sable," I pointed out. Winter's eyes widened at the information. She must not have retained everything I had told her while she was unconscious because after it had happened, I couldn't get to her room fast enough to tell her about it.

"Yes, but it wasn't to satisfy a true hunger. It's equivalent to giving someone a candy bar. It fulfills a limbic need, not a nutritional one. Just like a human can't survive on junk food without the risk of malnutrition. They would suffer the same fate."

"The only ones that we are aware of that can stop a reversion are humans, fae, and elves," Winter added.

"With the exception of dark elves," he added.

Dark elves? If any existed, they were so deep in hiding they might as well not. Their ability to cause death of body and mind with merely a touch was considered too big of a threat to be ignored. The elves weren't able to counter or control them. With the help of the witches, they'd been able to contain them. *Contained* was the nice word used in all the books for mass murder of a group of people. It was an agreement among the fae, elves, were-animals, and vampires that they would continue to assist in *containing* this problem.

It left a sordid taste in my mouth, knowing that a person, due to no fault of their own, was sentenced to death because of what they were. Because the abilities they possessed were so powerful and deadly, they couldn't exist.

"Well, you just assumed my mother was a witch. Could she have been a fae and that's the reason I can stop a reversion?" I was reaching, trying to make sense of something, or at the very least, trying to justify another anomaly in me that should not exist.

"Even if I was mistaken and she was a fae, which is highly unlikely because of the spell she did to ensure your survival at birth, it wouldn't change the fact that you are a were-animal," Josh said. His voice dropped and was now low and gentle, as though he was delivering bad news.

But it was Winter's response that surprised me. She was quiet. Concern draped over her face and lingered in her words as she spoke. "Perhaps the biggest thing you should be concerned about is Maya and her presence. She's supposed to be dormant, yet she seems to be anything but. Because of her, you're a were-animal that can do things with magic that even Josh can't, and now we know you're able to bring a vampire back from reversion. How many more things are you able to do that are abnormal for our kind? Most are uncomfortable with anomalies, especially if they prove to be a danger to many. You aren't part of this pack. Still, we will protect these secrets, but our reach is only so long and there is only so much we can do. The vampires are aware of some of your abilities, and once the alliance is over, I question whether or not those things will become a bigger concern to them."

"It will be to their advantage to keep it to themselves. I do not see why it would benefit them to do otherwise," Josh asserted. He had such an ability to swaddle his words with enough confidence and genuineness it was hard not to accept what he said with a fool's blind faith.

As I left, I wanted to believe him, and perhaps he was right. What did they gain by pointing out that little fact? So what? I could stop a vampire from reversion. Once upon a time, were-animals could only change when they were called, and now they could do it at will. Was I just the beginning of things to come? Was it actually confirmed that a were-animal couldn't stop a reversion? As far as I could tell, there wasn't anyone willing to do anything to confirm it.

I walked around the house for a few minutes, my tails just a few feet away, but it was easy to ignore them now. The nagging feeling I had about the platinum stranger wouldn't stop. He wanted to talk, and he was possibly the key to ending this while I remained at the pack's retreat hiding from him and Quell.

Once at Sebastian's door, my tail backed off. The door was slightly ajar. "Come in, Skylar," he said before I could knock.

His hands clasped behind his head, he leaned back in his chair as he glanced periodically at the open laptop, while I tried to read his scribbling on the notepad next to it.

"What?"

Oh Sebastian, you are so polite.

"I'm going home."

He pushed the rolling chair in front of his desk out with his foot. "Sit."

For a long time I stood, refusing to yield so easily to his will. His eyes were hard and uncompromising as the scowl deepened. Sebastian wore his authority so casually that it was hard to ignore.

Is a battle about a chair worth it?

I plopped into it and rolled closer to his desk. "I'm going home," I repeated, putting a little more steel in my voice.

Smug indignation formed a smirk that played at his lips. "Are you?"

I nodded. "He wants to talk, and obviously, he isn't coming here to do so...."

"No. That is not an option," he said as his gaze drifted to the door, an obvious invitation to use it.

Shrugging, I crossed my arms and rested back in the chair. "Okay, tell me how many more of your people need to die before it *is* one. Then let me know."

When he leaned into the table, his perceptive gaze remained on me for a long time before he spoke. "Why would you even consider doing something so dangerous? What are you trying to prove?"

"I have nothing to prove. If he wanted to hurt me, he's had two chances. In fact, many more, because he broke Josh's ward without much of an effort, so if at any time he wanted to hurt me, he could have done it without difficulty."

I saw the same inquiry on Sebastian's face that had crossed my mind many times since yesterday. *Why in the world would he want to speak to me?*

"I am sending Ethan and Steven with you."

"That won't work. Not only will you risk their safety, but I doubt he will be willing to talk with them there."

His chin rested on his fist, and it seemed like he held his breath for eternity as he considered everything. He walked to his storage credenza, opened the drawer, and pulled out a small silver device that he handed to me.

"It's a GPS, better than the one on your phone. We can find you anywhere. Keep it with you at all times, along with your phone."

I nodded. He frowned at the nonverbal response. It was an odd thing about them. They needed to hear, as though some binding agreement was made with your verbal acknowledgment.

"Okay."

"Talk to him, and if at any time you feel you are in danger, get away."

I knew he was offering his version of assistance, but this was plain offensive. Why didn't he just give me step-by-step instructions on the art of communication? Then go over basic life skills: don't walk down dark streets alone, fire is bad, look both ways when crossing the street.

"I know how to survive around dangerous people. I've had a lot of practice."

The amber rolled over his eyes, cold and hard. "You only think you have. Don't fool yourself. You haven't really *dealt* with dangerous people," he rumbled. He pulled another phone, old-school flip, and gave it me. "Keep this, too. My number is already programmed in it. So are Ethan's, Josh's, and Steven's. The moment he contacts you, notify me, preferably by text. I will make sure someone is close. If you feel like you need to bail at any time—do it. Okay?"

"And I shouldn't get in a car with him, and if he offers me candy I should say 'no,' and if he tells me he has a surprise for me and I just have to follow him to the dark alleyway ..." I quipped with a big smile.

He didn't find amusement in my banter. The stony face stared at me, not a hint of a smile.

"How cute. You think that a potentially dangerous situation that could lead to your death is a joking matter. Perhaps I will have a stand-up comedian rather than a priest at your funeral."

I didn't want to fight with him. He was worried about me, and I couldn't decide which was worse, his concern or disdain. Both seemed to teeter along the lines of irrational extremism. "Sebastian, I will be okay. He doesn't want me dead."

It was harder for Sebastian to grasp that than anything else. And perhaps I would have felt the same if I were him. It occupied all my thoughts as well. Why me of all people? It defied all logic and that was probably what was so upsetting.

CHAPTER 13

Whoever said the anticipation of something bad is always worse than the actual event wasn't waiting for the person responsible for killing some of the strongest were-animals and vampires in the country. I was pretty sure meeting him was going to be just as bad as waiting for him for the past three days had been.

The first twenty-four hours, I was relieved when he didn't show up. After forty-eight hours, I just wanted it to be over. Now, nearing the third day, I was a nervous wreck. Was he playing with me? Did he want me high-strung and agitated so I wouldn't think clearly? And most of all, why me? Of all the people he could have spoken with, why did he choose me? The constant analysis of it was giving me a stress headache with an intense gnawing, aching, tugging that was nearly driving me insane.

It started in the early morning and became progressively worse. It no longer felt like a headache. It was an unbearable tug. It felt like I was being pulled, a strong polarized jerk. I eventually realized it really wasn't just a headache, but someone calling me. Something had called me in this manner the year before and nothing good had come from the situation. I had found myself bound to an evil book that left me marked, forcing me to turn against the pack, and ultimately leading to Ethan stabbing me in the chest. No, I wasn't going to answer any force that called psychically or through any mystical means. *You want to talk, pick up a phone.*

But the gnawing persisted to the point that I couldn't function. My mind was unfocused, my head pulsated, and my body ached to respond. *Damn!*

Surrendering to it, I walked outside, got into my car, and drove, following the directions of the caller. My body was on autopilot. When the pull dwindled to a mild ache, I found myself in front of Quell's home.

He lay on the sofa, his body molded to the upholstery, in a state of exhaustion. He looked horrible: gaunt face, sunken eyes, tattered, dirty clothing. If it weren't for the soft sounds he made, I would have thought he was dead.

"Quell, what happened?" I asked, kneeling next to him.

"What are you doing here?" he asked in a hoarse whisper, making a poor attempt to sit up.

"You called me here."

He fell silent as he closed his eyes. Calling his name several times, I waited quietly for him to respond. Then I shook him, startling him awake.

"Go. I didn't mean to do it." His voice was weak, barely audible as he draped his arm across his face to shield his eyes from the light I had turned on. Dark bruising surrounded his wrist where he had been bound.

"What happened to you?" I asked.

"Michaela," he whispered through dry, chapped lips, laying his head back. He had been punished. Vampires punished their own through starvation and sensory deprivation, locking them away in a plain wooden casket, so heavily secured that escape was impossible.

"Why?" Knowing Michaela, it might have been for numerous

things, including not being crazy or malicious enough. I didn't expect a response. His eyes closed again and even the slight act of repositioning himself on the couch was an arduous task. He needed to feed.

I hurried to get him the Hidacus. Shards of glass and shaved metal were scattered at the end of the walkway leading to the greenhouse. And I was met with the noxious scent of sulfur and scorched material filling the air. Detail had gone into destroying the greenhouse. The beautiful flowers remained untouched, but would inevitably die without care and shelter. Parts of the greenhouse remained intact, while the side near the Hidacus was demolished. Portions of the plant had been ripped into shreds and the rest burned. The scorched branches that lay scattered about the destroyed room smelled like burnt flesh. The putrid odor of necrosis was sickening. I backed into the house, shaking my head, unable to fully grasp the maliciousness of the act. She had starved him and taken away his preferred means of nourishment. I had never been under any delusions that Michaela wasn't cruel. I just wasn't aware to what extent.

I went to Quell and could barely meet his dull gaze to tell him. But the look of desolation that fanned over his face made it apparent that he knew. It was at least six hours before he could go out to feed, and he looked so weak I doubted he could do it successfully. The vampires had a garden, a group of people who existed to feed them as needed. If I dropped him off at the Seethe's home, could he use one of them? But if that were an option, they wouldn't have left him here like this.

"I can help you," I said in a low voice, barely able to control it from trembling. "But what happened the other day can't happen again." If I was able to bring him back from reversion without losing too much blood, then feeding him shouldn't be a problem.

He jerked his head away when I placed my wrist near his lips.

"Just do it," I commanded in an exasperated voice, pushing my wrist closer to his lips.

With a great deal of effort, he pushed himself up, his eyes wide with apprehension. "You're the reason for this," he accused, shoving me away.

I sat back on my heels trying to process the information, feeling a brand-new pang from the guilt. "You were punished because of me?"

He nodded slowly. "Michaela had claimed you. I shouldn't have fed from you."

"It was to save your life!"

"It doesn't matter."

I hated how defeated he sounded. I couldn't decide what infuriated me most: the fact that Michaela had claimed me or that she was punishing Quell for saving his life and putting his needs above her desires. There wasn't enough hate in me to direct toward her. My anger was escalating into something so fierce that streaks of fire blushed against my cheeks. Unable to compartmentalize it appropriately, I lashed out. "Well, why don't you just tell that psychotic bitch I would sooner slit my wrists and bleed out before I would share a drop with her. You let her know that if she ever comes near me there isn't anything I will not be willing to do to make sure she never does it again and make sure it's the most painful thing she has ever experienced in her existence."

He was silent for a long time as he sank deeper into the sofa. Weak and exhausted, he seemed subdued to a point of no return. Based on the bruising, it didn't look as though he had conceded willingly to his punishment.

Forcing control of my anger and annoyance, I focused my attention back on him. "Is there someone else who can feed you?"

He shook his head slowly. It must have been like standing on the edge of a precipice, torn between loving a creator who was cruel, merciless, and unworthy of love, or denying it but being compelled to do so. He revered her, loved her solely because she had brought him into this world, this life, made him something other than human, the very thing he loathed. She hadn't earned it or deserved it, yet he gave it freely. It made me nauseous.

We sat in a long, uncomfortable silence. I moved closer and waited until his gaze met mine. "It's because of me this happened. Let me make it right."

I placed my wrist close to his lips, but he hesitated. "Take what you need to be strong enough to hunt at dusk."

The hunger lingered along his lips and eyes, yet he struggled adamantly to deny the urge. His self-imposed torment brought a sneer to his face.

"This is between us. No one will ever know. I promise."

Before I could finish my sentence, fangs sank into my flesh and his fingers wrapped around my wrist, gripping it roughly. You couldn't prepare yourself for the pain of sharp enamel searing through your flesh, no matter how you tried. I cringed, making long sibilant hisses the entire time.

He was careful, stopping periodically to gauge how I was doing. When he finally finished, he lay back against the couch, eyes closed. Pale fingers wiped across his lips, removing the rivulet of blood before brushing the remains on his pants.

"Thank you," he finally said. He opened his eyes, now an odd crimson, and met mine. He stood and went to his refrigerator as I wrestled with the urge to laugh at the image of a vampire peeking into one.

As he rummaged through the fridge, I realized the only reason he had food was for the person who tended his greenhouse. With the smell of necrotic flesh and sulfur still wafting through the air, my curiosity bested me.

"What happened to your gardener?" I asked when he returned with a glass of orange juice. His gaze swept to the hallway that had once led to his greenhouse. He shrugged. Just as I did, he probably assumed he was destroyed along with all the contents.

The thought of it made me sick to my stomach. "How can you not be angry with her?" I finally asked after taking several drinks from the glass, becoming acutely aware of his intense gaze on me, an odd blend of hunger and abhorrence.

"Why? It was just."

"No, it wasn't just. It was cruel and unnecessary. She punished you for saving your life, as though it wasn't worth saving. She's a vile monster unworthy of loyalty or your devotion!" I couldn't help but yell at him as he treated my rage as inconsequential, dismissing it with a plaintive smile.

"I should clean up. Will you stay?"

I shook my head and finished the juice. *No, I have to go home and wait for a psycho killer to show up—and talk.* "I can't." My body felt stiff and my wrist throbbed, a small inferno rising from the marks left.

"I should remove them."

I looked down at the two puncture marks and shook my head. "It will heal." Him feeding from me was bad enough, but closing the wounds seemed too intimate, crossing the obscure line I had drawn. "Don't call me anymore. It hurts if I try to ignore it," I stated, turning to him before I left.

He nodded slowly. "I will try. I'm not skilled at controlling it. You are my first—" He stopped abruptly. An acrid expression shadowed his face. "You're the first person I've had a blood connection with other than Michaela." He stared at what I was sure was a look of unadulterated disgust on my face; I held his attention for a long moment before he spoke. "But for you, I will try," he said.

I let out a string of curses as I pulled up to my house and found Steven's car parked in my driveway. I took the air freshener from the glove compartment and sprayed it on me until it was empty. Then I crossed my arm over my chest, hiding the bruising on my forearm.

Of course Josh would have told him how to disarm my ward. Most simple ones could be broken by were-animals, but the one Josh had created was far from simple and required a key word to disarm, which only Josh and now Steven knew.

He was sitting on the couch, arms crossed, and scowling when I opened the front door. Well, that answered whether he had duplicated the key.

"Eight missed calls, Sky," he growled through clenched teeth as I walked into the house. He tossed the phone to me. I barely caught it before it hit the ground. "You left the house without the GPS or your phone. The reason better be really good."

His tone was so rough and hard, I couldn't believe it was coming from him.

When I didn't respond, he walked toward me. Leaning in, he inhaled deeply, and then frowned. "Vampire and … what's that, citrus? Ah, refreshing." His cherub appearance hardened by the rueful scorn, he examined my neck, and relaxed a little. It wasn't until he looked at my arm that the anger returned, quickly squelched by frustration and dismay.

"It's not what you think," I refuted, pulling my hand away.

"Then tell me what it is. From the looks of it, you're feeding vampires. You want to tell me why?"

I didn't answer. I didn't know where to begin even if I wanted to tell him.

"Do you enjoy it?"

The longer it took me to answer, the harsher the creases turned down into a frown of disappointment. His hands washed over his face but didn't wipe away the emotions on it. "I'm not sure what is going on, but I hope you do. If things get bad, which I have a feeling they will, I can't help you—I won't," he said.

"It'll be fine." I stated it so confidently that I started to believe it myself. Steven wouldn't understand why my guilt made me feel responsible for Quell. I didn't quite understand it myself.

Quell's predicament was my fault. Perhaps he would have

preferred an end to his life rather than feed off the horrid blood of humans—or a mostly human. Maybe he was suicidal and too cowardly to take his own life. As the many thoughts whirled around in my head, compounding the guilt, I forced them aside. There were more pressing things to be obsessed about.

He gave me a wry smile and shook his head. "Let's hope so." He pulled out his phone and pressed a button. "She's here," he stated in a dry voice.

"Where the hell was she?" Sebastian's angry voice barked over the speaker.

Steven simply handed me the phone.

"Hello," I responded awkwardly, preparing myself for his castigation. Instead, I was met with silence—a long, uncomfortable silence.

"Where were you?" His deep baritone voice was commanding in a manner that was hard to ignore.

"I had something personal I needed to handle."

"Personal, like what?"

"If I wanted you to know I would have given you the particulars," I stated in the mildest tone. Poking the bear, or rather the irritated wolf, was unnecessary at this time.

How easily he slipped into that businesslike mode when necessary, latent with authority. This wasn't personal. It was about the pack and their protection and nothing else mattered.

"Skylar, I didn't give you this job—you requested it. If you want to bail, fine, but don't just flake. Honor your obligation as we always have with you," he stated.

I think I would have preferred if he yelled, screamed, and cursed me. Instead, he was disappointed and, for some reason, that bothered me. "Whatever obligations I commit to, I keep."

There wasn't any other rebuttal I could give. I doubted it would help if I told him the real situation. I had chosen Quell over my obligation to them, and there wouldn't be any redemption for that. The empathy and commitment I felt toward Quell would not be easily understood by him or anyone else in the pack.

I was unable to meet Steven's gaze as I handed back his phone, and he seemed to be at a loss for words as he walked out the door.

"Be careful" was the only thing he said before he closed the door behind him. His suggestion had more to do with Quell than my future meeting with the psycho that wanted to talk.

By the fifth day, I was tired of waiting and was about to give up when three abrupt knocks at my door ended the anxiety. Odd, amethyst-colored eyes stared back at me from the peephole. The platinum blond stranger was back.

"May I come in?" he asked through the door.

Did I really have a choice? If he wanted in, he was more than capable of letting himself in.

"If I said no?" I asked, testing the situation. He was calm and pleasant, which was more troubling. Calm crazies were by far the worst.

He chortled. "Then I will send my creatures out again. First, they will start with the coyote. He hangs around here a lot. You'd miss him terribly. Then I will send them after the snake, to finish the job. And the gorgeous redhead, the jaguar. I won't be so merciful this time. Then you can let me know which wolf you want to die first. I'll keep going until you feel a little more hospitable," he stated in a neutral yet terribly sadistic voice.

"Well, since you asked so nicely, please come in."

I sent Sebastian a quick text: "He's here." Then I whispered the words to disarm the ward and stepped aside.

Taking several steps back, I distanced myself until I was sitting on the couch several feet from him.

He walked confidently in front of me, periodically giving me what I suspected was his most charismatic smile. The steely glare I returned didn't seem to have any effect on him. He continued to wander throughout the room, taking slow, methodical steps and finding amusement in something he chose not to share with me. Somehow, I managed to remain calm as the lunatic made himself at home, taking a seat in the chair next to the couch. I inched around to face him.

"Finally, we meet again." He paused, raising his chin toward the air as though he were appreciating a welcoming breeze in a stifling room.

I had a peculiar, eccentric, raging psychopath in my home. *Can this go anywhere but downhill from here?*

I was nervous, running my fingers lightly over the screen of my phone, prepared to press the speed dial for Sebastian. Yet that didn't really give me any relief, either.

"We've met before?" I asked casually, shelving my uneasiness to appear more confident. Predators never responded well to anxiety or fear.

"Am I that forgettable, *amphora*?" he asked with a smirk. He stood up and continued pacing the living room.

I sent Sebastian another text: "I'm okay." I had a feeling if I didn't give him updates, a pack of were-animals would be busting through the door before I could get any useful information.

"How could I forget the werewolf that snatched my magic from one of my servants and nearly forced me out as though I were powerless? I enjoyed being linked to such untapped power."

The realization of who he was had me coming up with an escape plan fast. Ethos, the strongest purveyor of dark magic, was in my living room. I remembered that day well. I didn't take his magic from him. He had relinquished it willingly, allowing the full force of it to consume me, and if it hadn't been for Josh, I am sure it would have killed me.

When I first met him, he was a dark-scaled creature with horrid dark eyes. There wasn't anything human or humanlike about him. If given a thousand guesses, I never would have guessed this was him sitting in my living room. I glanced at the door several times, contemplating running. But if I had learned anything from every slasher flick ever made, the girl never makes it to the door.

He smiled when I looked at the door again. "If I wanted you hurt, rest assured, you would have known this by barely being alive. Please, have a seat. We have a great deal to discuss."

I stood. I wasn't going to run, but having him towering over me while I sat made me feel even more uncomfortable—trapped.

"You are quite the complex little vessel of magic. I can only imagine your potential. Good potential that I plan to use," he stated with delighted amusement as he made himself comfortable in the chair, relaxing back against it. His gaze shone with avid interest.

After a long moment of silence, I still couldn't help contemplating running out of the room as if an axe-wielding psycho were chasing me. I finally asked impatiently, "What do you want?"

He waved his hand toward the chair in front of him. "I want you to have a seat and stop being rude." A hint of frost lingered in his words.

I sat on the ottoman placed kitty-corner from the door and close to the window instead. If things went too badly, at least I had two quick exits.

Sighing heavily, he forced a smile. "That Josh has quite a temper. You should have seen how scared my poor little Pala was. She was nearly in tears when I asked her to return my magic. She actually refused me because she needed it to protect herself from your boyfriend."

"I can't believe Josh would get riled over a little thing like Pala betraying him, attempting to steal his magic, and then trying to kill him. How dreadful, a clear overreaction," I said sarcastically.

The amused smile on his face was dwindling. "She was quite ambitious, always wanting more. She was my most talented servant."

Was?

"My little run-in with you was quite an eye-opener. I was expunged by a novice. It was quite embarrassing. I had spread myself too thin, sharing my gifts with so many. Over the years, I traded reverence and worship for my power. You helped me realize that I can be celebrated and adulated without the sacrifice."

Does this soliloquy have an end? Get to the point already.

Sensing my impatience, he straightened, his face taking on a severe look. "The were-animals and vampires are like overactive children, running around aimlessly, fighting and vying for dominance. Sebastian is limited by his rules and structure, Demetrius by his impulses and desires. They need direction and a real leader."

"And you think you should be that person?" I asked incredulously.

"Of course. I should be revered for what I am, and they need to be controlled. A logical choice, don't you think?"

"And you think the way to gain that is by killing their people? Did you consider that would just really enrage them? I can assure you that showing you reverence is the furthest thing from their minds."

"The first ones were to make a point."

"Ever tried an Edible Arrangement? Those things really get your attention. They're fruit carved into cute little flowers. For a little extra, they can dip them in chocolate. They're the best. I just love them."

He chuckled and then clasped his hands in front of him. "On any given day, who is the most feared is a toss-up between the were-animals and the vamps, and they are a force. Sebastian, unlike Demetrius, could turn to the South for assistance. I took care of that, and now they are on equal playing fields. I've destroyed the Southern Pack and killed a substantial number of the Northern Seethe. They are weakened. If I continue, how feared do you think they will be when they don't have the numbers to make them a threat? Do they think they will continue to enjoy the luxuries of their power?"

I didn't have an answer. Instead, I listened as the psychopath laid out his well-constructed plan. Dealing with a psychopath was always difficult, but one with a plan was scary as hell.

Ethos seemed very interested in the appearance of his nails. He said, "The elves and witches are considering an alliance, are you aware of that? How hard will it be for them to subjugate a fractured power? The vampires are immune to fae and elven magic, the were-animals to the witches'. Apart, they are at a disadvantage. Together they are a force that most will not deny. But they are too foolish and arrogant to form a lasting alliance that will be invincible. They are in need of direction and a real leader."

"Again, you think it should be you?" I chuckled, an inappropriate burst of laughter that filled the air, sparked by nervousness and the pure absurdity of the situation. "For argument's sake, let's say they submit, and you become … president, prime minister, CEO, king, the big cheese, or whatever of the otherworld—"

"Lord," he interjected.

Is he kidding me? Lord of the vampires and were-animals? Wow, that is what you call a mega ego!

"Then what?"

"Everyone else will follow. With them under my control, the elves wouldn't stand a chance, and the fae would submit without much of a fight. Then the witches will have no choice but to follow. I need them because they have something that belongs to me that I would like back."

He wanted to be lord of the otherworld because the witches stole from him. What an overreaction!

"Why are you talking to me? Go call Demetrius and Sebastian and tell them your plan. Perhaps they will think it's a good idea and submit upon request. Clearly they would see that you are more qualified to lead than they are." I grinned, an attempt to soften my acrid words.

He smiled, baring his teeth like weapons. "I would like to keep you alive because you will prove to be very useful to me, but I will accept the loss if you can't control your tongue."

I inhaled a sharp breath at the beautifully worded threat on my life. "What do you want with me?"

"You will serve as my representative. Make them see that surrender is their only choice. I know you can do this."

I was too astounded to answer. Where was he getting his information from, Wikipedia? Demetrius still referred to me as "that pup." He held me in so little regard that he didn't even bother to learn my name. Sebastian saw me as a problem that had fallen into his lap and had proven to be nothing more than just that. And this egomaniac thought they would listen to me.

"Although you consort with them, you are not part of their pack and you seem to have established a working relationship with the vampires as well."

A relationship with one vampire among many was a "working relationship"? *Yep, he is definitely getting his information from Wikipedia.*

He delivered this as though he hadn't grasped the ridiculousness of his plan.

"You are bonded to both. They know your power, and they will listen," he asserted confidently.

He quickly came to his feet, his gaze unyielding and hard. "You have three days. If they don't concede willingly, then ..." His voice trailed off in an unspoken threat.

"They will not listen to me. Coming from me, it will be ignored. You want it to be considered, then you should meet with Demetrius and Sebastian."

He laughed. "You know a meeting between us would not be nearly as pleasant. How would anything be addressed with them looking for any and every opportunity to destroy me? No, I would rather not deal with such unpleasantness during a meeting."

Fine, deal with this truth bomb. "They'd rather die than be led by anyone other than themselves. They don't continue to fight for their leadership to hand it over to someone like a candy bar on Halloween. They would consider a brutal death more admirable than being considered a feckless and superable leader by submitting to you."

"It would be an easier transition if they did, but I am fine with getting rid of them if necessary." He shrugged his indifference. "You have three days."

"I will need more time," I blurted as he headed out the door. Days? I needed years, maybe even a decade or two, if he expected me to do this.

"No, three days. They either concede willingly or by force."

Great, I get to deliver that information. It must be Christmas.

CHAPTER 14

The large open space of the living room at the pack's retreat seemed smaller as I sat surrounded by an angered Ethan and Sebastian, an enraged Michaela and Demetrius, and an appalled Josh and Chris. As expected, they weren't handling Ethos's demands well.

When the yelling started, I wondered when someone was going to point out the old adage that you shouldn't shoot the messenger. No one did. Instead, I was tasked with answering a barrage of questions, which I couldn't possibly do. I listened for a long time as they made insults and incited threats directed at Ethos that he would never hear because I was his messenger, absorbing the rage that was rightfully his.

"Three days? I want him dead now," Michaela hissed angrily. Her typical lithe movements and graceful steps were reduced to stomps as she pounded across the floor. She was just short of throwing a tantrum. I had a feeling when she said she wanted someone dead, three days was as good as an eternity.

"How do we kill him?" Sebastian asked Josh.

Josh's eyes widened, shocked to the point of silence. After several long moments he spoke. "You want to know how to kill one of the rulers of dark magic who has existed longer than anyone in this room?" he asked in amazement.

"Doesn't mean he can't be killed. Just means no one has figured out how," Demetrius added.

Josh looked as though he had been slapped. They were asking him to go up against someone who had been practicing magic when his great-grandmother was probably just discovering she was a witch.

"He's no longer sharing his magic. He's at his strongest," I reiterated, since they were behaving as though they didn't hear me tell them that the first time when I had recapped my conversation with Ethos the psycho king.

"Can his magic be taken?" Ethan asked Josh.

Frustrated, Josh snapped at his brother, "If it was that easy, don't you think it would have been done years ago? Ethos has more enemies than the pack and the Seethe combined. There's a reason people don't screw with him."

"Then kill his creatures and the magic dies with him," Demetrius suggested.

Josh rolled his eyes. "Are you even paying attention? At the first sign of fatal injury, he retrieves his creatures for the magic to be returned. We are not dealing with an amateur here."

The room was getting heated with frustration and anxiety. Two of the most powerful groups in the otherworld rendered powerless. It was a hard hit to their egos, and they were having a difficult time dealing with it. Their limited knowledge of magic and ridiculous suggestions were only making a frustrating situation worse for Josh.

They were too focused on him and their anger that no one noticed or even cared when I slipped out to go to the library. Ethos had called me an *amphora*, which, when I Googled it, meant nothing more than a vase with two handles. There had to be more because he seemed very intrigued that I was one.

Chris was already in there, sitting on the table. Several books were sprawled around her, one in her hand as she perused the pages. She didn't seem to be looking for anything in particular, just browsing. She glanced in my direction, giving me a quick sweeping look before returning her attention back to the book. Whether we were standing next to each other or down the hall, it always seemed like there was an impenetrable wall that divided us. I didn't like her, and pretending I did just wasn't an option, but I had a feeling it was mutual. I stood at the door for a few minutes looking in her direction, building up the nerve to talk to her. Like her or not, she was knowledgeable. "What's an amphora?" I finally asked.

"A container," she responded dismissively without looking up from her book.

"I don't need the definition. I want to know what it really is. What does it mean to you?"

Distant hazel eyes briefly met mine before directing their attention back to her book. "It's an amphora because of the two handles on opposite sides. In the world of magic, the opposites seem to always have a common goal, to control which direction the amphora goes. The amphora is nothing, its contents ineffectual. It's the handle that has the real power and inevitably controls the contents. They never work together, always antipodes of each other: good and evil, light and dark." Her gaze lifted, watching me with intent curiosity. She spoke in a cool, neutral voice. "Interesting question. Is there a reason?"

I shrugged. "Just curious."

Her perceptive gaze stayed focused on me as she tossed the book aside and stood. "Did you ever find out why the vampires were able to use you for the ritual and not the others?" she inquired. That remained one of the things that made me a true anomaly, among my other odd things. The transference ritual that Demetrius wanted to use me for had been tried, unsuccessfully, on other were-animals. No one knew why the vampires assumed it would work on me. But because they went through such lengths to abduct me, Josh remained positive that they had irrefutable knowledge that it would.

I couldn't seem to escape her probing stare no matter how I wandered the room. Shaking my head I responded, "No."

Her full lips pressed into an unconvinced smile. "You don't lie as well as the others."

"If the handles never gain control of the contents, then what?"

She crossed her arms as a hint of a smile crossed her lips. "It's destroyed. Its only purpose is to act as a container. If it serves no purpose, then why should it exist?"

"So it just what—implodes, dies, vanishes from existence? What happens to it?"

She smiled. Did that mean I had some purpose and if it wasn't fulfilled, I was going to die or vanish? I didn't want to even consider that aspect of me imploding. Why didn't she elaborate? But I knew why as she studied me closely, assessing my reaction, questioning the motivations for my questioning. I hated this game of cat and mouse. I turned my back to her and focused my attention on the bookcase. I wasn't giving her any more information than she already had.

Josh entered. His presence broke the subtle tension that wavered between us. He was distracted and mumbling things under his breath, forced into a zone that left his mind in hyperdrive. His frustration level was off the charts, and it was something he wasn't skilled at hiding. Pulling books off the shelf, he just seemed to be tossing them randomly onto the table.

"What are you looking for?" Chris finally asked.

He continued throwing books on the table, too distracted to offer an answer. If we stayed in the room for a week with no sleep, food, or bathroom breaks, we never would get through the stack he had placed on the table.

"Relyn was the closest thing to ever exist that had power equal to Ethos's. Ask London how he died," Chris offered.

He stopped looking at the various titles of the books he placed on the table and focused his attention on her. "Why don't *you* tell me?" he responded in a dark, pithy tone.

They held each other's gaze for a long time. The passive looks spoke volumes as Josh subtlety challenged her and she submitted. But I wasn't sure why. I gathered that everything she did had a purpose and a carefully planned agenda. Was she offering the information to curry favor, or was it an acceptance of the challenge to display the depth of her knowledge?

"Marcia used the *Aufero* to capture his magic and then killed him. She's not nearly as harmless as people believe."

Josh hadn't learned the gift of stoicism. His face always displayed his emotions, no matter how slight. The knowledge that Marcia, one of the leaders of the Creed, the governing body for the witches, wasn't harmless didn't seem like new information. But the Aufero seemed to not only shock him but left him disconcerted. "The orb was destroyed—"

"It was supposed to have been destroyed when she gained possession of it nearly thirty years ago because it was being abused. It was intended to be used to punish your kind, which, in theory, was a splendid idea. It served well for that purpose, but then they started to abuse it to threaten the witches, coerce favors and behaviors. It was agreed that it needed to be destroyed, but do you really believe that it was? Marcia would never destroy something so powerful." Chris studied him. She smirked. "You know that's how she operates. If it's powerful and able to be controlled by her, it serves her purpose and remains. If it doesn't, then it is destroyed. Perhaps you should remember that, because I believe she regards you in the same manner."

His gaze was distant but he was reluctantly intrigued. "If the Creed has it, then where are they keeping it?"

She shrugged a response. I wasn't sure if she was lying or not. Unfortunately, she seemed to be as skilled as Ethan at keeping a look of apathy and making sure her vitals, movements, and voice never betrayed her. I didn't know why the

Aufero wasn't destroyed, but I knew where it was hidden. Well, not exactly. When we were in the dark realm last year, looking for the Gem of Levage, I had seen it. I assumed that it was the orb they were speaking of. At the time, I didn't know what it was used for, but since someone was hiding it using dark magic, I knew it wasn't good. The Creed guarded and controlled natural magic. I wasn't sure how they had used dark magic to hide such a thing. And, most importantly, why were they hiding it from their own?

I wanted to say something, to share the information, but as Josh's gaze lingered over Chris, it seemed as though he were trying to categorize her as friend or foe.

After long consideration, it looked like he had made a decision, but I wasn't sure which way he leaned. As he studied her through narrowed eyes, it was apparent that he wasn't happy with her level of knowledge.

With a half-smile, she matched his drilling gaze. She quickly pulled her attention from him to focus on Winter, who stood at the door. She looked better: a sun-kissed golden hue had returned to her face, her long charcoal hair was pulled back into a sleek ponytail, and her lips were glossed, showing no hints of the cracks and bluish discoloration that had been present just days before. Signs of fatigue and burden were still etched around her eyes. They were different now, holding the mild signs of defeat that made her appear softer, subdued. Her movements were lumbering and purposeful, without the smooth grace I had become used to.

When Chris had interacted with Josh, her features had been lax, displaying a warmth that I suspected was just camouflage. Now, she looked hard and keenly focused on Winter.

"You look well. I'm glad to see that you're doing better," Chris acknowledged in an overly cloying voice.

"Your concern is duly noted," said Winter.

Chris's head tilted, feigning faux sympathy. "You're the last one I would have thought to have been broken so easily. You've become quite fragile over the years. It's a good thing that Ethan would move heaven and earth to protect you."

"It's a good thing he's never had to."

"Well, now that he knows how delicate you are, things will have to change. Perhaps Sebastian can provide you with a bodyguard or something."

Winter's face was clamped so tight I thought it was going to shatter into tiny pieces. Pulling herself together, she forced a weak grin. "I would love to give you the opportunity to try to break me." If she wasn't just days from being out of a coma and still recovering from extensive wounds, that opportunity would have been now. Being a lesser species had its disadvantages, one being that they didn't heal as quickly as the others. Joan was doing well. One look at her, and you would have never suspected that less than three weeks before she had been moments from death.

Winter pulled her attention from Chris to look at Josh. "Your brother has horrible taste in women."

Chris shifted, placing an intense focus on Winter, bitterly roving over every inch of her. The chilling disdain was hard to ignore.

I had no idea why there was so much animosity between Chris and Winter. Perhaps they each felt the other vied for the position of queen bitch. Surely, they could share. Monday, Wednesday, and Friday, Chris could have it, and Winter could take the throne Tuesday, Thursday, and Saturday. On Sunday, they both could give it a rest.

Last year, Ethan had sent Winter after Chris when he found out she was working with the vampires. It didn't end well for Chris, and she still seemed to be harboring anger about it.

Chris bit down on her lip, but whatever she wanted to say was fighting its way to the surface, urging a release. It was then, at that tense moment, that Ethan stepped in, took one look at Winter and Chris glaring at each other in overt enmity, and looked as though he wanted to step back out. He didn't appear to want to be there any more than anyone else as his attention bounced back and forth between the two. The hostility was palpable, the revulsion undeniable. It was escalating to a whirlwind that would not be easily contained. Just when it seemed as though they were ready to give in to it, Kelly sauntered in, all smiles and ebullience.

"Here you are," she said to Winter. "Dr. Baker was about to send out a search party. You may be back to your old self, but he will not give up the chance to mother hen you some more. Just go humor him for me, will you? If not, I'll have to endure his ten-minute speech about how no one in this pack appreciates how hard he works and how everybody takes his talents for granted. Please don't make me listen to that speech again," she mused with a bright smile.

Winter eventually pulled her gaze from Chris and started to follow Kelly down the long hall but didn't seem to be able to leave before taking several more glances in Chris's direction and then giving Ethan a brutally harsh look. His lips pursed together, forming a thin line as his gaze lingered on her for a surprisingly long time.

Winter rolled her eyes away from him and disappeared down the hall behind Kelly. If this had occurred with anyone else, it would have been considered a challenge. Ethan and Winter's relationship was different. He had once said that they understood each other. I didn't know what that meant, but for some reason, the same rules didn't seem to apply with them.

After Winter left, Chris didn't seem to want to be near Ethan and couldn't get out of the pack's house fast enough. The moment her car sped out of the driveway, Josh guided me out of the house, and forty minutes later, we were outside London's home again.

He knocked and after several more went unanswered, he took out his phone to call her when the door swung open. "If this isn't a social visit, then you should just turn around and leave," she snapped.

He sighed, exasperated. "You know I wouldn't be here if it weren't important," he said quickly as she attempted to close the door in his face.

"It's always important. You keep hanging out with them, it will always be life-threatening and important. I know Ethan's your brother, but it doesn't mean you have to get involved with pack business. And now I hear you're dealing with the vampires, too. Whatever you're involved in, leave me out of it," she continued in a poignant tone as she attempted to close the door.

Grabbing the edges of it, he held it open. "More people are going to die if you don't help."

He nudged his way in, bringing me with him. "Please, just hear me out."

Stepping aside, she directed a cold glare at him that wasn't belied by the welcoming scent of honeysuckle from the candle burning in the far corner of the room. The lights were dimmed, and she had four small cauldrons sitting out on the table that she used during our earlier visit. It looked as though she had been practicing her magic. I'd known Josh almost a year, and with the exception of helping me use his magic, I wasn't aware of him ever practicing.

"This thing is a mess. I need you involved," he said.

She rolled her eyes. "You know why no one bothers me about magic except you? It's because I remain anonymous, and I go to great lengths to keep it that way."

"Pala's dead," Josh blurted.

London swallowed, and sorrow rolled over her. Her lips meshed firmly together and, for a long time, she was silent. No matter how she attempted to conceal the grief, it marred her features.

"It was only a matter of time," she stated in a despondent voice as her eyes fluttered, batting back the tears that had started to swell. When one managed to fall, she brushed it away quickly.

"It was Ethos," Josh continued in a mild voice. "You two were friends—best friends at one time. I need you involved."

"Friends? That was a long time ago, before she got caught up in that ..." Her voice trailed off, her words clipped by a suppressed sob. She started to pace, shaking her head slowly. "If Ethos, the were-animals, and the vampires are involved, this is something I need to stay away from—far away from."

"Do you seriously think he will just stop at the were-animals and vampires? You aren't that naïve."

London lifted her chin, meeting his intense eyes, seemingly unmoved by his entreaty as though she felt she would go unharmed, unidentified. In the world of magic, some would consider her barely worth mentioning. Her magic wasn't as strong as Josh's, but she was far more skilled than he was, which would make her a target. It was something that could not and would not be ignored.

Her face was laden with unyielding defiance. She wasn't going to help. "No."

"You don't want to be the person who could have helped but didn't," he informed her in a low, frustrated rumble. The determined look on her face disappeared as fear and apprehension emerged. I wasn't sure if it was the idea of making enemies of Demetrius and Sebastian or the repercussions of Ethos gaining more power that frightened her, but she was afraid.

She crossed her arms over her chest, and her lips tightened into a thin line. He hadn't changed her mind. She wasn't going to get involved.

Josh exhaled heavily. "When you needed our help, we did so without question. Why are you being like this?"

"Because last year I almost died repaying that favor. Or did you forget I was the one you asked to disenchant the Gem of Levage? You think I don't realize the severity of this? A few days ago, you brought me unsourced blood from a Tre'ase. Things couldn't get any better from there. Why can't you just leave me alone?" She paced nervously in the small foyer.

"If I had other choices—"

"You had other choices! When you were screwing around during training, you had a choice. When I offered to teach you three years ago, you blew me off every chance you had. There was your choice! Now look at you. You have me anchored to you, dragging me down with you. I am not an ally to the pack, I owe them nothing—I owe *you* nothing." She was flushed, her lips trembled lightly, and I could hear the rapid beats of her heart. Her fear matched her anger.

Josh bit down hard on his lips and his eyes withdrew, wounded by her explosive reaction. An uncomfortable silence chilled the room as they stared at each other. It was quite apparent that their friendship had never suffered a disagreement let alone succumbed to something as tumultuous as this.

He chewed on the nail bed of his finger as his gaze drifted away from hers to the floor. It was when frustration had gotten the best of them, him washing his hands across his face and London brushing at the hair that had fallen over her eyes, that I noticed they had similar body art on the inside of their forearms. Nearly identical tribal art covered a small area just above their wrists. The design was too unique to be a mere coincidence. Was this more than just a quarrel between friends, but rather a fight between lovers, ex-lovers?

London leaned against the wall, her right leg bent back propped against it as she exhaled, "What do you need?"

Josh went over everything that had occurred over the past weeks including the use of genums to make the creatures, them disappearing when injured, the self-inflicted injury by the other creature when he tried to source the magic, Ethos's plans to become lord of the otherworld and pursue his vendetta with the witches over an object they possessed that he desired.

She listened quietly, and her anger and fear transitioned into something far worse. Her skin blanched, and she looked as though she were going to be sick.

"That unsourced Tre'ase blood explains why Ethos could make such small creatures shift into larger, stronger things," she said as she started pacing again. "Tre'ases have the ability to shift and change appearances and with access to their blood, Ethos has that magical ability, too, and must be using it to manipulate the way the genums shift. This is so bad. You're not dealing with an amateur, Josh. I'm sure he's planned this for a long time." She shook her head, her voice weighted with concern. "You're messing with things beyond your capabilities."

"I know," he acknowledged. "What options do I have?"

Frowning, she glanced in his direction again before she left the room and returned with a silver rod with a smoky, lambent glow. "It's a *capsa*." She looked at it, face bitter with concern. "Magic isn't easily destroyed when the source is still alive, but it can be contained. If the capsa is in a closer proximity than Ethos when one of his creatures is destroyed, it will be drawn to the capsa. But if he is closer, it will always migrate toward his stronger presence. Do it enough times and Ethos will be made weaker and the capsa stronger, and you will have the advantage," she informed him.

Josh's gaze narrowed with a look of intrigue, but it was directed at London, not the capsa. It was the same look of profound interest that Demetrius had given him when he had discovered Josh could source magic. Josh seemed to become acutely aware that he had grossly underestimated her abilities. "This holds dark magic?"

She didn't hold his gaze long, letting it slip to the floor momentarily. "It holds *his* magic." She handed it to him but kept a firm grip on it. "You didn't get this from me. Do you understand?"

He nodded.

"When you are done with it, you destroy it. Understand?"

He didn't agree as easily. London watched him for a long

searching moment. I thought she knew, as I did, that Josh's fatal flaw was that he was drawn to magic, its power. She held on to it.

"Josh, you have to promise me."

He gave a weak smile and reluctantly, he promised.

As we headed for the door, he stopped. "Perhaps it's a good idea for you to pay your mom a visit—tonight."

"I'm not driving six hundred miles tonight."

He inched closer to her, just a step away. "You will have an airline ticket for tonight. Give me an hour and I will call you with the flight information. I know I shouldn't have brought you into this. At least let me protect you if things go bad. I owe you that much."

"You don't need to call, just text me the information," she said coolly.

I had the feeling she wanted to be as far away from this situation and Josh as possible. Before he left, he leaned in to kiss her on the cheek, but she stepped back, moving out of reach, refusing to look at him. The wounds of her rejection showed as he stepped away and started toward the car, glancing back over his shoulder several times to look at her. She closed the door without looking at him.

We didn't go back to the pack's retreat home. Instead, we ended up at Josh's condo. Most of the pack lived isolated from the population, in small towns or the country. Josh's high-rise condo was located ten minutes from downtown, a neighborhood crowded with constant activity. The luxurious setting didn't invite quiet or solitude. You weren't going for a run in animal form around his busy neighborhood or placing a cage in it. But the beauty of it, especially at night when the lights silhouetted the tall buildings that surrounded his apartment, seemed like a reasonable trade-off.

Stainless-steel appliances, hardwood floors, custom cabinets, and granite countertops didn't match his quaint furniture and décor, which fell somewhere between postcollege first apartment and frat house. Ethan owned the property but leased it to him. I doubt Ethan would have furnished it with the simplistic dark gray microsuede sofa, large cocktail ottoman, and decorative area rug oddly placed with the sole purpose of hiding stains in the carpet.

He stared at the capsa laying across his deep brown table that looked like it was used for more than eating. Small nicks along the surface stood out on its recently polished surface. He leaned low on the table, resting his chin on his arms, studying the capsa, in a state of quiet awe. He played with the delicate object, spinning it ever so gently along the table, wondering, I was sure, how his friend had learned to contain dark magic.

I watched him from the other side of the room, staying as far from it as possible. Dark magic and I didn't have a really good working relationship. I was able to convert it, something virtually unheard of, but I hated being near it. Now with it just a few feet from me, I had the same feeling I had when I was near Ethos, abysmal and overwhelming. Last year, I was connected to it, unable to expel it. I suffocated under its power and was dominated. Dark magic was different from natural magic, stronger and recalcitrant.

"Do you think it will be strong enough?" I finally asked, still tucked away on the far side of the room.

He shrugged. I didn't envy the position he was in. He was the go-to guy for all magic and intermediary for the pack. Just a year older than me, as a blood ally to the were-animals, he had more responsibilities than I knew I could handle. Most times, he handled it with finesse and ease, but now, he seemed heavy with indecisiveness.

Brushing his hand over the capsa, there was a distinct and unfathomable look of curiosity on his face. "We are going to make it stronger—make sure that it works," he said softly, his attention fixed on the rod on the table. This was his first time being around Ethos magic in a dormant state, without Ethos. Now he could study it, feel it, and possibly control it. Something he admitted he'd wanted to do.

"How do you plan on doing that?" I asked.

"You're going to convert it." He looked up and flashed me a small smile.

I took a deep, well-needed inhale because, at some point, I had started holding my breath, momentarily forgetting that I needed oxygen.

"You've converted dark magic to natural, now you will just have to do it again." Last year, when I'd done it, I destroyed the pack's infirmary in the process, and for several long moments, believed I was going to die. I waited for Josh to show the same fear that I was starting to feel. It wasn't that he didn't possess fear. He just ignored it more often than I did. Sometimes, I admired him for it. Today wasn't one of those times.

When he left and returned with a knife, I questioned whether his motives were selfless. I could sense his curiosity. Part of me possessed that same interest. Having access to his magic was one of the few things I enjoyed about being what I was. It was comfortable, enigmatic, and powerful, and I was able to manage it and, at times, control it—okay, maybe not control it, but I was able to avoid killing us while using it.

After he had explained his plan three times, I stood rooted in the middle of the living room, feeling overwhelmed and bombarded by information. It didn't seem any less dangerous or impossible. The only thing that flooded my mind was that curiosity killed the cat—or rather the wolf and warlock.

When I didn't respond immediately, he repeated the instructions again. He was going to loan me the magic but stay connected through physical contact. I was going to form a connection with the capsa, try to mimic its magic, and hope his would pull toward it, strengthening it.

It sounded simple, it should have been simple, but when I connected to the capsa, all hell broke loose, bringing its minions. There was a naïve part of me that expected it to be easy. No, it was Josh who had made me think it was simple. His confidence emboldened me, deceiving me into delusions of grandeur, making me believe there weren't too many things I couldn't do. But dark magic would prove otherwise. The smoky rod burned in my hand, scorching it, leaving blisters in its wake, as it snatched away my breath, forcing to me to my knees as I tried to pull in oxygen. Diablerie was powerful and innately draconian. You never really possessed it or controlled it. It used you to do its will, mastering its own fate, indulging its own pleasures, which seemed dark, violent, and malevolent.

But it didn't want me. It went for the gold, shooting through me with a torrential force. Josh ripped his hand away from mine as he was slammed back into the wall. Long, labored breaths were replaced with short gasps. His eyes didn't hold any evidence of their natural cobalt coloring. Now they were charcoal and bleak, and his body was rigid. Forced into an odd battle between pleasure and pain, he remained plastered against the wall. Sweat dampened his shirt. His chest rose in a slow rhythmic pace as the delineated lines of his abdominals relaxed and tightened.

When I started toward him, he raised his hand to stop me. I stood there, watching as he engaged in his own personal battle. Droplets of perspiration formed along his brow, his lips pressed firmly together, and then he collapsed to the floor. For ten minutes, it went on, and then finally, he stopped moving. His eyes were closed and he appeared to be asleep—or worse.

I shook him but he didn't wake. I shook him even harder. "Josh!"

He didn't respond.

I grabbed my phone out of my bag, shaking him with one hand, while I used the other to scroll through the numbers on my phone for Dr. Baker. Eventually, he stirred, and I exhaled the breath I seemed to have held since we started.

"That was … interesting," he admitted in a rough voice, running his fingers through his hair, shifting his body, trying to rid himself of the nervous energy that had taken over. But I couldn't ignore that he seemed like he was on edge.

Interesting! The new flavor of Doritos is interesting. This was freaking apocalyptic, insane, nuclear, shattering, and calamitous. *Interesting* lived four hundred miles and probably three states over.

I went over to the table, picked up the capsa, and slid down the wall, taking a seat next to him. We stared at it for a long time. It looked the same, felt the same, and made me feel the same. We hadn't accomplished a thing, except realizing how nefarious the magic we were dealing with truly was.

I wanted to go home, get away from the magic and the strange energy that had overtaken the room and was still strumming through it. Josh's appearance had lost that wayward nonchalance. He now looked harsh, concerned, and in need of an escape, too. But he didn't have the luxury of leaving the magic and its strange energy because it pulsed through his veins like his own blood.

"Stay here with me for a little bit," he requested in a quiet voice as his fingers interlaced with mine, holding the same hand he had used when we shared his magic. He dropped his head back against the wall. Magic was usually a gentle breeze off him, calming and neutral, but it had become a raging current, pushing off him with such force it was incapacitating. Instead of sharing his magic with me, he had relinquished it, expunging it in an effort to seek reprieve.

"We're not doing that again," I said firmly. It should have been obvious, but with Josh, you didn't know.

He didn't respond. His head lolled in my direction, firm fingers rubbed steadily against my hand, and a gentle gust hit my lip every time he exhaled, which was quite often. He didn't move for a long time, and when he did, it was to press his lips softly against mine. A dull spark singed them. I jerked my head back and pressed my finger to them. "Sorry," he whispered.

He was energy recoiled and blazing, and he was unable to release or control it. I felt bad for him as he sat next to me, uninhibited power surging through him. He relaxed his head back against the wall. His eyes closed as he slipped into a deep sleep.

I sat next to Josh for nearly three hours, watching him the first hour and then playing games on my phone until he awoke. He eventually took me home, but even in the sanctity of my house, I couldn't find sleep. Something felt weird, off. I was still holding magic—the wrong type, and no matter how I tossed and turned, it couldn't be relieved.

Tired of trying to sleep, I eventually found myself in the middle of my backyard, stripping out of my clothes preparing to force a change into wolf, just to rid myself of the jittery feeling, collateral damage from our experimentation today. I never would have thought I would find my wolf a welcome escape, but it was.

This was my third intentional change and it took me a while to do it. The other two times I had the benefit of help from Sebastian or Ethan. Now, I stood alone in the middle of the dank, cold woods, the cool air nipping at my skin, goose bumps forming small ridges along my arm and legs, a harsh reminder that I was outside naked and that I needed to do something. *Change*, I commanded myself, and still nothing happened. To help it along, I let the anxiety of everything that had taken place over the past few days flood and gain full range of my mind. The tidal wave of emotions washed over me, forcing me to retreat … retreat to her—my wolf. For some odd reason, she was my body's comfort zone. The human part of me was dismissed from dealing with the problems while the wolf faced them vigorously. It was her thing. She liked to make an appearance during times of distress.

The cool air bristled against my skin. The wind was soothing as it breezed over my gray fur as I ran through the bosk behind my house. The coarse grass scratched my paws as the intoxicating scent of pine and oak invigorated my senses. Keen night vision allowed me to course through the maze of trees, tall grass, and fallen branches with ease. I enjoyed every moment of it.

Running at full speed, I could feel the pent-up rage and anxiety being expunged, and it felt great right until the moment a sharp pop rang through the air and a bullet zipped past, barely missing my flank and embedding into the tree in front of me. I stopped abruptly, whipping around to find a rifle pointing at me. I darted behind the tree, trying to dodge the bullets that kept flying, missing me by inches as they picked off the bark of the tree.

The shooter, I knew him. I poked my head out to get another look—David. At his approaching step, I tried to force myself back into human form quickly. He found me before I could change. Aiming the barrel of the rifle at me, he prepared to take another shot. I needed to disarm him without injury and without getting shot or Ethos would be the least of my problems. Before I could move, the gun was snatched from him and he was thrown back hard against the tree.

Quell held David's rifle, aiming it at him with his finger firmly clenched on the trigger. I growled, my only way to communicate, urging him to lower the gun. He ignored me. Just as he was about the take the shot, I bit into his thigh. Cursing under his breath, he shook me off. When he didn't lower the rifle, I sank my teeth into him again, my growl muffled by the flesh crammed between my teeth. *Stop!*

Once he lowered the gun, I went over to David, who was lying next to the tree, eyes closed, taking short bursts of air. I nudged him several times with my nose. He still didn't respond. It wasn't until I laved my tongue over his face that he opened his eyes, startled. He was probably disgusted because I surely would have been. I didn't like it being done to me and I definitely didn't like doing it. Lowering my head and cowering, I tried to seem less threatening. He stared at me in awe before his attention moved to Quell, whose reproachful look made it evident that he wasn't happy with me stopping him. I growled, baring my teeth when he took several steps toward David. He stopped, shooting me a baleful glare as he retreated a few feet away where he stayed.

When I was sure Quell wouldn't attack, I went behind the tree to change. It took longer than I planned—close to ten minutes. I peeked out from the tree trying my best to hide my nudity while I talked to David. "It's me."

"Skylar?" He tried to stand, but his legs didn't cooperate as he quickly lowered himself back to the ground.

"Yeah, it's me."

He mumbled something under his breath, as more blood drained from his face and he gasped. "You … you …" The words disappeared as he rested his head back against the tree. I didn't want to tell him to breathe—that was stupid, and to my dismay, people always told distressed and shocked people to do it. You don't forget to breathe because it's instinctual. You just take too-shallow breaths.

"I need you to take several long breaths, please," I ordered in a gentle voice, giving me a chance to gather my thoughts. Where would I start? I explained to him I changed during a full moon and had recently learned to do it without. Information wasn't helping the situation. He was doing that weird breathing thing again, "Calm down," I instructed in a soft soothing voice. "You can't pass out on me."

I wondered what was going through his mind: How many people out there were like this? Could it happen to him? Were we cursed? The silence helped. Deep controlled breaths came at a gentle rhythm.

He glanced at Quell. "Are you an animal, too?"

Quell responded with an obsidian stare before he turned away from David and started toward me.

"Are you injured?" Quell asked, coming around the tree.

I pushed him back and wrapped my arms around my body, "No, but I'm naked." Before I could ask, he took off his shirt and handed it to me. I quickly slipped on the button-down, went over to David, and knelt in front of him. I gave him my most pleasant smile in an effort to keep him calm. This had to be hard for him. "How are you doing?"

He shook his head slowly, guilt replacing his fear. "I almost killed you.… I saw a wolf in our backyard … if I knew … I would never …" Then, as though he had just come to his senses, "You're a freaking wolf!"

I worked at a smile, and with effort, I gave him one. "Yeah." I eased in closer, aware that even though Quell had me by several inches, there was only so much of my body that the shirt could cover. I moved gingerly, making sure not to expose myself. I wished I could read David's mind and answer the most vexing questions that troubled him. He marshaled a brave face with much effort as he waited for me to speak.

For some reason, it didn't bother me sharing with David, but with Quell, I felt guarded, choosing what I revealed carefully. "My father was a werewolf, and of course, it was passed on to me," I offered. I figured David wanted to be sure that he was exempt from such a fate.

I shrugged off the despondent gaze that reflected back at me. "I guess that is what happened to me. My first change was at fifteen and every full moon, I change."

The silence remained for so long I thought he was going to dart away, screaming for the world to hear, "This woman is a wolf … a freak!"

His thoughts were working overtime, and when he closed his eyes, I could see them flickering behind his lids. "If you're a wolf

... what did you do with all that chocolate I gave you for Valentine's Day?"

Choking on my laughter, I wanted to hug him. Only David would respond like this.

"Oh, kitten," he said softly.

Kitten still? Even after the wolf thing?

I could still feel Quell's penetrating gaze on us—on David. It was making him nervous. I could hear David's heartbeat pacing at erratic speeds.

"Is he like you?" David asked in a low hoarse voice.

"Don't be concerned with what I am," Quell snapped.

Leaning into David, I said, "I need you to forget you saw him and my other half. You can't mention it to anyone, not even your partner. Understand?"

"Of course, you know I am a true guardian of secrets," he responded.

"No, you're not! You tell everything you think you know."

With his trademark whimsical smirk, he brought his hand to his chest in an overexaggerated display of umbrage.

A situation that could have gone terribly wrong; David had somehow made it into something that we could deal with. I knew the next time we had lunch it would be dominated by a million questions about this night, but at least for now he was handling it better than expected.

David looked over at Quell, whose affectless behavior came off far too unwelcoming.

"You should go home," I suggested to David, feeling Quell's eyes on us.

He nodded, his attention periodically moving in Quell's direction. He didn't know what Quell was, but at the moment he didn't like it.

. . .

"Why are you here?" I asked Quell as he followed behind me as I started toward the house.

"You're upset about something."

"You were rude to David. He didn't need that."

"He tried to kill you, and *I* was rude?"

"He wouldn't have done it if he knew it was me."

"Are you sure about that?"

My lips parted to make my case, but it was futile. Quell's perception of humanity was set in stone. A revulsion so deep-seated that even the thought of feeding from a person sickened him. My curiosity about what truly led to this dogmatic belief nipped at me, although I doubted I would ever find out the answer, and I was sure it wouldn't be tonight.

"You were upset earlier, too, before David. Who upset you?" he asked.

Earlier? Had he been there when I changed in the woods? He had just upgraded from odd to creepy. "I guess everything is finally getting to me," I admitted, giving him a partial truth. I didn't elaborate and tell him what had taken place earlier. Although he was trying hard to pay attention and appear concerned, he was obviously distracted. "What's the matter?"

"I have not fed since I last saw you."

"Why not?"

"I don't find feeding from you objectionable," he confessed.

"How flattering. Shouldn't such flowery words be accompanied by a box of chocolates, roses, or a stuffed animal?"

"Do you need to be flattered?" he asked earnestly with avid curiosity. I stopped walking to look at him. He had the social aptitude of a chimpanzee. "Is there a purpose for me to do so?"

I was fidgeting, trying to find the right words to tell the odd vampire that he was just weird. "You don't seem very comfortable around people or know how to interact with them," I pointed out.

"I don't want to be. I find comfort with others when I desire, and when there is no need—I find comfort in being alone. Do I comfort you?"

I gave up. There wasn't a way to get through to him. "You're odd, but I don't mind your company." I moved quicker toward the house. I really wanted a shower and something other than a shirt on.

"I don't mind yours, either," he said, but it seemed like a pained discovery. His steps were lithe, graceful, and unobtrusive as he followed me home.

The walk to the house was virtually silent. Occasionally, I found him staring at me, a perplexed look on his face. When I told him I needed a shower, I expected him to be gone when I came out. Instead, he sat in the chair in the corner, an odd image of beauty with an even odder nature. But there was something different about him. Even as I studied him from the corner, I couldn't quite put my finger on it. He seemed more like a vampire now—hauntingly dangerous.

When he stood and started to walk toward me, instinctively, I took several steps back. He took hold of my wrist. "May I?"

I was feeling less guilty about making him into what he had become. I nodded, and at my consent, his sharp fangs pierced my wrist. The pain pushed me back. I sank into the wall. He wasn't nearly as gentle as he had been before. When I sucked in a loud hiss, he stopped briefly, allowing me to soothe the pain, then he continued. When he finally stopped, he went to my fridge, took out a bottle of juice, and poured a glass for me. I had lowered myself to the ground, looking at my bruised wrist. I finished the juice he handed me in a couple of big gulps while he scrutinized me with that exanimate look that was no longer endearing but annoying.

"You're troubled. Why?"

"I don't like being vampire food." I looked down into my empty glass. I knew that if it hadn't been for me, he would still be feeding from the Hidacus, but it didn't make me feel any better about being part of his late-night buffet. I didn't like anything about this day, and feeding him was just the final straw.

"Okay," he said in a low, methodical voice. "I won't ask you again."

That was simple. "What will you do for food?"

"I'll do as the others," he admitted in a stolid voice. "You live in the sewer long enough, you learn to find the smell less offensive."

The fact that he was resigned to this way of life, though it was repulsive for him, drove my guilt right back home. "I'm sorry for what I did to you."

Taking my wrist, he leaned forward, and his tongue slid over the bite marks, removing them. "I'm sorry for what I did to *you*. Feeding us should be your pleasure, not an obligation." Then he was gone.

"I hate when people do that," I said to the empty space.

Late afternoon on the day after we had received the capsa from London, Ethan's arms were crossed over his chest, and the scowl on his face wouldn't ease. He remained unconvinced by Josh's false display of confidence when he told him about it. Lying in the middle of Josh's coffee table, it didn't look as intimidatingly powerful as it had yesterday. Josh needed to see if it would work on a creature before he presented the idea to anyone and was telling Ethan his plan as I stood on the other side of the room watching. Ethan listened, asking questions periodically. His confidence seemed to lie more in his brother than the tactic. Josh explained to him that, because of the capsa's affinity to dark magic, it could be used to track down the creatures. But he wanted to confirm it would work as intended. As long as Ethos was farther away than the capsa, it would draw the magic from the creatures before they could return to him. Josh hoped we could find enough of them to weaken Ethos to the point that he would be incapable of continuing the attacks. Although Josh would never admit it, I knew he wanted Ethos weak enough that he was no longer a threat to him, either.

While the pack held Josh in the utmost regard, Josh held himself to a higher standard and hated to be wrong. Dealing with Demetrius and his family had made him more cautious than usual. His failure would be seen as a pack weakness. Even during an alliance, there always seemed to be huge demonstrations of power, unnecessary posturing, and constant bravado that had roped in Josh. He had decided to withhold the information until he was confident of the results.

An impatient knock on the door pulled our attention away from the capsa. Chris eased past Josh when he answered, undeterred by his slim frame blocking her entrance. He turned, shooting a cool look in her direction while I surreptitiously slipped the gray rod off the table, placing it in the drawer of the console near the wall.

"London's gone," she stated.

"And?" Josh responded.

She smiled, warm and gracious. "You visited her last night—now she's gone. A less cynical person would believe that was just a coincidence." Her gaze brushed over him, then it moved to Ethan, whose face was stern. Perhaps he was angry with her intrusion, but he was probably a lot angrier at Demetrius's scent, which wafted off her skin and filled the room like a mist. It was thinly masked by the exotic floral fragrance of her perfume. Attuned to the subtle nuances that existed after she *traded,* I noticed her movements were lither, her gait sleek and stealthy, and there was a disturbing keenness to her gaze. She focused on Ethan and Josh, who had eased his way toward his brother.

She shifted her attention from them to me. "Skylar, what's going on?"

Why are you asking me?

She studied me as I made every effort to keep my face devoid of expression. I shrugged. Josh was on the fence about trusting her and I definitely didn't.

Josh crossed his arms over his chest. "Chris, I don't mind sharing information with you. In fact, you may be quite helpful in the matter. At this time, I have no new information for Demetrius. Are you here on your own or for Demetrius?"

She smiled. It was gentle, demure, and strangely disarming as she stepped closer to him. "I'm just a friend, stopping by. There's no harm in that, is there?"

"We're hardly friends. Chris, if you betray me—"

"You have my word."

He studied her for an excruciatingly long time. He couldn't determine lies by the subtle nuances that betrayed, and I doubt Chris had them anyway. But he was more perceptive than most. "Okay," he finally conceded.

Ethan hadn't relaxed. Before Josh could speak to her, he took her by the elbow and guided her into the next room. She snatched her arm away and started yelling at him for grabbing her as he attempted to close the door. It hit Chris's her and sprang open so I could see and hear them from across the room. Josh rolled his eyes, forcing out an exasperated breath before heading upstairs. I should have left with him or, at the very least, gone to the living room, found a nice spot on his comfy sofa, and entertained myself with the extraordinary view of the city. Josh lived half a block from a sports bar, next to a natural foods market, across the street from a pub. It was midafternoon on a Saturday. The streets were flooded with people bustling around enjoying their days off from a busy workweek. I could have entertained myself with people watching, but instead, I stayed fixed in that spot, watching the drama between Ethan and Chris unfold with avid interest.

They brought out my voyeuristic nature. I felt drawn by the enigmatic force that surrounded them. There was something always intensely intimate, strangely alluring about the way they interacted. Apart, they were both forces in their own right.

Combined, what they created seemed ineffable. Ignoring them wasn't an option. The odd dynamics that created their relationship girded around you, eventually sweeping you toward them. It was probably the same perverse reason we gawked at car accidents; stayed glued to the television to watch the most obscene, demoralizing reality shows; remained thoroughly engaged by trashy talk shows; and loved gossip magazines. Chris and Ethan were passion, violence, hate, love, betrayal, and sex all forced into symbiosis by them. It was a uniquely tragic situation.

Even as they stood apart from each other, Ethan on one side of the room and Chris on the other, it was as though they were close enough to embrace. Chris stood tall, her face set in defiance, waiting for Ethan's tirade or virulence. But instead, he remained silent, watching her. He rubbed his hands over his face then ran them through his hair several times. He was trying to assuage the anger, but it was a battle he didn't seem likely to win. He exhaled several ragged breaths before he was able to speak. "I know you well. Whatever you're sacrificing, tolerating, or dealing with to receive such considerations from *him* will eventually outweigh its benefits. I'm not sure when it will happen, but until then, don't you ever come around me, reeking of him. Do you understand?"

It was a long moment before she spoke. "You don't know me as well as you think, or you would know I didn't enter this foolishly or without considering the consequences. I can't keep having this discussion. I'm tired of it, and I'm sure you are, too. Make your decision now: either you deal with it and we don't have this discussion again, or you don't and we're through. Those are the only two options you have."

He inched close to her, and his lips brushed against her ear. Unresolved emotions coursed through his voice like ice. "I'm not the one who needs to make the decision—you are," he said firmly.

They were at an impasse.

I didn't see it being resolved any time this decade.

I understood the advantages of trading with Demetrius. In a

world where you dealt with creatures that moved as fast as a blinking eye with strength and agility that would easily leave you awestruck, you needed an edge. That I could identify with. But what I didn't understand was the *why*. Why did she choose to live in a world with creatures whose cruelty and malice surpassed anything you would ever see in humanity? How horrible had her existence in the human world been that she decided to consort with the creatures of the night, befriend the predators of the day, and interact with the supernatural world as though it were normal?

Chris was solely human—well, unless someone admitted otherwise. So why not dwell among the insipid and wholly human? Live in a normal world, do normal things, and remain oblivious to this world? If you didn't have to be here, then why do it? That was something I truly couldn't understand.

"Bored yet?" Josh asked from behind me, placing his chin on my head and wrapping his arms around me just above my breasts. He was watching the show, as well, but seemed disinterested and bored. After several minutes of scrutinizing them, he stepped away and I could feel him watching me as I watched them.

"I don't understand them," I finally admitted, pulling my attention away from them and walking toward him.

"You don't understand *them*, or my brother?"

"Both."

"Why do you need to?"

I needed to understand because I was cursed with the same curiosity that caused Pandora to open the box. It was a perilous desire that I just couldn't deny or ignore.

The silence between them was wrought with the same tension that would have been ignited if they were standing there screaming at each other at the top of their lungs. If Josh hadn't been there staring at me, I would have stayed watching them, but under his penetrating gaze, I felt the shame that I should have felt in the first place for standing there gawking at them.

When I headed toward the living room, Josh followed me. Even as he walked behind me, I could feel his deep inquiring eyes on me. He took a seat on the ottoman, directly across from the sofa that I slouched into.

"He doesn't like her trading with Demetrius," Josh said.

"She does it to have supernatural abilities. She turned to Demetrius because your brother wouldn't change her. This life is what she wants. Just give it to her. If I could change places with her, I would. Just have Ethan chomp on her or whatever he needs to do to change her and be done with it."

Josh chuckled grimly. "You've never seen someone changed, have you?" He didn't wait for a response before he continued. "When you are born that way, the body is prepared for the change and responds accordingly. Given years to accommodate to what you are forced into when called. Unlike the vampires, were-animals don't have the luxury of being dead before the change occurs. When someone is changed into a were-animal, the body is forced into something it wasn't prepared for. See one change and, believe me, you don't ever want to see another. Witness an unsuccessful one and you can go another lifetime without seeing it again." The look on his face changed from piqued curiosity to concern as he exhaled. "It is a constant struggle for them to maintain their calm temperament."

For the sake of argument, I let that statement go, but I hadn't met a were-animal that had an even temperament, with the exception of Joan, and her primal instinct far too often reared its head. They all seem to carry an air of coiled violence, possessing the primordial urges of a predator, even in the most unthreatening situations. It was the nature of what they were—what *we* were. I was no more exempt from it than they were. For eight years I sedated mine, ignored her, and hid her every chance I had. And still, I wasn't foolish enough to think it wasn't present in me, as well. But I was far more often on the receiving end of the were-animals' *temperament*. I had to remind myself that they were products of their nature, no more malicious than the lion hunting the gazelle, or a shark ravishing a seal. It was innate, something they could not ignore.

"I'm sure she's aware of what it involves. Can your brother, for once, let someone else make their own decision?"

Josh leaned forward, his elbows resting on his thighs while his fingers made random patterns on my leg. He wasn't one to stay still very long. At times, it was entertaining to watch him try to control it. Even in silence, the nervous energy pulsated through him.

He grinned. "My brother seems to be able to irritate the best of them. He can be a jerk and a raging jackass. If I'm not mistaken, that is how you used to describe him, but he is not often wrong. Changed were-animals have more problems than just the initial change. Imagine Gavin but less reasonable and far more petulant."

I didn't want to imagine such a creature, because someone worse than Gavin was inconceivable. Steven was changed, and he was the opposite of Gavin. But Steven had the benefit of having been raised by Joan and mentored by Sebastian. What would he have been like if Joan and Sebastian hadn't been there for him?

"Isn't that what the pack is for, to help her through the transition?"

"You think she would join *this* pack?" he asked incredulously as he stopped making finger designs on my leg and rested his palm on my thigh.

"Why wouldn't she? It's everything she would want."

The Midwest Pack was powerful, prestigious, and commanded a certain level of respect, fear, and consideration from most in this world. It seemed like it was right up Chris's alley. Would she join? They would probably have to fight to keep her from trying to take over.

When his cerulean eyes met mine, they seemed cool and distant, as though he sensed my supporting arguments. "You didn't."

~

After hours of driving and several false readings, we found where Ethos's creatures might be living. With the capsa in hand, we followed it as it led us blindly toward a similar source. I only hoped it didn't lead us to Ethos himself.

A strong magnetic pull guided us as the capsa desired to be near something that possessed more power than itself. We ended up in front of a large white house on a farm only twenty miles from the pack's retreat. The creatures slowly came toward the door, sensing our presence or the magic, drawn by an innate desire to migrate toward similar energy. It existed because they existed.

Six small beings, whose appearance reminded me of small primates, barely two feet high, wide-eyed and with broad gibbon-like features, slunk toward us. Focusing on Ethan, they changed. In the quadruped position, three of them advanced quickly in his direction. Their skin grayed, bristled hair covered their body, and long fangs sprang from their mouths, making it difficult for them to close them. Just feet from us, they assumed the bipedal position as their bodies quadrupled in size. They looked like large mangy wolves. The other three headed toward Chris, shedding their appearance like clothing until they matched something that was an oddly grotesque version of a human.

At their approach, Chris smiled, her eyes steeled and cold with an avid appreciation of violence, an unhealthy addiction to it. She drew her two guns simultaneously and pulled the triggers, bringing down three of them with three shots perfectly centered between the eyes as she had done before. She was a menace with firearms. That tidbit of information I made sure I remembered. I was glad this time she was on our side.

As the creatures fell, Josh ran toward them, placing the capsa next to them. There was a tug-of-war as they vanished then reappeared. When they remained corporeal, life escaped quickly from them. Thick, dark ether roiled above them then crept toward the capsa. The first creature caused the rod to darken noticeably. By the time the third had been captured, it was a smoldering black.

Ethan, Chris, and I killed the other three, which were quickly replaced by fourteen larger creatures that advanced toward us rapidly.

"I think we should leave," I urged as one of the things homed in on me. It took long strides, which turned into a full-out run only slowed by its constant transition to whatever it felt I represented: a mangy quadruped animal, a distorted human. Then it stopped for a moment and shifted to a grotesque scaled creature with charcoal skin similar to Ethos's natural form. Then embers formed into a body shaped by light. It was at that moment they all seemed to stop and gawk at me in disturbed awe.

I started backing toward the car, then ran with the others close behind me. I expected the creatures to follow us, but instead, they seemed frozen in an odd state of curiosity, which was fine because it gave us a chance to escape. The problem now: the quelling silence, furtive glances, odd looks of concern, and curiosity from the others that remained directed at me.

Several hours later, I wasn't surprised to have someone knocking at my door, I suspected it would be Josh, but instead, it was Ethan.

"May I come in?" he asked, more of a formality because it didn't sound much like a request. "Drop the ward."

I smiled and said, "Why don't you do it?"

Annoyance piqued as he exhaled an exasperated breath. He pressed his hand against the ward. It shrilled for just seconds, then lavender and gold lambent light wailed then faded. The ward dropped—no, it fizzled and collapsed upon his command. This was different from last year when he had broken Josh's protective field. Then it had taken force and great effort, crashing it into pieces. Now he seemed to have better command of whatever power he possessed and performed it with grace and deftness. It was fascinating.

Disregarding my curiosity, he stepped over the threshold. "We need to talk," he said.

I plopped down on the sofa and watched as he paced in front of me. Every so often he would stop to look at me. His eyes narrowed, watching me with a new ineffable curiosity and concern. I could almost see the information overload twirling around in his head, being moved, categorized, interpreted, and analyzed. "Where were you born?"

Okay, I wasn't expecting that. I expected his tried and true "What are you?" which only meant he knew something and was just trying to confirm.

"Ohio. I came to Illinois when I was six."

He bit down on his lips, his irritation more apparent now. It was the same look he gave me when he suspected I was lying.

"I am not you, Ethan. I have nothing to hide." The level of hypocrisy that I had experienced had whittled away at my tolerance.

He had moved so fast from his position across the room to kneeling in front of me it made me remember that, above everything else, he was a predator. "That's the problem. You have plenty you should be hiding, but you don't have the good sense to do so."

When he looked away, his face was strained. He closed his eyes; they were withdrawn, pellucid. "What do you know of your birth mother?"

"This is getting old. Let's drop the BS. Obviously, you know something pretty big or you wouldn't be here. So why not just tell me?"

"Last year, you spoke with Maya. Four days you were with her. That's a long time. What did she talk to you about?"

If he was going to withhold information, so was I. It was ridiculous that our interaction had been reduced to the childhood behavior of "you show me yours and I'll show you mine." But this was where we found ourselves. I sat up taller and crossed my arms. "Don't remember."

He came to his feet and as fluidly and quickly as he found himself in front of me, he was now at the door. "I do believe you will be missed when you're dead," he said as he started to leave.

"What is wrong with you? Why do you think that's an acceptable thing to say to someone?"

He slammed the door. The look that covered his face was hard to place. Hopelessness? No, that wasn't it. Sorrow? Perhaps. I could only compare it to the look someone might have just before they see a person hit by a car—a look of hopeless panic.

"She told me that she was murdered and was forced to live this life as a spirit shade. At first, she was only drawn to hosts with great power, but she soon learned that it was a miserable life because those with great power often possessed great evil. And she learned that those with power longed to host her because she enhanced their gifts. Then she showed me parts of my mother's life," I offered.

"You were born in Ohio. But your mother was born in Portugal, where she abandoned her responsibility as one of the five Mouras Encantadas. They guard mystical objects. Her job was to protect the Aufero, the very orb that Marcia currently has in her possession. Her death made her failure and responsibilities fall on the child she left behind. Right now, there are a select few that have this information, but I am the only one that cares whether you live past today. As I said before, you keep drawing attention to yourself, making it easier for the people she betrayed to find you. Your death will be no one's fault but your own."

He took a photo out of his pocket and handed it to me. "This is the Moura responsible for guarding the Gem of Levage."

Ethan watched me as I looked down at the picture. The woman was frozen in a state of shock and fear, arms outstretched, eyes vacant. It was as if someone had just snatched the life from her. It didn't look like a violent murder. In fact, it didn't look like a murder at all.

As the grating silence between us continued, I did what I always did—tried to read through the cold, distant eyes, vacant look, and detached personality, and as usual, I came up empty, my questions still unanswered. The only thing I accomplished was fanning the flames of my agitation. "Why would you tell me this information like this?"

In a low, exasperated voice, he said, "My fire-and-brimstone warnings went ignored and friendly advice doesn't seem to work, either."

He was quiet for a moment, and I couldn't figure out what was going through his mind. He said, "How does a person get through to someone like you?"

I'm sure the shock showed. Was this scathing, borderline barbaric, shock-and-awe delivery of information and treatment his way of helping? He didn't give me a chance to ask. He slipped into his car and sped away.

Even if I gave him the benefit of the doubt that he was trying to help and not decimate me with a single blow, I had no idea what to do with this information. Who would want me to pay for the transgressions of my birth mother? What were the other objects being guarded and who guarded them? Had they adhered to their responsibility or abandoned it like my mother? I had made a lot of noise, lacking discretion with so many things. Who did I need to tread lightly around, appear invisible, and slink into oblivion for?

Taking out the family-size bag of M&M's I hid from myself, I poured them into a large bowl, giving up the pretense that I was just going to have "a few," and put the rest up. The way I felt, I was sure I was going to finish them in the next twenty minutes. I grabbed my laptop and the book Josh had given me for my birthday. It was an interesting book and had held my attention for months after I received it. But it wasn't an easy read. Unlike the books in the pack's retreat, it was in English, which was rare for most of the mystical books that Josh used. Most were usually in Latin or Greek. This book spoke of objects, legends, and fairy tales as though you were reading folklore, but I knew better. It was only helpful if you were well versed in what the objects, legends, and fairy tales were. Scanning the book, I found the *Mouras Encantadas* only four times, not five. Each time I found the word, it described the object and stated that it was guarded by the Mouras: the Gem of Levage, Aufero, *Fatifer,* and *Clostra.*

The Clostra was a book or books. In Latin it meant "key." I wasn't sure what it was the key to, but since someone was tasked with its protection, it undoubtedly opened something horrid. My mother wasn't the only screwup. At some point, the protector of the Gem of Levage had failed, because last year the vampires had tried to use it to lift their restrictions. I really hoped the Moura that was protecting the Fatifer, "the bringer of death," was on the job and doing it well because it didn't need to fall into the wrong hands.

Despite the new information, I wasn't sure what Mouras Encantadas were and how they had come into existence. Were they being punished, or were they people born into this world with the sole purpose of protecting these mystic objects? Upon reaching adulthood, were they told that they wouldn't have a career, family, dreams, or their own lives because their entire existence was to protect these objects? And most importantly, were they just human? I knew my mother had had gifts. She could compel people to do things—anything she wanted. Josh wasn't sure if she had been a witch or not. But he suspected that was the reason I could change dark magic to natural magic and was convinced I could do the reverse. Well, we knew I couldn't compel people to act in the manner I wished, because if that were the case, things between Ethan and I would have gone a lot better.

Once I had looked the book over several times and couldn't

gather much more information, I went to Google. I was fluent in Portuguese, thanks to my adopted mother, who had forced me to learn it. Mouras was "moors," which didn't have pertinent meaning. In Latin it meant "death," in Greek it meant "destiny," and in Gaelic it meant "spirits." After perusing page after page, the only thing I gathered was that Mouras were "enchanted ones" and traditionally women. They were responsible for guarding charmed things, whether they were treasure, land, or objects. They took human form, which meant they could be fae, elves, or witches because, by all accounts, they had supernatural abilities.

Since my mother had abandoned her responsibilities, was it now my responsibility to take the Aufero from Marcia? If so, how was I going to do that? What, send the most powerful witch in the world a strongly worded card explaining that she had something of mine and had better return it—or things were going to get ugly? Yeah, that would work.

CHAPTER 15

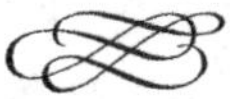

Chris had scanned the library for a long time, and each time she found herself in the vast space with rows and rows of books that flooded the shelves, she missed having total access to it. The Midwest Pack had the most extensive library she knew of. Even the fae, who prided themselves on being well informed, didn't possess this level of information.

Her Latin was rudimentary at best and she would have to rely on Google Translate to get through the book. But her curiosity was strumming at a high pitch. Skylar, the enigmatic new woman in the pack's life, seemed to have forged a new level of secrecy among them. Ethan tensed and became a prodigy of redirection at the mention of her name as he attempted to belie any curiosity she had.

Then there were the recent changes in Ethan that made her uneasy. Attuned to the minor undulations of his being, she could see them—they were subtle, easily hidden, and questionably deniable—but they were there. Now he was able to detect magic and breeze through wards. The benefit of being wholly human is that wards didn't stop you. He shouldn't have been able to follow her into her home without the ward being disarmed, but he could. It was a simple ward. She didn't expect anything dramatic, but it should have been enough to hold him off or, at the very least, give him room for pause.

She had pushed two of the books that had proven useless aside and was working her way through another when she felt Josh's eyes on her. They were icy, crushing into her.

"I knew this is where I would find you. Jeremy's looking for you."

She glanced at the arm that was injured earlier from her fight with Ethos's creatures. A claw had sliced into it before she could take the shot. Dr. Baker had cleaned it, closed it with Steri-Strips, and protected it with a layer of bandaging. Covered in blood, it looked a lot worse than it was. A shot of antibiotics, an assiduous cleanup job, and he was done.

"He wanted to give you something for the pain."

"I'm fine. I deal with pain pretty well."

His lips pressed into a frown. "Of course you do. You take as well as you give." His gaze shifted to the books in front of her, his disapproval apparent. She saw that he knew she was trying to figure out what it was about Skylar that made Ethos's creatures stop and why they had transformed multiple times to match her likeness. His look told her she was close. It would only be a matter of time before she figured something out, or at the very least, knew that Skylar was more than she appeared to be.

"Everything that occurred today will be kept between us. Okay?" he stated firmly.

Her lips curled into a cloying smile. "For you, anything. Today is as good as forgotten."

They both knew it wouldn't be forgotten, nor would she stop looking for the many questions left unanswered by today's events, but she would extend the courtesy of keeping the information to herself.

Returning her attention back to the books she was studying, she was aware of Josh's eyes on her as he settled back in the chair.

A white t-shirt draped over his lean body, the tattoos twitched and protracted with even the subtlest movements, studded earrings glinted, and the mussed hair as usual was a perpetual mess. All those quirky things were overshadowed by the power that permeated the room with his very presence. Before, it had been mild, inconsequential, something one would have barely noticed. Two years later, it was a force that was hard to ignore.

"What's the casualty count going to be when you two are done with this train wreck?"

She smiled a meager response to his question.

"We both know that's what it is. I'm not being controlled by my libido, so I can see it for the cornucopia of crap that it is," he said.

Chris maintained her silence. She was curious as to why a brother who was indifferent to so many things was concerned about her and Ethan.

"Do you love him?"

"Should we break out the cookie-dough ice cream and start braiding each other's hair for some real girlfriend time?"

"Dammit, Chris." His hand washed over his face in frustration, the table rumbled, and books trembled on the bookshelf.

She quickly came to her feet and moved away from the books and closer to the wall.

He massaged his temple and took several slow breaths. "Sorry. My patience has been tried quite a bit these days." When he finally spoke again, in a low desolate tone, he said, "He's not going to walk away, so you will have to. You are a liability. I don't know what it is about you that draws him to you, but you and him *together* isn't a good thing. His loyalties are tied to me and this pack, and I'm not quite sure where yours lie. As long as you are in the picture, Ethan doesn't act like himself. He denies it, but you are a weakness for him."

She slowly paced along the room, her nails dragging lightly across the table as she ignored his gaze. The harsher it became, the more difficult it was to ignore. She turned her back on him for a moment, something she would never consider doing with the other people she dealt with. He hadn't been hardened yet. There was still light and softness to his smile. Even angered, there was slight forgiveness and understanding in his gaze.

She turned and studied him with intent. He hadn't been in this world long enough to brew skepticism and anger. If he were angered, you had reached the extent of his mercy, which was probably quite extensive. If he betrayed someone, it was because he was cornered. If he killed, it was a necessity. Gifted beyond most people's knowledge, he had earned their respect but not their fear, dread, or malcontent. Josh was still what she considered only a minor threat. Known for his vast amount of power but limited skill, he wasn't considered a major player yet. She saw the potential. She didn't want him as an enemy, but something about him made her realize they might never truly be allies.

His induction into this world had been a result of his brother's desire to protect him. She doubted he ever assumed he would become such an asset to them. Like most abecedarians, there was still a level of novelty that made him seem like he was still prey wading into a pool of predators. He was strong enough not to be destroyed as a pack ally, but not enough to survive on his own.

"I believe you overestimate your brother's feelings for me. I think it's fair to say that most men who have claimed to love me have never tried to kill me."

"You betrayed this pack—"

"Betrayal can only occur when loyalty is expected. Sleeping with your brother hardly warrants eternal loyalty to this pack. The sooner you all realize it, the less indignant you will feel about my alleged betrayal."

"You're right. Your loyalty is to you and whomever is footing the bill at that moment. I understand that and, to an extent, can respect it. However, if you are in a relationship with my brother, your loyalty is expected, and acts against it will be treated as such," he stated acerbically.

"Now *that* sounded like a threat."

"Take it any way you like. But don't be foolish enough to believe that I can't see your effect on Ethan. Last year, he gave you a warning. When have you ever known him to engage in such banality? If what you did were done by anyone else ..."

Chris knew that and she suspected it might have partially been the reason Demetrius had believed she would be successful with the job. He was aware of their history, and as disgusted as he was about her "lying with dogs," he didn't mind exploiting their prior relationship, nor did she.

"Our situations aren't that different, you and I. What will you do when a conflict between the were-animals and the witches arises?" She watched the realization take over his mind. She thought it was a possibility that he'd ignored but was now forced to bring to the forefront. "You aren't so naïve as to believe it will never happen. What will your decision be when you are forced into loyalties? Whom will you choose? The witches because you are one, although, due to your mother's mistakes, they never considered you one of them, or the were-animals, who have treated you as one of their own but only because of who your brother is and the power you possess?"

"No need to be concerned about things that may never happen."

She spoke softly, barely a whisper, a conversation to herself that she allowed Josh to be privy to. "I don't suffer any delusions over the complexity of this situation." And she didn't. It was hard to remain indifferent, to split loyalties, to decipher which secrets were acceptable to keep and which ones were acts of betrayal. Ryan had warned her about getting involved with anyone in this world, and she had kept it a steadfast rule. She dated but never cared and definitely never loved. She wasn't foolish enough to believe that what she had with Demetrius wasn't a relationship.

With all its sordidness and dysfunction, it was still some form of a relationship where they fulfilled each other's needs. Despite it all, there was still a part of her that despised him because she knew that he was true evil and cruelty, and all he offered was an addiction that she wasn't ready to kick.

Her relationship with Ethan wasn't much better. Treading through the complexity of it, she could never deny that whatever amorous feeling she had for him, there was still a part of her that loathed him. The only thing she had ever asked of him was to change her to a were-animal and give her a better chance to survive in this world. His refusal was most detrimental, ruining her chances with anyone else. It was a tacit refusal from the others as well. Any of the were-animals she trusted to do it kept their distance from her as though she were laced with silver. Even Gavin, the petulant, denied her. In one single act, Ethan had ruined her chances of ever being changed to a were-animal.

"As our ally, you would never be betrayed. Can the same be said about Demetrius and the Seethe?"

She smiled; it was warm and sincere. "The only person I trust to never betray me—is me."

Josh held her gaze for a long time as she gathered her things and left.

Chris rolled her eyes as someone knocked at the door. *Dusk breaks through the day and the vampires come out to play,* she thought bitterly as she closed her computer and tucked the books that were spread along her sofa in the storage ottoman in the corner of the room. She had spent her time researching Skylar since she had returned from the pack's home. Her promise was that she wouldn't tell anyone what she had seen that day, but she was too curious to just ignore it.

Tension formed along her back and neck when she saw

Michaela standing at her door. This was the first time she had ever come to her home, and she couldn't help but be curious as to what warranted it now. Chris slid a stake into her back pocket, placed the M-9 into the back of her pants, and tucked away a small knife in her other pocket, preparing herself for anything. For a brief moment, she considered not letting her in, but she knew that if Michaela wanted to hurt her, she had plenty of other opportunities. And if she changed her mind and wanted to hurt her now, a little thing like keeping her uninvited into her home wouldn't stop her.

She swore under her breath. All these years she had managed to keep Michaela out of her home and had planned to keep it that way. Being around the unpredictable vamp was always a chore. There wasn't any rhyme or reason to her behavior, and Chris didn't want to have any part of it. Michaela was a vicious person, a skilled fighter, and malicious killer. She was used to dealing with that kind, but there was something different about Michaela. Her level of depravity exceeded most. She punished those she loved, tortured the ones she valued, and overall played sadistic games with anyone she chose. Whether you were her sworn enemy or her favorite created, you were treated relatively the same.

She opened the door but didn't invite her in.

"May I come in?" Michaela asked, her lips curved into a placid smile.

She stepped aside to let her in.

Michaela's smile widened, her voice cloying. "You know you have to invite me in, silly."

"Please, come in."

Michaela slipped past her, moving in an agile, lithe way that put her on the defensive. She walked throughout the room as though it were her own, then she disappeared into Chris's bedroom. She waited impatiently for Michaela to return. When she didn't, she went into the room, her hand discreetly placed behind her back, gripping the hilt of her stake.

Michaela lay across her bed, a distant look on her face, her body relaxed as her midnight hair fanned out over the duvet. It was Michaela who had urged them to start trading. Adamantly declaring Demetrius's responsibility to Chris, she had said, "Don't be cruel. You brought her from the brink of death just to leave her unguarded. You take care of her."

Chris didn't know the reason behind her benevolence, but she wasn't in any condition to deny it. In hindsight, she wished she had healed on her own.

"You please him a lot," Michaela stated as she rolled onto her stomach, stretching out on the expansive bed, her attention keenly focused on her. "He says he hasn't bedded you. Why? It can't be because you're not attracted to him. He's the loveliest thing I have ever laid my eyes on."

Yet he's not lovely enough to keep you out of others' beds, she thought contemptuously. If beauty was all it took to keep one's attention, then Michaela would have never strayed from Demetrius.

"My continued existence is not so much a result of Demetrius's actions but your graciousness. I appreciate your allowing Demetrius to trade with me. I would never disrespect your generosity by having an affair with him." Chris could barely get the drivel out without choking on it.

"An affair?" Michaela chuckled as she crawled across the bed and approached her. It was then she realized why Demetrius had fallen so hard for Michaela. The earnest and engaging way she looked at you was a siren's call, pulling you to her and stealing your will. The intensity of her gaze made you feel, if only for a moment, that you were the only person in the room. Movements so smooth and graceful were mesmerizing, absolving her of her cruel nature. But Chris couldn't. She was thoroughly and painfully aware of what Michaela was capable of and watched her carefully, her senses on high alert, ready to engage if necessary.

Positioning herself in front of Chris, Michaela stood close—crowding her. "You silly humans and the ridiculous labels you put on everything. It's just satisfying a craving, fulfilling the body's needs. Why consider it anything more?" She laughed softly, watching her tense. "He should be fond of you," she whispered, her fingers gently sweeping along Chris's cheek. "You're just a little spitfire, aren't you? It's cute."

As quickly as she was in front of Chris, she was back on the bed lounging lazily on her back as though she had never moved. Michaela's mood grew sullen. "You should have known him when we first met." Her voice softened, and her face held a look of bleak despair.

Chris didn't need to know him before. The stories of his brutality and violence were well documented and widely known. He was infamous for them. In his early years as a vampire, he had abandoned all acts of humanity, embracing dissolution and violence with a passion.

"He was so beautiful then. Being near him was the closest one could ever get to greatness. People feared him and worshiped him without question. Now, the longer he socializes with humans"—she frowned in disgust—"were-animals, and elves, the further he drifts from what he was."

"I assure you he has very little regard for anyone who isn't part of his Seethe, and his cruelty is second to none," Chris informed her, resting against the opened door as she wondered what was worse: a morose Michaela or an elated Michaela.

She shook her head, sounding desperate and lamenting. "Now he's complacent, exanimate, and amenable. We consort with animals and treat them as equals. Instead of forming alliances with them, they should be our pets, existing only to entertain us. It's so distasteful and embarrassing." Her lips twisted down into a disappointed moue. "And the fae, they don't fear us anymore.

They expect us to accumulate debts for their services. The elves, who once revered us, now play their silly games with us, displaying constant disrespect, even contempt."

She stood, pacing the area in front of the bed as she sank into her own melancholy world. If it were anyone else, Chris would have felt a twinge of sympathy for her apparent grief and sorrow. But there wasn't a place for sorrow or empathy for Michaela.

The long, yellow Bohemian dress swayed gently as she moved. Her limestone skin looked woefully pale against the thin material. Each step was soft and languid as she glided across the thick, carpeted floor. "Now he's just going through the motions," she whispered.

Once again, in a flash of a movement, she was in front of Chris, crushing her with a hard gaze. "But when he found you two years ago, broken, mere seconds from death, clinging to that pitiful little human life of yours, it ignited something in him. He was vengeful and angry—emotions I thought he had lost. It was deep, impassioned rage that burned through him like a wildfire. I hadn't seen the like in nearly sixty years. A beautiful glimpse of what he was. I've yearned for that for so long. You rekindled something in him that I thought he had lost. I deserve to have him back and to be truly happy."

She deserved happiness! The very idea that Michaela thought she should be rewarded in any way was absurd. She was cruel without cause. In the nine years Chris had been a Hunter, Michaela was still one of the most heinous things she had encountered, yet no one had ever put a bounty on her. It was only because Demetrius protected her when, by all accounts, she should have been punished by him. And if it were anyone else, Sebastian would have handled the matter, too. But if they destroyed Michaela, it would ensure a war, leaving both of them weaker and vulnerable to others. Reluctantly, everyone tolerated her behavior.

"I wish you could have seen what he did to those things that hurt you. It was macabre—a symphony of violence and pain. You gave him new life. I need you to keep him that way. Make him the person he used to be. I can't be with what he's become. He might as well breathe, breed, and eat. He's so human now."

Michaela held her attention. She stared into the face of Demetrius's lover, the Seethe's Mistress. Losing her human life before she had truly experienced true adulthood, she had replaced her lost humanity with a perpetual thirst for turmoil and violence as a way to make herself feel alive. It was at this moment that Chris was happy she hadn't allowed Demetrius to change her last year. If he had, what indulgence, addiction, or vice would she have chosen to help her deal with the lost humanity?

She spoke in a low, controlled voice, ignoring how irritatingly close Michaela was to her. "He is as I always remember. Perhaps you have become immune to him. He hasn't fallen from grace. His brutality and maliciousness are untainted. People still fear him, no one trusts him, and his name brings weaker men to their knees."

Michaela shook her head slowly, ruefully. "No, he's not the same. I can see it, feel it, and sense it. You've known him for only a few years. I've known him for a century." Her eyes lidded heavily with disappointment.

"I didn't create any emotions that he didn't already possess. Guilt evokes revenge. As a favor to him, I took a job I would have ordinarily passed on."

She scoffed, rolling her eyes. "Guilt. That was something he never would feel. Now ..." She sighed, shaking her head, and lifted her gaze to meet Chris's. "If Demetrius thought the were-animals had betrayed us, he wouldn't let something like that go unpunished."

"You want me to lie?"

Michaela's irritation flared. "Aren't you the noble one. I never said lie, but insinuations are just as effective."

"Why don't you do it?"

"Not very believable. I do my best to stay away from them," she stated venomously. Her lips had barely curled into a smile when they suddenly twisted down into a disgusted frown.

"What are you doing here?" Demetrius asked from the doorway. They turned toward the voice. Michaela's look was contemptuous as he stepped farther into the room.

"It's been less than twenty-four hours since you've last seen her. How envious your Elisabeth must feel, knowing you have cast her aside for another," Michaela cooed as her long delicate fingers ran along Chris's cheek. "And one who is not nearly as lovely as she is."

Chris had a hard time letting the insult roll off her and gripped the stake tighter in her hands, fighting the urge to shove it through Michaela. When she jerked her head away, Michaela drew her lips back, exposing her fangs as a warning.

Frowning, Demetrius's intense glare focused on Michaela. "Elisabeth continues to be the one in the garden who I value the most. That will never change."

Chris took slow, controlled breaths, trying to calm the anger brewing from the creatures of the night behaving as though she were an inconsequential thing that they possessed and controlled. She realized she was just a pawn to them, an inanimate object that spoke, moved, and performed for their amusement. They gave her so little value for no other reason than she was just human—no, because she wasn't a vampire. They held very little regard for anyone that wasn't part of their Seethe and even less for those that weren't vampires.

Michaela watched him for a long time and then smiled. "Did you know that your little pet has been playing on both sides of the fence? Perhaps you were wondering why she's so preoccupied these days. It's the wolf. She's rutting with him again. That's why she denies you. She prefers him to satisfy her lust."

Michaela kept a keen focus on Demetrius, watching his reaction, provoking him, hoping to ignite strife that would fuel her own selfish desires. "How embarrassed you must feel to know that she chose Ethan over you. Will she choose *them* over us?"

He inhaled a pseudo-breath as hard lines formed along his face. He scowled. His piercing obsidian eyes pressed into Chris, making her feel uncomfortable. She dropped her gaze from his. She shouldn't have had any feelings of guilt or shame, but, for some reason, she did.

Leaning back against the wall, he nodded for Michaela to continue.

"If things go badly, as they very well may, who will she side with? Will she repay your kindness with betrayal?" she taunted, watching his reaction, gauging his anger, instigating a volatile reaction.

Chris had a hard time trying to comprehend how Michaela could derive so much pleasure in antagonizing someone she claimed to love. She pushed past Michaela, ignoring the sharp look she gave her. "I'm confident that I won't have to make that choice. Josh is better than most give him credit for. When the time comes, I doubt you all or the were-animals will fail at ending this."

Michaela made a dark sound, clearly growing impatient with her.

Splitting her attention between Michaela and Demetrius, she inched toward the door. "Ethan and I have an understanding. We've always been rather casual. Our obligations have always come first. That has never been a problem between us."

She found her gaze locked with Demetrius's. He was still glaring at her as Michaela walked over to him and kissed him—a long, hard, lingering kiss. Chris looked away, and when her gaze finally returned to them, she found Demetrius's eyes open, staring back at her. His fingers ran along Michaela's face, gently stroking it, closing his eyes as he pulled her closer, his hands roving over her back. The kiss became increasingly heated and ribald. For a brief moment, Chris thought they had forgotten she was there.

But they hadn't. Human life was inconsequential to them—they just didn't care.

"Demetrius, Michaela, have a good night," she said coolly when they had finally pulled away from each other, dismissing them with a frosty tone and abandoning any pretense of pleasantry. She was tired and annoyed with them. Pacifying their massive egos by appealing to their arrogance didn't seem important at the moment.

After a long, uncomfortable silence, Michaela was the first to leave. Demetrius stayed longer, his gazed fixed on Chris in such a manner that she was starting to feel uncomfortable. She couldn't read him, which made her nervous.

"We'll discuss this later," he said finally.

"There's nothing further to discuss," she stated firmly, but she had a feeling it wasn't the end of this conversation.

CHAPTER 16

The next evening, Demetrius pushed his way past Chris when she opened the door. She didn't turn to meet his hard stare but she could feel it on her from across the room. "Shouldn't you be feeding or, at the very least, resting?" she asked in a stiff voice.

The last thing she needed or wanted was a visit from him. Six hours before they were all to meet at the pack's home, he decided to make a house call. Her focus remained on the plans for tonight: find the creatures and kill as many as they could find. The capsa was instrumental in the success of this. Ethos was expending too much magic to shapeshift, strengthen, and control his creatures. With the use of the capsa, they would weaken him to the point he was inconsequential, and capable of being killed. And if things went as planned, they would.

This was going to be over soon, and she couldn't wait. Playing peacemaker and soothing egos had devoured her patience. Demetrius and Sebastian could go back to despising each other from afar and occasionally fighting. There weren't any delusions that they would be able to maintain an ongoing alliance. The otherworld wouldn't know how to respond to it, would play them against each other.

"After tonight, you and Sebastian no longer have to play nice with each other," she said.

"Do you think it will really end tonight?" he asked. His eyes narrowed, watching her with the same intense manner he had since he walked in. His distrust wasn't from the lack of confidence in their potential to succeed but disdain at the very idea that if they did, it was ultimately because of the were-animals and their allies. It was a hard strike against his ego and that of his Seethe.

She turned toward him. "Josh wouldn't give you the satisfaction of his failure." She gave him a wry smile.

Demetrius studied her for a long time. His obsidian eyes were so cold and remote that she pulled her gaze away. "He is stronger than I believed, quite an asset to Sebastian," he acknowledged, unable to hide his envy that Josh wasn't his.

She shrugged. "He is strong but not as skilled as a witch of his level should be. He had assistance with this matter." Oddly enough, she wanted to protect Josh from Demetrius, who could be spiteful. He wouldn't think twice about destroying Josh and dealing with the consequences of the pack's wrath.

"Who?" His eyebrow raised as his curiosity piqued.

She knew that whoever was skilled and strong enough to help Josh, Demetrius would want for himself. He was never diplomatic with such requests. They were nothing more than poorly masked threats to comply. The person never walked away believing for one moment they had the option to decline.

Josh had informed her that London had made it clear she didn't want to be part of this world and went through great lengths to slip into oblivion. Chris wouldn't be the one to betray her anonymity. "She's gone."

"Dead or just gone?"

She finally lifted her eyes to meet his, smiling. "As good as dead."

He didn't look convinced; even her limpid smile didn't seem to win his trust. She was thoroughly aware of the attention he had placed on her, his gaze fixed sternly on her. For so many years, she had lived in this world as a ghost—her existence scarcely known. When a job was over, she vanished to return to her own life. Now, this world had her caught in it like a web. Each time she thought she was free, she found herself stuck somewhere else. One small mistake during a job, a slight error in judgment, and she was connected to Demetrius indefinitely.

"Michaela will not be joining us."

She didn't care to understand the intricacy of their relationship, but he protected Michaela at all costs. If there were a risk that she could get hurt, he wouldn't let her anywhere near it.

"My Seethe adores her. Chase, Gabriella, and Quell would be too concerned with her safety to be of any use tonight," he admitted as a subtle anger hardened his voice.

Chris wondered if the thought of their implacable adoration bothered him. Was he jealous? Or was it the adoration Michaela created that kept them together and drove him to protect her in such a manner? If she were ever severely injured, would they turn on him? Anyone who knew or felt hunger and desire knew that Chase wanted Demetrius's position. Unlike the were-animal, whose physical dominance played a large role in maintaining their position, the vampire's loyalties were an imperceptible game of politics. There was an ineffable loyalty held by the *created* for those who had brought them into the life, which explained why Michaela could be unnecessarily cruel to them without fear of retaliation. They would love her unconditionally. They understood the importance of having a leader who was strong, deft, wise, and when necessary, efficaciously brutal and cruel. Demetrius possessed that skill, but it wouldn't be long until others saw that Chase did, as well. They both had a fatal flaw—the women in their lives. Michaela had created Chase. He wouldn't do anything that would displease her, including vying for Demetrius's position in the Seethe.

Chris ignored Demetrius as he studied her, but soon it became so relentless that disregarding him was no longer an option. "I think you should leave, I have to prepare," she lied. The moment Josh had called her, she had cleaned her guns, sorted her ammunition, and packed everything she needed in her canvas bag.

He frowned. "Michaela is right to be concerned that you are lying with dogs again." He stepped closer, holding her gaze with relentless curiosity. "This thing with you and Ethan, I thought it ended years ago."

Her smile lacked warmth. "Since it hasn't affected my job, who I *lie* with isn't any concern of yours or Michaela's."

There was just a flicker of disdain. "You two shouldn't be together. I can't think of a worse coupling."

"Hmm, I can think of at least one. I appreciate your concern, but perhaps you should be less concerned about what I am doing and more concerned with *who* Michaela is doing. She runs through your Seethe as though she was getting mileage points for encounters."

He chuckled. "Michaela is not my concern at this moment."

"Why isn't she? You spend a great deal of worry on things that aren't your concern. Perhaps she is in need of yours. You claim to love her, but you spend your time entertaining yourself with others—"

"I love her deeply."

"You two have a strange way of showing it. At one time, you would have destroyed cities, killed hundreds, and changed the world as we know it for her. Now you stand here, with me, asking questions I have no intention of answering, concerned with things in my life that are really none of your business." She hated how close he was, and no matter how much she tried to distance herself, he invaded her space with his intense glower.

He smiled, but his eyes remained cold, hard. "We are not

human nor do we pretend to be. We don't put such limitations on our love, commitments, and desires. When you've lived as long as we have, you learn to put things in perspective."

"Or you end up no longer valuing them."

"This thing between you and Ethan, is it love?" he asked with a bemused cynicism.

Even if she wanted to answer the question, she didn't know how. Defining what they had was always a challenge.

He continued, dismissing the idea. "As if you two know anything of love. He comforts you, but you'll never truly give yourself to him. Eventually, the challenge of making you what he wants will tire him, and you'll grow weary of putting up a front. The happiest you will ever be is apart from him."

She couldn't give Demetrius the satisfaction of knowing that there was some truth to his words. Turning her back to him, she directed her attention to the window. It was pitch-black outside, and her image reflected back at her. Physically, she hadn't changed a lot over the years. The only changes were her eyes. They had become dark, hard, and cold: casualties of the world that she chose to continue to live in.

His chest pressed against her back, his lips nuzzling against her neck as he spoke. "If you had to choose …"

"My loyalties, as always, are to whomever employs me. Deciding between you and Ethan is not a choice you want me to make."

"But I want you to. Answer me."

She turned to face his inquiring gaze. "You are not my lover, my friend, or even one that I consider an acquaintance. You mean two things to me and nothing more: a paycheck and vampire blood. If you care to consider yourself anything more, then you are a fool. You have your answer."

If she were capable of such inane thoughts, she would have thought he looked hurt. But she knew better. Demetrius's arrogance and narcissism made him feel that he should be put above all others, and to be told otherwise was an assault to his ego.

She closed her eyes for a moment and tried to sort out how complicated her life had become over the last year. The pressure of it was weighing on her. She didn't want to deal with it anymore. She spoke slowly. "I'm not sure what Ethan and I have. Perhaps it's far worse than whatever you and Michaela have, but it's an acceptable complication, one that I am willing to deal with. But whatever this is between us has become something quite ugly and unacceptable, and it ends today."

A life that was always rather complex was further complicated by trading with Demetrius. The costs outweighed the benefits. It needed to be over.

With a wry smile, he asked, "*Over with?* What exactly do you want to be over?"

"Everything: the jobs, the trading, your invasion into my life, the ridiculous late-night visits, you trying to seduce me for kicks. You will not come here anymore. I am not available to you for any reason."

Stunned, his look blanched into dismay. When he spoke, his words were rough and commanding. "You'll walk away from my offering—my gift. Don't take it for granted because I will never offer this to you again. You think long and hard about this. Are you really prepared to go back to the way you were?"

"I was good enough before. I did my job well, you even said 'exceptionally.' I survived—"

"Barely."

Chris shrugged a response.

He smiled, stepping closer, and took her hands into his. Pressing his lips firmly into her forearm, his teeth grazed across the skin, beseeching her to do it one more time—for old times' sake. There was a smug confidence to his inquiry, as though she would never reject him. She was going to miss the enhanced abilities. She wouldn't deny that. But if she succumbed to it once, then there would be a twice, and she would never stop.

She shook her head. "No."

Demetrius's face tensed at her refusal before it melted away into acceptance. His gaze was gripping, deeply penetrating, and strong as it held hers, capturing her mind. No longer the master of her own accord, her volition was stripped from her at that very moment.

"*Chris, come to me*," he ordered as he took a seat on the sofa.

Unable to disobey his request, she was at his side immediately. He pulled her to him, setting her astride him before slowly unbuttoning her shirt and sliding it off her shoulder. His fingers dug into her skin as he pulled her to him. For a long time, he sat back admiring her, acquiescent for the first time since they had met. He kissed her gently on the lips, then the neck, before urging her closer to him. When his fangs sank into her skin, she whimpered, and he inhaled a ragged breath. With each deep draw, the pain intensified, and she was unable to stop the soft cries that only heightened his pleasure.

He fed for a long time, far longer than needed to quench his hunger. Afterward, he cradled her into him, caressing her against him. He kissed her again softly on the lips then on the cheek. Fully surrendered to him, her body rested against him, the coolness of his chilling her. When she shivered, he pulled her closer, his face tucked into the curve of her neck. He hesitated for a long time before he released her mind and her will.

Volition now hers again, she felt like she had plummeted into her being.

She looked down at her open shirt, exposed bra, his hands resting around her waist, and the rivulet of blood at the corner of his mouth. A rush of hatred and loathing sparked through her like an uncontainable fire. She jumped up in such a rush that she stumbled. He reached out to help her but stopped abruptly when he saw the look on her face. It was only then that he showed the slightest hint of remorse—just a flash. He would never give her the satisfaction of dwelling on it.

Anger ripped through her as she considered the defilement. She backed away from him until her lower back was just inches from the console at the other end of the room. The rage rode her hard. This level of fury was new to her and erased all logical responses. Her fingers stayed at the edge of the drawer, and when he took a step closer, they quickly slipped into the drawer, pulled out the 9mm Berretta, and aimed it at him. It wouldn't kill him, but it would hurt like hell. She wanted him to feel more than just pain. She wanted to kill him. Whether he killed her in the process or she became the target of his Seethe was the furthest thing from her concerns.

"Put it down," he commanded in a low voice. When she didn't move, he took several cautious steps toward her. "Be angry, but don't be foolish. I assure you, this isn't something you want to do." His voice was soft, genteel.

"You forced me!" She shook her head with disbelief.

"I didn't force you."

"The mind rape you pulled—it was force. Romanticize it if you want, but that is exactly what it was. You promised you would never do that to me!"

She was wound so tightly that the rage in her snapped—she pulled the trigger, squeezing off six shots. Demetrius moved fast but not fast enough. Two bullets clipped his shoulder, another grazed over his stomach. Reacting quickly, he closed in on her, pulling the gun from her. He threw it across the room then secured her against the wall. Pinning her arms across her chest, he immobilized her. His angry astonished face was just inches from hers as the pain from his injuries forced short, gurgled gasps.

She struggled under him, tugging, writhing, and twisting as she tried to break his hold. Her only thoughts were to get away so that she could get to a knife or a stake. "Get your damn hands off of me."

He stared at her for a long time—too long—fueling her anger with each moment. His face set, chin tilted high, gaze cool and unrepentant. His arrogant sense of entitlement made her body ache to inflict more pain.

"Behave," he urged, letting her go and stepping away.

Behave?

She rushed for the console, pulling the drawer out so far it dropped, emptying the contents onto the floor. Grabbing one of the blades and a stake that had fallen at her feet, she lunged at him. The idea that she could ever defeat Demetrius hand to hand was not a delusion she held, but anger had suppressed all logic as she reacted only out of fury and a need for revenge. Swinging the blade, she slashed at him, but he parried, and avoided her strike. A quick jab and the blade drove into rigid flesh of his stomach. He groaned. She retreated, ripped out the blade, and lunged at him again. He caught her hands in a firm grasp and backed her into the wall.

"Drop it," he ordered.

On autopilot, her body wouldn't give up until he was dead or as horribly injured as possible. He held her bound against the wall, she couldn't move. Pressed firmly against the wall, her options for defense were limited. The hard burst of breath from his gasp felt acrid across her lips. His fingers touching her skin made it crawl in disgust. She wanted him away from her—far away.

"I won't ask again." And he didn't. The pressure on her tendons increased, becoming too painful to endure. She dropped both the stake and blade.

"Get your hands off me."

It was a moment—a long moment—before he stepped away from her.

Her voice quivered as she spoke, anger sharpening her words. "As the leader of your Seethe, I realize, at times, you have to seem heartless. You need to appear ruthless, cold, to maintain your position and command their respect. I always assumed it was because it was necessary. But you are just cruel and ruthless for no other reason than you are a monster. You're right. You aren't bound by the same limitations as humans when it comes to emotions. It's not because they are inferior. You are a horrible, soulless thing. Get out!"

If Chris lived a thousand lives, she never would have believed what she saw on Demetrius's face—remorse. It was unmitigated, relentless repentance that eclipsed his features like a shadow. She looked away, refusing to feel sorrow or sympathy for him. She wanted to go to her grave hating him for the monster that he was.

He looked at the stake and blade dropped at his side. "I never planned it this way. Never with you and never like this."

"Get out!"

He stepped toward her, and she moved as far as she could away from him. Injured, he was unable to travel. He walked slowly out the door and slammed it behind him.

An hour later, she stood in the middle of her living room surrounded by shattered glass, splintered wood, and broken porcelain that covered the floor. After Demetrius left, she had taken the vase that he had given her, a unique blend of pearl and ocher blown glass, and slammed it to the ground. It was the first gift he had ever given her. It didn't relieve the deep-seated feeling of assault and betrayal that kept eating at her. He couldn't be like everyone else and place her payment in an envelope. Instead, it was sent over by courier with a vase filled with tiger lilies, which had been her favorite flower until she started dating Ethan and developed a special fondness for the moonflower. She wasn't sure how he knew that.

Pretentious bastard, she thought angrily.

Then she took the beautifully sculpted figurine he'd given her and threw it against the wall, raining porcelain throughout the room. She looked around for more of his pretentious presents. She grabbed a clay figurine. It was sculpted in her image, more weird than flattering. She broke it in her hands and stomped the remains into pieces. For a brief moment, she felt an extreme sense of satisfaction as she exhaled a ragged breath. It quickly vanished once she considered his violation. Her bad memories and demons that she had once buried deep and covered with activity, violence, and turmoil were now floating to the surface. Her breathing was shallow, her head pounded, and her only thoughts were to put them to rest once again. There were demons that she hadn't slain but put to rest and eased to the point she could live. Now everything was unleashed and she felt like she was being weighted down, submerged by them.

The walls were stained claret from the expensive bottles of imported wine, more gifts from Demetrius that she had tossed against them. She had destroyed everything he had given her and she still didn't feel any better than she did when she started.

Her life was a mess.

Chris walked into the pack's home. Sebastian sat on one end of the room and Demetrius on the other. The tension and thinly disguised hatred made it even more uncomfortable for her to be there. Demetrius's head tilted up, her scent announcing her arrival before she could make it into the room. He moved from the chair like a tenebrous wave. Clasping her by her arm, he pulled her toward the door. Sebastian appeared to have his attention elsewhere, but she knew he was aware of everything that was happening. It wasn't often he didn't know.

Demetrius moved in close to her; his lips brushed her ear as he spoke and she winced in revulsion each time it did. "Why are you here?" he asked in a forced whisper.

The idea of never working with him again was satisfying, and she would derive great pleasure in leaving. His Seethe would assume it was to protect her and wouldn't take kindly to knowing that he valued her safety, an outsider, more than theirs. That might be more than enough to ensure a coup and Chase competing for the position of the Seethe's Master.

But her skills as a sharpshooter were needed, and backing out at the last minute wasn't an option. Her career and the reputation she had worked so hard to establish would be irreversibly tarnished. Walking out on the job would ensure that the vampires would take great joy in trashing her. No matter what creative spin she put on it, her credibility would be ruined. The were-animals would never forgive her for the perceived betrayal, and Sebastian would undoubtedly want her to atone for it. No, she needed to complete this job. Walking away wasn't an option.

"You paid for a job, and I intend to complete it," she stated with a shrug.

His face pulled into a rigid grimace. "Your services are no longer needed or wanted. I want you gone."

"You want me to walk away from this, relieve myself of the duties I was hired to perform, while your people fight and possibly die? Do you really want to send me away and make me exempt from the dangers you willingly expect your Seethe to accept? Will you still have their reverence, their loyalty, their respect after such a betrayal?" Scrutinizing him for a long time, she finally asked, "Why are you doing this. To ease your guilt?"

His eyes narrowed to slits, and foreboding contempt forced a harsh frown on his face as he inched forward, closing the distance she had managed to get between them. "There isn't any guilt that needs to be assuaged. I saved you from death. Your life is mine to do with as I please." The rigidity of his face, the firmness of his tone, the steely coldness of his eyes let her know that he meant it. He felt it to his core, and despite any protests, he wouldn't soon change his views. Whatever remorse he had held earlier was now smothered by his arrogance and sense of entitlement.

Chris moved her hand from the gun holstered at her waist. She didn't have the temperament or control not to act on her feelings. A fine scene it would be for everyone to come into the pack's home and find Demetrius bleeding on the floor from gunshots. She pushed him away. "That's good to know."

His gaze remained on her as she crossed to the other side of the room where she turned, forcing herself to meet his gaze.

She smiled.

She was going to kill him tonight.

CHAPTER 17

Chris could barely see in the bleak night, murky with the heightened anxiety and anticipation of violence. The relief that after this moment they wouldn't have to be allies or deal with one another was so palpable it strummed through the air. With darkness shadowing the large area, Ethos's creatures' hideaway seemed more remote. The uneven terrain in the open area should have been plush with grass. Instead, it was crisp with dried weeds from the recent drought and poor maintenance.

She was perched in a tree about sixty feet away looking through the night vision scope on her M40. Because they had the element of surprise, they expected this to be a quick and brutal slaughter, but the creatures responded quickly with deftness and vigor. They swiftly changed to their massive size and responded to the attack viciously. Size and claws gave them the advantage—an advantage that would have killed less skillful fighters.

The first attack was on Chase, as a disfigured thing's slender fingerlike claws swiped at him several times. The last one was hard, grazing his clothes, missing the abdomen by a hair. One shot to the skull and the creature dropped at Chase's feet. He looked in the direction of the shot and nodded his appreciation.

Sebastian was art in motion, his movements graceful as he parried the monsters' advances. He moved with the graceful, quick movements of a person half his size. Whether using a sword or daggers, he was equally skilled. As he plowed his way through the pack of creatures, Chris was reminded of why he was the Alpha and why Ethos had kept him alive. He would have been a hard kill, and if you desired power, you definitely wanted Sebastian in your corner. His hands were his ammunition and his skills deadly weapons.

Sebastian, Ethan, Steven, and Gavin stayed in human form, directing the others and fighting hand to hand. The disadvantage of animal form against the creatures became evident quickly. They often went for the gut, slicing through it, which happened to a were-dingo. Ethan, with a sword in hand, clipped the thing at its knees, bringing it down. Josh was next to it immediately, siphoning the magic from it.

One vampire was killed quickly when a creature used its knifelike teeth to decapitate him. Another met his demise when a claw staked through his heart. His reversion was too fast to stop even if someone could have gotten to him. Demetrius's decades on this earth had made him adroit and a true menace. He preferred hand to hand and would only resort to weapons to inflict a greater depth of pain. The submission of Ethos's creature was swift and cruel, as he pinned him to the ground with a knife and dismembered him with a level of pleasure that only a sadist could have.

Chris's curiosity peaked as she watched the capsa responding to Skylar in the same manner it did to Josh. When one of the monsters tackled Josh, pinning him to the ground, he didn't have time to respond before Ethan crashed into it, dislocating the arm and severing its body down the middle. Skylar, moving quicker than Josh, retrieved the displaced capsa. As soon as she touched it, the magic was pulled from the creature.

"Hmm, that is interesting," Chris whispered but soon redirected her attention where it was needed. Seated comfortably in the large tree, nearly twenty feet off the ground, she peered through the scope. This was where she loved to be: in the middle of a battle, bodies collapsed around her, the violence, the pain, the adrenaline-induced high of being just minutes, if not seconds, from death. But she couldn't enjoy it because her focus was split between the creatures and Demetrius. She just needed one of the monsters to get close to him, which was a task in itself. As one of the best sharpshooters in the city, no one would believe a grossly inaccurate shot. Just one slightly off shot that was meant for one of Ethos's minions, but hit Demetrius, was believable. With the .50-caliber sniper rifle she used, the bullet would rip through his neck. It would be as good as beheading him, an unfortunate accident for which she would never be held accountable.

Shot after shot, creatures fell with a single bullet as she waited patiently for that perfect moment to kill Demetrius. And it occurred better than anything she could have imagined. One creature lay at his feet as he tugged at the sword, pulling it from its thick, putrid skin. Another approached him from behind. She needed it closer so she could take the shot. It would be perfect, clean, slicing through Demetrius's neck and hitting the thing, as well. It might not kill Ethos's minion but it would look believable. Demetrius's injury would be fatal, and he would go through reversion quickly. Even if she were off just ever so slightly, his injury would be too severe. He would need to feed quickly or suffer the fate of reversion. Chase was the closest to him and she knew she didn't have to worry about him making an effort to save Demetrius. Her lips kinked into a cruel smirk as she prepared to take the shot.

Her finger pressed against the trigger, she squeezed. At that moment, a sharp kick jabbed into her side. She lost her balance and fell back, crashing to the ground, feeling the sharp pains of bones breaking from the impact. Gasping for air, she tried to turn onto her stomach. A hammer-like jolt went through her hand as a foot slammed down on it. The bones in her hand were crushed, sending shooting pains through her.

Roughly flipped over, she was face-to-face with Michaela. Chris expected anger but she was met with a placid smile. With an open hand, she slapped Chris across the face. Without pause, she backhanded her and then pressed her hands over Chris's mouth, keeping her silent.

"I need him back, and you're the only way to do that," she said. She rained powerful relentless blows into her, driven by a rage that Chris couldn't understand. Her right shoulder had been shattered beyond use from the fall. She used her left hand to block the blows as the onslaught continued. Blood blurred her vision. She was able to return several jabs, but they weren't enough to deter Michaela. Her nails raked across Michaela's face. The vampire stumbled back.

"You bitch," she growled, grabbing Chris's hand and breaking the offending fingers.

When Michaela leaned over her again, Chris jabbed the heel of her hand hard against her chin, and her head snapped back from the impact. Michaela retreated just a few steps then kicked her in the side; ribs broke, puncturing her skin. Michaela continued thrashing blows against her as she attempted to roll away, protecting herself the best she could. Michaela's foot pressed into her back, planting her in place, and then she pushed it to nudge her over to face her before she slammed it hard into Chris's leg. The positional advantage made the leg snap easily. Chris's shrieks of pain were masked by the fighting occurring nearly sixty feet away.

The Seethe's Mistress stood over her, her face showing anger and pleasure. She watched as Chris struggled, making a feeble attempt to ease the pain. She could barely focus as Michaela spoke, a shadow of disdain lacing her voice, sharp and incendiary.

"He cares for you more than you deserve. Your death will hurt him, cause him great anger and regret. He will want someone to pay. The blame will fall on the were-animals because they failed to protect you. And he *will* make them pay."

When she inched closer, Chris made another weak attempt to move. Fighting past the pain, she used her fragmented arm to push her away. Michaela laughed at her efforts then wrenched the arm again until it lay limp at Chris's side. Using her fangs like a knife, she grazed them across Chris's neck. The pain seared through her, but she gritted her teeth, biting back the pain, refusing to give Michaela further satisfaction in her defeat. Blood spurted over Chris's face and chest. Unable to use her hands to slow the bleeding, she started to fade.

Michaela dragged her farther into the woods and away from everyone, ensuring that she would not be found. The natural predators of the night would find her defenseless and finish the job. She leaned down, speaking softly into Chris's cheek. "Nothing personal—just a means to an end. I *will* have him back."

Chris lay in the middle of the desolate woods, broken again, but this time beyond repair. She knew her death was inevitable, and she had never imagined it would be like this. The end was supposed to be something more climactic, a glorious fight that others would speak of long after she had been buried and mourned. She never imagined that she would fall victim to the wrath of the Seethe's Mistress, over Demetrius, just so her death could harden him, anger him, and make him wrathful.

Her breathing was now just shallow gasps. She expected to panic at the anticipation of death, but she didn't. There was a level of peace that she hadn't felt in her life in a long time. *Perhaps this won't be so bad after all,* she thought as she closed her eyes.

Blood dampened the ground, parts of the creatures' mutilated bodies were scattered over the area, and the smell of anger and violence permeated the air. The milieu of the vacant forest looked like a battlefield, yet it didn't feel like it was over. The sky, once dusky with a mere hint of light from the moon, became uncharacteristically stygian. I couldn't pinpoint the direction from which it came. The undulation of dark magic swept through the vast area in strong pulses. The others might have only felt the magic, but I sensed the darkness. Everyone stilled, waiting.

Hindsight being 20/20, I should have moved, even run like I was being chased by a hatchet-wielding monster, but like everyone else, I just stood and waited, transfixed, paralyzed by the amount of power Ethos still possessed, even though over forty of his creatures had been destroyed and their magic absorbed. He started to advance toward me in human form. Sebastian lunged at him, but with a wave of his hand, Ethos threw him back nearly twenty feet. The whole time, he didn't take his focus off me as he formed a thick, translucent bulwark around us that spanned over several feet, enclosing just the two of us in. Out of my peripheral vision, I could see Sebastian, Steven, and Gavin pounding at it with their weapons. With each strike, shards of energy, a shower of copper, pushed them back with as much force as they exerted. I backed away, forcing myself to the far end of the wall. My back pressed into it, but it wouldn't budge. Ethos was weakening. Every few steps, fragments of his human veil dropped and his real features resurfaced in bursts. As he inched closer, he was unable to hold his human form, and I was faced with the monstrous creature that haunted my nightmares.

Ethan slipped between us, breaking through the wall, which quickly reformed, blocking the three of us in. At the sight of him, the master of dark magic stopped, and taking several steps back, he hissed, a loud, reedy sound. The wall quivered, waves rolling over it, pressure forcing it to expand just to the brink of destruction before rebounding back. Deep vermillion eyes went blank as he pushed Ethan out of the space with such force it smashed me into the wall, keeping me plastered and immobile against it.

Come on, Josh. I hoped that with Ethos in a weakened state, Josh could defeat him. But he was nowhere to be found. I looked at all angles of the wall for him as the were-animals continued to try and shatter it, to get to me, a goal that the vampires didn't seem to hold.

Face-to-face, he switched to mildly less offensive human form. With a shattering crash, Ethan pushed through the wall again, but this time Ethos's response was less subtle. The features of his grotesque face became severe. What was it about Ethan that Tre'ases and powerful purveyors of dark magic didn't like? With a quick wave of his hand, he pounded Ethan's body against the wall until he went limp then expelled him through it again with such force it ripped a hole into it, which slowly resealed.

Ethos dropped to his knees, then skidded several feet away from me as flashes of light filled the darkened space around us. I didn't need to turn around. I could feel Josh's familiar magic. The strong neutral energy pulsated against my back. Josh's presence emboldening me, I moved fast, closing the space between Ethos and me. When he came to his feet, he was distracted. He was insulted by Josh's retaliation and ready to demonstrate the full range of his power—to test the levels of Josh's skill. His eyes became an abyss, empty and cold, as he called upon stronger magic. Opening his hands, he dropped small pods to the ground that formed into small creatures that breezed past me to get to Josh.

Distracted by his assault on Josh, he ignored me for the moment as he watched his creatures attack with amusement. I jabbed my knife into the soft part of his neck, sliding through it with ease, just inches from pushing through the other side.

Blood spurted as he clawed frantically at the knife. His abysmal eyes stayed on me as he gasped for breath, shifting between his human façade and true form. Stumbling back, he fought to keep from collapsing to the ground. It was intoxicating to know that I was the face of death to something that so truly deserved it. At that moment, I felt euphoric with an intense sense of satisfaction. Epic, heroic, valiant. Foolish, I was gloating in my own sense of grandeur when it came to an abrupt end.

Ethos pulled the knife from his neck and grabbed me. Pulling me toward him, his hands pressed firmly into my cheeks, forcing my mouth open. The injury made it difficult for him to maintain his misshapen human form. It melted away, exposing his real appearance: a scaled creature whose jaw was disproportionate, nose too small, eyes too large and awkwardly centered. Deep titian eyes penetrated me with anger.

He exhaled—expelling a thick fog that streamlined into a vapor as it forced its way through my mouth and nose. As I pulled for air, he vanished, but not like he'd done before. A vapor shaped into his likeness stood in his place, battling between various corporal forms, fighting to stay grounded, and then it was absorbed into air.

I wasn't sure what happened after that because my only objective was to gasp in enough air to breathe and survive.

My body rebounded against the ground as I hit it. I had been lucky too many times. There was no way I was going to survive this. Smothered, I hacked out gasps, which were the only sounds I could manage. Ethan and Josh stood over me. Josh looked panicked, his lips moving rapidly as he threw out spell after spell, switching between them and incantations that didn't work. His appearance was strained by concern and fear, but not Ethan's. He looked calm—too calm—as though he was prepared for this, expected it. Ethan leaned into him, instructing him quietly. He listened for a long moment then started to shake his head slowly. "That's a myth. It will never work."

"Just do it," Ethan urged, pushing him forward.

Josh leaned over me and began to chant, and then his mouth hovered over mine, never making contact. He inhaled then turned his head away from me before he exhaled a breath. Breathing came easier but it was still restricted. He did it again. Then breath came with ease. All I was left with was the intense feeling of energy—a new power that was unfamiliar to me. I went from gasping for my final breaths, as darkness and death pulled me under, to a sense of exhilaration and undeniable power. My body craved it more than the breath it needed to survive. And through all the trauma and pain, I knew, at that moment, it was something I wanted. Something I needed. I refused to be totally divested of it. It burned in my chest, tolled in my body, resurrected my spirit. When Josh hovered over me again to draw more out, I pushed him away. "I'm okay," I said, sitting up.

His look was challenging and unconvinced. "It's all gone?"

"I'm fine."

I looked around the area. Ethos was gone and so were the rest of his creatures, with the exception of the ones we had killed. The ground was crimson and damp with the blood of those that hadn't survived. Clothing, bullets, broken weapons, and trampled vegetation covered the ground. The battle was over.

Josh didn't seem to care about anything other than me, as his attention remained focused intensely in my direction. I tried to ignore the inquiring gaze.

"I'm fine," I stated again.

He studied me for a long moment. Then he smiled, but it was weighted and forced. "Of course you are." He came to his feet and backed away from me.

Did he know? Could he sense it? My thoughts were interrupted by Demetrius barking through the dark crisp air. "Where the hell is she? Find her now!" Since all the major players in Demetrius's Seethe were in sight, I figured he was looking for Chris.

Josh's attention was pulled from me as he started his search for her. I followed him, helping with the search. I thought I would feel different—stronger, mystical, powerful—but everything felt the same. Staying close to Josh, when he went straight I went to either his right or left. We moved through the field, calling her name, traipsing deep into the copses.

Ethan searched the other side of the woods. The calm front that he wore like a mask melted quickly, giving way to panic.

"She's here," Josh called out from deep inside the woods. "She's here," he repeated, but now it sounded strained. Wide-eyed and mouth gaping open, he simply stared at the body. When I moved closer, I saw why he looked so mortified. She didn't even look like a person. Covered in blood and dirt, her body was so mangled, I had no idea where to start. She made gurgled choking noises in place of breathing. Josh seemed frazzled as he stood over the body, at a loss for a plan of action. Ethan stood next to him, painfully stilled as he looked at the battered figure in front of us.

Demetrius took one look at Chris and directed his rage at Ethan. "How could you let this happen!"

Josh pressed his finger along her carotid, feeling for a pulse. Then he tried her wrist. His face quickly went to defeated resolve as Demetrius and Ethan threw a barrage of insults and threats at each other.

Josh didn't bother trying to intervene. Instead, he knelt down next to her. "I have to take her to the house and see what Dr. Baker can do."

But he didn't sound confident that anything could be done. It took him a moment to try to position her crushed body in a manner he could travel with her.

As Ethan and Demetrius continued their fighting, spewing insults and blame, the area quickly became divided: were-animals on one side and the vampires on the other. Each side waited for the other to make the first move, leading to a battle that would be a detriment at this time.

"This isn't helping," I snapped angrily. I didn't necessarily like Chris, but no matter how I felt about her, she didn't deserve that. I directed my attention toward Ethan. "You go to the house and see after Chris." Then my gaze swept the rest of group. "And the rest of you go home. It's over." There was enough venom and anger in my command that they actually listened to me. The insults and posturing stopped, and eventually they left.

Demetrius and a large number of his Seethe showed up at the pack's retreat. After several hostile negotiations, Sebastian's only concession was to allow Demetrius to enter alone. Demetrius didn't seem at all concerned for his own well-being and dismissed his Seethe without hesitation.

I was able to slide through unnoticed because of the commotion caused by Josh, Steven, and Sebastian trying to keep Ethan and Demetrius away from each other. There wasn't a doubt that, if left to their own devices, they would have tried to kill each other. After a lot of encouragement, Ethan was on one side of the room, Demetrius on the other. It didn't take a psychologist or someone extremely adept in understanding behavior to realize we were dealing with very similar emotions—men in love. Or maybe it wasn't love. Neither one of them struck me as the type that could grasp the concept of something as ineffable as love or capable of ever really feeling it. Perhaps they were just men enthralled or maybe even men in extremely complex versions of like.

As I watched Demetrius's distraught appearance and sorrowful eyes, I wondered if Chris would be better off dead. Did Michaela know of his feelings? I doubted it. She didn't strike me as the type of person who would be okay sharing the same glass with someone, let alone sharing a man. And Ethan, his tumultuous relationship with Chris was anything but ideal. It was only a matter of time before they actually killed each other.

After nearly an hour working on Chris, Dr. Baker's frown lines were so deeply embedded they didn't seem like they would ever relax. Kelly had started her on an IV, then she attached her to a monitor while Dr. Baker assessed her and started trying to address her many wounds. When he had treated Winter, Joan, and the other were-animals for injuries just as bad or worse, he didn't have the same defeated look on his face as he held now. Maybe because with were-animals had a chance—a much better chance than Chris with her wholly human body.

When Dr. Baker was finished, she was medicated and attached to a monitor and infusion pump. The room was quiet. Just a series of swooshes, light interminable thumps, and clicks filled the silence.

As the various emotions of tension, anger, and worry permeated the room, it was Kelly's that shocked me the most. Splitting her attention between Chris and everyone in the room, the look of disgust finally shadowed and hardened her soft features.

"Whose genius idea was it to have her out there?" Her voice sliced through the silence. It sounded even harsher coming from her, whose voice was always a gentle banter.

I could understand her anger. We seemed cruel and uncivil as though we had forced her into a battle where she was outmatched and defenseless, and this was the result. Looking at Chris in this state, it was easy to forget that she was capable of many forms of violence, malice, and cruelty herself. She was a predator in her own right. But in her quiescent state, lying on the hospital bed, she looked fragile, weak, and diminutive. It washed away all those memories and made you feel immense sorrow for her.

She went into cardiac arrest. Everyone panicked except Dr. Baker and Kelly, who responded quickly. On television, it always looked intense and exciting. Someone started compressing the chest in rhythmic, forceful bursts while breathing life into the person. Then a wonderful angel of life brought a defibrillator and screamed, "Clear!" The body jerked and spasmed and then the person was breathing again. The only thing those shows had right was that everything became uncharacteristically silent and everyone seemed to be moving in slow motion. No matter how quickly they moved, it just wasn't fast enough.

If she managed to survive, she would be okay. Five minutes, that was the magic number that a person could be without oxygen to the brain before there was irreversible damage. It was a tidbit of information I always kept stored away, because when I was forced into my wolf during emotionally turbulent moments, I always felt like I was going into cardiac arrest. My mother, a pathologist, had always assured me I wasn't, but I was never convinced.

Dr. Baker had a difficult time stabilizing Chris, and she went into cardiac arrest two more times. The intensity of the emotions heightened to the point where it felt strained and uncomfortable. Demetrius slipped out of the room soon after the first cardiac incident. I could see him through the small glass window walking the hallway, drawn deeply into his own thoughts. I was having a hard time dealing with all the uncharacteristic and conflicting changes in my own emotions. I felt concern for Chris, empathy for Demetrius, and fear of Kelly, who looked like she was ready to give everyone in the room a thorough tongue-lashing.

"So guys, what's the end game?" Kelly finally asked, her hard gaze meeting everyone's for a brief moment. It swept from Josh, Ethan, Dr. Baker, Sebastian, and then back to Ethan.

"We'll change her," Ethan finally resolved.

Dr. Baker shook his head. "She will never survive it. Even a lesser species will be too hard for her body to endure. I don't think you realize how bad she is."

Look at her. He knows how bad she is.

Josh stepped over to his brother, silent for a long time, and then he exhaled. "You have another option," he offered. He was suggesting turning Chris into a vampire.

Ethan considered the option for a long time. Well, as long as he was capable of thinking about it, which was only seconds. "No."

"Ethan." Josh turned to face his brother once again, their eyes locked in that place where the two of them seemed to go when they had their nonverbal conversations. After a long moment,

Josh bit down on his lip as he stepped closer to his brother. "You'll regret it if you don't," he finally whispered.

"I've learned to live with far worse."

Josh waited, wide-eyed, his attention focused on his brother, who seemed too steadfast in his decision. "Ethan," he said softly in a final plea.

Although he hated Chris and Ethan being together, like Kelly he couldn't let her die. Not here and not like this. I wondered if, like Kelly, his feelings softened seeing her lying on a hospital bed, battered and defeated. It was easy to forget at that moment what she was really like.

Ethan shook his head and turned from Josh's entreaty. After moments of silence, Josh looked at Sebastian then Dr. Baker and shook his head.

Sebastian nodded once, accepting Ethan's decision. "Don't let her suffer," Sebastian said to Dr. Baker. *Translation: When we leave, let her go as gently and quickly as possible.*

"You're going to let her die?" Kelly asked softly, the anger replaced by sheer horror and repugnance.

Their silence was a tacit confirmation. Kelly stepped back, her focus sweeping throughout the room, then it stayed fixed on Sebastian. She waited, just as I did, for that hard baritone growl, the acerbic response that made challenging his decision impossible. All he had to do was object and it would veto Ethan's decision. But he didn't, and part of me knew he wouldn't. Chris was a liability, and there was some solace in her death. Ethan hated vampires, Demetrius to be more specific, but changing her still left her out there and a possibility in Ethan's life. I doubted vampirism would stop it.

Whether Ethan chose to admit it or not, she was his weakness, and everyone else could see it. If he were a junkie or an alcoholic, she was the next fix or drink. I didn't think Sebastian had ever liked her because he saw her for what she was to Ethan and the pack—a liability. Knowing that, he still wouldn't have been the one to pull the trigger. If he had, there would be animosity and distrust between them, inevitably weakening the pack. Everything Sebastian did was for the good of the pack. Letting Chris die was good for them.

Unable to take her eyes off Sebastian, Kelly was in an intense state of awe, lips parted in shock, eyes wide and glistening with disbelief. "Sebastian," she said in a barely audible gasp.

He started out the door but turned to face Kelly, who had sagged into the wall as though someone had smothered her with the apathy that filled the room. The shock of realization shadowed her face, and she displayed it clearly. We were monsters—heartless, unconscionable monsters. The realization of it hit hard and she was at a loss for words.

Before she could find them, Sebastian spoke, his tone soft, a gentle induction into the darker part of this world that she hadn't seen. "Sometimes, what seems like the cruelest thing is the best option."

He gave the air of compassion, I believe, for Kelly's benefit. He kept a careful eye on her, but because of the indeterminate way she gazed at him, her emotions were hard to read. Perhaps she had slipped into her version of Neverland, where people didn't let someone die if there were alternatives. Where puppies and kittens bounced around and babies were dressed up like an Anne Geddes photo. I hoped she had found her happy place, because right now she needed to be somewhere. She was broken.

All the petals had been plucked off her rose of innocence and she had been truly initiated into this world. It was cold, hard, reprehensible, and, at times, disturbing. When you found the ability to trudge through the darkness and accepted how things worked, you still felt like you'd crawled through filth. They all had been dwelling in the swamp so long that it was just another decision that benefited the pack. Whether it was by association or innate, I wasn't that far from it myself.

Dr. Baker detached the monitors, removing the many lines

attached to Chris, all while Kelly continued to look at us like we were fiends without a conscience. We all watched for the subtle nuances of life: the gentle rise of her chest as she breathed, the slight flutter of her eyelids, the light thump of a barely functioning heart.

All the signs of life held, but they were faint. She would be dead soon, but she was a fighter, clinging to it longer than anyone expected.

"Ethan." It was Josh's final request.

Ethan turned briefly to look at his brother with a cold, hard intensity, making it clear that he wasn't going to change his mind.

With the mask of indifference covering his face, Ethan stepped out the double doors and came face-to-face with Demetrius. "Go home," he said.

Preoccupied by the sight of Chris's nearly lifeless body on the hospital bed, he didn't bother to be insulted. He stepped closer to the door, peering past Ethan to get a better look. Ethan shoved him back. Demetrius snarled, drawing his lips back and baring his sharp canines like daggers, ready to defend. He pushed Ethan skidding farther into the room, crashing into the far wall. Ethan rebounded quickly and started toward him in long, hard strides. Kelly stepped between the two of them, her arms outstretched, separating them. Ethan stopped abruptly to keep from crashing into Kelly.

She looked at Demetrius for a long time as his attention diverted from Ethan and returned to Chris.

Kelly frowned. "Why can't he at least say good-bye? Doesn't he at least deserve that much?" she asked Ethan, her voice just a whisper, so subdued and disenchanted she seemed shattered beyond repair.

Ethan kept his opinion to himself, although his look spoke volumes. The alliance was over, the perpetrator handled—they owed Demetrius nothing.

It took a long time before he answered. His lips were pressed tight. "Say your good-byes and leave," he said, taking a quick glance at his watch.

Demetrius was at Chris's side before he could finish. We stepped out to give him privacy, but Kelly wasn't able to move too far away. She watched him from the other side of the door, through the small window. On her toes, her face pressed close into the glass peering at them in complete silence. When she looked back at Dr. Baker, her eyes glistened. "What will happen to her when he is done?"

Dr. Baker responded quietly, "She will be relieved."

Disgust and disappointment molded over her features like a cast. "Relieved? You mean you will kill her."

He looked uncomfortable under her deeply disappointed gaze. His scowl deepened, reaching his eyes, filling them with concern. "Yes."

She returned her attention back to the window, unable to look at him. He stepped closer to her and she tensed. Then he moved away, giving her the space she desperately needed.

It had only been five minutes, but Ethan had grown impatient waiting. He stepped out of the hallway to the main house. Josh followed behind, probably to make a final effort to try to persuade him. Sebastian paced the long hallway, unusually patient with Demetrius's extended good-bye. He didn't seem concerned about Demetrius, just annoyed.

Fatigued from battle and in need of feeding, they knew he wouldn't be able to leave with Chris, and he wasn't in any state to successfully turn her. They seemed to be more concerned with Kelly. Dr. Baker watched her as he leaned against the wall just several feet from her.

Kelly divided her attention between Demetrius and Sebastian, carefully watching Sebastian as he wandered the length of the hallway, growing more impatient with each step. By the time he reached the far end of it, she slipped into the clinic.

The moment she moved, Sebastian was in front of the door

just in time to hear the clank of steel locking and sealing her in with Demetrius. She closed the curtain, shutting us off from them. Sebastian slammed against the door. He had a dejected look as though he knew the locks wouldn't give. The room that he had taken special care to equip with doors and locks strong enough to withstand the most violent and vicious attacks, for the protection of the pack, had been turned against him, restricting his access. He pounded on it, yelling for Kelly to open the door.

The door strained under the full-fledged attack but didn't give. Dents formed on metal, the hinges creaked at the assault, but the locks wouldn't give. Ethan was suddenly next to Sebastian. Most of the locks in the house had iridium in them, preventing them from being penetrated by a witch. Josh was no use in this matter. He wasn't as strong as the others, but he helped as they all pushed into the door, trying to force it open. Finally, after intense effort from Sebastian, Ethan, Gavin, Josh, Steven, and Dr. Baker, the door broke in half, although the locks still held.

The room was empty except for Kelly.

She walked around the bed, cleaning the area. Guilt was a heavy shroud that forced a frown on her face. A fresh bite mark covered her neck, shadowed by light raspberry bruising.

"Where are they?" Sebastian asked through clenched teeth. He stepped closer, amber rolled across his eyes in waves, his hands fisted. Just seconds from striking, he held on to his patience a few moments longer.

Her attention remained on the tasks: stripping the sheets away, discarding soiled medical instruments, and sanitizing the area.

"Answer me," he demanded with the authority only he could have.

She stopped abruptly and looked afraid. She opened her mouth several times, but her words were lost, swallowed by her fear.

Sebastian stepped closer. "I need you to tell me where they are."

He knew where they were—we all knew. I wasn't sure why he needed her to admit it.

More tenacious than courageous, she backed away from him and glanced around the room. Surrounded by a group of angry were-animals whose fury was directed solely at her, she was unremorseful—afraid, but unremorseful. Taking several slow breaths, Sebastian seemed to be working hard to douse his growing ire. All the times I had angered him, I thought I had felt the apex of it, but this was it in its most intense, raw form. He didn't speak for a long time, focusing on her with such intensity. His fury didn't need to be voiced.

Kelly eased closer to Dr. Baker, but he was like an iceberg, unable to provide her the comfort she sought. The bravado and defiance that had plagued her far too often slipped away, and she cowered.

The seconds of silence turned into minutes before Sebastian exhaled a deep breath. "You wanted her here, then you need to handle this," he said firmly to Dr. Baker, working hard to subdue his anger. He turned and left the room, but it was with great effort, stopping several times to look back at her. His lips coiled tightly into a sneer.

"Please excuse us," Dr. Baker said to us, his hands trembling as they ran through his silver hair. His narrow face and stately features looked severe. It was only then, when Kelly saw the disappointment and frustration that covered his face, that she showed even a hint of remorse.

Everyone else left quickly. I hesitated. Dr. Baker was angry. There was a part of me that wanted to stay and protect Kelly, but I knew I couldn't. Dr. Baker waited patiently for me to eventually leave. I backed out slowly, hoping to catch at least the beginning of whatever was about to take place. Nothing. He waited until I was out the door.

It was nearly fifteen minutes before Dr. Baker emerged from the clinic with Kelly just steps behind him. I had a feeling she didn't get the reprimand she deserved and wouldn't ever get it from him. He left the house, keeping his back to her as though looking at her was too hard. She lingered behind. The tote that she always carried was pulled close to her as she waited for him to leave.

I thought she would make it out the door without having to deal with Sebastian, but just as her hand touched the knob, he came out of his office and called her back into the house. It took a long time before she turned around and even longer for her to muster the courage to make eye contact with him.

"I'm sorry." Her tone was flat as she neared him. She couldn't have sounded any less sincere if she had tried.

He stepped out of his office. His face a placid mask as his gaze roved slowly over her for several long moments and eventually settled on the bite mark. It seemed to ignite his anger all over again. "No, you're not, so you can keep your damn apology. If given the chance, you would do it again. That's why we have a problem."

"I couldn't let her die," she said softly, looking down at the floor.

"She's still dead!" he snapped. When he spoke again, he was calm, too calm—the quiet before the storm. "Let's just put aside your paramount betrayal to this pack. You fed a vampire—a powerful one—who, less than two weeks ago, was so enthralled by you he had to restrain himself. Or have you forgotten that so quickly? I realize in your idealistic, naïve world, you believe that he wouldn't *call* you, strip you of your will, and force you to do whatever he desired. History has proven otherwise. He doesn't possess that level of control. He is and always has been a servant to his lusts."

He waited a moment, allowing her to truly grasp the magnitude of what she had done. The memory of that night when that vampire captured her mind, rendering her helpless, must have flashed into her head because the same look of fear and dread rekindled on her face.

"I couldn't let her die," she repeated softly.

Despite what she had subjected herself to, I didn't think she was capable of letting someone die if there were other options.

She finally lifted her eyes to meet his. They were dark, disappointed. "You should have felt the same way. I expected better from you." Whatever expectations and standards she had for him, he had drastically fallen short.

"Then it's a good thing your happiness isn't predicated on me living up to your expectations. We can stand here all day and discuss how I have insulted your moral sensibilities, but I have neither the time nor the desire to do so. Since you didn't really think your little plan out, let me tell you what is going to happen now."

He couldn't take his focus off the bite mark on her neck that was now highlighted by bruising. "For the next five days, you get Gavin as your guardian. By then Demetrius should have lost the ability to call you. Don't even consider sending Gavin away during this time."

Talk about cruel and unusual punishment—sticking her with Gavin, who would undoubtedly hate the undertaking and would make her aware of it in every possible way. The next five days were going to be as good as torture for her.

She opened her mouth to speak, and his eyes narrowed, silencing her with a quelling look. He looked ferocious—deadly. If at any point Kelly had underestimated the seriousness of the matter, she couldn't at that moment. He stepped close to her, his face inches from hers. When she tried to step away, he pulled her closer. "If you ever do anything like that again, it will not be as easily forgiven or as kindly handled. Are we clear?"

"What are you going to do, kill me?" she asked coolly, stepping away from him as he released his hold.

His lips curled, but there wasn't anything pleasant about it. There were probably hundreds of things a person could do to you that would make you wish you were dead. I was sure Sebastian knew most of them. His gaze was intense, a silent promise that if she ever betrayed them in such a manner, death would be the least of her worries. "Are we clear?" he repeated, his voice a deep rumble.

He didn't wait for a response. He returned to his office and closed the door, leaving her staring at it with a look on her face that wandered between immense fear and indignation. It was as if she were torn between knocking on Sebastian's door to tell him off and cowering in a corner.

Self-righteous indignation won by a landslide. *Silly woman.* Kelly was about to knock when I said, "I wouldn't." Perhaps she heard the subtle warning in my voice, but she tugged her bag closer to her, walked into the living room, sat on the couch, and waited for Gavin.

CHAPTER 18

It was a little past midnight, and I found myself searching for Quell on a small trail not far from my house. It had been three days since I had allowed him to feed from me. The bruising was gone. I wasn't sure if his ability to call me had strengthened. I was stronger—or so I thought. But even with the dark magic tightly wound in me, the only thing I could manage to do with it was make my clothes dance around in front of me like I was stuck in a mawkish Disney film. I couldn't perform a strong protective field, bring down the ward at my house, or do any of the cool things that I had seen Josh and London do. I had taken the risk for nothing—a useless endeavor.

Now Quell's pull lured me to a rough terrain, a favorite spot for mountain bikers and light trail runners. The Midwest wasn't known for its acclivity, and it would never suffice for a true enthusiast. But nature runners and hikers found it acceptable. With fall in bloom, it was hard not to appreciate the flourishing colors of autumn foliage: orange, claret, yellow, and transitioning green. Instead of the redolence of the trees or the small brook that merged with the land at the end of the trail, there was a strong scent. It was bleak, murky, and dissolute.

I hated that I couldn't resist him calling me and endured its shrilling nuisance for the greater part of an hour, but as the intensity escalated, it was hard to ignore. Quell stood across the clearing, his head dropped, posture guarded. Inching closer, I could see the strained lines forming on his forehead and weighted frown. Did he know what he did to me?

"Quell?"

He responded with a start, so distracted that I actually caught him by surprise. Something was off with him. He looked taxed. "What are you doing here, Skylar? Go home."

"Always so hospitable," I muttered under my breath. "Stop calling me and getting cross when I show up," I snapped. "You may not need sleep, but I do."

"We rest."

I didn't care, and in my foul mood, I didn't have a problem voicing it. "I don't care what you call it. You do it in the morning. I do mine at night. Do whatever you need to do and stop calling me! It's one o'clock. I'm tired."

"She's dead—really dead. She can't be turned."

I heard Chase's voice but didn't see him until moments later when he emerged from the bosk, his shirt bloodstained, his ebony eyes deep and intense. "Just as the heart stops, you have to feed them, then—" He stopped when he saw me standing next to Quell, then he pulled back his lips and bared his teeth. I think it was a smile, and had I been in better spirits, I would have taken it as one. Now it seemed like a snarl, maybe even a threat.

I focused on the wooded area he'd come from. The pungent smell of spilled blood and death was stronger now. Stepping closer, I passed Chase, who looked annoyed by my intrusion. A woman lay stilled on the grassy plains, her dark brown hair fanned out from around the olive-toned tearstained face. Her expression was frozen in that liminal state between pain and shock.

Quell wore his guilt like a scarlet letter.

"What have you done?" I said.

He didn't answer. Instead, he stood there with a vapid look on his face that just tweaked at my anger.

"What have you done?" I pushed him, and when he continued staring at me in resolute silence, I shoved him even harder. "Say something!" But he didn't. Anger made me want to assault him with a barrage of punches. Instead, I shoved him again, harder, trying to force an answer. Chase grabbed me from behind. Strong arms encircled my waist and pulled me away. I jabbed my elbow into his face, and when he stumbled back, I returned my ire back to Quell. Chase regained control of the situation quickly, hooking his arm around me and crushing me against him as he pulled me back several feet. I didn't give in willingly, bucking against him, my fist batting at any body part I could contact. I thrust my head back and it pounded into bone, but it was his cheek, not his nose as I had hoped.

"This little poodle may be more bite than bark." Chase chortled, amused. The pressure around me increased, my ribs screamed for relief. "I am going to ask that you calm down, and I only plan to ask once."

My struggle came to an immediate halt. It was a few long moments before he released me.

Quell stepped closer. His face was still vacant, his attention focused on Chase briefly. "Thank you for coming," he said quietly, dismissing Chase.

Once we were alone, he inched his way toward me. There was such a thing as emotions being too calm. It always seemed like it was the calm period before the torrential storm.

"How many has it been?" I could barely force the words out through my disgust.

It took too long for him to answer. We stood in the middle of the stygian woods as the smell of blood and death crept through the air, the result of Quell's bloodlust. Each minute that I stared at that stolid mask made me angrier and sicker. What was taking him so long? Were there that many? "Answer the question!" I snapped angrily.

"Whether it is one or one hundred, it will be too many for you," he admitted in a dejected voice.

I wished I had come armed with something—anything. Every fiber in my body wanted to hurt him—kill him. The impassive look that didn't hold any remorse for the lives lost made me want to brutalize him until they mattered. "How many?"

"Five."

Three days since he had fed from me and he had killed five people already. "Is this what you are now, a murderer?"

His face hardened, rage flashed across it and settled hard as his lips folded down into a frown. Before I could react, he was right in front of me, towering over me.

"I am what you made me. Sixty-nine years I went without the taste of blood—no desire, no urges. Now I can't make it go away. I can't ignore it. It's a craving that stabs at me and I'm not strong enough to stop it—"

"You're going to have to stop it. I can't let you kill another person just to satisfy a lust you are too weak to control."

His lips pulled back into a snarl, his eyes cold and angry. Fear crept up, covering me as I realized that I couldn't stop him if he decided to make me his next victim. I was sure he could hear the pounding of my heart. Instead, he looked out toward the woods where the dead body laid—the result of his lust. Abruptly, his face relaxed into an odd calm. When he spoke, his voice lacked inflection. "You want it to stop? Make it stop."

And with that, he was gone.

My hand was starting to leave a deep crease in my forehead as it pressed against it. I looked up briefly when Steven opened my front door. He had a television in one hand and was pulling a large suitcase behind him with the other. The amused grin stayed on his face as he sauntered into the guest room, where he stayed for a few minutes. I heard the suitcase zipper, then clothes rustling around.

"I'll be in Georgia for the next few weeks or so. The cable guy will be here Monday for an install. I can't believe you don't already have it in here. Way to make your guest feel wanted," he stated from inside the guest room—or rather, his room.

He was still chattering, but I was only half listening. When he sat next to me, I could feel the weight of his eyes on me. My head lolled onto his shoulder and I closed my eyes. "Are you moving back to Georgia?" I asked, unable to mask my disappointment. I didn't want a roommate, but I couldn't imagine what my life would be like without him.

He sighed heavily, resting his head against mine. I clenched my hands into fists to keep from wrapping my arms around him. "I wanted to and put in my petition for a transfer. My mother's first official act as Alpha of the Southern Pack was to reject it," he stated dejectedly.

I pretended to be just as disappointed as he was. "Then you are definitely coming back?"

"Definitely. My mother wouldn't have it any other way."

We fell into a comfortable silence as we often did. As much as I tried to divert my attention to the television, my thoughts remained on Quell. I wished I could tell Steven. I knew he could make things better. But this was my problem. I had created a potential serial killer and now it was up to me to make things right. I knew what I needed to do; however, finding the tenacity to do it was something entirely different.

"Look at me."

When I did, he rested his forehead against mine. "Tell me what's on your mind," he requested in a low, mesmeric voice.

I wanted to, but I couldn't. "I can't."

The small smile on his face was forced, but he nodded slowly. "Sometimes, the things that seem the cruelest are the right things."

Was that the pack's mantra to justify acts that others would deem atrocious?

There was that part of me that felt it wasn't my place to correct this. Quell was a vampire. I expected him to feed from humans, and unfortunately, I expected that there would be accidents. It was the unavoidable cruelty of their existence. Most vampires fed without killing, and I wished that could be true of them all. Then there were those that held so little value for human life that slaughtering their food was just inevitable. That was the harsher side of their existence that I tried to pretend didn't occur.

If Quell got too out of control, either the pack would handle it or Demetrius would, as he had with the others. I didn't know what warranted pack involvement. Was it the heinousness of the act or the quantity? Demetrius and his Seethe only cared if it affected them. If a vampire started feeding excessively, killing people in droves, drawing too much attention to them, then they would intervene. But what they considered excessive exceeded my expectations.

No matter how I tried to push the responsibility off on someone else, my conscience wouldn't let me. I was going to have to stop this and hope that Michaela never found out it was me. The breath I inhaled seemed rough and sharp as it slid down.

Make it stop. I could hear him saying it repeatedly in my head. Now I had to make him stop.

Hours after I had decided to do it, I stood at the back entrance of Quell's home with several stakes on my waist holster and a couple more in my shoulder bag. I also had a gun, which would just hurt him, but the large knife would definitely do the job.

The erratic thumping of my heart wouldn't cease no matter

how controlled my breaths became. I was terrified. I was about to kill Michaela's favorite, and with Demetrius so distracted with Chris's transformation, I wondered if she would use revenge against me as a way to pass the time. Storing that thought underneath the many others that had occupied my mind, I inched closer to his house, slipping into the eclipsing darkness as I waited for him to appear.

If I was going to be successful, I definitely wanted to get him before he fed and before dusk, when he was at his weakest. I opened the door. Vampires didn't lock their doors. Why would they? A burglar would be getting far more than what they bargained for if they ever dared to steal from them.

"Are you waiting for me?" asked the low, remote voice. I spun on my heel. Unable to aim the stake, I still shoved it in his direction. He grasped it between the palms of his hands, blocking it from striking. Almost simultaneously, we looked at it. My aim was off. If I had struck, it would have impaled him just shy of his left shoulder. Grasping my hand, he directed it over the apex of his heart. "Now," he stated.

Does he realize this will kill him?

He was staring at me, waiting, urging. I gripped it tighter, pulled back and struck. I expected him to move, to fight back, or at the very least stop me. When he didn't, the stake plunged into the side of his chest, missing his heart by just inches. His face twisted in pain as he dropped to his knees then fell back on the ground, taking several ragged, pained gasps. His head pressed hard against the terrain as blood spilled from his chest. The gasp dwindled into low, labored breaths. "You missed," he said in a rough voice.

"No, I didn't." I pushed the stake in farther and he hissed in pain again. Leaning over him, I gripped the hilt harder. "I can't let you keep killing like this."

"I can't get rid of the hunger," he admitted in a strained voice, his teeth clenched as he attempted to ease the pain. I pushed the stake in farther and he screeched. If I couldn't make myself kill him, I wanted to hurt him so badly that he would remember this moment, relive it in his nightmares.

"Why can't you just stop? You did it for decades before. Why can't you go back?" I tried to sound authoritative, but it sounded more like I was pleading with him to behave.

He closed his eyes, seemingly recalling the time he had been ruled by other things than hunger. "I've descended so far. I thirst for it. Even the thought of their moral depravity isn't enough to deter me anymore."

He was killing innocent people to satisfy his lust, and he still considered himself morally superior. Vampires. It was a harsh reality check. I had underestimated him from the beginning, but Michaela hadn't. Initially she might have been drawn to his apparent beauty, but she saw through it and knew the insensate potential. She lay in wait for him to expose his dark, lethal side.

"I realize you need to feed. It's the only way you can survive, but you don't have to kill. You've done it before, with me." As he held my gaze, I could see the struggle and as much as I wanted to hate him and have no sorrow for him—I couldn't.

"I can't kill you. You are as much my creator as Michaela. She took away my humanity. I'm indebted to her for that, but *you* brought me over."

Oh great! I sat back on my heels, weighted down by my own conflicts. I didn't know what to do. I was responsible for what he had become. Before me, he had been content being a plant-sucking vampire and would have been content dying that night. Perhaps, like Michaela, he knew what type of monster he would become if he tasted blood. Could it have been the fear of what his existence would become that kept him from feeding rather than his overwhelming disdain for humanity? I had saved and ruined him in one sweeping act.

"You should have let it end that night." He pulled himself up to sitting.

"Yeah, but I didn't. You needed to be saved. I didn't know that was a bad thing," I admitted, washing my hands over my face. "You have to go back to the way you were. Go back to feeding from the Hidacus."

He shuddered at the thought, then he frowned. "Michaela has forbidden it. I lost that privilege when I fed from you."

"It was to save your life!" I couldn't understand why Michaela kept punishing him for me saving his life. She wanted him like this: hungry, rabid, and uncontrollable with only one option, feeding that would inevitably lead to deaths—lots of deaths.

"Doesn't matter," he snapped as he came to his feet.

I came to mine, too, keeping a substantial distance from him, but he started toward me. It was so abrupt and aggressive that I positioned the stake to strike, if necessary.

"I won't risk Michaela's anger and her punishments just to go back. You want it to stop? Then make it stop," he challenged again.

Kill him. There was that inhumane part of me that indulged my most primal, savage urges, and it was pushing me to accept his challenge. I wanted to listen to that part of me: drive the stake straight through his heart, decapitate him, and walk away from the wreckage without any feelings of remorse or guilt. Now how did I stop being me for the next few minutes in order to do this?

As he spoke, there was sheer desperation and sorrowful distress as he conceded to what he had become. "I've tried to use animals, but it doesn't satisfy the longing anymore. I need human blood. It's a hunger I can't and won't deny."

I knew that hunger from my visit with Gloria the Tre'ase last year. I felt the bloodlust and I knew it was hard to ignore. It pulled at your existence, called to all the urges beseeching you to respond. I couldn't resist it then. How could I expect him to do so now?

Perhaps, in some warped way, *I* was his creator. And now he was asking me to kill the person I essentially created. I felt so responsible for him, and I didn't know how to make that feeling go away. "You can use me," I finally said. "You won't kill me, so you can use me. Not forever, but until you can get things under control. I will help you with that."

I sure had a lot of things on my plate: werewolf, host to a spirit shade, amphora, and now vampire mentor.

I thought the remote, empty look on his face would change, show something—perhaps relief or appreciation, but instead, he looked troubled. "May I?" he asked, taking my wrist.

I nodded. The lump in my throat kept me from speaking. Fangs pressed into my wrist, but it wasn't a bite, just a small prick. Blood bubbled to the surface, running down my arm as the Lost One stared at the red stream. He inhaled. Inching closer, he inhaled again before his tongue laved over the stream of blood, removing all traces from my skin. There was a look of horror and relief on his face, and I couldn't discern why.

He kept my hand close to his face. "I won't abuse your kindness," he stated earnestly.

I believed he meant it, and maybe he would try, but he wouldn't last long. I could see the hunger in his gaze as it draped over the corners of his lips and lingered in his onyx eyes.

Pulling my hand away, I nodded. The vampires might no longer consider him lost, but he was, and he was taking me with him.

CHAPTER 19

Josh reluctantly laid the capsa in the basin. It had taken me three days of persistent calls and inquiries about the capsa to get us here. But now, after much encouragement from me, Josh and I stood in the library of the pack's retreat, staring at this cylinder filled with the dark magic used to sustain an army of Ethos's creatures.

Just minutes before, we had had one of our many conversations and debates about it. Josh wanted to keep it "for future use" as another weapon to protect the pack. His desire to control dark magic had become his obsession. He wouldn't admit it and did a good job of hiding it, but I knew. I could feel it. The lust and desire ensorcelled him, blazing in him like wildfire. It didn't help that Ethos had dominated him, intensifying his already heightened curiosity and desire to learn to manipulate and control dark magic, to never be defeated by its power again. Fueled before by curiosity, now by pride, he had been beaten in the field and his ego was bruised by it.

Now I had to add "sponsor for magic addicts" to my list of responsibilities. I wallowed through my own hypocrisy to be his anchor into reality, and reinforce that we could not keep the dark magic even if we believed it could be of any use in the future. Not only had he made a promise, he had an obligation not to be reckless.

"How do we destroy it?" I asked, my hand gliding over it. It didn't make me recoil like it had before. Instead, I touched it gingerly, feeling that kindred energy we possessed. It hummed lightly against my finger, a last plea not to be destroyed, and I answered by pushing the basin away from me to the middle of the table.

"As with most things, ice and fire." His pale blue eyes were entreating and his voice was like satin as he made a final plea. "I don't think we should destroy it."

I looked at the capsa. It glowed, flickering at a steady pulse, ever so enticing, an appeal for clemency.

"London: lover or friend?" I inquired.

It took him a long time to answer, and I knew he was considering how he would categorize the complexity of what they had. "Friends," he finally said softly, as his gaze faltered from mine, "and occasionally more."

Of course, why wouldn't they be? He was an alluring warlock with beckoning blue eyes and defined features that were often shadowed by a beard from constant missed shaves.

Everything from his body art, sly wayward grin, incessant violation of personal space, and denial of conformity set off all types of internal alarms that he was trouble. But he was also charismatic and charming, and he possessed a confidence that was just shy of being arrogant. He was hard to walk away from.

People betrayed lovers more often than they cared to admit, but friendships seemed to forge a bond that most were reluctant to break or betray.

His attention had long left me, focused on the strobe of power on the table. The codependent relationship that we had developed would eventually break from the constant abuse inflicted on it. When he was weak, I needed to be the voice of reason.

"You made a promise to your friend that you should keep," I stated firmly.

London had made it clear that she wanted to remain invisible. If we kept this, it could very well fall into the wrong hands or be discovered, and eventually, it would all come back to her. She deserved her privacy and her wishes respected. We would not have defeated Ethos without her help.

His lips curled slightly, reluctantly surrendering. He whispered several chants and the wand frosted over. Cool vapor radiated off it, chilling the air. Then, with another chant and a wave of his hand, it burst into flames. But instead of diffusing into a vapor, the flames smothered and the ice melted from the capsa, returning it to its previous form. The lights faded into darkness and the floor rumbled under our feet, a warning. It would not die easily, fighting for its existence to the bitter end.

Josh placed his hands on the table and it shook. As his eyes eclipsed to black, he called forth stronger magic, but unlike before, nothing happened.

"Try it again," I said. I placed my hand over his on the table as he recited the incantation again. Sharp sparks came flying out of the capsa. It rattled, screeching as it iced over, ignited into flames, and drifted into a mist. All evidence of its existence blew into the ether.

"Thank you," he stated softly, "she wouldn't have forgiven me."

I shrugged, becoming increasingly aware of him as he moved his hand from under mine and turned to face me. Usually, Josh's magic felt calm, a gentle untainted breeze. But now, it seemed sordid. Attuned to the subtle nuances of it, I seemed hyperaware of how truly powerful he was. His power was something of beauty. You didn't want to just appreciate it like art, but it sparked an intrinsic need to devour it, possess it as your own.

Standing just inches from each other, unrelenting surges of power kept us at a distance. Now I knew why Pala had to have his magic, craved it to the point where she had betrayed him. I couldn't fight it. I wanted more of what he possessed. If it were in my power to do so, I would have taken it. It was a feeling that no matter how I fought to suppress, kept emerging.

As if he had read my thoughts, felt my desire, and knew my ill-intentions, he stepped closer. A small smirk formed on his lips. He whispered the same incantation he had earlier with Ethos as he stood just inches from me. His hands wrapped around the nape of my neck, pulling me closer to him, our lips just inches apart, his breath warm against my lips. I should have given in to it, because I could feel how the dark magic had changed me, made me want more—willing to do anything to get more. It was an indulgence that was hard to deny. But instead, I erected a protective field, separating us. It looked a lot more intimidating than it was, a thick translucent wall with shimmers of light reflected off it. It pushed at Josh, shoving him back.

He admired it for a long time then focused on me through it. I thought for once I had formed a strong protective field, a delusion he allowed me to keep for a few minutes. With a miscreant smile and very little effort, he touched it and it crumbled. He continued toward me as I accepted the inevitable.

I closed my eyes and waited. He had to know now that I had held on to some of the dark magic, and I waited for him to make things right. Nothing. When I opened them, he looked strangely intrigued, and once again, I felt like I was being gawked at by observers, but this time—I proved to be interesting.

He smiled. "It becomes you."

Then he was gone.

Denial had become the security blanket that I clung to every chance I could, but after five days, it had lost its appeal. I needed answers, and the best source would be from the one person who had proven to be as different as I was—Ethan. That's how I ended up at his front door seven days after I had killed Ethos. It would have been sooner, but I wanted to give him time to do whatever he had to in order to deal with what had happened to Chris. He didn't strike me as the type that grieved, so I wasn't sure what he did exactly.

I knocked on his door with hesitation, the book that Josh had given me for my birthday in hand. It was my undeniable evidence that Ethan was more than he pretended to be and that we were one and the same.

When he opened the door, he didn't look surprised to see me. In fact, he looked expectant. Giving one quick look at the book, he stepped aside to let me in.

"What do you want?" he asked impatiently when my attention jumped from him to the laptop and the three books lying next to it on the sofa. I recognized them from the library of the pack's retreat.

"Not going to offer me a glass of water or something?" I asked in a saccharine tone.

"What. Do. You. Want?"

"Why do you care that I am a Moura? And how does it affect the pack? You've called me naïve and foolish more than once, yet I am not foolish or naïve enough not to realize that what I am affects the pack. I suspect that what I am affects you as well. So, what are you?" I challenged, scrutinizing him as I waited for the inevitable lie.

"You know what I am."

"No, I know what you claim to be—a werewolf—just like me. I know that you seem to have a lot of information about me that should otherwise be unimportant. I know that when Gloria met you, she wanted to get as much distance as possible from you, and so did Thaddeus. Ethos was repelled by you and couldn't get you away from him quick enough, but with Josh, he just wanted to play magical one-upmanship. Why?"

Once again, there was that vacant, obscure look, the breathing that stayed steady and rhythmic, the heartbeat that kept perfect time—which meant by all accounts a person was going to offer you the truth. But with Ethan, it meant he was probably going to lie through his teeth.

His lips drew back into an amused smile. "A lot of people are afraid of me. I don't think that's cause for suspicion."

Everything about him was cause for suspicion, and my only goal today was to get him to admit why. "You effortlessly breeze through wards that even Josh has trouble with," I added.

"So?" His amusement turned to disinterest.

"I think there is more to you. A great deal more."

He smiled. It was a cold smirk, a challenge. "What, do you think I'm like you?" he inquired, his eyes narrowing with interest.

I nodded. "Yes, something like that." I didn't think we were exactly alike, but he was probably the only person I'd met who was remotely similar to me and that was the only reason he cared so much about what I was. There was a common link no matter how much he denied it.

An air of smug contempt remained on his face as he inched closer to me and leaned in. I could feel the warmth of his breath on my ear as he spoke. "What's the matter, Skylar? Do you hate being alone—the only one of your kind in this big bad world? Do you need someone to hold your hand through it, coddle you, and tell you that you're a special little snowflake and everything is going to be okay?"

What an ass!

I attempted to appeal to a civil, humane, kinder side of him that was probably being held hostage by this jerk. "Yes, I hate knowing that when I stand in a room full of were-animals, I am still different. Sometimes it's thrilling, but most of the time, it's really scary to know what I can do with magic, and I can't help but wonder if it will help me or destroy me. And it sucks that the more I find out about myself, the more I feel like my birth mother sentenced me to something far worse than death by letting me live. So yes, I hate being out here alone."

He watched me for a long time, carefully and with interest. "You and I are nothing alike. There is no one else like you. You're not about to be soothed, pampered, and told that everything's going to be okay, because it's not. Get over it. Grow a pair and deal with it. Let's just hope that when everything hits the fan, you are still breathing afterward, or at the very least, your death is simple and not some torturous revenge," he said.

The nice part of him wasn't being held hostage by the jerk. Apparently, he had assassinated him years ago, and this insolent jackass was all that remained.

Evasion was Ethan's weapon of choice too often. And it had worked too often.

"Well, I don't think we're that different at all." I believed it the more he denied it. "You can't be a witch, or at least you will never admit it. Is it because you are afraid of them, what they will do to you, or to Josh, for not exposing you?"

The smirk remained. "One thing we don't do is underestimate the witches. If I had shown signs of being a witch, I would not be standing here with you. No, I am not a witch."

With pseudo-confidence, driven more by curiosity and determination, I challenged him. He seemed to know a lot about me, and now it was my turn to learn about him. "In all the time I have spent with Josh, he's never mentioned the protected objects."

"Perhaps you two were so busy with other things that the subject just never came up," he stated derisively.

I was really starting to hate him.

When I spoke, I made my voice hard, rigid, and challenging. "I'm tied to the Aufero. What are you linked to?"

The small deviant smile just curved even more. His platinum gaze became penetrating and intense. I continued, "The Clostra?" Was he linked to the key, and if so, what exactly did it unlock?

"The Fatifer?" I asked again. Ethan associated with something with the sole purpose of bringing death wouldn't surprise me.

Now he stared at me with incited amusement, his arms crossed over his chest.

"You said there were five Mouras Encantadas, which means there are five mystical objects in need of protection. I only found four, and since we destroyed the Gem of Levage, that makes only three. One is missing. What do you know about the elusive fifth object that even the books have no knowledge of?"

And there it was, that ever-so-subtle skip in the beat of his heart, the ragged breath that seemed edged in the back of his throat. It was the closest thing I had ever seen to a flinch from Ethan.

His face curled into an indecipherable smile. I couldn't quite put my finger on it: Fear? Concern? Guilt?

He shrugged. "I made a mistake. Perhaps there were only four."

Ethan didn't make mistakes like that. He was hiding something—he was always hiding something. I should have just let it go, but I couldn't. "You have a lot of information and know a hell of a lot about me. What are *you* hiding?"

As always, I would be met with either a glare or silence. This time, he chose silence.

"I'm going to find out," I told him firmly, stepping closer to him to drive the point home.

He chuckled, a dark, ominous sound. "You do that." He took off his shirt and started toward the back door. "I'm going for a run. Unless you plan on joining me, you can let yourself out."

My attention went to the books lying on the sofa. I just wanted a peek and had every intention of having one the moment he left the room. As if he sensed my intentions, he walked past the sofa, closed the laptop, and gathered the books, taking them to a room to the right and shutting the door.

"Are you joining me or not?" he asked, unbuttoning his pants then slipping them off along with his underwear.

Ethan was too comfortable with his nudity and knew that I wasn't. This was his less-than-subtle way of forcing me to leave. I stood fixed in my spot, my gaze planted on him, refusing to look uncomfortable. *It's just a naked man,* I told myself.

Who was I kidding! I had seen only seven men naked in my life and all of them were part of the Midwest Pack. For a brief moment, I looked away but forced myself to hold his gaze as his man parts jaunted out as he approached.

It's just a naked man, I reassured myself.

As usual, Ethan and I were engaged in a juvenile game of chicken. My gaze breezed over him with full intensity, yet he didn't feel ashamed

"In or out, Sky?" he asked, walking toward me.

It's just a naked man walking toward me, I reminded myself. My unwavering gaze focused on his. I refused to let him know how uncomfortable I was.

"I'll just wait here until you get back," I said. I had plans. They all started with the books he was hiding and whatever was on his computer.

"That wasn't an option."

"I'll pass."

The cynical smirk remained even as he walked toward the back door. He stopped and remained still for too long. I knew nothing good could come of it.

With his back to me, he turned to look over his shoulder. "Ethos could have killed you at any time. Do you wonder why he didn't?"

Consistent with his m.o., he planted the seed of devastation and curiosity and watched in amusement to see what grew. But he was too late. Although I didn't have any answers, I had thought about it more times than I could remember. I replayed that moment over and over. Ethos didn't succumb to my strength. He surrendered, and I didn't know why, but I was willing to bet there wasn't anything good behind that door, either.

CHAPTER 20

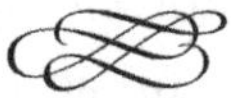

If you had told me months ago that I would be willingly standing in Sebastian's office late on a Saturday night, I would have pointed you to the nearest psych center. He was giving me that same look he always did, a mixture of annoyance and boredom with both fighting for dominance. I wondered why the hell I was there. Oh, that was right; my life was in the crapper: people were more than likely going to start looking for me and possibly trying to figure out the many ways to make me pay for my mother's failure. I stupidly harbored dark magic, my life was a big cauldron of the unknown, and the only people whom I semi-trusted and had helped me so far were associated with this pack. Despite Ethan's denial, there was a link between him and me and the mystical object. The pack was a wealth of untapped information, and I had every intention of getting it.

I grappled with the dichotomy of my feelings for the pack. Although I wasn't part of them, they protected my life, shared information, and made sure I was safe at all times, despite their personal feelings toward me. The pack represented power, strength, and stability—things I desperately needed. In contrast, they were cruel, held a selfish commitment to their pack, and had the type of ethics that bordered on criminal. Sadly, the very things I hated, I might well need in the future. If someone did come looking for me to pay for the shortcomings of my mother, or if I couldn't help Quell and had to kill him, I would need refuge from Michaela's and the Seethe's wrath. If the dark magic became too much for me to handle—or worse—I would need Josh and probably Ethan, as well.

As Sebastian waited for me to speak, he looked like himself: confident and lethal. "What?" he finally asked, settling back in his chair.

Had either he or Ethan ever learned the word "Hello," or were greetings too pedantic for them?

"Last year you invited me to join the pack—"

"I'm quite aware of the invitations I make. I don't need a reminder. Why are you here?"

"Does your offer still stand?" I asked softly.

I expected him to tell me to leave in no uncertain terms. After all, it had been over a year since he had asked.

"You never formally declined. The offer still stands."

"I would like to accept."

I'm not sure what I expected: a smile, a greeting, a simple nod that cordially said, "Welcome to the pack, your new membership packet will be mailed to you," or something along those lines. Instead, I only received a cool look of indifference.

"Okay," he responded as he returned his attention to anything that he deemed more interesting than me, which could have been the half-bent paperclip to his right.

When I didn't move, he looked up. "Good-bye."

He drew his attention back to whatever held it before I walked into his office, but before I could back out the door, he asked, "What changed your mind?"

My answer didn't seem to be of great interest because it didn't warrant him lifting his head to look at me.

"You let me handle the situation with Steven."

He looked up, intrigued, his eyes narrowed with curiosity.

"Whatever issues you have with me, you put them aside and let me help with Steven. You didn't send me away. Despite your feelings about me, you are always there to protect me, even if it's from my own foolishness. I admire and respect that." I admitted my partial truth.

As I turned for the door, I nearly tripped over my conscience. Guilt forced me into full disclosure. I needed to tell him everything. Well, most of it, or rather, a CliffsNotes version of my truth. I gave him enough information so that he knew what he was inheriting by letting me into the pack. I left out the parts that I was still feeding Quell, that Ethan was something like me, that I was hell-bent on finding out what, and that I had kept part of Ethos's magic.

After I finished, he regarded me for a long time. If he was shocked, amazed, or even remotely interested by my revelations, he was hiding it well. His look was just shy of being bored to tears, and I wondered if I gave him the information while standing on one foot, juggling six knives while singing the "Star Spangled Banner," would he have been the least bit interested?

His half-smile curled into a devious grin. Relaxing back against the chair with his hands clasped behind his head, he said, "I assure you that it will be my pleasure to direct anyone who cares to inquire about the Aufero to Marcia."

His eyes darkened to the point they looked sable, and there was an uncharacteristic calm to his appearance. "Five protected objects, Skylar? I believe there are only four, three now that the Gem of Levage has been destroyed."

You have to be kidding me! Everything in me wanted to tell him to take his pack membership and shove it, along with that huge lie. I wasn't sure why the story had changed, but at the moment, I needed them more than I needed the truth. Now, my only goal was to learn how to read through the deceit in order to find out what the fifth object was, where to find it, and why they were lying about its existence.

When I didn't leave immediately, he watched me then shot an expectant look toward the door. *Mr. Hospitality.*

"Skylar, whatever you have going on with Quell, I expect you to handle it discreetly and quickly. I don't want a mess that I will have to clean up."

Did I seriously think Sebastian wasn't constantly aware of what went on around him and the people who associated with his pack? He probably knew exactly what Ethan was and what he was hiding. But before I could ask, he looked up with that hard, reproaching gaze that didn't welcome further questions.

"And whatever issues you have with Ethan, I advise you to drop them, understood?"

There wasn't any room for misinterpretation. He was telling me to stop all inquiries about Ethan, which only heightened my curiosity.

Pack life was going to be quite interesting.

EPILOGUE: AWAKENING

Chris opened her eyes. The realization that she was in Demetrius's personal home wasn't a big surprise. She lay motionless against the cool, silky sheets on the king-sized bed trying to get used to the extreme clarity of her vision. The pores and the subtle imperfection of the champagne-colored walls were clear, blemishes on what before had looked perfect. The colors of the canvas art were too intense, disfiguring the images on it. She squeezed her eyes closed, preparing herself for the way things now appeared to her. Her expectations, now different, made it easier. "That's better," she whispered.

Adapting to the way her body moved was difficult. It felt foreign to her, her movements quick and precise, smoother than she could have ever imagined. The various scents of the room roved over her in spells, overwhelming her senses. The mauve linen dress draped her frame but didn't keep her body warm. Unable to move from the edge of the bed, she remained there like a stone, trying to find a purpose to move. *Vampire.* It tasted worse against her palate than it felt. The ache in her stomach wouldn't stop.

She wasn't dead. It should have unburdened her, but it didn't.

She was a vampire. The only remnant of her human existence was the erratic beat of a heart that continued to linger. Pressing her hand against her chest, she waited to feel the familiar pounding again.

"That will go away the first time you feed," Demetrius said. He stood against the frame of the door. His lips curled into a smile as he walked into the room. Everything seemed so new, different, and unfamiliar.

She shut her eyes again. The memories became jumbled pieces as she struggled to hold on to them. One stuck with her, clinging on the precipice of the very moment that brought her to this point.

"Are you okay?" Demetrius asked gently, his fingers brushing lightly against her cheek. The arrogance faltered, replaced by surprise when she shifted from him. Cupping her face into his hands, he stared at her for a long time, his gaze moving slowly over her face, admiring his work. "How do you feel?"

She bit down on her lip, not very hard, but blood trickled into her mouth. Her tongue ran across the long incisors. *I have fangs now.* She kept running her tongue over them, strangely fascinated and repulsed by them. "Hungry," she admitted.

"Of course you are. Your process took longer than most. If it were anyone other than you, I would have allowed them to perish," he admitted softy. "I needed your human body to heal first. I wanted you to be whole—healed and unmarked—before I changed you." His hands roved slowly over her body, hitting each spot, taking moments to appreciate it before placing a light kiss on her forehead. "Now, here you are—perfect."

She knew that his words weren't an admiration of her appearance but a declaration of his skills as her creator.

The redolence of human blood permeated the air. She cared less about what he was saying and more about the hunger pains that were getting worse. She darted toward the smell, but he grabbed her before she could make it, his arm a firm loop around her waist.

"Wait."

Tugging at his arms, she was feral. When he didn't release her, she clawed at the restrictive hand, pushing toward the alluring smell, as the gentle thumping of a human heartbeat continued to beckon her. Her mouth watered at the thought of sinking her teeth into the jugular vein.

"I said wait," he commanded softly against her hair, pressing her even closer to him.

She pulled away and started toward the door again. And once again, he grabbed her before she could make it. With his arm wrapped around her, he guided her back to the bed. His voice was a gentle purr as he comforted her. "It's Elisabeth. She's my favorite. If you go in there like a rabid animal, you will kill her, and I will not be happy with you," he stated sternly.

Positioning her on the bed, he knelt in front of her, "Do you remember the conversation we had before you were to be changed the first time?"

Chris's lips pressed into a formidable line. She didn't want to become one of those that killed their donors. It was an idea that had always bothered her.

She nodded.

"Very well. Calm down and you will be rewarded, but if you can't, then you will have to wait," he stated firmly.

She closed her eyes and took slow breaths until she was in a better state. The fact that she didn't want to kill Elisabeth helped, but it was still a challenge. Preserving human life didn't seem so important at the moment.

The scent came closer, aromatic and sweet. When she opened her eyes, the honey-colored woman approached her. Elisabeth's long black hair was pulled back into a tight bun, exposing her long, languid neck. She approached Chris slowly while Demetrius stayed at her side.

Chris went for her neck in a lurch and he pulled her back before she could get to her.

"Slow. Sit down with me," he urged, pulling her into his lap. Elisabeth sat next to them. When she extended her arm, Chris took it quickly before she could settle in comfortably next to her. As Chris's teeth pierced her skin, taking a long draw from the vein, she sucked in breath through the small gap in her teeth.

Chris's fingers pressed harder into her wrist. The blood tasted better than it smelled.

Demetrius gently tugged at her. "That's enough."

Chris wasn't amenable to stopping and shot Demetrius several dirty looks as he forced her to stop.

"Thank you, Elisabeth. Send Daniel in," he said, kissing her lightly on the cheek.

Chris sneered at him.

"Jealous?" he asked, amused.

She was, and it bothered her. For a long time, she simply stared with confusion.

"I'm your creator. There is a strong connection in the beginning, but regretfully, it will pass," he admitted with a smile.

At least someone is enjoying it, she thought angrily. She wished she could quash the feeling when an earthy cedar-toned man entered with hair cut skull-short, leaving only small waves that clung to his scalp. His topaz eyes were bright, lips kinked into a crooked grin as he approached her. Everyone in the Seethe's garden was there voluntarily, but she had always believed there had to be something that had forced them into this perverse life.

The moment he entered the room, she pulled him to the bed and sank her fangs deep into his carotid. He didn't even gasp out in pain or seem shocked by the roughness of her attack. Instead, his hand entwined around the nape of her neck, pulling her closer. She fed from him far longer than she had fed from Elisabeth. Demetrius didn't seem to protect him in the same manner.

Eventually Demetrius coaxed her off him but it was too late.

His long, thin frame lay flat against the bed, skin pallid, eyelids tightly closed. He wasn't dead but he was barely alive. Chris understood the draw of feeding from a troubled mind. It was intoxicating. A fabulously turbulent roller-coaster ride, producing a feeling far superior to endorphins or anything narcotics could offer. It was too hard to resist.

"Chris, you must learn to control yourself," he scolded. "If you can't take better care of the ones in the garden, then you will be prohibited from using them. You wouldn't want that. They are quite convenient."

She stared at him, finding the irony in him chastising her about control. He was the epitome of self-indulgence and poor self-control. She nodded slowly, but she couldn't keep her eyes off Daniel.

The amused look on Demetrius face turned to flashes of anger. "You like him?"

She knew that if Demetrius was jealous of him, this probably would be the last time she saw him. She definitely wanted to see him again. She shook her head, giving Demetrius her undivided attention.

He watched her for a long time, looked down at Daniel, and frowned. "We all have our favorites."

She kissed him lightly on the cheek and then softly on the lips. "You saved my life, again. I have a favorite. It's you," she said softly.

Demetrius smiled. "If only it would stay that way. But for now, I'll take it."

The week since she had been changed went by at a snail's crawl. She hated that she was still in Demetrius's home, forbidden to leave, restricted from experiencing the new novelty of the world, and unable to efficiently feed herself. Now she was waiting for the light to fade into dusk so that she could at least leave for the night.

Demetrius was gone. One of the benefits of being an aged vampire was that you weren't as restricted by the light. You weren't going on any daylight power walks, but the moment the sun started to set, you were free.

Yesterday, Chris had allowed her cabin fever to get the best of her and discovered the repercussions.

She looked out the window with longing, considering how long it would take her to adjust to this new life. It wasn't a matter of *if* she would adjust—just when. Her life had always been a series of adjustments. She wouldn't expect anything less from her death.

The steps were soft, barely audible as they approached her. She turned to find Michaela just a few feet from her. "You seem to be doing well," Michaela acknowledged in a cool voice with a venomous smile.

"I am. Demetrius has been very helpful during my transition," she responded, her smile matching Michaela's.

"Of course. It's you. Would he be any other way?" Michaela offered, watching her attentively.

"He does seem to go out of his way to protect me. I doubt he would be pleased to know what you did to me," she acknowledged, slowly circling Michaela, keeping her eyes on her the whole time and prepared for anything that she would offer.

Michaela's unfathomable look quickly turned to pure callousness. "He would be angry for a while, because I hurt *his* Chris. But I've done far worse and have been forgiven without consequence," she stated coolly with undeniable confidence, her midnight eyes hard and unyielding as they held Chris's. "Don't take it personally. You were a necessary evil. If things had gone as intended, then I would have had him back—the *real* him. Instead, we have you. I failed. That should offer you some consolation."

Chris was amused that she was on the receiving end of a

necessary evil. It was something she had always believed in, and she had considered trading with Demetrius as one of them.

She inched her way closer to Michaela, who didn't seem bothered by their extremely close proximity. Her fingers ran along the fabric of Michaela's blouse, near the collar. "There is no need to bring Demetrius into this. What you did to me will remain our little secret." She reached up and stroked Michaela's hair, twirling strands of it around her finger. Leaning in, her lips brushed against Michaela's ear as she added in a low frisson tone, "Just like what I plan to do to you will remain mine."

MESSAGE TO THE READER

~

Thank you for choosing *Darkness Unchained* from the many titles available to you. My goal is to create an engaging world, compelling characters, and an interesting experience for you. I hope I've accomplished that. Reviews are very important to authors and help other readers discover our books. Please take a moment to leave a review. I'd love to know your thoughts about the book.

For notifications about new releases, *exclusive* contests and giveaways, and cover reveals, please sign up for my mailing list at McKenzieHunter.com.

Made in the USA
Monee, IL
22 February 2025

12739316R00215